# Strong is the
# A Novel of Ancient Egypt:
# Book 1: The King

**By Max Overton**

Writers Exchange E-Publishing
http://www.writers-exchange.com

**Publisher note:**
**Due to formatting issues symbols such as ü, ä, é and ö have been replaced with the simple letter u, a, e and o. We apologise for this necessity.**

Strong is the Ma'at of Re, A Novel of Ancient Egypt: Book 1: The King

Writers Exchange E-Publishing
PO Box 372
ATHERTON QLD 4883

Cover Art by: Julie Napier

Published by Writers Exchange E-Publishing
http://www.writers-exchange.com

ISBN **ebook**: 978-1-922233-91-2
**Print**: 978-1-925574-14-2 (WEE Assigned)

# Map of Ancient Egypt (Kemet)

# Simplified Family Tree of Usermaatre Ramesses

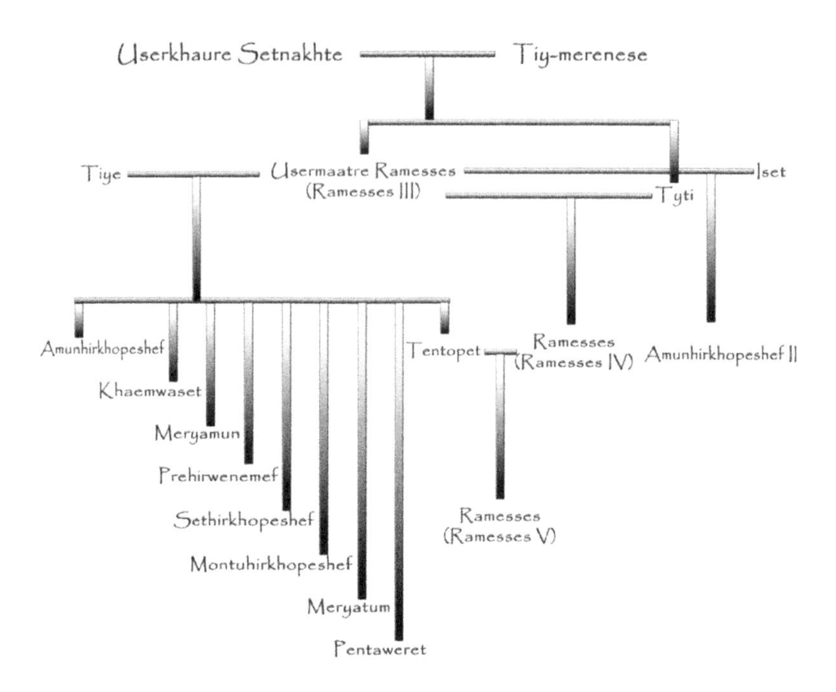


# Simplified Family Tree of Ament & Tausret

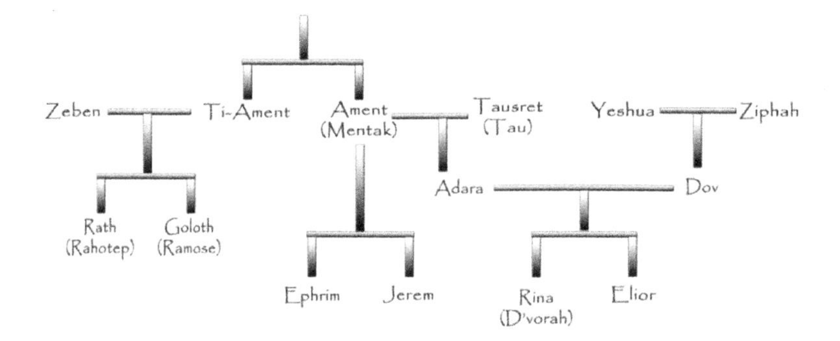

# Prologue
# 1 Shemu Day 26, Year 1 of Usermaatre Ramesses

The morning was cool with a fitful breeze off the river through the Eye of Re, shining down from a cloudless sky, promised heat as the day progressed. A slim man approaching middle age sat on a throne on a raised dais in the forecourt of the Great Temple of Amun in Waset, hearing the sonorous phrases of the priests but not really listening. His own thoughts occupied his attention, and the ceremony conferring on him the Double Crown of Kemet and godhead as Son of Re was little more than an anticlimax after the events of the last three years.

The dawn of that day had seen the new king washed and purified in the temple lake, presented within the dark recesses of the temple to the cobra goddess Wadjet and the great god Amun, and now he sat in state while crown after crown was placed on his head and the blessings of the gods invoked. It was a ceremony the king had seen performed on four men and one woman before him, on Baenre Merenptah, on Userkheperure Seti, on Akhenre Siptah, on Sitre Tausret, and most recently on his own father Userkhaure-Setepenre Setnakhte. The first two coronations he had watched with interest, the third with feelings of disdain and the fourth consumed by anger. Only that of his father had made his chest swell with pride and love and anticipation.

"Let this be an end to it for the lifetime of the youngest person here," he murmured to himself as the priest droned on, placing one crown after another on the new king's head. "The Great Usermaatre reigned for sixty-seven years and I mean to do the same. Kemet has had its fill of kings being crowned every few years..." He broke off as he realised the priest had stopped talking and was looking apprehensively at him.

"Son of Re?"

"Continue."

Five priests now confronted him and addressed the man sitting on the throne.

"Let Heru empower you," cried the first priest. "Your name in Heru shall be Kanakht Aanisut, Strong Bull, Whose Royalty is Great."

The man knew that Strong Bull was a common title, necessary to highlight the king's fertility that would reflect upon the kingdoms; whereas the other phrase served to emphasise his royalty, necessary as his family had only just risen to the pinnacle of power from their former obscurity.

"Nekhabet and Wadjet name you also," the second priest said. "Your name of Nebty shall be Werhabused mi Tatenen, Great of Hebsed like Ptah-Tatenen."

This title had given the uncrowned king many sleepless nights as he wrestled with a way to convey his intentions regarding his reign. He was determined to rule for a long time, making the Hebsed festival of thirty years a regular feature, just as the Great Usermaatre had done. Ptah the Tatenen as god of the primordial mound would signify he also was a creator, fashioning Kemet anew from the chaos of the previous years.

The priests continued their acclamation of the king's names. "The gods recognise you as their son on earth," called out the third. "Heru Nebu names you Userrenput mi Atum, The golden falcon, rich in years like Atum."

Another creator god, this one based in Iunu. Three gods, Amun for Waset, Ptah for Men-nefer, Atum for Iunu. The king knew that the forms were important, that names carried power and by naming the gods in his throne names, he would bind them to his rule.

"Nesut-byt, King of Ta Mehu and Ta Shemau, North and South, cried the fourth priest. "Usermaatre Meriamun, Strong is the Ma'at of Re, beloved of Amun."

*Let the Ma'at of Re be strong within me*, the king thought, *just as it was for the Great Usermaatre. Let Amun and Amun's City welcome me. Waset, so important and yet so dangerous.*

"Sa-Re, Son of Re," the fifth priest said. "Ramesisu Heqaiunu, Ramesses, Ruler of Iunu."

As the last words of the priests fell into the silence of the forecourt, the crowd of watching nobles and priests, sons of the new king and army officers, and as many of the common citizens of Waset as could fit into the temple grounds, raised up their voices in praise.

"Usermaatre, Usermaatre, Usermaatre!" Waves of sound crashed into the temple walls, spilling out through gates and between the great pylons, washing over the high walls and disturbing the swallows nesting in the eaves. They flew out, twisting and turning as a thin black cloud in the azure sky, twittering their unrest before returning to their nests and roosts.

Usermaatre Ramesses, son of Setnakhte, stood and surveyed his people, savouring the moment. Three years before he had been just an army commander, today he was King of Kemet, the most powerful nation under Re.

He stepped down from the dais, the tall double crown high on his head, the symbolic beard jutting from his clean-shaven jaw and the robes and emblems of state draped about his muscular limbs. The crowd parted before him and he strode through them, across the forecourt, out through the temple pylon and into the dusty streets of Waset. A roar went up from the common people as they saw their king walk among them, men cheered, women shrieked their delight and called out blessings, and the Medjay ran to keep up, to form a protective cordon around the Son of Re.

It was unexpected. The ceremony had called for the newly crowned king to board the royal barge moored at the temple dock and return across the flooded river to the palace on the western bank. Instead, Ramesses chose to walk the dusty streets of Waset, communing with his people, and they loved him for it.

*I am king*, he thought. *Like the Great Usermaatre before me, and like him I have strong sons to succeed me, even named for his sons.* Ramesses smiled and as if he was turning to offer his countenance to the cheering crowds, looked behind him to where his sons walked. *Boys, but they will soon be men, Amunhirkhopeshef my first-born, Khaemwaset marked for glory as a priest like his namesake, Meryamun the cheerful one, and Prehirwenemef my serious boy.*

Ramesses turned off the main thoroughfare, letting his feet guide him into the streets dedicated to artisans. The shopkeepers gaped at the sight of their king, before breaking into cheers that shook the dust from the linen awnings lining the street. From there he continued on through the broad and narrow streets of Waset, the Medjay jostling the crowds as they pressed close to their king, and on to the palace of the Governor. On the steps of the palace, he stood for a time and basked in the adulation of his people, at last turning his steps toward the docks and the royal barge that would carry him across the river.

*I will model myself on him, but I will not fail like him. The House of the elder Ramesses fell, but mine will not. I will leave strong sons behind me to carry my name into eternity. In a hundred years, men will name me Great Ramesses.*

This day, all men would see him up close. In days to come, he would withdraw from the sight of common men, assuming the distance and dignity that was expected of a king, of a god, but this day he was their saviour, a king to unite the kingdoms that had been strained and shattered since the glorious days of the Great Usermaatre.

*Those days will come again...*

# Chapter 1
# Year 1 of Usermaatre Ramesses

"I have ordered the construction of my Mansion of a Million Years."

The three women present in the private quarters of King Ramesses looked at each other, but said nothing for several moments. Then the oldest of them inclined her head and said, "That is as it should be, my son, but how does that concern us?"

"It will not just be a funerary temple where priests will offer up sacrifices to me and for me for eternity, but a palace as well. I have it in mind to construct a new residence worthy of me."

"It will be costly," murmured a middle-aged, rather portly woman. "This palace is quite comfortable and..."

"I am not concerned with the cost, and this palace is old, well over a hundred years. I want something new that will reflect my glory." Ramesses glared at the woman. "I don't expect you to understand that. You have always thought small, but you are no longer the wife of a mere army officer. Learn to think like a royal wife."

The Lady in question visibly flinched, but said nothing.

"I am sure that the Lady Tiye meant nothing by that remark, Son of Re," said the youngest woman. She was fourteen years old, and already displayed a beauty that eclipsed both her mother and the king's wife. "We all think only of your well-being, brother."

Ramesses smiled at the young woman. "I know you do, Tyti. Both you and my mother understand what it is to be royal, but you must no longer call me 'brother'. I am now 'Son of Re' or 'Majesty'...or perhaps just 'my lord'. Even to you."

Tyti smiled and bowed her head submissively, though her eyes flashed her annoyance. "Let it be as you say, Son of Re."

"And what of me, my son?" asked the older woman. "Will you insist that the mouth that kissed you as a babe must now utter formal phrases instead of endearments?"

A smile tugged at the king's lips. "You are Queen Tiy-Merenese, Great Wife of my royal father. I will make an exception for you, in private."

"And...and I?" Tiye whispered. "I am your wife and I alone have shared your bed these last fifteen years. Am I not a Queen also and exempt from having to utter these formal titles?"

Ramesses pursed his lips and looked at Tiye thoughtfully. "You are the wife of my youth, and were content to be the companion of a lowly army officer. You have borne my sons and stood by my side all these years and thus will always stand high in my estimation..." His voice trailed off.

After a few moments, when the king seemed disinclined to continue his thought, Tiye cleared her throat and prompted her husband. "I will always stand high in your estimation, my lord?"

"Yes, but a wife and a Queen are two different things." Ramesses sighed. "You were born a commoner..."

"As were you, my lord," Tiye blurted. She went pale and her eyes opened wide as she realised what she had said, but forged ahead, determined to make her point. "We were all born common, my lord, but now we are royal."

Ramesses frowned. "I am the son of a king, this lady here..." he gestured toward Tiy-Merenese, "is mother of a king, and Tyti is daughter and sister of a king. What are you?"

"I am the wife of the king," Tiye said. Her voice trembled slightly but she held her head up.

Ramesses nodded. "And you will always be wife of the king, but a king has responsibilities to the kingdoms; responsibilities that he must face no matter what are his personal inclinations."

"What are these responsibilities, my son?" Tiy-merenese asked.

"I am Bull of Heru, and I must be seen to be fertile, more fertile than those around me..."

Tiy-Merenese and Tyti nodded, murmuring, "It is the king's responsibility."

Tiye looked stricken. "I have given you four healthy sons that live and five daughters, though only two yet live. What are you saying, royal husband?"

"I am saying that as king I must plough many fields. A king must have a Per-Khemret stocked with many women to bear the king's children."

"Even your father took other women when he became king," Tiy-Merenese conceded. "I would expect no less of you, my son."

"The king may do as he pleases," Tyti agreed. "There are no limits placed on the person of the King."

"Of course you will have concubines," Tiye admitted. "Lesser women on whom to father children to become scribes, priests and court officials. It is expected."

"Not just concubines," Ramesses said. "A king may have more than one wife, and I mean to."

"You promised me when you first brought me to your father's house that I would be your only wife," Tiye whispered.

"You are talking nonsense," Tiy-Merenese snapped. "My son was a lowly army officer at the time, but now he is king. It is his right to enjoy as many women as he pleases."

"I agree," Tyti said. "My brother the king...Son of Re...knows his duty. He will have many wives and father a great sheaf of sons. Have you picked out your new wives yet?"

"I have picked out one."

"Will you tell us, Majesty? Is it perhaps some young woman of the court in Waset who has caught your eye? Or in Men-nefer?"

Ramesses smiled. "She is in Waset."

"She is well born?" Tyti asked. "Of course, she would have to be if you mean to make her your wife." She turned to her mother. "Who do we know that is noble enough to be joined to the King's House?"

Queen Tiy-Merenese laughed. "There is only one woman of high enough birth to marry a king and become not only a wife but also Queen."

"Who?" Tyti demanded. "Who is this paragon...?" Her mouth gaped open as she stared at her mother and then turned to face her brother. "Tell me, brother."

"You know who it is, Tyti my sister. Do you think I would let just any man marry my sister and join his blood to ours? No, you will be my wife and my Queen, Tyti, and have many sons with me."

"But she is your sister..." Tiye murmured.

"Foolish woman," Tiy-Merenese said. "What is forbidden to common men is the purview of kings. What could be more fitting, a royal wife for a king?"

Tiye looked at the young girl in some distress. "You cannot agree to this..."

Tyti shook her head, setting the gold beads in her wig softly clattering. She turned to Ramesses. "I will be Queen?" she asked. When the king nodded, she grinned and bowed. "Son of Re, do with me as you will."

Behind her, Tiye wept softly.

Work started on the Mansion of a Million Years, and on the adjoining palace, walls of stone and mud brick soaring upward as a thousand workers transformed the bare soil of the western shore. Further inland, in the dry, dusty valley of Ta-Sekhet-Ma'at, the king's tomb proceeded apace with the specialised tomb workers transforming bare cut rock into majestic chambers and corridors, walls already ablaze with coloured inscriptions and images. Work had started on it in the days of his father Userkhaure-Setepenre Setnakhte, an open entryway followed by a corridor with two side chambers, and another corridor with eight chambers leading off it.

Tyti, daughter of Userkhaure-Setepenre Setnakhte, married her brother Usermaatre Ramesses, though the event attracted little notice. Typically, a woman moved from her father's house to her husband's house, taking her personal possessions and a symbolic pot of fire from the family hearth. There was no ceremony, civil or religious, though the scribes made the appropriate notations in the temple records. Tyti was already a part of the king's Per-Khemret, or Women's Residence, the wing of the palace where the women lived. She merely changed rooms, moving from the suites that housed a dozen women of the king's household into one that befitted her new station as King's Wife. The best room in the Per-Khemret was occupied by the king's mother, Tiy-Merenese, and the second best by Tiye, but when Tiye returned to her suite the evening of Tyti's elevation, she found many of her sumptuous furnishings had been removed from her rooms.

Tiye grimaced and stamped her foot in annoyance, but there was nothing she could do. The items had been removed on the king's orders, so she just had to make do with whatever she could take from women lower down the social order. She stalked from room to room, servants in tow, and removed a chair here, a wall hanging there, ignoring the protests of their owners. One item could not be replaced though, a small table inlaid with turquoise and malachite that had been a wedding gift from her father many years before. This loss was not to be borne, and the next day she set out in search of the king to protest its confiscation.

She found the king at his noon meal, and entered the room boldly, though her confidence received a jolt when she saw young Tyti sitting on a couch with the king. The king and queen were feeding each other morsels of food, making a game of it.

"My lord." Tiye bowed as required when entering the king's presence but rose again quickly.

Ramesses did not appear to notice, wiping a spot of grease off Tyti's lips with clean linen. "Have you come to join us, Tiye? I would have you be friends with Tyti."

"As my lord commands, but I came to ask for the return of my table."

"What table is this?" The king selected a ripe fig from the plate on a side table and broke it open, revealing the pink flesh inside. He fed half to the young woman beside him and bit into the other half.

"The turquoise and malachite inlaid table that was removed from my room. The servants said that it was removed on your orders and taken to the rooms of...of your new companion."

Ramesses smiled at Tyti. "You have such a table, my love?"

"I believe so. It is a very nice table."

"Well, I did tell my servants to find the very best furnishings for you."

"My lord is most kind," Tyti said.

"But do I get my table back?" Tiye asked. "It was a gift from my father."

Ramesses frowned and touched the corner of his mouth where a fig seed had stuck. "Is a gift from your father, who was, after all, a commoner, more important than a gift from the king? I have given it as a gift to my queen as a token of my love. Would you have me go back on my word?"

"My lord, it...it was not yours to give..."

"Not mine? Are you mad, Tiye? Everything in Kemet belongs to the king. The contents of this palace are mine, and if I choose to give something in it to someone, that is my right. No one could possibly..." Ramesses broke off as Tiye started sobbing. "What is this, Tiye? What is the matter?"

"It...it was a gift, my lord, from my father. Now that he is dead, I have nothing else of his, and I desired that it should remain with me in my rooms until I died, at which time it should be buried with me."

Ramesses sighed. "I have already gifted it to another."

Tiye thought for a moment as she wiped the tears from her eyes. "Yet by your words the table remains your property, my lord, as do all things in Kemet. You could just give it back to me."

"But then I would be deprived of its use," Tyti remonstrated.

"Your words have merit, Tiye," the king admitted. "As do yours, my beloved Tyti." He frowned in thought. "Will you give the table back to Tiye, my Queen?"

"Is this your wish, my lord?" Tyti asked.

"It would keep the peace within Per Khemret, preserve the Ma'at of the palace and soothe my spirit."

"Then I will be glad to do so, for your sake, my lord. Only..."

"Yes?"

"Allow me to keep the table for one more day. It is pleasing to the eye and I would gaze upon its beauty once more."

"That seems reasonable. You agree, Tiye?"

"If it pleases my lord."

"It does please me. Return the table tomorrow morning and I shall commission another table for you that will be twice as beautiful."

The table was returned the following morning, but one of the legs now had deep scratches on it, and several pieces of the stone inlay had been loosened or were missing. Tiye glowered at the servants who delivered it, but said nothing, knowing she would lose standing if she railed at them. They were only servants, after all. Instead, she sent for a scribe and had him pen a short note thanking Tyti for its return, and including a small gift of jewellery. It was a minor victory of the spirit at best, but Tiye felt better for it.

There was peace for a time within the Per-Khemret of the Waset palace. Ramesses spent many nights with his new wife, so it was no surprise that within two months of the marriage, Tyti was with child. She was examined by the court physicians and her urine taken for testing; the chief physician being delighted that he could report to the king that the grains had germinated in such a way as to indicate the child would be a boy. The king's delight at this news caused Tiye to scowl once more and berate her servants.

"Why does the king delight in this news of a son?" she asked. "Have I not already given him four strong sons in whom to rejoice?"

Of course, there was nothing the servants could say to this, or even dared to, should they be so inclined. This was wise as it was well known that the king did not look kindly on any criticism, and their wellbeing would be in jeopardy should word of an ill-judged comment be reported to him. So they kept their counsel and waited for the storm winds of a slighted wife to blow over.

Word of Tiye's anger reached the king's ears, however. Whispers ruled the palace, so it was inevitable that his wife's words would be reported eventually. Ramesses was inclined to send for her and berate her, but then thought it over.

"It is hard for her to grasp as she is of common birth," Ramesses told his Tjaty, "but a son born to me and my sister-wife is of great importance to the kingdoms. I can see she feels this as a slight, though it is not intended as such. I will make it up to her."

"Your words are wisdom, Son of Re," the Tjaty said.

# Chapter 2
## Year 1 of Usermaatre Ramesses

The old palace of Waset, these days used as the Governor's mansion, had been taken over by the king and his family for the coronation celebrations. Servants swarmed like the distraught inhabitants of an overturned beehive, hurrying hither and thither with linen cloths, utensils and food, and all chattering about the recent ceremony and the new king. Usermaatre Ramesses, the new king, was now in the inner chambers, bathing to remove the dust and sweat clinging to his body, after which he would refresh himself with the choicest foods and wine. All attention was focussed on the divine person of the king, and little thought was spared for the four young sons of the king.

They had walked in the procession behind the throne bearing their father, and had revelled in the adulation of the crowds, buoyed up by the excitement of the occasion, and only just becoming aware of their exalted position in Kemetu society. Yesterday, they had been sons of the Heir, and only two years before had been merely the sons of an army officer. The eldest son, Amunhirkhopeshef, could clearly remember those days, as could his brother Khaemwaset, two years the younger. Even the babies, younger brothers Meryamun and Prehirwenemef, said they could remember visits to the barracks in Waset. Those days had evaporated, though, their futures as ordinary soldiers dissipating like the river mist in the heat of the rising sun. Now their futures would be far grander, as generals, as priests, as important officials in the court of the king their father.

"I am the heir to the throne of Kemet," Amunhirkhopeshef declared, stripping off his sweat-stained headdress and throwing it carelessly to the floor. One of the ubiquitous servants snatched it up and hurried it off to the palace laundry, but the young princes paid the servant no attention.

"Not yet, you aren't," Meryamun said. "Father has to declare you the heir."

"And he will. I'm the eldest. It is my right, so I will be king one day."

"It's not fair," Prehirwenemef said. "I want to be king too. Why shouldn't I be the heir?"

"Silly boy," Amunhirkhopeshef muttered. "Go play with your toys."

"It's not the way it works," Khaemwaset said gently. "The eldest brother is always...well, usually anyway...the heir to the throne. Father has to announce it to make it official, but it is almost certainly going to happen."

"There's no 'almost' about it. I will be heir. So don't you go getting any ideas above your station."

"I don't want to be king," Khaemwaset said.

"Of course you do. Anyone would."

Khaemwaset shook his head. He took his headdress off, wiped his face with it and held it out for a servant to take. "I'm going to be a priest."

Amunhirkhopeshef stared at his brother. "Why? Because father named you for that other son of the Great Usermaatre? That's no reason to throw your life away."

"I want to be a priest."

"But you could be a soldier," Meryamun said. "I'm going to be a great general and defeat the Nine Bows."

"So am I," Prehirwenemef added. "I bet I'll kill more enemies than you."

"Won't."

"Will."

"Seriously, Khaem', you actually want to be a priest?" Amunhirkhopeshef asked.

Khaemwaset nodded slowly. "I've spent time with the priests in the Great Temple of Amun. The sanctuary is awe-inspiring. I was even there one time when the god spoke. It made me think..."

"The god spoke? Truly?"

"Well, I only heard a grating noise like a heavy statue being dragged over stone, but the priest with me declared it was the voice of Amun. He said it only sounded like a noise because I was uninitiated."

"What did the god say?"

"I don't know. The priest wouldn't tell me. That's one of the reasons I want to be a priest--so that I can hear the gods clearly and know what they are saying."

Amunhirkhopeshef whistled. "I wish I'd heard the god." He shrugged. "Still, I suppose when I'm king I'll be a god too, so I'll be able to understand when the other gods talk."

"That will be years away."

"Of course. I would not wish ill to our father. I have no doubt he will reign for many years."

Servants took away the stained clothing of the princes and brought them fresh linens, which they changed into there and then, unmindful of the presence of male and female servants. Nakedness was not something to trouble their minds, and it had not been many years since they had run around without clothing. Other servants brought a selection of plain armbands and pectorals for the older children, as well as reed sandals and fresh headdresses.

Prehirwenemef stopped in the middle of fastening his kilt and looked at Khaemwaset, who stood naked as he selected an armband.

"Your thingy looks funny, Khaem'. What have you done to it?"

"What are you talking about?"

"Your thingy...your member."

Khaemwaset looked down, his eyebrows drawing together in a frown. "My penis? What do you mean? It doesn't...ah, I see; it's been cut."

"Cut?" Preherwernef looked horrified. "How did you cut it?"

"He didn't," Amunhirkhopeshef said. "It was cut for him by a priest of Min." The older boy chuckled. "You have that to look forward to, Preher'."

The two younger boys gaped, and Prehirwenemef went pale.

"This...this is a joke, isn't it? Why would a priest of Min do that to you? Have you told father? He'll punish him."

"Stupid boy," Amunhirkhopeshef sneered. "Haven't you heard people talk about circumcision? That's what being cut means."

"It's a ceremony that happens about the same time as the shaving of your side lock," Khaemwaset said. His hand strayed to his shaved head. "You must have heard of it." He took a clean kilt from a servant and fastened it around his waist.

"Yes, but I didn't know what it meant."

"And it's performed by the priest of Min because he's the god of sex," Amunhirkhopeshef said. "You've seen men and women do that, I know, and one day you'll do it too."

"But...but what do they cut off?" Meryamun asked. His hands cupped his genitals protectively and he looked around furtively as if expecting a priest of Min to leap out at him.

"Just the skin at the tip of your penis," Khaemwaset said.

"Though sometimes the flint knife slips and they cut the whole thing off," said Amunhirkhopeshef, grinning. "Then they whip off your sack too and make you a eunuch in the Per-Khemret."

Prehirwenemef started crying.

"Stop it, 'Herke'," Khaemwaset said. "You're just frightening him. It's all right, Preher', when your time comes it will all go well, I promise you. The priests are skilled and hardly ever make a mistake. And they'll be extra careful with the son of a king."

"Does it hurt?" Meryamun asked.

"Dreadfully," Amunhirkhopeshef said. "You'll scream for days."

"Don't pay any attention to him," Khaemwaset said. "He's just being a beast. It hurts for a time, but not too much, and if you remember why they are doing it, it's bearable."

"Why are they doing it?"

"To make you a man. Same as shaving your side lock off. You put away your toys and the symbols of your childhood and become a man."

"Do...do girls do it too?"

"No, stupid," Amunhirkhopeshef laughed. "They don't have anything to cut, and they can't become men."

"Girls do other things," Khaemwaset said. "Don't ask me what, though."

"When do they do it?" Meryamun asked. "The cutting?"

"Getting worried? You've got a while yet; you're only a baby. Khaem' had his done a few months back and he's only just turned eleven. Another year, maybe."

"I don't want it done at all," Prehirwenemef said.

"You've got to."

"Not everybody has it done," Meryamun said. "I've seen some of the servants, fully grown men, and they...they didn't look like that."

"That's true," Khaemwaset said. "It's mostly the nobles that circumcise their sons. It's a sign of godly favour to offer up your skin on the altar of the god Min."

"Well, I don't want to."

"How can the people ever know you're suited for nobility and a life of service if you can't show you can put up with a little pain?" Amunhirkhopeshef asked.

"I'll do something else then. I've seen soldiers that looked like me down there."

"You can be a common soldier, but you could never be a General. And I doubt if they'd let a son of the king refuse to be cut."

"If I tell father I don't want to..."

"He'll think you're afraid. He won't want a coward as a son."

Meryamun started sniffling, and soon both younger boys were sobbing.

"Now look what you've done," Khaemwaset said.

"What did I do? I just told them the truth. If they're too much of a baby to face up to it, that's nothing to do with me."

"Well, I think it was a nasty thing to say, and I'm going to tell father."

Amunhirkhopeshef scowled. "Don't you dare."

Khaemwaset made a face and turned away. His older brother reached out to restrain him, grabbing an arm.

"Let go of me."

"Not until you say you won't tell father."

"Tell him, Khaem', Meryamun sobbed. "He's bad and father will whip him."

"You be quiet too, or I'll...I'll do...something."

Khaemwaset tried to pull free but Amunhirkhopeshef seized his brother and started to drag him away from the door. Meryamun tried to interpose himself and even Prehirwenemef tugged at Amunhirkhopeshef's kilt. The servants looked worried, but none dared intervene physically, and the most senior one present sent a man to notify the king.

The older boys were wrestling on the floor, with the younger ones plucking at limbs and kilts in half-hearted efforts to separate them, when the surrounding servants melted away and the room grew quiet.

"What is the meaning of this?"

Meryamun and Prehirwenemef shrank back, brushing away tears, and the two older boys looked up and hurriedly disengaged. They remained kneeling on the floor and looked up at the angry face of the king.

"What is the meaning of this?" Ramesses repeated. "Amunhirkhopeshef, you are the eldest; tell me why you are fighting."

Amunhirkhopeshef glanced at his brothers, and then faced his father, head held high. "They would not obey me."

"Why should they obey you?"

"I am the eldest; your heir."

"You are my eldest son, but who made you heir?"

Amunhirkhopeshef looked down at the ground, unable to meet the king's stare.

"Well? Who made you heir?"

"The eldest son is always heir."

"Not always, but even if you were to become my heir, it would happen when I say so, not before. Do you understand?"

"Yes, father."

"Now tell the king you understand."

"Wh...what?"

"This is a matter concerning the king and the kingdoms, not just a dispute between father and son. Tell the king you understand."

Amunhirkhopeshef stared in some confusion, but Khaemwaset leaned closer and whispered, "Yes, Son of Re."

The elder prince glanced at his brother for a moment before comprehension washed over him. He turned and bowed to the king. "Yes, Son of Re. I understand."

"Now, in what way would they not obey you?"

"I...I'd rather not say."

"He was bad, father," Meryamun piped up. "He was saying nasty things...ow." He shot an aggrieved look at Khaemwaset as the boy lightly cuffed his young brother.

"A prince does not go telling tales."

"But you were going to. You said you were going to tell father..."

"I would not have done it."

"Enough, all of you," Ramesses said. "You will tell me now what you say you would not have told me."

"It was nothing, father," Khaemwaset said. "Youthful teasing, nothing more. If our younger brothers believed us, then I apologise, but..."

"Khaemwaset had nothing to do with it," Amunhirkhopeshef said. "I was the one teasing them, and Khaem' was trying to stop me."

"How were you teasing them?"

"I described the circumcision ceremony in such a way as to inspire fear."

"He said the priest might cut everything off," Prehirwenemef said, sniffing loudly.

Ramesses looked from one to the other before replying. "I am disappointed in you, Amunhirkhopeshef. As the eldest son you have a responsibility to look after your younger brothers. You want me to make you my heir, but an heir becomes a king and a king must learn wisdom. The kings of Kemet rule by the will of the gods, and the love of the people. To achieve both, you must have peace within the kingdoms, and this quarrelling is not the way to achieve peace. I, as king, seek ma'at within the kingdoms. You, as my sons, must seek ma'at within this palace. How can I rule properly over my people if my sons are rebellious and fight among themselves?"

"I am sorry, father," Amunhirkhopeshef said. "I will try not to disturb your ma'at again."

"See that you do not. I will be watching you as I consider who will become my heir. As for you, Khaemwaset, it was bravely done seeking to take the blame upon your shoulders, but it was still an ill-considered action. How is your brother to learn if he allows another to pay for his actions? It was only his nobility of spirit that led him to own up." The king turned to his two youngest sons. "And you Meryamun...Prehirwenemef...you must learn discernment. How can you possibly think that I would allow harm to come to my sons? I will ask the Nem-netjer of Min to describe to you the ceremony of circumcision. He will allay your fears, so that when the time comes for you to offer up your foreskins on the altar of Min, you will see it for the honour it is."

With that, the king told his sons to report to the scribes in charge of their education. "Not even the coronation of your father should get in the way of your lessons. Go now, and behave as young princes rather than unruly boys."

"Yes, father," chorused the four of them. The older two bowed respectfully, but the two young ones hugged their father quickly before scampering from the room.

# Chapter 3
# Year 1 of Usermaatre Ramesses

The flood ended and the king made preparations to sail north from Waset. Before he left, he visited the west bank once more and toured his rapidly rising Mansion of a Million Years. He pored over plans and made suggestions that the architects were quick to incorporate, pacing out new courtyards, tearing down newly erected walls and ordering in fresh loads of building stone. The size of the adjoining palace was increased, with gardens to be laid out for the enjoyment of the residents of the Per-Khemret.

The royal barge was outfitted and readied for the voyage north, cabins being erected on the deck for two passengers.

"I am leaving you in charge of the Waset Per-Khemret, mother," he informed Queen Tiy-Merenese. "And I am leaving Queen Tyti behind too. She is with child and I desire that her son be born in Waset."

"As my lord commands. Will you be taking any women with you for your comfort?"

"There will be women in the north, but I will take Tiye with me. She is feeling slighted by my attention to my sister-wife."

"That is wise, my son," Tiy-Merenese murmured. "An unhappy wife sours the lives of those around her. Tiye is the wife of your youth and if you smile on her as you once did, she will rejoice."

The royal barge pulled out into the current, its red-tipped oars thrashing the water into foam as it steadied itself for the voyage north. Sunlight caused the gold on its prow and sides to flash and gleam, creating a spectacle that raised a cheer from the watchers crowding the docks of Waset. A light breeze blew from the north, dispelling the odours of the city and bringing with it aromas redolent of growing things and the fresh waters of the Great River.

Ramesses stood beneath an awning that had been erected over the rear deck, feeling the slight tremor that ran through the planking when the oars bit into the water. Now that the current had gripped them, the oars were only used to modify their course when the steering oars at the stern were insufficient to the task. Tiye stood beside him, her face carefully neutral while she tried to work out why the king had invited her along on the voyage. She was not left in doubt for long.

"I have been neglecting you, Tiye."

Tiye bowed her head to hide a smile. While it was gratifying to hear her husband admit his fault, she knew that the king must not be seen to take the blame for anything.

"My lord, you have been busy with affairs of state, and any attention you pay me fills me with delight."

"Nevertheless."

Ramesses turned and contemplated the vistas of water, sky and growing things that spread out before them. Rippling waters, spreading waterlilies, reed-lined banks and grassy fields beyond abounded with wildlife, ducks and egrets, jumping fish and the disturbance where a crocodile or a pehe-mau slipped below the surface of the water. Above everything, in the clear heat-hazed air, hawks and vultures wheeled, and the twittering of birds carried across the waters from the reed beds.

"Our lands are rich indeed," he murmured.

"My lord?"

"Can you not see how we are blessed by the gods? They give us a river that supplies our every need, its life-giving waters growing every good thing, its wide expanse allowing us to travel freely the length of the kingdoms. Gold and silver and copper, good building stone abounds, a population with every skill necessary for our high civilisation and a good source of labour. Nations on our borders that fear us." He looked at Tiye again and smiled. "Do you see what this means?"

"No, my lord."

Ramesses nodded as if she had supplied the answer. "It means that I can become the greatest king that Kemet has ever seen, that the world has ever seen. I grew up thinking that my namesake, the Great Usermaatre Ramesses, was the greatest king ever, but I see now that I have it in me to excel all his feats. I will lead the armies of Kemet to victory over the Nine Bows, fill the kingdoms with beautiful temples and shrines to all the gods, have every mouth uttering my praises, and leave my kingdoms to my strong sons that they might reign after me for a thousand years."

"Yes, my lord," Tiye agreed. "You will be the greatest king of Kemet and *our* sons shall rule after you." She stressed the possessive modifier. "Amunhirkhopeshef, our eldest son, will be a worthy successor."

"He is young yet."

"Thirteen years, but capable. His father's son."

"True, but the future lies with the gods."

"I have given you four strong sons, my lord. One of them will reign after you."

"I may have more sons."

"I hope I will bear you many more, my lord, but these four will always be your eldest."

"You are concerned that I will favour the son of my sister-wife Tyti over one of your sons?"

Tiye hesitated. "My lord will do what is right."

"You need have no fear on that score. Besides, who knows what the future holds? I intend to be on the throne for fifty years at least. My sons will be old men by the time they inherit."

"May that day be far removed indeed, my lord." Tiye got slowly to her knees and grasped her husband's knees, kissing them. "Thank you, my lord. I feared you had turned your face from me."

Ramesses bent and drew his wife to her feet again, kissing her forehead. "Never may that happen, beloved. You are the wife of my youth and none can take that from you." He regarded Tiye quizzically. "You think I put my sister before you?"

"You made her Queen, my lord."

"Yes, I did, but I have explained this to you already. She is the daughter of a king and deserves no less."

"But I do?" Tiye asked boldly.

"You are the mother of my heir. In time you will be King's Mother. Let that content you."

Ramesses stroked his wife's cheek and kissed her. Shortly, he took her into his cabin and ploughed her fertile field vigorously. He left her lying languidly on his bed and washed before donning a fresh kilt, sandals and nemes headdress. Then he went onto the deck and sat in the front of the barge drinking river-cooled wine and thinking his own thoughts.

The banks of the Great River were dotted with villages and towns, each dependent on the farms that sprawled across the low land at the water's edge. Hemmed in by cliffs and the desert beyond, the kingdoms unfurled as a green ribbon of fertility of varying width set in the red desert. The populace of town and farm spilled out to watch the royal barge pass, and if the vessel passed close to one shore or the other, cheers floated across the dark waters to lift the spirits of the king.

When he saw a temple, either within the town boundaries or alone on a mound or clifftop, Ramesses would, as often as not, instruct the barge captain to turn aside and moor at the local docks. The king would then walk through the streets, accompanied by a small cordon of sailors, and worship at the local shrine or temple. Amun, Heru, Re, Min, Ptah, Het-hor or Set were all fellow gods and the king's presence brought honour to their local cult as well as paying his respects. The priests bowed and danced in attendance, and were rewarded by gold or the promise of it. Ramesses took notice of any temple disrepair and promised help, saying that his masons would restore each temple and shrine to its former glory.

Tiye joined him for some of these forays ashore and women crowded the streets to see the king and his wife walk together. Stories had spread through the kingdoms of the king's new wife, his sister Tyti, daughter of the old king, and many had wondered whether this had put a strain on the relationship of the king and his first wife. It was now evident that it had not, and that the king loved Tiye as much as he ever did.

The barge came to Men-nefer many days later and they broke their journey there. Tiye welcomed the opportunity to bathe properly and sleep in a bed that did not move, to walk about in gardens and talk to other women. She consulted with Tjayiri, who was also called Userkhaurenakht, the Great Overseer of the Per-Khemret in Men-nefer, regarding the dispositions of the rooms, and necessary modifications that would have to be made to the gardens and pools within the tiled courtyards. If she was required to spend time there, Tiye was determined it must meet her standards of comfort. Pere, junior scribe of the Per-Khemret, took down copious notes and had them drawn up into a series of instructions for the masons and gardeners.

The king, meanwhile, consulted with court officials and received reports of the affairs of the northern kingdom and the state of the borders. Tjaty Herwernef called together the Great Khenbet Council to discuss these matters and received reports from the assistant to the Assistant Overseer of the Treasurer, Mentemtowe, as to the financial state of the kingdoms. Priests of all the major gods were present to report on the state of the temples within the city, and Ramesses honoured his second son Khaemwaset by allowing him to sit in on the deliberations of the Tjaty's

Council in Waset. Khaemwaset was only eleven years old but was almost ready to enter the temple of Ptah as an acolyte. The king was encouraging him to emulate the son of the same name of the Great Ramesses who had become a Sem Priest of Ptah.

After two months of activity within the northern capital, Ramesses felt restless, and was determined to carry on with his tour of the kingdoms, carrying on downriver to Per-Ramesses with a view to inspecting the northern corps. Tiye asked to be excused, and did so with a triumphant smile on her face.

"I am with child again, my lord." She clasped her as yet unrevealing belly as if cradling a future heir. "I feel sure it is a boy, another in the quiverful of sons I will produce for you."

"I am overjoyed, my beloved," Ramesses said, taking his wife in his arms. "You shall want for nothing while I am away. I put the Per-Khemret of Men-nefer in your charge. Do with it as you will."

"Hurry back, my lord, for I greatly desire you to see your son when he is born."

"I shall be back long before then. A month or two at the most."

# Chapter 4
# Year 2 of Usermaatre Ramesses

The king had sailed north to Men-nefer with his mother months before, and now word had come south by messenger commanding Amunhirkhopeshef to join him in the northern capital. Trepidation and excitement filled the prince in equal parts for although he had never left the comfortable confines of Waset, he had often dreamed of taking his place in the wider world of the two kingdoms.

"How will I go?" he asked Tjaty Hori, on being told the news. "Along the desert road? By chariot with soldiers?"

"By barge," Hori said. "The road is long and dusty and beset by bandits."

"I am not afraid. I will scatter any bandits and trample them beneath my horses' hooves. The heir of Usermaatre can do no less."

"I did not imagine for one moment that you could, young sir," Hori replied, hiding a smile. "I do this more for myself. How could I explain to the king if I put you in the path of danger?"

Amunhirkhopeshef scowled. "I can drive a chariot...and I am skilled with the bow."

"I know you can do all those things, and I am sure that your father will see fit to give you opportunities in the future, but for now you must put your desires to one side. King Usermaatre Ramesses calls you north by water and you must obey. It is my duty to ensure your prompt obedience. The barge leaves in two days' time."

And so it was. Amunhirkhopeshef stood on the wooden wharves of Waset suddenly overcome by the realisation that he was bidding farewell to everything he knew and was familiar with, facing an exciting but uncertain future. The only things that stopped him from exhibiting his fear, beyond a slight tremble of his lower lip, were the presence of his brothers and a large segment of the city population. Meryamun and Prehirwenemef wept openly, and Khaemwaset was even more solemn than usual. Amunhirkhopeshef would have liked to hug his brothers and would not have minded dampening their shoulders if they had been alone, but the presence of so many others was a restraining influence.

The city population had turned out in force, eager for any show, and while many watched silently from behind the cordon of soldiers, some called out loudly for bread and beer to be dispensed in honour of the occasion. Tjaty Hori sent a few Medjay into the crowd to crack a few heads with their staffs. Priests were on hand too, ever ready to pray for the safe passage of the heir in the hopes of having a little more gold passed their way, but the hand of Amun lay heavily on his city, and his priests controlled the farewell.

One thing that made the voyage less daunting was the presence of a friend. Panhesy, the local garrison commander in the city of Waset was sending his son Ptahmose north to join the Amun corps in Men-nefer, and had prevailed upon Tjaty Hori to allow his son passage on the barge that carried the heir. Ptahmose and Amunhirkhopeshef had known each other for several years, and while their futures were going to be very different, that had not impeded their friendship. Ptahmose was a very junior officer, but his filial connection to Commander Panhesy offered many opportunities for future advancement. The young man was aware that friendship with the heir could be very important, but his duty was made easier by the fact that he genuinely liked the eldest son of the king.

"Come, my lord," Ptahmose said. "Your barge awaits."

Amunhirkhopeshef raised an eyebrow at the formality, but allowed himself to be escorted aboard the vessel. The barge captain showed the prince to his quarters just forward of the steering oars and to Ptahmose's sleeping mat just outside the reed screen door.

"That won't do at all," Amunhirkhopeshef said. "Ptahmose is my friend. He sleeps inside with me."

"My lord, it is not seemly," the barge captain protested.

"It's all right, Hirkho," Ptahmose murmured.

"No, it's not, Mose. Have it done, captain."

The captain capitulated, telling a sailor to transfer the sleeping mat to the prince's quarters. Then he excused himself and gave the orders to cast off.

Naked sailors leapt to the dock and unwound the heavy ropes while others raised the gangplank. Temple horns sounded and the crowd cheered. Dock workers pushed the barge away with poles, and as a water gap appeared, oars were thrust into the water.

"Farewell," shouted the young princes on shore.

Amunhirkhopeshef lifted a hand in acknowledgement, but otherwise tried to appear aloof and regal, though tears flooded his eyes. Ptahmose stood a pace behind his companion, and kept his own counsel, not wanting to intrude on what was apparently a sorrowful occasion. He grinned as the deck lurched beneath his feet, the current catching the vessel as it drew away from the dock.

"We're on our way, Hirkho," he murmured. "Glory awaits us both in the north."

Amunhirkhopeshef brushed the tears from his eyes and nodded. "A few years and we'll both be leading corps into battle. This is the start of our lives, Mose."

The barge moved out over the expanse of green water, eased north by the current. A steady breeze blew in their faces, but this did not matter as the sails would not be used on the voyage. Steering oars and the occasional use of the main banks of oars were sufficient to enable the shallow-bottomed vessel to make its way.

Both youths had ventured out of Waset before, but neither had experienced the vistas that opened up before them as the barge drifted north on the current. The river was a broad expanse of water bordered by vegetation and beyond that the yellows, browns and reds of the desert. At times, cliffs raised themselves high, crowding the fertile land, and at other times they withdrew and diminished, allowing arable land to spread almost as far as the eye could see.

Amunhirkhopeshef stood in the bow, eyes wide as he drank in the unfolding wonder that was Kemet. Ptahmose stood beside him almost silent, similarly overcome. From time to time, one or other would point out something of interest--a swirl where a crocodile or pehe-mau broke the surface, a flock of birds rising like thunder from the reed beds as the barge passed, the way the sunlight lit up the painted walls of a temple or drew shadowed patterns on high sandstone cliffs. Fishing boats peppered the water surface close to villages, the white sails sweeping them away from the barge's route as their owners caught sight of the royal flag flying from the mast head.

Odours assailed their nostrils--a swirling mix of growing things, the wet smells of water and mud, scent trails from orchards and less salubrious ones from village middens, the acrid overlay of desert dust, and closer at hand the sweat of sailors after a stint at the oars.

At first it seemed as if the barge travelled in silence, so intense was their concentration on the visual, but after a while the noises of their passage grew on them. The hull of the boat hissed through the rippled water, the breeze in their faces gusted with the faintest of sighs, mingling with their breathing; timbers creaked, while mutters of soft conversation arose from the oarsmen awaiting the next command. Across the waters, they could hear the splash of fish leaping, the cries of water birds, and high above them in the hazy blue shell of the sky, a hawk circled and uttered shill cries. Sometimes, when the barge drew closer to land, muted voices drifted across the water, the sound of mattocks striking earth, and the lowing of cattle.

It was almost too much for Amunhirkhopeshef. He turned away, a stricken look on his face. "I...I had no idea Kemet was so large. It's overwhelming."

"We've only seen a little bit of it," Ptahmose pointed out. "We've got days to go yet."

"I know, but...I'm not sure I can explain, Mose. I've really only seen the city and the palace, together with a few visits to farms and temples...but all this..." he waved his arms expansively. "My father is king of all this...there's so much of it. It fills me and...and I've only seen a tiny part. I don't know I can take it all in."

"It is impressive, I admit, but we'll get used to it. Let's get a drink and something to eat. Perhaps if we concentrate on our bellies, our hearts will make sense of all we've seen." Ptahmose looked round and called to the captain, "Hey, Captain. Can we get something to eat?"

The prince and his companion ate well on cold roasted goose, crisp vegetables and bread baked only that morning in Waset. They were offered cool river water, but being young men, turned it down, preferring to quaff long draughts of foaming beer. After eating, they sat in the shade of an awning erected in the stern and watched the interminable banks of the Great River slide past.

"You know, Mose, it's made me think," Amunhirkhopeshef said.

Ptahmose picked with a fingernail at a bit of goose flesh caught in his teeth. "What's that?"

"All this out there...the size of Kemet."

"Um...all right...what are you thinking?"

"The king made me his heir officially before he went north, and I started to think what it would be like to be king. Not that I want to be any time soon, of course," he added hurriedly.

"Of course not. The king is still young and will likely reign for many years yet."

"Even so, as heir I have to think about the future. I only knew the city and the palace...almost nothing about the rest of Kemet beyond the fact that it was there and that people from all over petitioned the king and that the Nine Bows are out there somewhere...anyway, I suppose I thought that Kemet was just a slightly larger version of Waset. Now, seeing it spreading out all around us, I wonder how any man can possibly control it all. When my time comes to mount the throne, how can I possibly rule all this?"

"That's why you have a Tjaty and Governors," Ptahmose said.

"What do you mean?"

"Well, a king has a Tjaty of the North and a Tjaty of the South who act for him, right? They are like little kings. Then there are the Governors of the forty-something sepats up and down the length of Iteru--they rule over their own sepat in the name of the king. Below them are the mayors of the cities and towns, the elders of even the meanest village, all controlling their own little kingdom and reporting upward. As well as all that, you have thousands of priests and a host of government officials all ruling their own pieces, with the army and Medjay keeping order."

"It sounds complex."

"It is, but it works. Think of the army as an example. How could it work if it was just a mass of people with bows and spears? Every man would just fight where he chose or go home; nothing would be achieved. Instead you have corps commanders, troop commanders, and leaders of fifty, ten and so on, all acting to maintain order--to maintain ma'at, if you will. The corps is Kemet's weapon and the king wields it, directing it at the enemy. Or think about this barge. What a waste of time and effort it would be if the king had to tell every oarsman when to pull on his oar. Instead, you have a captain who does that because the Tjaty told him to take you to Men-nefer, and because the king told him."

"So it's a series of hierarchies?"

"Exactly."

Amunhirkhopeshef frowned. "You make it sound as if the king has nothing to do."

"The king has plenty to do, but all the people who work for him take the drudgery of everyday concerns from him. He doesn't have to deal with all the little things that happen each day. Tjaties and governors and mayors and officials and priests do all that."

"So what does the king do?"

"You know that already," Ptahmose replied. "A king is the High Priest of every god. He is the Son of Re and through him, the gods bless Kemet.

He is the final arbiter of every dispute, and his strength of arms keeps Kemet safe against every foreign enemy. Without him, Kemet would descend into chaos."

Amunhirkhopeshef thought about this. "How is it you know so much about it when I, as heir to the throne, do not?"

"I am older than you, and have turned my mind to governance. I am an army officer, though only an aide, but I hope one day to command a corps or even become a general."

"If you are not already a general when I am king, I will make you one."

"Thank you, but as you are likely to be old when you become king, I'll probably be dead by then."

"Then I'll give you a splendid funeral, lavishing much gold on your tomb."

"You are very generous, O Son of the Son of Re," Ptahmose said with a grin. "However, you should be careful what you promise, as circumstances might change. I put it down to your extreme youth. When you are as old and wise as me, you'll realise..."

"Enough of your boasting, Mose," Amunhirkhopeshef cried. "You are but a year older and certainly no wiser. As for other things, you may be an army officer but I can outdo you in the use of weapons."

"Prove it."

"By the gods, I shall." Amunhirkhopeshef sprang to his feet and hailed the captain of the barge. "Ho, captain, take us ashore. I wish to hunt for wildfowl in the reed beds."

The captain had no option but to pull into the western shore just upriver from a great spread of reeds that lined the bank. In the pre-dawn chill of the next morning, small boats were launched and the two youths were paddled into position. There they crouched, shivering, while they waited for the sun to lift above the eastern horizon and the flocks of ducks roosting in the reed beds to arise.

As the first rays touched the western shore, the ducks awoke and took to the air, their wings sounding like a storm where the rushing wind beats down the trees and flattens the crops. Amunhirkhopeshef offered up a muttered prayer to Re and stood, sending arrow after arrow into the massed flocks wheeling above him. Ptahmose did the same, laughing with delight as birds started falling into the water and reed beds, from whence naked sailors retrieved them.

The arrows used in the competition had coloured threads attached to them so a score could be kept, and the ducks were laid out on the barge in two long rows. Sailors had started the day in high spirits, yelling out as each stricken duck was retrieved, but as the minutes passed, they grew quieter, looking apprehensively at the prince as Ptahmose's line grew longer.

The surviving ducks had winged away to the croplands on the eastern shore, and the last of the victims retrieved, when the two youths boarded the barge. Ptahmose saw at a glance that he had won the competition. Ordinarily, he would have exulted, but he saw the anger that washed over his friend's face. He walked down each line of corpses and thought hard how he could salvage the situation.

"These birds have not been sorted properly, Hirkho," Ptahmose said. "A duck pierced through the wing without an arrow in place cannot be counted."

Amunhirkhopeshef scowled but nodded, allowing Ptahmose to throw aside these birds. He brightened when he saw that many more were taken from his opponent's line than his own.

"Further," Ptahmose went on, "a bird pierced in the body is worth more than one pierced in the wing. It is the difference between skill and luck."

"Luck comes from the gods."

"Indeed, but it does not outweigh skill. Look, Hirkho, if we count a body blow as worth two, then you have clearly won this contest."

"I suppose so..."

"It is obvious," Ptahmose said forcefully. "I merely loosed my arrows into the flock above us. They were so tightly packed I could not miss, whereas you placed your arrows precisely into the breasts of each bird. That is more than luck--that is skill and luck together--truly a princely attribute. Do you not agree, captain?"

The captain nodded sagely and the sailors cheered the result. Amunhirkhopeshef smiled and accepted the praise of the crew, now examining each bird carefully and boasting about the numbers struck firmly in the breast. While he was engaged thus, the captain drew Ptahmose aside.

"That was wisely done, lad."

"He is the better archer, captain. I saw no reason to let my luck get in the way of the heir's enjoyment."

"Whatever you say, but I saw you in action, and you had the better technique."

"He is the heir."

"Indeed he is, and that means more than skill or luck."

Ptahmose nodded. "And we shall eat well tonight. I'll suggest it to the prince that we celebrate by letting the crew feast. I think we have killed enough to let each man have a duck."

# Chapter 5
# Year 2 of Usermaatre Ramesses

Ramesses sent word by fast chariot that he would be arriving in the north shortly, and that he desired all his army generals and commanders to be on hand for his inspection. His eldest son Amunhirkhopeshef, newly arrived in Men-nefer, would accompany him as the king thought it time that the youth get his first experience of the army. In a private ceremony attended only by the Tjaty and General Hori, he made the inexperienced youth a General of the Army.

"You are my eldest son and heir. One day you will be king but before that you must learn of war. I am making you a General."

"Does that mean I can lead the army into battle?" Amunhirkhopeshef asked excitedly.

"Indeed it does, my son, but you would be wise to accept the advice of a more experienced commander. You are only thirteen and have never led men against the enemy."

"I shall be like a lion taking down a wild ass," boasted the boy. "Men shall fall before my bow by the hundred; I shall crush them beneath my chariot wheels and win a mighty victory for you, father."

"The Nine Bows will tremble at your name," Herwernef observed with a smile.

"What it is to be young!" General Hori exclaimed.

Ramesses laughed and embraced his son. "We must find you a worthy enemy, but in the meantime, learn the craft of war from General Hori here, and my northern commanders."

Amunhirkhopeshef wanted to travel north by chariot rather than by barge, so Ramesses indulged him. The king ordered out the chariot squadrons of the resident Ptah corps and, after being ferried across the river to the eastern bank, took the road north and east. Ramesses led the squadrons, driving his own war chariot, and Amunhirkhopeshef proudly drove his own chariot, refusing to have a charioteer drive him, and keeping a scant horse's length behind his father.

Ramesses saw the barely contained energy within his son and allowed the boy to vent it from time to time. He would slow his own chariot and wave his son onward, calling to him to scout the way and report back. Three or four chariots would always accompany the prince, driven by trusted men; men who could be relied on to keep the headstrong youth from harm. At other times, king and heir would drive well ahead of the other chariots, whipping their horses to greater efforts while the other charioteers allowed them some privacy.

They stopped at Iunu one night, and king and heir visited the temples of the Nine arranged on their spiral roadway, ending up at the temple of Atum. Here they offered to the creator god, but Ramesses was also careful to avoid offending any of the other eight gods, paying special attention to Set.

"Set is the god of armies," Ramesses explained to his son. "You are named for Amun and when you are king you will have a special relationship with Re, but as a General, you should never forget Set."

"I won't father, but when do we reach the corps? I want to lead my army."

"In a few days. First we must go to Per-Ramesses and inspect the fortifications there."

The city that had been built by the Great Usermaatre dominated the eastern part of Ta Mehu, its high walls and fortifications acting as a bulwark against any foreign invasion. Another corps was to be found housed in its barracks, but the identity of the corps was never certain. The corps that guarded the northern borders took it in turn to come back to Per-Ramesses, ostensibly to man its walls as part of the defensive wall of Kemet, but in practice as a much-needed break from the onerous duties of the corps in the field. So it was that the first sight they had as they drove their chariots in through the southern gate of the eastern city was of drunken soldiers.

Ten or more soldiers spilled out of a tavern roaring out a drunken song. Two of them grabbed a passing woman and started fondling her body despite her loud protests, while the others gathered round and cheered them on. A few townspeople gathered in groups, but none seemed prepared to aid the woman. They and the drunken soldiers failed to notice the chariots of the king and his son as they came to a halt near them.

"What are they doing to that woman?" Amunhirkhopeshef asked. He looked around for the other members of the chariot squadron and for the first time regretted having outpaced them so comprehensively.

Ramesses did not answer, but the muscles of his jaw tightened. He leapt down from the chariot and strode forward, shoving men aside, and hauled one of the men off the crying woman.

"Here, what do you think you're doing?" the man cried out as he staggered back.

Ramesses stooped and dragged the other man off and shoved him aside. "Get out of here before I call the Medjay."

The first man laughed and looked at his fellow soldiers for support. "You think they're going to trouble the fighting Herus? They know better than to mess with us."

"You are men of the Heru corps? What are your names?"

"What do you want to know for?" called out one.

"And what business is it of yours anyway?" asked another.

"Soldiers do not go around attacking Kemetu women," Ramesses said.

"He's a lord of some sort," said one of the men. "Thinks he's better than us."

"We're only having a bit of fun, now stand aside, whoever you are."

"Give me your names."

"I'm getting a bit tired of your attitude," said the first man. "You nobles are all the same; driving around in your chariots lording it over us, while we're the ones who win the wars for you lot. If you don't believe me, ask our commander."

"You tell him, Beku," called out one of the other soldiers.

Beku grinned and stepped forward, poking Ramesses in the chest. "There, now you know my name. Last chance, fellow. Walk away or get what's coming to you."

Ramesses slapped the man's hand away. "You dare lay a hand on me? On your knees, Beku of Heru. And the rest of you," he added, looking at the other soldiers.

The tone of command cut through the fog in the minds of some of them, and one or two started shuffling backward. Beku laughed and raised his fist, but a voice pitched high with nervousness stopped him.

"Do not lay hands on the king," Amunhirkhopeshef cried. "It is death to do so."

"Eh, who's that?" Beku asked, looking toward the two chariots. "What's that whelp chattering about?"

"He says he's the king, Beku..."

"Don't be stupid. Where's his crown and gold jewellery? He's just some minor lord in a dusty kilt."

"He has the look of his father..."

"Nonsense, the king's in Waset. Besides, he travels around with lots of people, not just with a boy..."

The roar of chariot wheels and pounding hooves drowned him out as the chariot squadron raced through the gate and pulled up in the wide street in a cloud of dust. Men leapt down and ran forward, swords drawn. The drunken soldiers tried to run, but any who did so were cut down, and the rest fell to their knees and held out their hands, begging for mercy. Beku went pale and prostrated himself in the dust.

"F...forgive me," he stuttered. "How was...was I to know?"

"Arrest all these men," Ramesses ordered, "but these two..." he pointed to Beku grovelling at his feet and the other man who had been assaulting the woman, "...keep them separate." He stepped over the prostrate man and returned to his chariot, urging his team on toward the Governor's residence. Amunhirkhopeshef followed his father but he said nothing, the words he had meant to say dried up by the look of fury on the face of the king.

The commander of the Heru corps knelt on the stone floor of the audience chamber, his outstretched hands trembling. Commander Nakhtmin was new to the position, having replaced Merymose only a year before when the man's loyalty was called into question. Nakhtmin had seen first-hand how ruthless the ruling family could be when it came to stamping out opposition. Now he was in fear for his life, all because of some drunken soldiers.

"I am disappointed, Commander," Ramesses said. "I had been led to believe your corps was one of the best. Instead I find it populated by drunken oafs who rape women and assault their king. Are you incapable of maintaining discipline or do you just not care for your good name and that of your king?"

Governor Kamose sucked his teeth and watched keenly, wondering how Nakhtmin would crawl out of this latest dilemma. Admitting incompetence could lead to his dismissal, whereas bringing shame on the king's name could lead to a worse fate.

"I am waiting for your answer."

"Your pardon, Son of Re," Nakhtmin said. "I feared to interrupt your Majesty. I, too, am sorely disappointed in the behaviour of what is a very small number of men in the Heru corps. My men have returned recently from duty on the northern borders and succumbed to drink and the desire for women. Their conduct is inexcusable, of course, and I will deal with it firmly."

"How?"

"How will I deal with them, Son of Re? Well, er...it is my understanding that eight men did no more than stand around. I thought perhaps a reprimand and..."

"They spoke disrespectfully to me and encouraged the other two."

"Er...a whipping? Ten lashes each, Majesty?"

"Make it fifty. Next, the rape of the woman."

"They did not actually..."

"The intention was there. If I had not stepped in they would have raped her. You know the penalty for rape."

"Yes, Majesty. But what of the one who laid a hand on you? The penalty for that is death, but if he is already to die for rape..."

"I cannot kill him twice, so the manner of his death must serve as a lesson. Assemble the corps and punish the guilty men. Fifty lashes each for the lesser charges, death by beheading for the rapist, death by impalement for the one called Beku."

"And er...burial, Son of Re? Are they to be denied?"

Ramesses considered for a few moments. "I am feeling generous. Let their families claim the bodies for a proper burial."

"Yes, Son of Re."

Nakhtmin remained on his knees, not having been dismissed. Ramesses regarded him thoughtfully.

"What should I do with you, Commander? Some of the responsibility for the actions of your men must lie on your shoulders."

"I am at your mercy, Son of Re."

"I will consider the matter," Ramesses said. "Go now and attend to your duties."

Nakhtmin rose to his feet and stumbled backward, his head bowed as he left the presence of the king. When he had left the chamber, Ramesses turned to Governor Kamose.

"What have you to say on this matter?"

Kamose bowed, but hid any fear he might have been feeling. "I am the civil authority, Son of Re. I have limited control over the military. Had you not intervened, the woman might have complained to me, whereupon I would have acted to limit further harm, probably in consultation with Nakhtmin. I have Medjay to keep some sort of control, but they are helpless against seasoned troops, even drunken ones."

Ramesses nodded. "Maybe the punishments will discourage further abuses."

"I shall pray they do, Son of Re."

Kamose hesitated, waiting to see if the king had anything further to say on the matter, and when he had not, spoke again.

"I would be honoured if you and your son would join me at dinner this evening, Majesty. A mere fifty or sixty guests, but one you might find interesting, a Syrian princess has fled the Hatti and seeks refuge in Kemet. I have granted her temporary accommodation, dependent on your final decision, of course."

"A princess of Syria? Well, they breed like conies up there, so I won't attach too much importance to it."

"She is rather good looking, Majesty."

Ramesses looked at the governor. "And?"

Kamose smiled. "If you were looking to stock your local Per-Khemret, she might be a suitable addition. I am sure she would consider it an honour to become your concubine. Her daughter too, for that matter. Sixteen years old and untouched; a dark-haired beauty."

"I shall look upon her...upon them...with interest."

The feast took place at sunset, in an open courtyard of the governor's palace. Each guest was greeted by servants and allowed cones of scented beeswax to be strapped to their heads. The heat of the evening would gradually melt the wax, letting it drip flower scents through the plaited wigs, down the bodies of the guests and their clothing.

Ramesses and Amunhirkhopeshef sat on couches with Governor Kamose beneath a spreading tamarind tree. Small birds swarmed in the branches, twittering deafeningly as they settled for the night. Debris and droppings rained down, but the Governor had erected wide linen awnings so that none would soil the feasters below. As the light faded from the sky, little bats flitted and darted in the evening air, their high-pitched cries heard only by the younger guests.

Off to one side, cooks gathered around cooking pits, putting the finishing touches on a variety of roasted meats. The arriving guests stood and took in the beauty of the surroundings, inhaling the aromas of the meats. These, mixed with the scent of fresh baked barley bread and the perfumes of the beeswax cones, assailed their nostrils most pleasingly.

Men and women gathered to either side of the royal party, seating themselves on couches, chairs or cushions according to their rank, and servants moved among them dispensing watered wine from the Governor's own vineyards, freshly brewed beer, cool river water or milk, warm from the udders of cows or goats. Other servants brought out roasted meats in great platters, fatted beef, lamb and goat, goose, pigeon, duck and, for the royal party, more exotic bird flesh from Kush and the north. There was fish in abundance, both saltwater and river varieties, either whole or stewed in milk and spices, baked in thin pastries and drizzled with honey and herbs. Bowls of oils were presented, pastes of chick peas, crushed sesame seeds and sweetmeats prepared from dates, almonds and honey. Fresh vegetables were served to cleanse the palate, lettuce, cucumber, onion and radish, and a multitude of fruits.

Ramesses ate sparingly, casting his eyes over the guests, while Amunhirkhopeshef ate greedily, exclaiming over every new dish and praising the skill of the Governor's cooks. Kamose himself picked at his food, paying attention to the needs of his royal guests and signing to his trusted servants to bring the choicest viands and the best wine. As the tempo of the feast slackened, when bellies became filled with good food and the drink induced a pleasant haze, when the perfumed beeswax cones dripped delightful scents down backs and breasts, then Kamose signalled for the entertainment to begin.

Musicians hurried out and struck up a lively tune on reed pipes, a variety of stringed instruments, some curved with many strings, others long and straight with one or a few taut strings running their length. Other musicians shook sistra and two blew softly on horns. The feasters clapped time with the music, and then the dancers came out, young girls wearing nothing but a thin string around their waists. They swayed in time to the music, bending and clapping their hands, lifting their feet high and stamping on the hard-baked earth of the courtyard. The flickering torchlight accentuated their movements, casting moving shadows on burnished bodies, and quite plainly exciting the onlookers.

The king seemed preoccupied despite the entertainment, and Kamose leaned close to ask if the banquet was not to his liking.

"I have never eaten better, Kamose, and the music and dancers are second to none, but I cannot see this Syrian princess of whom you spoke."

"Ah, Majesty, Princess Hemdjert and her daughter Iset asked if they could meet you after the feast..."

"Hemdjert? Why such an ill-omened name?"

"The king of Hatti murdered her husband, his own son, Majesty, causing her to flee for her life. She still mourns him, hence the name she has taken. It is Habadjilat or some such barbaric name in her own tongue, which translates as Hemdjert in the gods' tongue."

"What is her real name then?"

"I believe it was 'meadow flower' or some such, but she has renounced it along with her position when her husband died."

"And you want me to take a woman with such an ill-omened name into my Per-Khemret? Whatever possessed you, Kamose?"

"She is very beautiful, Majesty. I thought...well, a temporary dalliance..."

"I like the sound of the daughter better. She is beautiful too?"

"Iset? Yes, indeed, but she is only sixteen."

"Tyti, my sister-wife, is only now fifteen, Kamose."

"Of course, Majesty..."

"I wish to see her now."

"Er, yes, of course..." Kamose summoned a servant and sent him running to warn the Syrian ladies of the imminent presence of the king, then he stood, clapped his hands for silence, and informed the feasters that the king wished to retire and that everyone should go home. He led the king back into his residence and to a small audience chamber.

"The lady and her daughter will be brought here, Majesty."

"I only want to see the daughter."

"Princess Hemdjert does not allow her daughter out of her sight."

"What? Even when I request it? This girl must be a prodigy of beauty indeed."

The Governor's servants ushered in two ladies dressed in the northern fashion, with folds of garments covering almost all their bodies despite the warmth of the evening. Both women were veiled, concealing their features. They advanced toward the king and dipped into a curious gesture that incorporated a half squat and a bow, before straightening and standing before Ramesses.

"My lord king, Son of Re, Lord of the Two Lands," said one of the women. "I am Hemdjert, daughter of Mursil, lately wife of Amalek the fifth son of Suppiluliuma, the king of Hatti, and this is my daughter Iset Ta-

Hemdjert. We throw ourselves on your mercy, asking for refuge from those who mean us harm."

"You are welcome in Kemet, Lady Hemdjert, as is your daughter," Ramesses replied. "I have heard tales of your beauty. May I gaze upon your countenance for myself?"

"As your majesty wishes." Hemdjert lifted her veil, followed a moment later by Iset. Both women stood there in the audience chamber looking boldly at the king of Kemet. "Well, Majesty?" she asked softly.

Ramesses stared at Iset's face. He dragged his attention to her mother when she spoke, but quickly returned to his contemplation of the daughter.

A small smile tugged at Hemdjert's lips. "I see my daughter has gained your approval, Majesty."

"In truth, the tales I heard did not do your beauty justice...either of you." Ramesses stepped closer and stared into Iset's eyes. The girl did not lower her eyes deferentially but met the king's gaze openly. Her full lips pursed slightly and then creased in a welcoming smile.

"How may we thank you for offering us refuge, Son of Re?" Hemdjert asked.

"I wish to take Iset as my concubine," Ramesses replied.

"No."

"What?" Kamose cried. "You refuse the king? This is a tremendous honour, and..."

Ramesses cut the Governor off with a gesture. "Why do you refuse me, Hemdjert?"

"My daughter is a Princess of the royal house of Hatti..."

"Unacknowledged, and liable to execution if your father-in-law catches you."

Hemdjert inclined her head. "Indeed, Majesty, but royal blood flows in her body. It would be beneath her to become anyone's concubine..."

Kamose hissed at the insult, but Ramesses just nodded.

"...even yours, O Lord of the Two Lands. She is made for bearing strong sons to inherit their birthright."

"Marriage? You want me to take her as a wife? I have two already."

"Only two, Majesty? I understood that the Bull of Heru fathered sons on a hundred women."

Ramesses laughed. "You understand correctly, but only those born to my wives may be my heir."

"And Iset will bear your heir or not at all."

Ramesses turned back to the young woman. "And what do you say, Iset Ta-Hemdjert? Do you have a mind of your own? Will you come to my bed willingly?"

"As your wife, Son of Re, I would do all things willingly," Iset said. "As for the rest, it is as my mother says."

Ramesses shook his head and turned away. "You would bend the King of Kemet to your will? There are a hundred girls as beautiful as you, a thousand even, who would be willing to spread their legs for me, for no greater reward than the honour I do them."

"Then may I suggest you take one of them, Majesty," Iset said. "For I have told you under what circumstances I will spread mine."

"I do not even know if your body matches the beauty of your face or the fire of your mind," Ramesses grumbled.

"Nor will you, Majesty, before marriage. A princess of Hatti is modest and chaste. If you seek casual pleasure, then you must look elsewhere. If you want a Queen and mother to your heirs, then you will find no better."

"I have a Queen already, my royal sister Tyti. And heirs too, four strong boys. Why should I need others?"

"A king cannot have too many sons. Look at your namesake Usermaatre Ramesses. Who was it who inherited the throne upon his death? It was Merenptah, his thirteenth son. You are still a young man, Majesty. Who knows how many sons you will outlive?"

"You are well informed for a foreigner."

"Where else should a Syrian learn about but Kemet, the most powerful nation under the sun? What else should a princess learn about than the royal family of this most powerful nation? And who else should a young girl learn about than Kemet's young and virile king? You are the most powerful king in the whole world, and I want to be your Queen."

Ramesses stared and then laughed. "I like you, Iset Ta-Hemdjert. Very well, you shall be my wife and my other queen, for as you no doubt know, the Great Usermaatre had two queens and indeed, one of them was called Iset as well. I shall marry you and sow sons in your belly to reign after me."

# Chapter 6
# Year 2 of Usermaatre Ramesses

Ramesses took Iset Ta-Hemdjert to be his wife at an informal gathering of local nobles and officials three days later, and in an elaborate ceremony an hour later, raised her to the status of Great Royal Wife alongside his sister-wife Tyti. Then he took her to bed, and her body proved to be every bit as enticing as her face. He remained closeted with her for two days, and then only stirred outside the palace for short periods.

The king's planned inspection of the northern corps was put on hold, and his son Amunhirkhopeshef was left to his own amusements. He moped around the palace for a few days before asking the governor to organise a hunt in the local reed beds. Kamose could see nothing wrong with allowing the youth his way, as his father was almost certainly going to be occupied for the next few days; rumours were circulating that the Bull of Heru was proving exceptionally virile.

Ta Mehu comprised a vast triangle of flat well-watered land, intersected with the wide flowing branches of the Great River as it made its way to the sea, and by numerous canals that connected the cities to the river. These canals had to be extended from time to time or re-dug at long intervals as the very course of the river changed, though no man knew why. The result was that a large part of the land was low-lying and often marshy, and water birds flocked to the region by the tens of thousands, sometimes darkening the sky as they passed over.

Kamose instructed his hunters to lead the young prince to the largest flocks of waterfowl. They were charged with making sure that he had a good day's hunting and that nothing happened to him. The Governor, with a smile upon his face, told them in graphic detail what would happen to them if harm befell the young prince. The hunters blanched, but bowed respectfully and backed out of their lord's presence.

They set out from the palace at Per-Ramesses on foot while it was still dark, the stars in the body of Nut still bright in the cold clear air.

Amunhirkhopeshef shivered, wishing that he had worn a woollen tunic instead of succumbing to vanity in an effort to appear manly. He noticed that the hunters were well wrapped up against the night air, and scowled. There was nothing he could do about it though, unless he wished to draw attention to his plight, so he strode along rubbing his bare arms and casting anticipatory looks at the eastern horizon.

The hunters led the prince north from the city, following the course of the river. Several small boys tagged along, eager for adventure and the opportunity of a good meal after a successful hunt. Mud squelched underfoot as they crossed open fields and dew-soaked pastures, the damp adding to the Amunhirkhopeshef's discomfort. At last, a faint tinge of greyness hinted at the approach of Re's solar barque, the stars fading out before his godly presence. The hunters halted and started preparing for the hunt.

"There lie the reed beds, my lord," said Bak, the chief hunter, pointing. "With your permission, we will station you just there, near that dead tree. Den will stay with you. The rest of the men will circle around to the far side, and as the sun rises, beat the reed beds and make a loud clamour. You should have fine sport as the birds fly out and over you."

The eastern horizon coloured up as Amunhirkhopeshef waited, having strung his bow and checked his arrows. He still shivered, his clothes wet and clinging to him, while a thin chill breeze made his jaw tremble. Occasionally, he would slap at biting insects that arose from the swampy ground to feast on their blood. Den the hunter waited with him, occasionally murmuring encouraging phrases, telling the young prince of the huge number of birds he would undoubtedly slay. After a short time, Amunhirkhopeshef snapped at him to be quiet, and the first rays of the rising sun lit upon two silent watchers.

With the dawn came a low babble of sound from the reed beds as the waterfowl awoke to a new day and prepared to fly to their feeding grounds on the pastures and tilled fields. A few arose, wings whirring as they lifted into the air. Amunhirkhopeshef lifted his bow.

"Wait, my lord," Den whispered. "These few are widely spaced and alert. Wait for massed birds."

A few moments later, shouts and calls split the morning air and, with a roar like falling water or a sudden thunderstorm, a great flock of birds arose from the reeds, their beating wingtips brushing, and soared up in a mass so dark, Amunhirkhopeshef thought it really was a thundercloud.

"Strike now, my lord," Den cried.

Amunhirkhopeshef needed no further encouragement. He loosed an arrow into the flock and saw a bird falter in its flight, loosed another and saw a second bird plummet back toward the ground. A third, a fourth, a fifth followed, and so thickly did the birds flock that every arrow found a mark. The hardened wooden tips of the shafts pierced feathers and flesh, killing some outright and sending others spiralling into the river or reeds uttering plaintive cries.

The prince ran out of arrows and stood grinning as the last of the flock wheeled overhead and swept out over the river and away. From the direction of the reed beds came the happy cries and splashes of small boys and some of the more enthusiastic hunters as they waded through the shallow water, recovering corpses and wringing the necks of any birds that still lived. They emerged from the reeds triumphant, holding aloft dead birds and laying them down on the grass in front of the prince. Almost every arrow was recovered too, though six or seven had disappeared and three were broken, having hit a bone as they killed.

The heat of the morning sun dried the dew and started to warm the shivering prince, so when Bak the hunter suggested they move on to hunt geese in a nearby field, he was eager to do so, despite feeling very tired. He moved off after the hunters, scratching at the insect bites on his bare arms and legs.

They found the geese, a small flock wandering over a field of young wheat seedlings, tugging at the tender green shoots as they fed. A few of them raised their heads as they spied the men at the edge of the field, and uttered a few honks as a warning to the rest of the flock. The hunters squatted, motioning the prince down beside them.

"We must keep low," Bak said. "Geese see a man standing and are afraid, but they do not see a man when he crouches down."

"Not see him?" Amunhirkhopeshef asked, puzzled. "How can that be? I can still see them clearly; how can they not see me?"

"Forgive me, my lord, if I did not say it right. Yes, the geese can still see us, but as long as we crouch down, they do not recognise us as men, and do not see the danger. We can crawl much closer to them than we could walk."

Bak led the way again, crawling on hands and knees in the general direction of the grazing geese. One or two still looked toward them and uttered an occasional honk, but it was a cry of curiosity rather than alarm. The hunters did not crawl straight toward their quarry, but angled first to one side, then the other. In this way, they approached the geese quite closely. Bak stopped and held up a hand.

"This is close enough, my lord," he whispered. "Any closer and we will alarm them."

Amunhirkhopeshef nodded and sat back on his haunches, fitting an arrow to his bow. He aimed at the nearest goose and released. The arrow flew in a flat trajectory and buried itself in the earth a pace from the bird. It squawked and flapped its wings, stretching out its neck to stare at the stick that had suddenly appeared, but after a few moments it shook its feathers and resumed grazing.

The prince tried again, correcting his aim slightly, and this time the arrow flew true, piercing the bird and bowling it over. It cried out and beat its wings for a few moments before lying still, and nearby geese looked round for danger, uttering a series of soft honks.

Den reached out and touched the prince's sandal and when he had the boy's attention, pointed at two geese that were moving in their direction.

"They will see us, my lord, and raise the alarm. Take them next."

Amunhirkhopeshef turned and raised his bow again, just as the nearest goose flapped its wings and stretched out its neck, bugling a loud alarm call. The prince released the arrow immediately, transfixing the bird's breast, but the damage had been done, the rest of the flock was taking to the air, calling out their distress as they beat their way aloft. The prince leapt to his feet, rapidly loosing arrow after arrow into the departing flock. Three birds fell, their wings broken and bodies pierced, two on land, but a third splashed down in the river. The hunters ran, chasing down the wounded geese and wringing their necks, before turning their attention to the one in the water. It swam in circles some fifty paces from shore, one wing and a foot pinned to its side by the arrow, honking its distress.

"Someone will have to swim out and get it," Den said.

"Send one of the boys," Bak agreed. "It's their job."

One of the small village boys was tasked with the duty and he grinned and dived in, splashing vigorously as he made for the stricken bird. It swam slowly, beating the water with its uninjured wing and slowly drew further from the boy.

"Keep going," Bak yelled, encouraging the boy to greater efforts.

Amunhirkhopeshef's attention was drawn to a swirl in the water further out in the current and he grabbed Den's arm, pointing.

"What's that?"

"What, lord?" The hunter shaded his eyes, staring out over the water and suddenly stiffened. "Crocodile. Look there, Bak, it's a crocodile."

The reptile moved swiftly through the water, barely breaking the surface as it arrowed in toward the commotion in the water. The hunters and other boys yelled to the boy to come back, and Amunhirkhopeshef so forgot his dignity as to join in.

The small boy had almost caught up with the wounded goose when he saw the ripple in the water and stopped swimming. For a moment he just bobbed there, treading water, and then with a yell of terror threw himself backwards. As he did so, the ripple died away and for a moment the surface of the water was still save where goose and boy still splashed some ten paces apart.

The stillness and uncertainty lasted no more than a dozen heartbeats. Then the crocodile broke the water surface beneath the goose, lifting it aloft on a cushion of water before its jaws closed around the hapless bird and dragged it under. Bak called to the boy to redouble his efforts, for he had spotted another crocodile approaching. The hunters moved down until they were shin-deep in the water, yelling for the boy to swim faster, the other boys screaming and crying as the reptile got nearer.

Amunhirkhopeshef fitted an arrow to his bow and muttered a prayer to all the gods, including Sobek, the crocodile god. He aimed, just over the head of the swimming boy and loosed an arrow. It skimmed past the bobbing head and thwacked into the water no more than a handbreadth in front of the crocodile, which came on undeterred. He shot again, and at the short distance now to the target, hit the crocodile on the snout.

It bounced off, but the crocodile seemed to pause, and in that breath, Bak and Den reached down and grabbed the boy, hauling him bodily from the water and throwing him back onto dry land. They scrambled after him and stood panting with emotion and effort as the crocodile turned and swam off.

"My lord," Bak said to the prince. "Your actions have saved the boy's life."

"A mighty hunter indeed," Den added. "And one who looks after his people."

With an effort, Amunhirkhopeshef maintained a serious demeanour, though his chest swelled with pride.

"Come," he said. "Let us prepare the spoils and feast, for today we have shared danger and lived to boast about it."

The hunters gathered up the fallen geese and they returned to the field where the ducks lay. They prepared a fire, plucked and gutted the birds, and roasted them above the coals. Eaten hot from the fire, with fat and juices dripping from fingers and chin, the prince thought it was the most delicious meal he had ever eaten, and praised the hunters as skilled cooks. Den gathered some plants from the water's edge and the crisp leaves and stalks cleansed their mouths of the meat juices and refreshed them.

They returned to the city and palace with their shadows long beside them, and the hunters sang the prince's praises to everyone they met, recounting his hunting exploits and how he had driven off the crocodile as it was about to devour a boy. His father Ramesses was still ensconced with his new wife, which disappointed Amunhirkhopeshef, who wanted to boast. Instead, he went to bathe and change into clean clothes.

The prince sat in the water of the bathing pool while servants poured cool water over his head and shoulders, thinking back over the day, and absently scratched at an insect bite on his thigh. He shivered, as if the chill of the morning was still lodged within his bones, and ordered the servants to bring linen towels. The meat he had eaten earlier sat heavily in his stomach and he could not face another meal, so he went to bed.

Amunhirkhopeshef woke with a fever the next morning.

# Chapter 7
# Year 2 of Usermaatre Ramesses

The king stayed in the city of Per-Ramesses for a month, enjoying his new wife, and then went north to the borders to inspect the troops guarding Kemet's frontiers. He did not take Prince Amunhirkhopeshef with him as he had originally planned, as the boy was sick. The court physicians had explained that the boy had gone hunting in the reed beds where a demon must have entered into his body. They had treated him with emetics and purgatives and fed him all manner of noxious things designed to drive the demon out. Priests had joined in the battle, offering up sacrifices and prayers for the recovery of the king's heir, but to no avail. It was believed now that the demon had been sent by Sobek, as the crocodile that represented that god had been robbed of its prey by the prince's actions. Ramesses sat with his son as he slept, and left orders that no expense was to be spared in finding a remedy.

"Find an acceptable replacement for the boy he saved," Ramesses instructed, "but if all else fails; sacrifice the boy he saved to the crocodiles. It is better a commoner dies than my son and heir."

With that, Ramesses gathered his chariots and sped north, his mind focussed once more on the military might of Kemet and whether it was of sufficient strength to match the feats of the Great Usermaatre. He went first to the string of forts along the Way of Heru, the military road along the coast. These forts were the main line of defence for the rich lands of Ta Mehu, and guarded against incursions from the lands of Kanaan, Amurri, Hatti, the Syrians and, more recently, the Sea Peoples.

The king travelled fast with his squadron of chariots, descending upon a fort in the light of dawn, surprising the guards and catching the commanders napping. He inspected every aspect of the fortifications, every stitch of clothing and piece of equipment, eating with the men to judge the quality of the food, and issuing stern orders if any detail did not match his expectation. Some commanders and officers were commended, others castigated, and a few replaced, but each time the king swept out through the gates with his squadron, heading for the next fort, he was satisfied that he left Kemet's defences stronger.

He deigned to explain his thinking to one fort commander. "How can I think about attacking Kemet's enemies, if our defences are lacking? I must attack from a position of strength."

From the forts, Ramesses moved on to the corps patrolling the borders. He had already dealt with the lack of discipline in the Heru corps back in Per-Ramesses. Corps Commander Nakhtmin had been left in charge of his corps, and he had preceded his king to his station on the frontier. Now Ramesses gathered his four local commanders together and outlined his thoughts for the future.

"Not since the glorious days of the Great Usermaatre have Kemetu armies stamped their enemies into submission. There have been rebellions and minor incursions by the Ribu in the west and south, and the Sea Peoples here in the north, and the kings that followed the Great Usermaatre, Baenre Merenptah and Userkheperure Seti, merely fought to contain these enemies. My own father, Userkhaure-Setepenre Setnakhte, was unable to end these threats to Kemetu peace as he was kept busy destroying the remnants of internal instability. The pretenders that followed the legitimate descendants of the Great Usermaatre ripped the kingdoms apart and set brother against brother. My father brought an end to this, and left it to me to deal with Kemet's foreign enemies.

"I will soon lead the armies of Kemet against the Ribu, destroying them utterly; against the Sea Peoples, shattering their confederacy and incorporating them as vassal states; and against the Amurri, the Hatti, and the Syrians should they set even one foot upon soil that rightly belongs to Kemet. Before I can do this, however, I must take the corps that have fallen into disuse, have become pale imitations of the corps that served the Great Usermaatre, and create them anew. I have recently seen what happens when a commander loosens the hand of discipline on a corps and I give you all fair warning, I will not tolerate further failures. Let any commander who believes he cannot control his men step down now. Let any commander who believes he cannot fashion his men into an efficient fighting force, hand over his command to another."

Nakhtmin, Commander of the Heru corps, stepped forward and fell to his knees in front of his king, stretching out his hands in submission.

"Hear me, Son of Re," he said. "I was that officer that failed in my duty down in Per-Ramesses, yet you extended to me the hand of mercy and allowed me to retain my command. Know this, merciful one; I will not fail you again. The Heru corps and I stand ready to do your bidding, even unto death. Command and I shall obey."

"Arise, Nakhtmin," Ramesses said with a smile. He embraced his commander. "Never fear, I will ask a lot of you, of all of you. Do my other commanders stand ready to obey me?"

"Amun stands ready, Son of Re," Senedje said.

"As does Re," Khay declared.

"And Set," Hori said fiercely, pushing past the other commanders. "Command and we obey."

Ramesses started his inspection of the corps immediately, starting with the Heru corps. He was thorough; examining the men's equipment, asking the men questions that revealed their knowledge of what might be required of them, testing their responses to shouted commands, the dip of banners or the sound of rams' horns. To the officers he asked different things, seeing if they understood basic tactics and firing difficult questions at them. As soon as the other commanders saw what was happening with Heru, they surreptitiously sent runners to their own corps to prepare their own officers and men.

The king progressed by degrees through the ranks of foot soldiers and onto the archers and the chariot squadrons, instructing the corps's scribes to take down any faults he found, or places where he thought improvements could be made. As the day progressed, the list got longer and longer, and Nakhtmin's spirits got lower and lower.

"He'll never survive this," Khay whispered to Hori. "The king means to make an example of him."

The camp itself and even the camp followers were inspected, Ramesses showing great interest in even the lowliest servant and the most mundane piece of equipment. He went through the horse lines, studied the horse feed and tested the tackle, and then did the same thing in the cooking areas, going so far as to taste the food and weak beer offered to the men.

"See about changing your source of flour for the bread," he told Nakhtmin. He held up a chip of stone that had jarred his teeth. "I want all the men in good health. A cracked tooth is painful and distracts a man whose mind should be focussed solely on the enemy."

Nakhtmin called the overseer and gave him the king's instructions.

"We grinds the barley ourselves, sir," said the overseer. He eyed the other men standing around but did not recognise any of them. "Besides, teeth always gets chipped, don't they? Seems stupid to worry 'bout that."

"Insolent dog," Senedje snarled. "That man needs a good flogging."

"Enough, Senedje," Ramesses said quietly. "Your name, overseer?"

"Huni, but who are you?"

"I am Usermaatre Ramesses, Huni, and if I want the flour free of stone chips, then it is your job to make it so."

Huni frowned, and recognition of the name if not the face crept over his features. He threw himself to the ground and wailed aloud.

"Forgive me, Majesty, I didn't know. O gods of earth and water, I've got a wife and three children who depend on me. Don't deprive them of a father just because he's a fool. I shoulda seen, majesty, you with all these gents and thems so quiet an' all. Oh, say you won't have me killed, Majesty, please."

"Get up, Huni."

With a little prompting from his commander, who nudged him with the toe of his sandal, the overseer rose to his knees and fearfully raised his face to his king. His tears formed muddy streaks in his dust begrimed face and his lip trembled.

"Huni, I forgive your transgression because you acted in ignorance. However, I want you to take my words and store them in your heart. You are to dispose of your old grinding stones and use new ones that are not chipped and cracked. I want no stone chips baked into the barley bread you serve the men in this corps. Do you understand?"

"Yes, Son of Re, but..." Huni licked his lips and looked down at the ground.

"Yes?"

"H... how do I pay for new stones, Majesty? Do I sell the corps's stores?"

"Order the stones and give the bill to your commander. He will get the required silver from the Treasury."

When the overseer had scurried away to do his king's bidding, Ramesses turned to his commanders. "Note my actions and words carefully. Every part of every corps is to function as well as it can. If equipment is broken, mend it or buy it anew. Look after your men and horses, treating them as if they were your own horses and children. I want my corps to be well fed, well equipped, well trained, and healthy, and I will judge my commanders on how well they carry out my orders."

The king looked around his anxious looking commanders and smiled. "Now, who is next? Khay of Re, I think."

When every corps had been thoroughly inspected and changes initiated, Ramesses started the corps on military exercises, concentrating on having the soldiers carry out complicated manoeuvres without falling apart. They practiced with spear and axe, sword and staff, even fighting without weapons. Archery was practiced and the chariot squadrons worked hard on charging en masse. It was a long time before the king professed himself satisfied.

"You have made a good start, gentlemen," he told his commanders and senior officers, "but there is a long way to go. I want the Kemetu army second to none."

Military matters were not the only things to hold the attention of the king over these many months on the northern borders. While the Tjaty and Great Khenbet Council of each kingdom governed on a day-to-day basis, all matters of importance were still referred to the king for his approval or decision. A steady stream of messengers connected the king, wherever he was, with the governance of every sepat. Every day, Ramesses sat in his command tent with his scribes, going over the messages and writing out replies, orders or suggestions.

A message came from distant Waset, informing the king that Queen Tyti had given birth to a healthy son. She wanted to name him Ramesses, and petitioned the king for permission. He readily gave it, as the Great Usermaatre had also had a son called Ramesses. The king was in a good mood that day and celebrated with his commanders in the evening.

Another day, a messenger arrived from Men-nefer, with the news that his wife Tiye had also given birth, though only to a daughter. She had named her Tentopet, and asked the king if this met with his approval.

"Why should I care?" Ramesses asked of the scribe after the man read out the letter.

Wisely, the scribe held his tongue.

"Daughters are trouble," the king mused. "Look what disaster befell Kemet when a woman tried to take the throne. I have many sons, though, so that will not happen to me. I can always marry her myself or give her to one of my sons."

A letter arrived from Per-Ramesses, from his new Queen Iset. She sent a long message declaring her love and then reported that she was with child and hoped to bear the king a son. The Queen's mother, Hemdjert, petitioned the king in the same letter to raise her daughter to the status of God's Wife of Amun.

"Give a woman everything and she wants more," Ramesses observed. "Is the title of Great Wife no longer enough for her?' He thought for a few moments. "Well, it is easy enough to grant. Let her be God's Wife of

Amun in Per-Ramesses, just as Tyti performs that role in Waset. If I can have two wives, so can the god."

Another letter arrived from Governor Kamose reporting on the condition of Prince Amunhirkhopeshef. The boy had recovered fully, but had then had a relapse and was once more sick and feverish. Physicians and priests continued to attend upon the king's heir.

Each Tjaty operated an extensive spy network within his kingdom, rooting out unrest and dissatisfaction, and within the nations of the Nine Bows. These spies reported back when they could, and trusted scribes within the palaces of Waset and Men-nefer collated the reports so that the Tjaty could gain an overall picture of any threat to Kemet. These threats were then sent to the king wherever he was. Each report on the Nine Bows was read over carefully for any signs of preparation for war. There seemed to be little on the horizon at the moment, but Ramesses knew war was inevitable and wanted to be fully prepared.

He was fond of telling his generals, "If war does not come to us, I will take it to all of Kemet's enemies. A nation crushed into the dust will no longer trouble us."

A curious report piqued the king's interest--a report of possible trouble that stemmed from within Ta Mehu, from near the city of Per-Bast. Spies reported that an old enemy had been seen in the city, General Ament, who had been the principal supporter of the woman who called herself Sitre Tausret and pretended to be King of Kemet. Tausret and Ament had been defeated and had fled for their lives. None knew if they had lived or died.

"They must be dead," Ramesses muttered. "And if not, what would he be doing in Per-Bast? There's nothing for him there...ah..." He frowned, thinking hard. It had been five years or more, but a memory tugged at his attention. "He had a sister there. Could he have returned to visit her? It is possible..." Calling for his scribe, he had him pen a quick letter to Tjaty Herwernef, bidding him search the property of Ament's sister and arrest the former general if he was found. He ended the letter by telling the Tjaty to take whatever steps he deemed necessary to prevent a resurgence of rebellion. Then he forgot the matter as his attention was taken up by other problems.

Another letter shattered the king's equanimity. It came from Governor Kamose and concerned the king's own son Amunhirkhopeshef. The scribe scanned it quickly and went pale, hesitating to read it.

"Majesty, I...I do not...it is bad news."

"Read it," Ramesses commanded.

The scribe licked his lips nervously, and after a false start, read the letter from Governor Kamose. "'To King Usermaatre Ramesses,' it reads. 'Son of Re, Lord of the Two Lands, High Priest of Every Temple, Life! Health! Prosperity! From Governor Kamose of Per-Ramesses, Fan-Bearer on the King's Right Hand, Greetings.

'Son of Re, it is with great sorrow that I must report on the death of Crown Prince Amunhirkhopeshef, Heir to the Two Lands. The illness which beset him many months ago relented its hold on your son, but then returned in full force. Though there were many days when he seemed to recover and live life to the fullest, he relapsed into fever.

'Son of Re, be assured that the physicians and priests of every god offered up continual efforts to save your son from death, but it was not to be. He passed into the West after a restless night, seemingly without pain, on the twelfth day of Peret, this second year of your majesty's reign. The whole city mourns him, and as soon as the news spreads abroad, every person in Kemet will mourn him. We pray each day for the good health and fortune of King Usermaatre Ramesses, Life! Health! Prosperity!'"

Ramesses said nothing. He sat in his command tent, his eyes unfocussed as the scribe read the letter. After a few moments of silence he lowered his head into his hands and groaned.

"Oh my beloved boy," he murmured. "My firstborn, my hope for the continuation of my House, I grieve that you have been snatched from me. Truly I am the Great Usermaatre come again, for in like fashion his eldest son was taken from him."

He groaned again and sighed deeply. "Have my chariot prepared. I leave for Per-Ramesses within the hour."

# Chapter 8
# Year 3 of Usermaatre Ramesses

The presence of Queen Tyti within the palace at Waset brought pressures to bear on the three surviving princes, the sons of Tiye. Tyti made no secret of the fact that she regarded her own infant son, Prince Ramesses, the rightful heir to the throne despite the king's pronouncement. A messenger had delivered the dreadful news of the death of the young heir Amunhirkhopeshef, plunging the palace and city into grief. Priests had stripped gaily coloured banners from the temple walls and even the business of the city merchants had slowed for a time. Things returned to normal, particularly after the entombment of the prince's embalmed body, but the brothers reacted in different ways to his death.

Meryamun had a cheerful demeanour, and the death of his brother depressed him for a while. His natural high spirits took over though, and he soon cast aside his grief, seeking delight in the exercise of his martial skills. Prehirwenemef took the news hard and kept to himself, shunning the normal company of Meryamun. He had had the misfortune to suffer the flint knife of Min only half a month before the news of Amunhirkhopeshef's death, and though he had faced circumcision bravely, he used this as an excuse to keep to his rooms.

Khaemwaset suffered the most. A quiet and studious young man who sought nothing more than a life of service to the gods, he now found himself thrust to the forefront of society. Tjaty Hori called the young man into his presence following the funeral and handed the youth a scroll from the king.

"What's this? Couldn't it wait?"

"Read it, Prince Khaemwaset," Hori said.

Khaemwaset scanned the scroll, easily reading the scribe's formal writing, and his brow furrowed as he read.

"This can't be right."

"Do you doubt the king's word?"

"No, but...this names me heir and First Born Son."

"You are the king's eldest son...now."

"It doesn't seem right. Amunhirkhopeshef was First Born Son and the heir. I cannot strip that from him."

"Not even if the king your father commands it?"

Khaemwaset was silent for a time as he considered the document and exactly what it meant for him. "I don't want to be heir," he said at last.

"You have no choice," Hori said. His voice was tinged with compassion. High office called for ambition rather than reluctance, and the throne was as high as one could aim.

"There's always a choice. I could refuse."

"Really?"

Khaemwaset shrugged. "Perhaps. I'm not sure I could face my father and tell him that." He was quiet again.

"If you are not heir, then whom?"

"Meryamun is oldest."

"With respect," Hori said, picking his words carefully, "Prince Meryamun will make a fine soldier, but the throne calls for more. Balance is needed."

"Prehirwenemef then."

"Balance again. Prince Prehirwenemef is prone to depression. The throne cannot just lock itself away in a room in times of adversity."

"Perhaps Queen Tyti is right, and young Ramesses should be heir."

"He is a baby, Prince Khaemwaset. No, you cannot avoid your duty; you must accept the privileges and responsibilities of being Kemet's Crown Prince."

"I want to be a priest like my namesake."

"We do not always get what we want," Hori said.

"I will be a priest," Khaemwaset said.

"The king is High Priest of all the gods. I cannot see anything wrong with being a priest and heir, but then again, I am merely Tjaty of the South. Talk to a priest or two; find out what it is really like to be one. Fairly dull, I'm sure."

Khaemwaset nodded. "I will talk to the priests, but what do you make of the other title the king seeks to place upon my shoulders? Is it a mistake? Have I misunderstood?"

"First Born Son? It is strange, I admit. Amunhirkhopeshef was your father's firstborn, without doubt, but he must have some reason for it." Hori coughed delicately. "Er...is there any reason to think you and Amunhirkhopeshef do not share the same mother?"

Khaemwaset stared at the Tjaty. "No, that is not possible."

Hori had the grace to look embarrassed. "A king is allowed to have more than one wife."

"But my father was not king when I was born. He had one wife--my mother Tiye--and was faithful to her. I am his son... his second born son."

"Then there is another reason he calls you First Born."

"What reason?"

"He seeks to bind you close to him by elevating your status. No longer are you Second Son, the second choice as the heir, but he names you First Son."

"Nonsense."

"Perhaps...but consider. You are certainly now the First Born Surviving Son, but we have no title that incorporates 'Surviving', so that aspect is dropped from formal inscriptions."

Khaemwaset shrugged. "I don't suppose it matters. It's what the king wants and I can live with that."

The prince found himself much lauded in the city on those occasions when he took a ferry over from the palace on the West Bank. People would flock to the wharves if there was any hint of his arrival, and follow behind his chariot, cheering and calling out blessings. It was heady stuff for a youth, and he started to think that maybe being heir was not such a bad thing after all. He still had to reconcile his newly acquired future with his previous intentions, however, so took himself off to the Great Temple of Amun to discuss the matter with the Hem-netjer of the god, Bakenkhons.

Bakenkhons welcomed the prince, acutely aware that for the time being the fortunes of the House of Amun relied on the goodwill of the House of Ramesses. He ushered Khaemwaset into his private quarters and sent an acolyte for wine and honey cakes. When they arrived, he served the prince with his own hands and sat him down in the most comfortable chair.

"Now, to what do I owe the honour of your visit, Prince Khaemwaset?"

"I am the one honoured that you see me, Hem-netjer."

"I am the spokesman of the god, but the god holds a special relationship with the kings of Kemet, so in whatever way I can help, I will."

"Thank you, my lord, but I seek help personally, rather than for the family."

"Speak then, Prince Khaemwaset, and I will attend."

Khaemwaset sipped his strong wine and nibbled at a honey cake while he considered his words. "You know that I am named for the son of the Great Usermaatre?"

"Indeed, and when I was young, I actually met that first Khaemwaset."

"You did?"

"Briefly. I was no more than a junior priest at the time so did not speak to him, but I saw him and listened as others spoke."

"What was he like?"

"He was a great man who had time for everyone. Soldier, scholar, priest... Crown Prince even. But you would know this. The gods loved him, for he loved them, and restored many temples and shrines. Had he lived, he would have become a good king."

"He was Sem-Priest of Ptah."

"Yes. His duties related specifically to funeral rites, especially where the deceased had no living male relative. He took their place, representing the heir and introducing the dead person to the gods. It is a very responsible position."

"That is what my father wants me to do--to become a Sem-Priest of Ptah, like the first Khaemwaset."

"A commendable ambition, my lord, but is this because you want it, or because your father seeks to have you follow the path of your namesake?"

"Does it matter?"

"Yes...and no." Bakenkhons smiled and passed the plate of honey cakes to the prince. "Yes, in that service to the gods should come from the heart; no, in that service to the gods is good of itself."

"Well, I want to become a priest. I always have...but, now my father names me heir."

"The first Khaemwaset was both priest and Crown Prince."

"So there is no conflict?"

Bakenkhons leaned back in his chair and sipped his wine, marshalling his thoughts. "What do you know of the general office of priesthood, my lord?"

"Not much. I know they serve the god in many ways--feeding and clothing the images, carrying them in processions, burning incense. Things like that."

"That is how an outsider sees the priesthood, but there is far more to it. Every aspect of the running of a temple is performed by priests, even the menial tasks such as..."

"I thought you had servants for that," Khaemwaset interrupted.

A flash of annoyance was quickly hidden.

"Most of those you think of as temple servants are in fact priests and acolytes. Priests prepare and serve the food, bake bread, brew beer, do the accounts, make beds, clean and scrub, carry away night soil. Every aspect of a priest's life is governed by service to the god and to other priests. Even when he no longer works within the temple precinct, he labours as a farmer on temple lands, tilling the soil or minding the flocks. One month in three a priest serves within the temple, two months out of three he serves as a common labourer."

"Even you?"

"No, not me. By the time you rise to become a Prophet of the god, your sacred duties outweigh all others. When I am not serving the god directly, I am involved with the running of the temple and temple lands throughout the kingdoms."

"What about a Sem-Priest?"

"A Sem-Priest is expected to perform subsidiary functions, like other priests." The Hem-netjer regarded the prince with a critical eye. "Does that influence your desire to serve in a temple, my lord?"

"Surely as a son of the king, as the king's heir, I would not be expected to perform menial tasks?"

"The Hem-netjer often brings the god his food, the God's Wife clothes him, and even the king has been known to offer him wine. Do you regard those as menial tasks?"

"Well, no...so I would do those things?"

"What about gathering up the food the god does not eat, and taking it to the temple refectory? Would that action be beneath you, my lord?"

"No, I suppose not."

"That is good, because the least thing done in the service of the god is counted as an action that reduces the weight of your heart when it comes to the final accounting. When your heart is weighed against the feather of Truth and Ammit stands ready to devour your heart, will your service to the gods save you from eternal wandering? If you doubt that you can stand humbly before the god and serve him in any way he chooses, you should choose another path through life."

"No, I...I want to serve the god, but...but which god? The first Khaemwaset served Ptah. Should I not do the same?"

"Amun is the god of Waset," Bakenkhons pointed out. "The most powerful of the gods in this city."

"And Ptah is the god of Men-nefer. How does that help me?"

"What does your heart tell you?"

Khaemwaset sat and looked at the Hem-netjer of Amun. He reasoned that it would please Bakenkhons if he chose Amun, but there was something about the god and the Great Temple in Waset that gave him pause. He had been in the inner parts of the temple, and the atmosphere there had engendered awe and dread, which he supposed was only fitting for the holy place of the god, but it filled him with fear too. The temple dedicated to Ptah in Waset was small, unlike the magnificent edifice of the god in Men-nefer, but even the small, cramped shrine in Waset brought him peace. How much more would Ptah's grand temple in Men-nefer bring him?

*Will I make an enemy of Bakenkhons if I choose Ptah?*

It was as if the Hem-netjer read his thoughts in his eyes. "Do what your heart tells you, Prince Khaemwaset. The gods often speak to us through the ears and eyes of the heart. To which god do you feel an affinity?"

"Ptah, Hem-netjer."

"Then you have made your choice."

Khaemwaset hesitated, trying to choose his words carefully. "Uh...you have...the god Amun has no objection?"

"You will become a priest of Ptah, but when you mount the throne you will still accept the crown from the hands of Amun as your father did before you?"

"Of course."

"Then Amun is content."

# Chapter 9
# Year 3 of Usermaatre Ramesses

The king did not remain in Per-Ramesses long, staying barely long enough to mourn his eldest son and see him safe into the hands of the embalmers. He spent some time with his Queen Iset too, commending her on her fertility, and making sure she had everything needed to deliver a healthy child.

"The first of many," Ramesses declared.

"And what will you name him?" Iset asked, her hands clasped about her belly.

"You seem very sure it is a boy."

"Oh yes, my lord. It is a boy who will rule after you."

Ramesses smiled but shook his head at the same time. "Well, we shall see. He will have five older brothers..." His smile slipped. "Four now...if it is a boy as you seem to think, call him Amunhirkhopeshef."

Iset grimaced. "It is bad luck to name a boy for a dead child."

"Not in Kemet. A new son is often named for one who has gone before. My eldest son Amunhirkhopeshef was a fine young man and would have made a fine king. It is an honour for our new son to bear his name."

"I would rather name him something else."

"No, you will name him as I have said."

Iset burst into tears, clinging to her husband and begging him to take back his word. She sobbed that it was tempting the gods to name a child thus, wetting the royal shoulder quite thoroughly.

Ramesses left the Queen's presence after adjuring her severely to name the child exactly as he commanded. He underlined his displeasure at her protests by not taking her to his bed again, enjoying instead other young women of the Per-Khemret. Ten days more and he was gone, driving his chariot down to Men-nefer.

Tiye was scarcely more welcoming, being overcome with grief at the death of her eldest son as well. Ramesses commiserated with her, and made an effort to remain civil when she took him to task for what she perceived as betrayals. She made no secret of her anger that her husband had not only taken another wife, but had made her a queen as well, a Great Royal Wife.

"I have explained this to you before," Ramesses said patiently. "When I married my sister Tyti it was to honour her by raising her to full royalty, not just as a daughter and sister of kings, but as Great Royal Wife. It was expected of me."

"And marrying this Syrian whore was expected of you too?" Tiye asked. "Could you not just bed her and allow me to keep what dignity I still possess, instead of making her a queen above me?"

"She is a princess, Tiye, and the granddaughter of Hatti's king. She deserves more, so I married her."

"And wounded me deeply."

Ramesses sighed. "I am the king and sometimes I must do things for the good of Kemet rather than concern myself with feelings."

"It was not for the good of Kemet, but rather for your carnal pleasure..."

"Enough, woman. I am the king and I do as I please."

Tiye scowled. "She is expecting a child, I hear."

"Yes, she thinks it will be a boy."

"I have given you boys."

"Yes, you have, and they are my heirs. And of course Tyti has given me a son too, and named him Ramesses."

"He will only ever be a child when my other sons are men. They will rule after you."

Ramesses nodded. "One of them will, at least. I suppose I shall make Khaemwaset Crown Prince now. I must make an announcement to that effect."

"He will make a good king."

"Perhaps, though I thought to make him Sem Priest of Ptah, like his namesake, the son of the Great Usermaatre."

"He could be more than that, my lord. Forget this desire to imitate your grandfather and let my sons make names for themselves that owe nothing to another's accomplishments."

"The Great Usermaatre Ramesses was Kemet's greatest king, and that is why I took his name. I mean to be as great as him and be remembered as long. He obviously pleased the gods with his victories over our enemies, with his many sons dedicated to so many offices, for they allowed him a long and illustrious life. If I do as he did, in every respect, the gods will smile on me too."

"I shall pray that they do so, my lord. Will you take me to your bed?"

"You wish it?"

"Yes, I know you leave for Waset in a few days and I want you to give me another son to match those given you by your other wives."

"Gladly, beloved, but you do not need to match them for already you excel. My three eldest sons are yours and nothing can take that from you. You are my first wife, the wife of my youth, and I am glad the heir comes from your belly."

True to his word, Ramesses sailed from Men-nefer on the royal barge a few days later, and rapidly put all thoughts of his wives from his head. He spent most of the next twelve days sitting under an awning on the deck and dictating thoughts on the future of the kingdoms to one of his scribes. Accompanying the king, and acting as a financial adviser, was Assistant Overseer of the Treasury Peyferewy. This man had with him, as his own assistant, Mentemtowe, who was the one who delved into the scrolls and records when the king desired some pertinent fact. The actual Overseer of the Treasury, Ruma, remained in Men-nefer putting together the latest details of revenue from the kingdoms.

"I wish to leave my mark on the kingdoms as a builder," Ramesses said. The scribe hurried to write down his words, while Peyferewy just nodded sagely.

"To this end, I will cause temples and shrines to be built from Napata in the south to the Way of Heru in the north, further afield even, when the territories under the sway of Hatti come under my control."

"That will be costly, Son of Re," Peyferewy said.

Ramesses waved the observation aside. "The conquered lands will yield much gold. Now, I shall inspect my Temple of Millions of Years, and my tomb, when I get down to Waset. Work should be well along with those already, but the tomb for my dear son Amunhirkhopeshef must be completed quickly, and tombs for my wives and other sons started."

"Amunhirkhopeshef's tomb is well advanced, Son of Re," Peyferewy said. "The latest accounts from the Place of Truth arrived just before we left. Almost all that needs doing are the identificatory inscriptions in the first corridor."

Ramesses nodded and thought for a moment. "Hereditary prince foremost. Royal scribe also and...yes, he looked forward to becoming a chariot commander, so let the title 'master of the horse' be his too. Make it known to the masons."

Peyferewy nodded to Mentemtowe to make a note in the treasury records for extra expenditure to be allocated in the Great Field for tombs.

"I intend to build a temple to Amun in Waset, and a separate one to Mut. They may be husband and wife but they deserve separate residences as well as the one they share."

"A noble intention, Son of Re, but again, it will be costly."

"I do not care about expense, Peyferewy, for the gods appeared to me in a dream and asked me to build their temples. Asked, mind you, not demanded, by which I understood they regarded me as an equal."

The Assistant Treasurer's eyebrows lifted, but he said nothing. Mentemtowe nudged him and whispered, "Did you know he was a god?"

Peyferewy saw that the king was bent over the scribe's shoulder, correcting something he had written, so he risked a response. "I have heard rumours."

"A god-man I can understand, all kings are that, and a god after death when they become one with Re, but to be a god during one's lifetime..."

"What are you whispering about?" Ramesses demanded.

"Your pardon, Son of Re. We were just debating where we could most easily obtain the funds for your many building projects."

"Well, do it later. Anyway, it won't be as expensive as all that. There are plenty of good quarries for stone, and besides, many existing temples and Mansions have spare blocks lying around. I suggest you send masons to the Mansions of my predecessors and see what stone blocks or carved reliefs they can spare. I am sure they will be quite generous toward my living godhead."

Peyferewy bowed. "I am sure that will be the case, Son of Re."

Ramesses retired to his cabin for a sleep shortly thereafter, so Mentemtowe had a chance to ask Peyferewy some questions.

"Tell me I misunderstood the king's commands, Peyferewy. He seemed to be saying we must rob the funerary temples of other kings to build his own."

"That is indeed what he was saying."

"But that is wrong, it is impious and..."

"Hush," Peyferewy said quickly. "The king cannot be wrong, particularly if he is a god. The other kings won't miss a few blocks; their priests will gladly give up some nice reliefs that can be easily reworked. And it will save the Treasury much gold, which in turn means the king can build more temples."

"It will still be very expensive."

"So we must find ways of cutting costs. Pay the builders less, perhaps."

"Then they'll buy inferior stone, build too quickly, and risk the whole thing falling down."

"Indeed," Peyferewy said, "but not for several years. In the meantime the temple has been built and the king can move onto other projects. He means to repair lots of temples to show his piety, so if one or two fall down he can gain further credit by repairing them."

Mentemtowe considered this bold plan, but although he saw flaws, he kept silent, happy to let the burden of blame fall on Peyferewy's shoulders.

Once in Waset, the king hurried to view his partially constructed Mansion of Millions of Years, with adjoining palace, and let the Assistant Treasurer contact the city's builders, architects and masons to get some of his building projects started. The king roamed the huge construction for some time, making suggestions and criticising the architects over this part or that, and had his scribe take copious notes. From there, he went to Ta-Sekhet-Ma'at where he examined the work being done on his tomb, and directed the masons to hurriedly finish off the tomb of Amunhirkhopeshef. Only after these things had been carried out did Ramesses repair to the palace to see his newborn son and his Queen Tyti. All things were done in accordance with custom, however, and his first action was to greet his mother Tiy-Merenese as the senior lady of the Waset Per-Khemret.

"Greetings, mother, all is well with you?"

"Ah, my lord and son, it is good to see you. Yes, all is well with me, though these bones are getting no younger and I ache every morning."

"Age comes to us all. And the Per-Khemret? How are the women of the palace?"

"They are well, my lord son. Three of them have borne children since your last visit, Aya, a girl; Het, a girl; and Tyti, a boy."

"My sister-wife is well? And the boy?"

"The Queen is...well, I will let her answer for herself. She was ever a headstrong girl and becoming a mother has not softened her. As to the boy; he thrives."

"Then let them enter before me," Ramesses said. "I would greet my wife once more and hold my son."

"Of course, my lord son." Tiy-Merenese ordered a servant to run to Queen Tyti and tell her that the king required her presence at once.

While they waited for Tyti, they refreshed themselves with wine. Ramesses told his mother of events in the north, and of the sad news of his eldest son's death.

"The City of Amun grieves with you," she observed. "For he was named Amun is his Strength."

"Unfortunately, Amun was not his strength, or rather, Amun was not sufficiently strong for him."

"Perhaps if he had been closer to Amun's City when he fell ill..."

"Perhaps."

An Overseer of Per-Khemret entered and bowed. "Son of Re, Queen Tyti requests you receive her."

Ramesses nodded and stood to receive his sister-wife. Tyti entered with a baby in her arms and bowed slightly to Ramesses before holding the child out to him.

"Son of Re, Usermaatre Ramesses, this is your son, named Ramesses, for like you, Re fashioned him and he will be a great king after you."

Ramesses frowned at her words, but took the baby and held him close, examining him for any fault. He could see none, and nodded. "He is a fine boy."

"Worthy to be your heir, my lord husband."

Ramesses shrugged. "Maybe one day. He has three older brothers."

"They are sons of a commoner..."

"And a king."

"Of course, my lord husband, but they have royalty on just one side, whereas little Ramesses descends from kings on both sides. He is far worthier of being king."

Ramesses sighed. "We have been over this before. Tiye was my wife before even my father became king. She married me about the time you were born, Tyti, and has been a good wife through all the troubled days when the House of the Great Usermaatre fell. She can never be Queen, as she is not royal, but she will always be my wife and her eldest son shall be my heir. Amunhirkhopeshef has passed into his tomb, so Khaemwaset is now my heir."

"What sort of a king is only half royal?"

"Our father was only half royal, did that lessen him?"

"And what of the son of your Syrian wife? Does he also take precedence over my son?"

"Iset has had a son? What have you heard?"

"Nothing official, my lord, but rumours abound. If it is indeed a son, will he too inherit before my son?"

"He is younger than little Ramesses, so no."

"I am glad of it," Tyti said, "but you say Tiye's eldest son will be heir. Does that still apply if she has other sons born after Ramesses?"

"My eldest son by a wife will be heir, no matter who is the boy's mother. Now let that be an end to it. I dislike women vying for power through their sons as if I am already dead."

The king showed his displeasure by not taking Tyti to his bed for several days, instead taking pleasure with other women in the Per-Khemret. This in turn angered Tyti, but her mother Tiy-Merenese dissuaded her from expressing her thoughts, impressing upon her the fact that the king could do as he liked.

As usual, royal messengers travelled throughout the kingdoms, transmitting information from the governors of cities and sepats to the Tjaty of the North or South, and from those officials to the king himself. The King's Son of Kush, Ramesnakht, likewise sent messengers to the king, but his letters mainly concerned the status of tribes in the hinterland and the production of gold from the mines.

A sheaf of letters arrived from Tjaty Herwernef in the north, dealing with all manner of local business, most of which were just reports of action already taken on a variety of issues, but one caught the king's attention. It was a short report that had come through one of many spies who roamed Ta Mehu, searching out dissatisfaction and the seeds of rebellion. This particular spy, Bebi, in Per-Bast, reported that one of his men claimed to have seen General Ament, the noted traitor and fugitive, in the city.

Herwernef had ordered a clandestine investigation, but nothing more could be added to the report. The Tjaty asked the king what action he should take.

"Is it possible?" Ramesses asked of Tjaty Hori.

"Neither his body, nor that of Tausret, was ever found, Son of Re. I suppose they could still be alive six years on, but what would they be doing in Per-Bast?"

Ramesses shook his head. "I can only think of one thing that would bring Ament back, he is hoping to raise a rebellion among disaffected elements."

Hori opened his mouth and then hesitated, uttering only an indistinct "Uh."

"What? Speak to me, Hori."

"Son of Re, I do not like to contradict you, but...er...there is another possibility."

Ramesses frowned but waved for Hori to continue.

"Er... I believe Ament was Overseer of Vineyards in Per-Bast..."

"He can scarcely think to take up his duties again."

"No, Son of Re, but the reason he was given that position was because his sister owned a vineyard near that city."

"Yes, that's right. I remember now. You think she might be working with the traitor?"

"Or conceivably he is just visiting family."

"A dangerous course. It is more likely he hopes to raise rebellion."

"I am sure you are right, Majesty."

Ramesses considered the notion for several minutes, then nodded. "Have a letter to Tjaty Herwernef drawn up. He is to investigate the possible sighting of Ament in the light of his sister's ownership of a vineyard in Per-Bast, and is particularly to determine if she might be using her resources there to aid in a revolt by her brother."

"It shall be done, Son of Re," Hori said.

# Chapter 10
# Year 3 of Usermaatre Ramesses

Tjaty Herwernef read the letter from his king, and though he thought it unlikely that Ament was in Per-Bast at all, let alone to seek support for a rebellion, he sent for the spy Bebi and gave him his instructions.

"How far am I to go, sir?"

"What do you mean?"

"Well, I can watch the sister's farm, perhaps talk to some of the workers in the vineyard, and make cautious enquiries about this man Ament, but unless I actually find him, nothing much is going to come of it."

"The king wants to know if the man has been there and if he is making trouble. Do whatever you have to."

"The sister may need persuading to reveal anything about her brother, sir."

"I realise that." Herwernef read the king's letter again, trying to read between the words. "Use your own judgment. If you cannot find out anything by asking around, arrest her and have her interrogated. Don't harm her unless you have to, but you may be able to find something that will loosen her tongue."

"May I have that in writing, sir?" Bebi asked. "Just in case someone disputes my right to act."

Herwernef grimaced, but nodded. "I'll have my scribe draw up the necessary documents."

Ti-ament missed her brother and had worried about him ever since he and the woman who had once been Queen of Kemet (king too, some said) had left their vineyard and disappeared into the north, together with their adopted boys. For a long time, nothing more had been heard of them, and then a cryptic letter arrived, written not in the language of Kemet, for Ti-ament was unschooled in the arts of reading and writing, but rather in the language of Kaftor, one of the Sea Peoples. She had taken the letter to her husband Zeben who deciphered it. He was Kaftor, though it had been many years since he had betrayed his nation for the love of a Kemetu woman, and been rewarded by Baenre Merenptah. Now, he tended the vineyard he had been given and raised children with the sister of once-General Ament.

"What does it say, husband?" Ti-ament had asked.

"It does not say much," Zeben admitted. "It says, 'We are safe and well...' that must mean your brother and Tausret..."

"Shh, my love. She is just Tau."

Zeben nodded. "'...and have a daughter Adara...' ...strange name. It is neither Kemetu nor Kaftor... 'If you ever need to send me word, ask of Dan-el the Potter in the town of Urit, and use the name by which I sign this.' That's all," Zeben finished, "except for a word that makes no sense, 'toothfish'."

Ti-ament had thought for a moment and then laughed. "You know our father was a fisherman? Well, when Ament left to join the army, we called him 'toothfish' because that is a fish that can bite hard and wound you, just like a soldier. The letter is from Ament, it must be."

"It is good to know they are safe. Do you want to write back? I can write something."

Ti-ament had thought about it but shook her head. "It is enough to know they are safe. If we write to them, then others may find them."

After the initial interest shown in her situation by the soldiers of the new king, nothing more had happened. Months, and then years, passed. Userkhaure Setnakhte ruled Kemet with a fist of granite and then his son Usermaatre Ramesses had followed him, and the hostile eyes of the new rulers of Kemet had turned elsewhere, leaving them alone. Recently, however, Ti-ament had felt those eyes turn toward her once again and then, without warning, the soldiers arrived.

They burst in upon them as they ate their evening meal, throwing open the door and rushing in with swords drawn. Zeben leapt to his feet and grabbed a knife, but Ti-ament screamed and held him back.

"We offer no resistance," Ti-ament cried. She could see the men bore the insignia of one of the corps and guessed they were there on the king's business. "We are honest folk, sirs, and pay our taxes. Why have you attacked us?"

The officer stared at her. "You are Ti-ament, sister of Ament, the rebel and traitor?"

"I am Ti-ament," she confirmed, "but my brother was a General and loyal to the crowned king of Kemet."

"Yes, you're the one. Where is your brother?"

"I haven't seen him these past six years."

"Perhaps not, but you know where he is?"

"No sir."

"Who are these others?"

"Zeben, my husband; also my sons Rath and Goloth. These are my daughters..."

"What sort of names are those? You are not Kemetu."

"I was a Kaftor," Zeben said. "Until Baenre Merenptah rewarded me with this land. My sons are named for a good friend, and for my father, both Kaftor."

The officer grunted and moved across to the table, fingering the meat, bread and vegetables. "You eat well, better than my men. It's not right that Kaftor should eat so well when honest Kemetu do not. How can you afford to?"

"Our vineyard is productive and we work hard."

The officer shook his head. "I think you are taking Kaftor gold and spying for them. The penalty for that is death."

Ti-ament gasped and gathered her small daughters to her skirts, while Zeben moved his sons back behind him.

"We are not spies," Zeben said. "We are honest Kemetu and loyal to the king."

"Well, that's for a court to decide," the officer said. "Arrest them and put them in the prison in Per-Bast for now. The Tjaty will decide their fate."

"All of them, sir?" asked a soldier.

"Just the men." The officer looked at Ti-ament. "If you want to see your man and boys again, you'll remember where your brother is."

The soldiers bound the arms of Zeben and his two sons and led them off. The girls started crying, but Ti-ament calmed them and followed along, accompanying the soldiers and their prisoners into Per-Bast. They arrived at a stone building that formed part of the Mayor's residence and the prisoners were pushed inside. Zeben started to call out to his wife to petition the Tjaty, but a blow silenced him.

Ti-ament waited outside for a long time, waiting for someone in authority to come out. At last, the Mayor of Per-Bast arrived, with his guard, and she knelt in the dust, stretching out her arms in supplication.

"Hear me, my lord, for I am your humble servant."

The soldiers of the guard rushed forward to drag her back, but the Mayor stopped them.

"Who are you, woman, and why do you accost me in the street? If you have a petition, present it at the proper time and place." He started to move past.

"My lord, my husband has been wrongfully arrested, along with my two young sons."

The Mayor regarded her thoughtfully. "You are the wife of the Kaftor spy?"

"I am Ti-ament, wife of Zeben, who used to be a Kaftor, but is no spy. We own a vineyard on the east side of the city, gifted to us by Baenre Merenptah himself."

"I know the property. It is a fine vineyard, but it will be confiscated as the proceeds of the crime of treason if the court finds your husband guilty."

"He is innocent, my lord, as are my two young sons who are Kemetu-born and could not possibly be spies."

"I am told that you possess information that would prove your husband's innocence," said the Mayor. "Tell the authorities what you know and he will be released."

"My lord, the officer who arrested my husband asked the whereabouts of my brother Ament, but I don't know where he is. I haven't seen him for six years."

"He hasn't written to you? Communicated in any way?"

"No, my lord."

"Then you have a problem. As matters stand, your husband and sons will be tried for treason before the Tjaty and when found guilty, for there is no evidence to the contrary, will be punished appropriately."

"I... I'll petition the king."

The Mayor laughed. "You can try, but I can't imagine he'll hear you. No, get used to not having a husband or improve your memory, that's my advice to you." He started to move away again, but turned back. "Oh, and find somewhere else to live. I will be sending a bailiff round to take possession of your vineyard."

Ti-ament took her daughters and returned home, packing up a few belongings and some food before the bailiff arrived to prevent what would then be regarded as theft. She had just finished and was standing on the road outside with a milk goat on a rope and her daughters clutching a duck apiece when the bailiff and his men arrived.

"Here, those are not yours," said the bailiff. "Put them back immediately."

"You have only just arrived," Ti-ament replied. "Up until this moment the vineyard and everything in it belonged to me and my husband. You have no right to anything not within the vineyard boundaries."

"And I say I do. That goat and those ducks for a start, and whatever you have in that basket."

"Then you'll want my dress too. It came from the estate." Ti-ament put the basket down and started taking off her dress while her daughters looked on bemused.

"Here, stop that," cried the bailiff. "What do you take me for, a tax collector? Put your dress back on and get out of here. Go on; take your belongings and go, before I change my mind."

Ti-ament went, though unhurriedly, and thinking about her options. Her daughters trotted along beside her, their arms locked around the ducks, and after a bit, the eldest one, Taui, tugged on her mother's dress.

"Where are we going, mother? Are we going to see father and Rath and Goloth?"

Ti-ament stopped and looked around, tugging on the rope as the goat kept going. "Not right now," she said. "We have to find somewhere to stay."

"Forever?" asked six year old Ini.

"No, not forever. Just until they let your father and the boys out of prison."

"Did they do something wrong?" Ini asked.

"No, silly," Taui replied. "It's all a mistake, isn't it, mother?"

"That's right," Ti-ament said. "Now, we'll go to Matia the washerwoman. She knows us and will take us in." She said it confidently, but was inwardly not certain of their reception. Matia was kind enough, but if she believed Zeben's supposed crime might taint others, she would shut the door in their faces, friend or no.

Matia listened on her doorstep, a worried look on her face, as Ti-ament explained their predicament. Ti-ament sent her daughters off to graze the goat and ducks on a nearby piece of wasteland, while she talked to the washerwoman.

"I will not hide it from you, Matia. My husband is innocent, but we may not be able to prove it. I don't want you to suffer, but I ask for my daughters if not myself, that you let us stay in your courtyard for a day or two, a few days at most."

"And I will be honest with you in turn. I like you, Ti-ament, you have always been a good neighbour and generous on holy days. I have heard nothing one way or the other concerning your husband, so as far as I am concerned, I am just extending hospitality to a neighbour. If the soldiers demand your eviction, I may have to do it, but until then, you are welcome."

"Thank you, Matia."

Matia's only surviving daughter had married and moved away several years before, so the house seemed spacious. After Taui and Ini had their supper and been put to bed, the women talked quietly beside the cooking fire in the courtyard.

"What will you do?" Matia asked. "Stand by your husband?"

"Of course, but I don't know what I can do to help. The Mayor said he would be tried before the Tjaty and sentenced. I don't even know the penalty if he is found guilty."

Matia shook her head. "Don't think about it, Ti. You are inviting trouble if you think about it too much. Keep yourself busy and perhaps petition the courts for the return of your property."

Over the next few days, Ti-ament helped Matia with her washing work, while her daughters looked after their goat and ducks, as well as a cow that Matia owned, taking them out to graze and bringing them back at night. Ti-ament kept thinking about what she could do, and went to the prison daily to see if she could see or talk to her husband and sons. On one of these visits, she saw the prisoners being taken out to witness a flogging being inflicted on some miscreant, and got close enough to exchange a few words with her husband. She told him where they were staying, and hoped they would be released soon when they saw nothing was happening.

"There are only two choices, wife," Zeben said gruffly, drawing patterns in the dust with a toe. "Either give Ament up, or contact him. Tell him what is happening and he may give himself up to save the boys at least."

Ti-ament refused to contemplate giving up her brother, but after thinking about it, decided to try and contact him. She scrounged a piece of papyrus from near the temple of Bast, and made her own ink from soot mixed with plant sap. At night, after Matia had gone to sleep, she composed her message, writing in the few words of Kaftor she knew and hoping whoever read it (Ament hopefully) would be able to decipher it.

'Toothfish,' she wrote. 'Husband, two boys in prison, not right. Want catch you. Please help.' She signed it 'Sister' and read it over carefully, wishing she knew enough about languages and writing to make the message more intelligible.

"If I could use a scribe to write in Kemetu my message would be plainer," she muttered, "but if the message was intercepted they'd know who I was writing to. At least in Kaftor, few people in Kemet will be able to read it."

Delivery was another matter, but she hoped she would find a merchant in a caravan going north to carry the letter to Dan-el the Potter in the town of Urit. After that, she would just have to wait, and it might take many months for the letter to be delivered.

Ti-ament yawned and went to bed. There was nothing else she could do.

# Chapter 11
# Year 5 of Usermaatre Ramesses

Throughout the previous year, the Sea Peoples had been making forays along the coast of Kanaan, landing where they could. They burnt a few villages and towns, rounded up a few herds, took some captives and disappeared out to sea at the first sign of Kemetu soldiers. Increasingly, their ships were seen off the mouths of the Great River and urgent appeals found their way to the court of Usermaatre from governors and lesser officials from the border north into Kanaan. The corps had done their best to protect the inhabitants and cultivated lands, but the Sea People had refrained from direct confrontation, melting away in the presence of opposition and taking to their ships again. They could move much faster by sea than could the corps by land, so wherever they landed, it was always some time before the soldiers of Kemet reappeared.

Kemet had a navy, but its ships were small and carried few people. They could shadow the Sea People's fleet and give warning of its appearance on the coast, but were powerless to stop it. All they could was alert the army as to its movements.

Now, as the flood waters abated in Year Five, reports came in of a large fleet making its way along the coast toward the land of Kemet. Ramesses immediately convened a meeting that comprised not only the Great Khenbet Council, but also the military leaders of the Kingdoms. Ptahmose the Royal Scribe of Memoranda presided, with a phalanx of lesser scribes present to take notes or research pertinent points.

The king's eldest son, Khaemwaset, attended as a nominal General, being First King's Son, but as he had little experience of leading men and none at all of battle, his father told him to pay attention and keep his mouth shut. Also present were Hori, son of Bekamun, titled Great General of the Lord of the Two Lands, and Djehutemheb, General to His Majesty. Both had risen quickly to positions of power in the troubled days following the death of King Userkheperure Seti and the rise of the new House of Ramesses. Likewise, both were experienced only in civil actions restoring peace within the kingdoms, and neither had faced a foreign enemy in strength. Still, they had experienced officers under them.

Tjaty Herwernef called the Khenbet Council to order and outlined the reports of the approach of the Sea Peoples.

"We are facing a major invasion of the diverse nations known to us collectively as the Sea Peoples. Specifically, we have identified the Peleset and Tjeker peoples, and elements of the Sherden and Shekelesh. These and other groups have recently laid waste to many lands in the north, decimating the Hatti and destroying Karkemish and Qode. Now they have cast their envious eyes upon the riches of Kemet and desire to take all things for themselves.

"A large fleet of nearly fifty ships has sailed south and is even now landing an army in Kanaan. Reports from spies indicate that the assault on Ta Mehu will be two-fold, by land along the Way of Heru, and by sea as their fleet forces the mouths of the Great River. Together, they will deal death and destruction to the cities and cultivated lands in the heart of the northern kingdom. This we cannot allow, so we must decide where we meet the enemy and what forces we have at our disposal to utterly destroy them."

Ramesses thanked his Tjaty and called for General Djehutemheb to enumerate the strength of the army.

"Son of Re," Djehutemheb replied. "The northern army of Kemet stands ready to destroy the enemy."

"I do not doubt it, General, but tell the Council why you feel so confident."

Djehutemheb bowed and faced the Khenbet Council. "We have six corps available for the northern army, Amun, Re, Ptah, Set, Sobek and Heru, nearly eight thousand men in all. They are well trained and well supplied, thanks to the foresight of His Majesty. I am confident that we can face any army the Sea Peoples choose to set before us, and defeat them."

"And General Hori," Ramesses said. "What of the defences within Ta Mehu? The Sea Peoples mean to sail into the Great River. How have you prepared for that?"

Hori got to his feet slowly, a worried frown on his face. "We have corps within Ta Mehu," he said, "but the real problem is getting to grips with the enemy. They are on the water, whereas we are on land. They can disembark troops anywhere, and we must hurry to keep pace with them on both shores of the river. Thus we divide our forces and they can concentrate them at will."

"You are saying you are incapable of defeating the enemy, General Hori?"

"By no means, Son of Re. I merely wish to point out that our task within the northern kingdom is completely different from the task facing General Djehutemheb and the corps. We face a mobile naval force and must adapt our forces accordingly."

"How?" Ramesses demanded.

Hori licked his lips and cleared his throat. "There are two possible lines of defence, Son of Re. One is land based and depends on a string of small forts along the shore lines, so that no matter where the enemy fleet lands, there are always men on hand to repel them. Watch fires can be built to alert neighbouring soldiers as to the enemy's disposition."

"And the second line of defence?"

"A proper navy that can engage the enemy before they ever set foot in Ta Mehu."

Ramesses frowned. "That will be no easy task, General Hori. Kemet traditionally has an army and fights on land. We only have troop transport barges and small fishing boats, neither of which is suited to a naval engagement."

"We would have to build ourselves the ships needed, Son of Re."

"An expensive undertaking," Tjaty Herwernef observed. "The Treasury officials will bear me out, I'm sure."

"The alternative is to leave ourselves open to attack by water," Ramesses said. "The Sea Peoples are coming and I will not allow them to set foot on Ta Mehu soil."

The Council sat in silence for a few moments, wondering how they could carry out the task set them by the king. If the enemy did land on Kemetu soil, it would be because they had failed in their duty.

Khnumhotep, Overseer of the Treasury, cleared his throat. "What sort of ships is His Majesty contemplating for our navy?"

"You are my Council," Ramesses said. "What do other nations have? The Sea Peoples for instance?"

"They have big ships, Son of Re," Hori said. "Many oars on each side, filled with sailors and can carry a hundred soldiers besides."

"I have heard of other ships that throw grappling hooks and board enemy ships, putting the crew to death," Herwernef added.

"How big are these ships?"

Hori started to shrug but realised that gesture was not suitable when talking to the king, so turned it into an awkward bow. "Perhaps the size of the royal barge, Son of Re."

"The Treasury could not afford more than a handful of those," Khnumhotep said. "Ten maybe if we broke up smaller vessels, but it would take a year or more to have them ready."

"We do not have that long. Find me another solution."

Another silence enveloped the Council.

Prince Khaemwaset got up and hesitantly approached the throne, bowing submissively. "Son of Re, Illustrious Father, may I speak?"

"What is it, Khaemwaset? We are busy here. Do you want to be excused?"

"No, Son of Re. I have an idea concerning these ships."

Ramesses sighed. "Well, I do not see anyone else putting ideas forward, so speak." He leaned forward and looked into his son's eyes. "But do not waste my time."

"Thank you, father." Khaemwaset bowed again and half turned so he could include the Council in his speech. "It seems to me, from listening to the learned members of the Khenbet Council that we cannot afford big, expensive ships like those of the Sea Peoples. Even if we could afford them, it would take a long time to train sailors and soldiers alike so they could fight effectively..."

"That is what has been said," Ramesses said impatiently. "If you have nothing new to add..."

"Forgive me, father, but I have," Khaemwaset interrupted, earning him an angry look. "We are a nation that boasts many fine archers, and numerous fishing boats that are skilfully sailed on the river. Could we not combine our skills to produce a navy of small boats that can move fast and sting the enemy, withdrawing before their larger ships can retaliate?"

"What damage could a fishing boat possibly inflict?" Ramesses asked. He looked at the Council members. "What other ideas do you have? Workable ideas?"

Khaemwaset flushed and sat down, keeping his face averted. There was another period of silence, this time rather uncomfortable as the men there felt compassion for the young Heir.

General Hori cleared his throat. "Prince Khaemwaset may actually have come up with the solution, Son of Re."

Khaemwaset looked up, eyes wide, and rewarded the General with a broad smile.

"Explain yourself," the king demanded.

"We cannot compete with the Sea Peoples on their own terms, Son of Re. They are seafaring nations with a lot of experience and a lot of ships. If we are to successfully counter them, we must devise something new. We have ships already, well, hundreds of fishing boats anyway. Perhaps these could be modified so as to be militarily useful."

"How exactly?"

"Well, I'm no sailor...or even fisherman, Son of Re, but it seems to me that one or two men could steer a boat close, and an archer in the boat could pick off a handful of the enemy, fleeing when they try to retaliate."

"What if the wind is against them?" Herwernef asked.

"A couple of extra men to act as rowers."

"Already the ships must be built larger," Khnumhotep observed, "and thus more expensive."

"But possible," Hori persisted.

Ramesses frowned and stroked his chin. "I am unconvinced."

"Let me gather a few men who work with boats, Son of Re. We will see what can be done and report back to you in a few days."

"Very well, you have three days. Do not disappoint me, General Hori."

"We have another concern, Son of Re," Tjaty Herwernef said. "Men to defend Ta Mehu. The corps of the northern army can counter the enemy's land forces, but we have fewer to counter their fleet. Admittedly, we can strip the land of peasants for a short time, but not for long, else we shall all starve. We need men; several thousand."

"I am sure you will find them, Tjaty," Ramesses said. "There are thousands of merchants, artisans, builders, even labourers from the quarries."

"Indeed, Son of Re, but we need strong men. The quarrymen may suffice, but the others are unsuited."

"Send to Kush for fierce tribesmen."

"Undisciplined, Majesty. There is another source of labour though, the prisons."

"You would trust murderers and thieves to defend our land?"

"It is not unheard of," murmured Scribe Ptahmose. "Perhaps not murderers, but those convicted of lesser offences have been offered freedom in return for service in the past. If we emptied the prisons, we could probably find a thousand strong men to defend our shores."

"Look into it," Ramesses said.

Tjaty Herwernef had the easier task. He did not spend much time debating the issue, but instead sent orders to the governors, mayors and elders of every sepat, city, town and village, instructing them to scour the prisons for any persons willing to exchange their present situation for voluntary service defending Kemet. Before a month had passed, he had nearly two thousand volunteers.

General Hori gathered together men from the ship building guild, from the fisherman's guild, and invited Prince Khaemwaset to sit in on the deliberations. He presented the problem to the people most concerned with boats and sat back as they argued over whether it could be done and what final form the naval vessels would take.

Three days after the Khenbet Council meeting, General Hori and Prince Khaemwaset reported back to the king and showed him drawings of the ships they believed would be able to withstand the attack of the Sea Peoples.

"You shall have your navy, Son of Re," Hori said. "Most of the vessels can be constructed from already existing ones, and others can be modified as auxiliary boats."

"How long?"

"Six months, Son of Re."

Ramesses nodded. "A navy is not a suitable occupation for an army general, though. Who should head this effort? What do you say, Khaemwaset? You thought of this."

"Make General Hori your Admiral of the Lord of the Two Lands, father."

"What say you, Gen...no, Admiral Hori?"

Hori bowed low. "I am deeply honoured, Son of Re."

"Then let it be so."

# Chapter 12
# Year 5 of Usermaatre Ramesses

As time went by, Prince Meryamun grew closer to Prince Prehirwenemef. Since the death of their older brother Amunhirkhopeshef and the new heir Khaemwaset having vanished into the north to take up duties with their father the king, the two boys had been thrown on their own resources. They were different in temperament--Meryamun being boisterous and bold, while Prehirwenemef was inward looking and cautious. One thing united them though, and that was the hunt. That--and the competitive spirit that ruled them.

As sons of the king's body, few people were prepared to deny them, and though Tjaty Hori was tasked with their education, he was often too busy to keep them under his direct control. In the absence of his heavy hand, the princes would flee the city in their hunting chariots and seek out game in the eastern or western deserts. Unknown to either prince, Hori's hand still lay over them as the soldiers detailed to guard their royal persons came from the local Mut corps, and they had strict orders to let no harm befall them.

A report came in from a local hunter that gazelle were plaguing the farmlands near Ta-senet, and that although numbers had been killed or driven off, there were still many to be found. The princes immediately started making plans to escape the city and go hunting for gazelle.

"And who knows," Prehirwenemef said, "where there are gazelle, there may be lion."

"Hori will never let us hunt lion," Meryamun said.

"He won't know."

"We have to tell him. Ta-senet is too far to just sneak off to. We'll need a boat to get there, and we can't just take one."

"He'll stop us going. As you said, he won't let us hunt lion."

"Yes, but as you said, he won't know," Meryamun said. "Look, we don't know there is a lion anyway--just gazelle. We tell him gazelle are destroying crops and ask him--ask him, mind--to let us go and help the farmers. How can he refuse such a selfless act?"

Such was their enthusiasm that they ran off immediately to find the Tjaty. He was presiding over some small disputes over boundary stones in the Hall of the Law when they burst in upon him. The farmers and land-owners involved bowed and drew back in deference to the young princes, but Tjaty Hori held up a hand to cut off their excited chatter.

"Prince Meryamun," he said, addressing the older boy. "Please withdraw until I have finished my work here. Your interruption is unseemly."

Abashed, Meryamun withdrew, dragging his younger brother with him.

"Now look what you've gone and done," Prehirwenemef said. "He'll never give us permission now."

"Well, you were with me too, so I can't see that it's all my fault."

Tjaty Hori sent for the princes at midday, and had them stand before him in silence for several minutes while he just looked at them.

"Do you know why I said your interruption was unseemly?" he asked at last.

Prehirwenemef looked down at the floor and shuffled his feet, but Meryamun looked boldly at Hori. "We are sons of the king. Why should we not speak with you, who are just his minister?"

"You are sons of the king," Hori agreed, "but in the king's absence, I stand in his stead. Moreover, he has given me authority over you. Do you think he will support my authority or your rudeness?"

"How were we rude?"

"You interrupted the farmers and land-owners that had come to me for adjudication in their disputes."

"They are just peasants, whereas we are nobles who..."

"Who should know better," Hori said. "Meryamun, you and your brother rank high in Kemetu society and will, no doubt, hold responsible positions when you are men, but what have you done that is worth what these farmers do every day of their lives?"

"What do you mean? How can you compare a lowly farmer with the king's sons?"

"You are who you are because you were born to it. You did not earn your rank or your place in society, whereas that farmer that you look down on worked hard to produce the very food that graces your table each day. Has he not performed a service deserving of praise rather than ridicule? What have you ever done for him that equates what he has done for you?"

Meryamun scowled but said nothing.

"Eh? What was that? I couldn't hear you, Prince Meryamun."

"I said nothing, Tjaty Hori."

"No, because you can say nothing. Until you start to serve Kemetu as these common farmers do, then you cannot justify saying anything."

"But must we then be farmers?" Prehirwenemef asked. "I don't want to be a farmer."

Hori shook his head. "Of course not. When you are a man you will be a priest or..."

"I want to be a general," Meryamun said.

"There you go interrupting again," Hori said. "I was about to say, you are likely to either be a priest or join His Majesty's army and fight his enemies."

"Let our brother Khaemwaset become a priest. I'm going to be a general and crush the Nine Bows beneath my chariot wheels."

"Me too," Prehirwenemef said.

"Very commendable," Hori said drily. "Let us hope you learn some sense of decorum too. The king will not want his generals rushing off without proper planning, without gaining some sense of the occasion."

Meryamun shrugged. "You are right, Tjaty Hori. My brother and I are sorry we interrupted you during your law sessions."

"I was not inconvenienced, though the farmers were. It is to them you should apologise."

Meryamun snorted. "I would not so lower myself."

"Well, that is your choice," Hori said. "I cannot force you to." He looked from one brother to the next. "That is all I wanted to say. I dare say you have things to do; I know I have."

Prehirwenemef grabbed his brother's arm as the Tjaty turned away. "What about the hunt?" he whispered.

"Ah...er, yes... Tjaty Hori. I have...we have a request."

Hori stopped and turned back, raising an eyebrow. "A request?"

"Yes. We have a report that gazelles are plaguing the farmers of Ta-senet and we thought we should go there rid them of this nuisance."

"We would be helping the farmers," Prehirwenemef added. "Just like you said, we would be serving the common men of Kemet."

"Selfless service of the kingdom?"

"Well, er...no. Not just that. You know we like to hunt and we thought...we hoped...you might let us go."

"I am surprised you are asking permission," Hori said. "You usually just sneak away."

Meryamun blushed. "We didn't think you'd mind, but Ta-senet is a bit further away, so we thought we'd better ask you."

"So can we?" Prehirwenemef begged.

"You will take hunters knowledgeable in the area? Soldiers? Servants?"

"Yes, Tjaty Hori."

"Then I see no reason you cannot help the farmers of Ta-senet..."

Prehirwenemef let out a whoop of joy, and Meryamun nodded fiercely.

"...providing," Hori went on, "you do not hunt lion."

"There's a lion?" Prehirwenemef squeaked. He grabbed at his brother's arm. "See, I told you there was a lion."

Meryamun clapped a hand over his brother's mouth. "Of course we will not go out to hunt for lion," he assured Hori.

Tjaty Hori smiled and left the room.

Prehirwenemef looked dejected. "I wanted to hunt a lion."

"Perhaps we shall."

"But you told him we wouldn't."

"I said we wouldn't go out to hunt for them, but if we cross their fresh trail...well, they could be about to attack the farmers' flocks and herds. We'd be honour bound to protect them then, wouldn't we?"

Prehirwenemef grinned. "When do we leave?"

They left the next day, armed with their favourite bows and quivers of the straightest arrows they could cajole from the armourer in the Mut corps. Groomsmen led the finest horses from the stables, hitched to lightweight hunting chariots, and a squad of soldiers assembled by the south gate. A small train of four wagons joined them, carrying such comforts of home as the princes would need, even on a hunting trip. Townsfolk gathered to watch the princes depart, and cheered them on their way, enjoying the spectacle and the infectious enthusiasm of the youths.

Meryamun had opted to take the eastern land route south rather than the western route through farmland or the river. He had sent a messenger ahead to commandeer boats to take them across the river to Ta-senet, and now looked forward to a little light hunting in the dry scrublands that lay between Waset and the ferry point.

Each prince rode in a chariot with an experienced charioteer at the reins, and four other chariots followed at their heels. Mennefer was the officer tasked with guarding the royal youths and the responsibility gnawed at him. His squad of men would follow at a run, but he and the best of his archers would ride in the other chariots and attempt to provide protection for the princes. It would be no easy task, as Meryamun often behaved as if he was king, or at least Crown Prince, imperiously ordering men around and insisting that he alone should venture out of sight of the accompanying guards. Prehirwenemef was more cautious, but even he sometimes took it into his head to take off into the desert in pursuit of some animal or other. Mennefer knew that if the least harm came to either prince, it was his hide that would suffer for it, so he kept as close a watch as he could on his charges.

The first part of the journey was straightforward, the road running straight and firm through a thin skein of farms before they petered out on the edge of desert scrub. Here, Meryamun sent out his hunters to search for game, and they returned soon enough with news of a small herd of antelope moving slowly away to the east. Immediately, the princes ordered their chariots in pursuit with Mennefer scrambling to send an adequate guard after them.

Prehirwenemef's chariot surged ahead of his brother's early on, but Meryamun was more daring and kept yelling at his charioteer to drive faster, and even when they had overtaken his younger brother's chariot, spurred him on to greater efforts. The hot desert wind blew in his face as he grasped the light wicker railing to prevent himself being thrown off, and he yelled with excitement as the wheels bounced across the desert floor, sometimes lifting completely clear of the ground. Sweat from the horses speckled his face and body, but still he urged the charioteer onward. When the first of the racing antelope came in sight, a small herd of some eight or ten does led by large-horned buck, Meryamun glanced behind to see where his brother had got to, but the other chariot was a hundred paces or more to the rear.

"They are mine," he yelled. He wedged his feet under a leather strap that ran across the floor of the chariot, freeing up his hands to grasp his bow.

Meryamun pointed toward the fleeing buck and fitted an arrow to his bow, holding it with one hand and steadying himself with the other as the charioteer guided the horses across the path of the antelope to approach the buck from the left. The prince grinned despite the dust and sand thrown up by the hooves of the antelopes and horses, and braced himself again, raising and sighting his bow.

"Keep it steady," he muttered. The charioteer knew his trade though, easing the chariot alongside the sprinting buck.

At the moment the prince released the arrow, one of the chariot wheels hit a small hole and the arrow flew low, almost grazing the antelope's belly. The buck raced on unhurt while Meryamun cursed the charioteer. Now the buck veered away, heading for a thicket near a dry stream gully, and the charioteer urged the horses on their new course, coming up alongside the fleeing animal once more.

Meryamun glanced around and saw that the does had scattered and that his brother's chariot was pursuing one, rapidly overhauling it as it sought cover in denser scrub. He hauled his attention back to his present problem and readied another arrow.

"I'll have the skin off your back if you spoil this for me," he muttered. Then, as the gully and trees leapt at them, he released.

The arrow, buck and trees intersected and the charioteers hauled the horses round desperately. Meryamun was almost thrown out as the chariot bounced over the edge of the gully as the horses leapt into it, then tumbled to the sand as they pulled up in a cloud of dust.

Meryamun staggered to his feet and stared toward the thicket. "Did I get it?"

The charioteer calmed his shaking and blowing horses, and then made his way into the thicket, with Meryamun close behind. They pushed through vegetation in almost complete silence, the only sound a slight crunch of sand beneath their sandals and the swish of leaves against their bodies. Crushed plants released a spicy aroma into the hot, still air, and somewhere ahead of them Meryamun smelled blood mixed with a musky odour.

"I did get him," he whispered.

The charioteer motioned for silence and stood listening. He knew he might get into trouble for ordering a prince, but the youth's safety was his prime concern. If indeed they smelled the buck up ahead, it may be that the beast was only wounded and approaching it carelessly could result in injury. Then there was always the possibility that a predator--lion, leopard or wolf--might be sheltering in the thicket. He moved slowly forward, but Meryamun pushed him aside impatiently, and thrust through the intervening bushes.

The buck lay on its side, panting for breath with the arrow deep in its side. Bloody froth bubbled at its nostrils and when it saw the men it struggled to rise, but the charioteer ran forward, grasped the horns and pulled the beast's head back, drawing a copper knife across its throat. The antelope's feet kicked as its lifeblood soaked the sand, and then it died, eyeballs rolling up in their sockets.

"A fine kill, my lord," the charioteer said, wiping the blade of his knife on the animal's hide.

The two men returned to the chariot and with some coaxing, led the horses out of the gully, where they waited as the other chariots in the party came up to them. One was Prehirwenemef's, and the young prince looked smug as he jumped down from his chariot.

"Missed your buck, eh, Mery? I got my doe, so we'll eat well tonight."

"Oh, I got him. He's still in the thicket where he sought to hide, but my arrow found him out."

Meryamun signed to a couple of men to fetch the buck, and grinned as his brother's smug look evaporated as they dragged the buck into view.

"Never mind, little brother. I am the elder so it is only fitting I killed the buck."

"It was only because your team was faster. Next time, I'll get there first."

Meryamun laughed. "Of course you will. Now let's get back on the road. The gazelles of Ta-senet won't wait forever."

The dead antelope were loaded onto the chariots and they all made their way back through the desert scrub to where the road lay. As they neared, Meryamun shaded his eyes against the westering sun and peered at the waiting wagon train.

"What's happening?" he called across to Prehirwenemef.

They were not left in doubt for long, as a horse raced to meet the chariots. Meryamun was astonished to see one of the aides of Tjaty Hori astride it, looking most uncomfortable. The man slid off and bowed to the princes before addressing the elder one.

"My lord Meryamun, Tjaty Hori sends his felicitations and requests your immediate presence in Waset."

"Do we have to go?" Prehirwenemef asked. "I was looking forward to our hunt."

Meryamun ignored his brother. "What has happened?" he demanded.

"A courier from the north," the aide said. "It is no secret that the Sea Peoples are sailing toward Kemet's coast, and..." The man hesitated and lowered his voice. "My lord, the Tjaty will need to confirm this, but you have been summoned north by the king."

"Me too?" Prehirwenemef asked.

"I believe so, my lord."

"What does it mean?" asked the younger prince.

"Is it not obvious?" Meryamun said. "War is about to break out and the king summons us. It can only mean he intends to make us generals...well, me anyway."

"Then let's get back to the city," Prehirwenemef said.

Leaving the wagon train and other chariots to follow, the princes turned their chariots toward home, while Mennefer took pity on the aide and took him back in his chariot. The army officer had his own hopes that the Mut corps would be called north too, to take its part in the war against the Sea Peoples.

# Chapter 13
# Year 5 of Usermaatre Ramesses

The waters of the Sea of Kinnereth were almost calm, tiny wavelets hissing over gravel on the shores as the sun beat down from a cloudless sky, sending shards of white light shimmering over the surface. Some two hundred paces offshore sat a small fishing boat, rocking slightly as the two men in it worked on a tangled fishing net. A spread sail hung limply, there being no breeze to catch, and it served only to cast a tiny patch of shade.

The younger man sighed and threw down the patch of net he was working on. He flexed his fingers and stared at the many cuts and abrasions on his hands.

"I think Ephrim must have deliberately tripped and broken his arm. I feel like doing it myself, just to get out of doing this."

The older man ceased his own repairs and smiled. "I suppose herding goats is easier?"

The young man shrugged. "It doesn't rip my hands up like this. Did it do the same to you when you were young?"

"For a time. Your hands will get callused after a while."

The younger man returned to his task, making exaggerated movements as he caught a cut finger on a cord or rubbed an abraded hand. "Ephrim will lose the goats or worse," he muttered.

"You worry too much, Jerem. Anyway, your sister Adara will help him."

"She's only eight. What could she do if a leopard attacked the herd?"

"There hasn't been a leopard in these parts for years. Besides, she's good with a sling and a well-aimed pebble will dissuade most predators." The older man turned and looked toward the shore, shading his eyes from the sun's glare. "That's Adara now."

Jerem stood up, rocking the boat so he had to grab hold of the mast. "She's in a hurry. I wonder what's wrong."

"Grab the oars, we're going in."

The fishing boat slowly swung round as oars dug deep into the clear water, and the older man gathered up the net neatly and stowed it in the stern. Adara had now reached the shore and stood ankle-deep in the cool water, hopping from one foot to the other and waving her arms above her head. As soon as the boat got close, Jerem shipped his oars and leapt over the side, dragging the boat closer. The older man helped him drag the boat up onto the shingled shore, and then turned to the girl.

"Now, Adara, what's the matter?"

"A letter, father. From Kemet." Adara looked puzzled when her father gasped and she turned to her brother. "What's wrong, Jerem? What has upset father?"

Jerem ignored her, looking with concern at his father. "It might be nothing, sir. If the king knew where you were, he'd send soldiers rather than a letter."

The man nodded. "Well, I'd better find out, hadn't I? Bring your sister along." He hurried off.

Jerem and Adara followed at a slower pace.

"Why would the king of Amurru send soldiers for father?" Adara asked.

"Not Amurru; Kemet. We used to live down there long before you were born, and father used to be a great General in the Queen's army. Ament was his name then. The present king of Kemet hates him, and if he ever found out where he lived, he'd send soldiers for him."

"Why has he changed his name? I like 'Mentak' but if he's really 'Ament' then we should call him that."

Jerem stopped and dropped to one knee beside his sister. "That's a secret, Adara. You must tell no one."

"I won't, but does this mean we'll have to move away? I like it here."

"Let's see what the letter says first."

Their parents were inside their small mud brick home when they arrived back. Adara ran inside immediately, but Jerem paused, looking at the neat animal pens and vegetable garden, the small orchard which had yet to bear fruit, and the single gnarled olive tree that bore a good harvest every year. He shook his head, sincerely hoping that they would not have to move away. He would miss it as much as Adara.

His parents looked up as he entered. They stood beneath the central skylight, a ray of bright sunshine illuminating the letter his father held in his hands. Ephrim his brother sat on a chair with his right arm in a sling, and Adara stood beside him.

"What does it say? Who is it from?" Jerem asked.

"It's from my sister," Mentak said. "And written in Kaftor. It says, 'Toothfish, husband, two boys in prison, not right. Want catch you. Please help.' She signed it 'Sister', so I know it's from her."

"Who's Toothfish?" Adara asked.

Mentak smiled. "That was her name for me when I stopped being a fisherman and became a soldier. It's a fish in the Great River of Kemet that can give you a nasty wound if you're not careful."

"Like a soldier," Adara said, clapping her hands. "But why did you change your name from Ament, father?"

Mentak looked at Jerem and frowned. "You told her?"

"She should know. She's old enough to know the reasons for secrecy."

"I won't say anything," Adara assured them. "But why did you?"

"You started this, Jerem," Mentak said. "You might as well tell her the rest."

Jerem nodded. "All right. Adara, your father was once General Ament, the foremost soldier in the army of Queen Tausret of Kemet, your mother."

Adara gaped at her mother. "Mama's a queen?" she squeaked.

"I was once, but now I'm just plain Tau, a woman of the Khabiru," her mother said with a smile.

"And...and my brothers are...are princes? I'm a princess?"

"I'm afraid not," Ephrim said. "Jerem and I are just Shechemite boys rescued by General Ament and..."

"Just Mentak the fisherman now."

"And his wife Tau."

Jerem smiled and finished off his brother's thought. "Mentak and Tau adopted us, and then after we had fled from wicked King Ramesses, you were born, Adara, so I'm afraid you are not a princess as your mother was no longer queen, just an ordinary Khabiru tribeswoman."

Adara looked crestfallen for a few moments but then laughed. "I wouldn't know how to be a princess anyway, but I didn't know you had a sister, father."

"Ti-ament," Jerem said. "We used to live with her."

"It seems she is in trouble," Mentak said. "Her husband and two oldest boys have been arrested, and she has asked me to help."

"How can you, though?" Tau asked. "It would mean death for you if you set foot in Kemet again."

"Only if they caught me, my love."

"You're not seriously considering it?"

"I have to. If Zeben and her two sons...what were their names? Goloth was one, I think."

"Rath was the eldest, Goloth the younger," Jerem said. "I remember them."

Mentak nodded. "I can't leave them in prison."

"And how do you intend getting them out?" Tau demanded. "You have no authority in Kemet any longer."

"That is true, and also in truth, I must try. She is my sister."

"Then I am coming with you."

"No, my love, you are not. You are needed here to take care of Adara and Ephrim. Jerem will help you with this, while I..."

"You dare to deny me this?" Tau demanded.

"You are no longer queen, my love," Mentak said gently. "I know Kemet and with my new features..." he stroked his bushy beard, "...I will not be recognised. You, on the other hand, are still the beautiful queen that so recently reigned over the kingdoms. Somebody would recognise you and then all would be lost." He gazed at his wife as the anger drained from her face. "You know the truth of it, my love, don't you?"

"Yes, curse it," Tau muttered. "Well, if you must go, go swiftly and may the gods of Kemet and Kanaan both, look after you."

"Let me come with you, father," Jerem said. "You need a companion."

"No, it's too dangerous."

"If it's that dangerous, you're not going," Tau said.

"I have to go. I won't be recognised."

"If they won't recognise you, father, how much less will they recognise me? I was a boy when I left Kemet, and I too have a beard, though..." he grinned, "...not as luxurious as yours. But seriously, father, you need an extra pair of eyes, and another good right arm."

Mentak shook his head, and opened his mouth to repeat his refusal, but Tau interrupted. "If you must go, then Jerem should go with you. I don't like the idea, but someone needs to keep an eye on you."

"You'll need him here..."

"You don't think I'm capable? I have Ephrim and Adara to help me."

Mentak grumbled a while longer, but he eventually relented in the face of his family's determination.

"When do we leave?" Jerem asked.

"As soon as possible. Who knows how long this letter has been on its way."

"What route will you take?"

"Walk to Urit and then see if we can join a caravan heading south. With luck the traders will hire us to help with managing the beasts and their burdens."

Mentak and Jerem left two days later, walking west from Kinnereth toward the coast of the Great Sea. They were not alone on the road as many people trod the route between Kinnereth and the fishing village of Semak, nestled at the foot of the Mount of Marduk, sometimes called Karem El by the resident Khabiru. The town of Urit lay at a crossroads near Semak, and the road north and south was a busy highway carrying trade goods through Kanaan.

The road south was also frequented by troops and posed some slight danger, but Mentak preferred to risk that instead of journeying by less used roads and risking bandits. He found Dan-el the Potter in Urit and thanked him for passing the letter along.

"I thought I might see you, Toothfish," Dan-el said. "You are heading south to Kemet?"

"You read the letter?"

Dan-el shrugged. "It was not sealed, and how else could I tell who it was for? No doubt many read its message, but the meaning was lost to all who did not know you."

"I am grateful, Dan-el, and when I return from Kemet I will bring you a gift."

"No need, my friend. How will you travel?"

"Can you find us a caravan? My son and I are willing to work our way south."

Dan-el considered the request. "Can you handle a sword?"

"Moderately well."

"Then I might have just the thing. A friend of mine travelling from Sydwn has lost some men at Akko. Turns out they were on the run and they were recognised and carried off by the local troops. He's looking for reliable guards. Shall I tell him you're interested?"

Mentak thought for a moment and then nodded.

The caravan was an unwieldy hundred heavily laden asses with a score of men to look after them. An Akkadian called Lipit-Ulmash was the owner, a tall, full-bearded man with a haughty demeanour. Mentak thought he did not need extra guards after he saw him and his sons Bin-kali and Ali-kali in action. Bandits surprised them half a month south of Urit, when a dozen men blocked the road, armed with a variety of weapons and demanded a toll. The Akkadians did not even bother to discuss terms but leapt into the fray with blades flashing and rapidly killed four men, driving the others off. Mentak wounded one other and earned a nod of appreciation from Lipit-Ulmash.

Mentak kept his distance from the other men in the caravan as much as possible, and deflected interest in his son Jerem from the younger Akkadians. They had a certain reputation and Mentak made sure he was close to Jerem at all times. The other men were rough but friendly enough, and respected their privacy. Apart from the initial disturbance of the bandit attack, the journey down the length of Kanaan was uneventful, until they reached the Way of Heru.

Kemetu troops stopped them at the first fort and ordered all goods to be unloaded and inspected. Every man was scrutinised, but as far as Mentak could tell, they were not looking for anyone in particular. He decided to risk asking a junior officer.

"You have a Kemetu accent, though you are impossibly hairy," said the officer.

"I have made this trip many times," Mentak replied, "but have never been searched like this. Are you looking for something?"

The officer shrugged. "You have come from the north. Have you seen any troop movements?"

"Kemetu, you mean? No."

"Not Kemetu. I would know about that. Any Sea Peoples?"

Mentak shook his head. "We kept away from the coast and saw no armed men except for some bandits near Urit. Do you want to know about them? We saw them off, but..."

"I have no interest in any cursed bandits. On your way." The officer stalked off.

The caravan made its way slowly down the Way of Heru and into Ta Mehu. They were not stopped again, though several times soldiers watched them move past. Mentak knew some of the units they encountered and thought he recognised a few men, but kept his face carefully averted, though it was unlikely anyone would recognise him with his full beard and unkempt hair.

"We are going to have to be careful," he told Jerem. "This war with the Sea Peoples means we could get pressed into the army. Probably our greatest protection is that we look foreign, so play that up if you are approached. Don't speak in Kemetu, shuffle your feet and gape as if you're an idiot."

Lipit-Ulmash was taking his caravan down to Men-nefer, but stopping first at Per-Ramesses and Iunu. Mentak considered just slipping away when they reached Iunu, but he decided to confide in the Akkadian as he hoped he might be able to link up with the caravan as it made its return north in a month or two.

"I'll be sorry to see you go, Mentak," Lipit-Ulmash said. "You've done your bit on the journey south, and I can always use a good fighter. If you're here in Iunu when I return, I'll take you on again." He showed his appreciation by handing him a small amount of silver.

Mentak and Jerem crossed the river at Iunu, and made their way across the well-watered lands to Per-Bast and the vineyard where his sister and her husband had lived. Strangers were in residence, so without letting on who they were looking for, made their way into the city, and to the central market where many of the traders set up their stalls.

"How do we find her?" Jerem asked.

"We know what she looks like, so we'll just have to roam the streets until we see her."

"Couldn't we just ask people? I knew a few people here from when I lived with her."

"If she's being watched, we could find ourselves arrested. No, we'll have to wander around. You stay here, near the markets and I'll try the wells. If she's still here, she'll need to eat and drink. One of us should see her."

"And if we do? How do we let the other know?"

"Meet back here at sunset."

They were unsuccessful that first day, and slept behind the animal pens in the meat market, gaining a little body heat from the animals and also a few lice. Scratching and yawning the next morning, they bought some food and ate it near one of the wells, scrutinising the women as they came to collect water.

"That one looks familiar," Jerem said, pointing to an older woman. "I can't think from where, though."

"Could you have seen her at the vineyard?"

"I don't think so, but I have seen her."

"Follow her. I'll keep watch here."

Jerem went off and followed the woman, while Mentak maintained his watch at the well. A number of women collected water, and some washed clothes or infants in the stone troughs nearby. One or two looked like Ti-ament, but when he looked closer, Mentak saw the resemblance was only superficial. The morning passed slowly and he started to wonder where Jerem had got to.

He heard a commotion and saw Jerem running toward him, with a big grin on his face. "I found her, father," he called.

Mentak stepped forward and grabbed him roughly. "Be quiet. Who knows who is listening? You found her, you say? My sister?"

"Yes, that woman we saw is Matia the washerwoman. She lives near where we used to live and Ti lives with her now...and the girls. I scarcely remember Taui, you know, and the younger one Ata died. Ti was only expecting Ini when we left and..."

"I know, I was there, remember. Did you talk to Ti or just see her?"

"Talked to her, father. Come on, she's expecting us."

Mentak looked around carefully, but nobody seemed to be paying them any attention. He nodded and clapped Jerem on the shoulder. "Lead on then, son."

# Chapter 14
# Year 5 of Usermaatre Ramesses

A merchant vessel plying the coastal routes brought a report to the court of Usermaatre Ramesses in Men-nefer of a fleet of the Sea Peoples off the coast of Kanaan. The king at once dispatched messengers to warn the coastal communities along the edge of Ta Mehu, and to carry orders to the northern army. They were to send swift scouts by land to detect any landings by the enemy, and to send back reports of the fleet movements.

General Djehutemheb received his orders at the hand of the king himself and sped north to take up his command. He was to find, but not engage, the enemy; and send word to the king. Ramesses was determined to bring the enemy to battle personally and inflict a defeat that would make his name as illustrious as that of the Great Usermaatre.

Admiral Hori also received his orders, but they were somewhat vaguer as the military might of the newly constituted Kemetu Navy was as yet untried. He was to take his little fleet to the mouth of the easternmost branch of the Great River and there engage in exercises to test tactics.

"You have the men you need?" Ramesses asked.

"Yes, Son of Re. We have emptied the prisons of men willing to fight in exchange for freedom. Some of them may even make good soldiers and sailors."

"If they are criminals they need serve only to die," Tjaty Herwernef said. "They will scarcely be missed."

"Any man who dies to make Kemet secure is worthy of praise."

"Of course, Son of Re. I did not mean to make light of their condition."

"I know the capabilities of the corps, Admiral, but not of your new navy. I shall go to Per-Ramesses in a few days on my way to command the army, so you will show me your men's capabilities then."

Admiral Hori begged leave to join his navy in preparation for the king's visit and was given leave to depart. Prince Khaemwaset served as the general's aide, and accompanied him north, having sent word to all the units of the fleet to assemble at Per-Ramesses.

Commander Merikare had been put in charge of the criminals drafted into the land-based units of the navy. They would serve to support the small boats as they fought the enemy in the lower reaches of the river, and the most effective way of doing that was with the bow and arrow and slingshot. Every man who came out of prison was interviewed and placed in a unit where his skills, if any, would be put to good use. There were few men with useful skills though. Most of the common criminals were layabouts who had avoided honest work, though a few had been soldiers or fishermen. These latter ones were sent off to the naval units. The unskilled were placed where the most likely outcome was death at the hands of the enemy. Their deaths would, however, serve to protect their more skilled brethren.

When the officials had come to the city of Per-Bast, they had found only a handful of prisoners willing to exchange the relative security of the prison for the dangers of service. A man and his two sons were among those to volunteer, and Commander Merikare interviewed them himself.

"Your names?"

"Zeben, Commander. These are my sons Rath and Goloth."

"Strange names. You're not Kemetu, are you?"

"I was born a Kaftor, sir, but I married a Kemetu woman and settled here in Per-Bast."

"What were you before you married? A soldier, by any chance?"

"A charioteer, sir."

"Excellent. We have a use for you. What about your sons? What skills do they have?"

Zeben shrugged. "They are young, sir, and mostly worked with me in my vineyard."

"A pity, still, they can no doubt hold an axe and swing it at an enemy soldier."

Zeben grimaced and thought hard. "Rath is good with boats, sir. Is that any use?"

Merikare nodded. "Could be. What about your other son? He must have some skill."

"He hunts ducks in the reed beds with bow and throwing stick. He would be wasted as an axeman."

The Commander considered the man and boys before him and nodded. He needed every able-bodied person he could find; it was just a matter of where to use them most effectively.

"Very well, I will accept your service. You, Zeben, shall enter my personal service as a messenger, seeing as how you can drive a chariot. Your eldest... Rath, was it? I'll send him across to the naval..."

"Sir, please...can we stay together? They are young and I worry about them."

"This is not a feast day or a trip to the menagerie, fellow. You will go where I say or rot in prison. Your choice...quick about it now."

"Yes, sir. Sorry, sir. We'll do it and gratefully."

"Good. Your eldest will join a naval squadron and your youngest will become an archer. These men..." Merikare gestured his guards forward, "...will take you to your units. Fight well, and you will be released at the end of the war."

Commander Setau had the large fleet of small boats at his disposal. A former fisherman himself, he was familiar with the ways of the water, but less skilled at managing so many independent minds. Each man, often commandeered along with his boat, had his own idea about how best to sail it, and never mind what everybody else was doing. Setau had made savage examples of a score of the worst offenders, and now the others were at least obeying him, even if somewhat reluctantly. New recruits flooded in from the squads scouring the prisons of Ta Mehu, and Setau weighed up their experience level and inserted them into the fledgling fleet where he thought they would do most good.

A vast number of small fishing boats had been broken down and reconstituted as larger fighting vessels. They bore two large steering oars and a large rectangular sail. They were very dependent on wind direction and were not manoeuvrable in crosswinds, so oarsmen were added, up to ten on each side for the larger ships and these provided forward motion as well as changes of direction. A manoeuvrable ship was useless without some means of attack, however, and this problem had given the new naval officers a headache. Armed men were often clumsy within a ship in motion, and had to loose arrows wildly in the gaps between the rowers and the sail.

Setau had solved this himself, and his solution had earned him his promotion to Commander. He had ordered a flat platform to be constructed above the level of the rowers and archers and slingers stood here with an almost unobstructed view of the enemy once the sail was lowered. A low railing enabled the archers to brace themselves when they released their arrows, and after they had done so, could either release more over the stern as the rowers sped them away, or could lie flat to present less of a target to enemy archers. It promised to work well, but it had not yet been tried under warlike conditions. The arrival of the king in Per-Ramesses would change that.

He accompanied his fleet downriver to Per-Ramesses and beyond, finding a stretch of water where he could demonstrate their budding naval capabilities. He settled on a stretch of placid water by rich flat meadows where the fresh water of the Great River first met the salt of the Great Sea. Five barges were designated as enemy ships and hoisted red banners. His own smaller ships flew green banners so that watchers could tell them apart, though size alone was sufficient for that. Land-based squads crouched down in the cover of shrubs and reeds, out of sight of the 'enemy' barges, while the fighting ships of the Kemetu navy waited upriver. All that was needed was the arrival of the king.

Ramesses arrived the next morning along with an entourage of officials and army officers eager to see the new tactics devised by Admiral Hori and his Commanders. The Admiral greeted him nervously and conducted him to a comfortable chair set up in the shade of a small awning. An assortment of common stools was available for the king's companions and some squabbling arose as they all tried to find a stool and seat themselves near the king. When Ramesses had been settled and refreshed with wine, Admiral Hori nodded to Prince Khaemwaset who waved a banner to set the battle in motion.

The barges thrashed their way past the sand bars at the mouth of the river and made their way into a broad expanse of water. Oars threshed the water into foam and the sound of a drum beating time for the oarsmen carried to the watchers on shore. As they started to draw level with the king, a host of small boats sped round a bend in the river, some taking advantage of fluky wind gusts, but the majority rowing to battle. The two fleets closed rapidly, and small flights of arrows lofted and fell all around the barges. Archers on the barges replied in kind and the small boats were peppered with missiles, though the faster and more manoeuvrable fishing boats turned about and withdrew whenever the 'enemy' archers found their range.

"It looks dangerous," Ramesses commented. "I hope the casualties will not be too high. I can't afford to lose men in an exercise."

"The arrows are blunted, Son of Re," Hori replied. "I dare say there will be some injuries, but none should be too serious."

"What are they doing now?" Ramesses pointed to where the fleet of small boats had split into parts and had worked their way between the barges and the shore, keeping up a steady stream of arrows.

"Small boats by themselves cannot harm the barges, Son of Re, so they seek to bring them within range of...ah, see? It is working."

The barges turned clumsily to follow the smaller craft in toward the shore, their oars stirring up the mud as the water shallowed. At the last minute, when it looked as if the fishing boats would be pinned against the river banks, they darted out of the way, and hundreds of men rose from their concealment amongst the shrubs and reed beds. A storm of arrows rose and fell and stones from slingers thumped against the barges' wooden sides and clattered across the decks.

Cries of alarm and pain arose from the 'enemy' sailors, and the barges lurched and wallowed as they tried to extricate themselves from the shallows. One stuck fast on a mud bank and the soldiers on shore rushed it, splashing through the shallow water and boarded it. Hand to hand fighting broke out and the sailors were thrown into the water amid general laughter. The other barges beat their way out into deeper water and turned for the river mouth, pursued by a ragged fleet of small fishing boats. There were fewer arrows loosed now as stocks were running low, but there was no doubt in the watchers' minds that the 'enemy' had been routed.

Ramesses sat in silence for a time and watched the small boats returning from the fray, and the soldiers leaping and shouting on the shore and on the captured barge. At length he nodded, and the watching officials breathed a sigh of relief.

"It looks promising, Admiral Hori," Ramesses said. "But the river is wide here. What would you have done if the barges had not followed the boats into range of the soldiers on shore?"

"One can never be certain what an enemy commander will do, Son of Re, but if this had been a real battle, I would have had those same barges packed with men and archers, and they would have sailed close to the enemy ships. It would have been the same as them coming close to shore."

"It would seem that you have done well, Admiral Hori. Has my son, Prince Khaemwaset, performed creditably?"

"Indeed, Son of Re. With your permission, I would make him a commander in the navy."

"I doubt he would settle for that as he already holds the rank of General in my army."

Hori bowed. "Of course, Majesty."

Ramesses returned to the city and made his preparations for moving north. He visited the Per-Khemret and commended Queen Iset on having borne a fine young son. While he was there, he bedded her again, desiring to leave another son in her belly who would be a companion for the infant Prince Amunhirkhopeshef. Iset would like to have enjoyed more of the king's attention, desiring to attend feasts and priestly plays, but resigned herself to being there solely for the king's pleasure.

Khaemwaset surprised him when it came time to join the northern army, by asking to be left behind.

"You do not need another General when facing the Sea Peoples, father. Your presence will be all our men need, but your navy should have a royal representative too, to encourage and persuade them to greater efforts. Let me join Admiral Hori."

"This naval experiment means that much to you? Very well, I will make you Admiral of the Lord of the Two Lands and put you in charge."

"Not that, father, for I lack experience and it would distress me if my inexperience caused the fleet to be defeated. Make me a Commander under Hori instead."

Ramesses hid a smile, but he was secretly pleased at his son's words. It was only his due that the Prince hold high rank, but he was displaying maturity in his decisions. He would make a good king when his time came to mount the throne of Kemet.

News arrived of an army of the Sea Peoples landed on the coast three days north of the Way of Heru, and Ramesses mobilised his forces in preparation of joining his corps. Elements of the enemy fleet hovered offshore, so Khaemwaset hurried off to join Admiral Hori and prepare their navy to meet the foreign ships. By land and by sea, Kemet was under attack, and both army and navy would be necessary to stop them.

# Chapter 15
# Year 5 of Usermaatre Ramesses

Ament had an emotional reunion with his sister, after she got used to the idea that this unkempt, bearded man was the same army general she had once known. She cried, and then wept with joy, and her little daughters howled until she comforted them. Jerem played with them and soon had them laughing, but they still looked askance at the wild-looking man in their midst.

"You couldn't get here any sooner?" Ti-ament demanded. "I wrote to you nearly a year ago."

"I only got your letter a month ago. It must have been held up, otherwise I'd have come sooner."

Ti-ament nodded and brushed away tears. "Can't be helped. You're here now."

Matia the washerwoman had welcomed them into her house for the sake of her friend Ti-ament, but looked nervous. Ament had to assure her that they would keep a low profile and hopefully would depart very soon.

"As far as anyone is concerned, I'm Mentak, a Khabiru goat herder interested in supplying the corps with meat. My son Jerem is helping me."

"I'm not sure anyone would believe you, brother," Ti-ament said. "Couldn't you have chosen an occupation you know something about?"

"I am actually a goat herder these days," Mentak said. "And a fisherman. But come now, tell me what has happened to your husband and boys."

"Soldiers came looking for you again, brother. You and that lady of yours must still scare the king, because he hasn't stopped looking for you. All it takes is some fool thinking he's seen you somewhere and soldiers arrive. This time they carted my men off to prison hoping it would loosen my tongue as to your whereabouts."

"You should have told them what you know. It's little enough."

Ti-ament nodded. "Urit, and Dan-el the Potter. I thought about it, but I couldn't have your deaths on my conscience. I hoped if I obviously didn't know, they'd release them."

"Perhaps they will."

"No, it's too late. They've emptied the prisons because of this war against the Sea Peoples and drafted the prisoners into the army and navy."

"You know this for a fact? That Zeben has been pressed into the army? Or navy?"

Ti-ament nodded again. "Zeben and Goloth are in the army, and Rath has joined the navy. I don't know what units, though, or where they've been sent."

"It might be possible to find out," Ament said cautiously, "but then what? Encourage them to desert, I suppose."

"I hoped you might have a plan," Ti-ament said.

Ament shook his head. "A bit hard to do that without knowing the situation. The first thing to do is find out where they've been sent. Once we know that, we might be able to think of something."

"They can't stay here though, can they?" Jerem asked. "I imagine deserters are treated harshly if recaptured."

"That's true," Ament confirmed. "You'll have to leave Per-Bast, probably forever."

Ti-ament groaned. "I hadn't thought that far ahead, but where could we go?"

"You could always join us in Kanaan," Ament said.

"It's such a long way... I can't make that decision. Zeben will have to make it."

"All right, let's leave it for now. I'll make enquiries and see if I can find out where they've gone, and worry about what to do later."

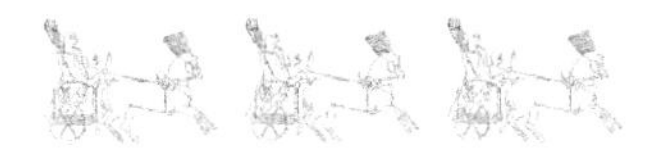

Ament could not just ask at the local army barracks, so he took himself down to the taverns and made the rounds, sitting quietly with a foaming mug of beer and listening to the other drinkers. Whenever he overheard a conversation that pertained to military matters, he insinuated himself into the group and, by buying drinks, was able to pose a few questions. After a few days of this, he found out what he needed.

"War's coming," an old man said. "The king's taking the corps north to fight the Sea Peoples. I'd go myself, but my leg..." he slapped the offending appendage with one hand and took another drink.

"We've heard it all before, Ahtep," said his fellow drinker. "Wounded at Perire saving the old king's life. It's always seemed to me that if you had, Baenre would have rewarded you, yet here you are cadging drinks off your friends and strangers."

"Ah, you're a good friend, Nakht," Ahtep said. "And you, stranger..." he hiccupped. "What was your name?"

"Mentak."

"Foreign, eh, with a name like that?"

"Khabiru. I herd goats and I'm looking for a market for my meat. I thought with a war on..."

"You're looking in the wrong place," Nakht said. "The army doesn't get its meat from Per-Bast. You'll need to see someone in Men-nefer or Per-Ramesses."

"I was given false information then it seems. What does Per-Bast produce?"

"Not much. Men for the army and that newfangled navy, and wine. There are some good vineyards hereabouts."

Ament nodded sagely. "Army officers will always want wine. I should have owned a vineyard here instead of a herd of goats."

"Wouldn't stop you being pressed into the army though," Ahtep said.

"What? Even landowners? I thought they'd be exempt."

"Most are," Ahtep agreed, "but not if you're foreign."

"Zeben's as Kemetu as you," Nakht said. "He might be Kaftor born, but he's as loyal as any man. Rotten what happened."

"Who's this Zeben fellow?" Ament asked.

"Local vineyard owner," Ahtep said. "Decent enough fellow, despite being Kaftor born. He was arrested, along with his sons...what? Must've been close on a year ago now? Anyway, they were arrested and then pressed into the army."

"That's right," Nakht said, "and his only crime was being married to that woman of his who was sister to a traitor."

Ament desperately wanted to know which corps they had joined, but couldn't think of a subtle way of asking. "I passed a couple of corps on the way down here," he said. "Funny if this fellow had been in one of them. Heru, I think one of them was... and Re, possibly."

Nakht shook his head. "Nah, Commander Merikare wasn't sending men to the frontline corps. It was a local one, I think."

"Just as well," Ahtep added. "He'll stand a better chance of surviving, what with him being a farmer instead of a soldier. His boys too, I'd say."

"They have a local corps?" Ament asked.

"They made one especially for prisoners and the like. Calling it the Hapi corps as it's supposed to work with the navy."

"And based in Per-Bast?"

"Nah, it's down in Per-Ramesses, I think."

Ament found an excuse to leave shortly thereafter, and hurried back to find his family. He told them of his findings and Jerem added a little bit of information he had gleaned from listening to the local fishermen.

"They're upset that all their wooden boats have been taken," Jerem said. "They're having to make reed ones now, which aren't as good...though I suppose they're cheaper to make... Anyway, they say the new navy is based downriver from Per-Ramesses, so that's where Rath will be."

"Can we do anything?" Ti-ament asked.

"I'll try, but the first thing I have to do is make sure you and the girls are safe. I think we need to take you north into Kanaan."

"I'm not leaving Kemet while my husband and boys are in danger."

"I can't protect you and look for them at the same time," Ament reasoned. "Unless... Jerem, you could take them north while I try to get into the army."

"Father, no," Jerem protested. "You'd be recognised."

"It's a new corps that's been formed. With luck, there'll be nobody there who knows me. Anyway, I can't think of a better way to find them. But the rest of you have to leave Kemet. I can't be worrying about you as well, and if I do find a way to prise them free, we'll have to leave in a hurry. Little children would only slow us down."

Ti-ament continued to argue, but her brother wore her down and eventually she agreed. Jerem was not happy to be tasked with the role of escorting her to safety rather than helping his father, but he too agreed, though grudgingly.

They said their farewells to Matia, and set off on foot to Iunu, and then on to Per-Ramesses, travelling as a family group of foreigners. Their trip was without incident as, although there were plenty of troops on the move, nobody was looking for fugitives and Ament's appearance bore no resemblance to the man he had once been. In Per-Ramesses, Ament spent the last of his silver buying a donkey and provisions for the journey north.

The Akkadian caravan owner was still somewhere in the south, so he could not secure their passage north with him, but he found a small caravan willing to take them.

Then Ti-ament changed her mind and flatly refused to go. To Ament's annoyance, Jerem supported her, saying that as Zeben and the boys were supposed to be in or near the city, they should at least look for them before contemplating their exodus. Ament pleaded, then shouted and stamped out of the room they had rented, before realising that nothing he could say was going to change their minds.

"Very well," he said. "A month, no more. If we haven't found them in that time, I want your promise that you'll go, with no more argument. Jerem will accompany you."

Ti-ament smiled. "You'll find them, brother. I know you will."

It was not hard to find the Hapi corps as the whole city was like a kicked ants' nest, with soldiers everywhere, merchants bustling around trying to sell their wares to the army overseers, and seemingly the entire population of Per-Ramesses in an uproar. Harder, though, was to track one man, or rather two, amidst this hubbub. Ament tried asking a few soldiers if they knew a man called Zeben, but quickly realised that as the whole corps had only recently been put together, it was unlikely that anyone knew more than a handful of other men. A better hope was to ask an officer, though there were dangers inherent in this approach. Officers would likely have been drawn from other corps, and the chance of someone recognising him despite his changed appearance was that much greater.

He decided to risk it, and found the military headquarters of Commander Merikare. The corps commander was elsewhere, but Ament looked for officers he did not recognise and followed them, waiting until they were off duty before asking questions. He received a variety of responses.

"Zeben? Never heard of him."

"You think I bother myself with every soldier in the corps? Be off with you."

"No. Why are you asking?"

"Try his Troop Commander. No, I don't know who that would be."

"Who are you? Why aren't you in the corps yourself?"

Ament hurried away from this last officer, muttering that he was a foreigner, and returned to the military headquarters. It was apparent that few officers were familiar with the troops under their command as yet, and that if he wanted to know, he would have to persuade the scribe of the corps. He thought about the problems involved in penetrating the army headquarters and decided he would just have to walk in boldly and brazen it out if he was challenged. The only advantage he had was knowledge of army procedures and the way junior officers reacted to new situations.

"Where is the corps's scribe?" he demanded of the first junior officer he saw. "The Commander told me to find him and give him a message."

"Uh, down that hall."

Ament nodded but did not thank the man, letting him assume that despite his appearance he was someone of note. He sauntered down the hall as if he had every right to be there and asked again at the end of it.

"Scribe of the corps?"

"Why do you want him?"

"That's my business...and your Commander's. Shall I tell him you held me up?"

"In there," the man said, pointing.

There were several men in the room, some of them scribes, others mere helpers who were involved in sorting scrolls into baskets. None of them looked up when he entered.

"Who is in charge here?" Ament demanded.

An older scribe put down his pen and raised an eyebrow at Ament's bearded face. "I am. What do you want?"

"It's not what I want; it's what Commander Merikare wants. He sent me."

"And what does our esteemed commander want?"

"He wants the list of the men pressed into service in Per-Bast, and the units they were assigned to. Produce them immediately."

"Why would he want those?" The scribe shook his head as Ament opened his mouth to speak. "Just thinking out loud. Min, look in that basket there...the one labelled Per-Bast. There should be a scroll in it with the symbol for prison. Bring it here."

The scribe looked back at Ament. "You're not a soldier are you, though you have the manner of one? What are you; a spy?"

"Would I tell you if I was?"

The older scribe shrugged. "Here's the scroll," he said as Min trotted over with it. He unrolled it and scanned the lines of common script. "I wrote this down myself, you know."

"Give me the scroll." Ament held out his hand.

"You can't take it with you."

"Commander Merikare wants it."

The scribe shook his head. "Commander's orders, personnel scrolls are not to leave here. Every prisoner pressed into service must be recorded and his behaviour noted. How else is the Commander going to tell if the man has earned his freedom when the war's over?"

"The scroll won't be lost. The commander will have it."

"You have that order in writing?"

Ament shook his head. "Now I'm going to have to waste time going back to get written permission. He's not going to be happy."

The scribe shrugged. "Not my problem. You should have thought of that."

Ament cursed softly, and felt his spirits fall. The information he needed was right there, but he couldn't... "Could you look up a name for me? Three names?"

"I thought Merikare wanted all the names?"

"He does, but I know he has three he was most curious about. If I could at least take that information back to him, he might forgive my lack of the scroll."

"I suppose so. What were the names?"

"Rath and Goloth, sons of Zeben."

The scribe perused the scroll. Yes, here we are... Goloth... Hapi corps, Blue Troop. What was another name?"

"Rath, and Ze..."

"One at a time, one at a time. Rath, you say? He's in the Heron squad of the Iteru fleet. And the third name?"

"Zeben. Father of the other two."

"Zeben?" the scribe frowned and traced his finger down the list of names. "Merikare wants to know where this Zeben of Per-Bast is?"

"Yes."

The scribe grunted and called Min over, whispering in his ear. Min looked startled, but hurried out of the room.

"Where's he going?" Ament asked.

"There's another scroll in another room. I think this Zeben is on it."

"I thought you said you had written this scroll yourself? If Rath and Goloth are on it, then Zeben must be too."

The scribe smiled and shook his head.

Ament noticed the other scribes were now looking at him and he had a sudden feeling something was wrong. "Never mind," he said. "I'll take these two names back to Commander Merikare, and return for the other one later." He turned away and strode for the door.

As he reached it, two armed men burst through it, with Min on their heels. "That's the man," he cried. "The bearded one."

Ament froze, a bronze spear point pricking his chest. The scribe got up from his seat and approached him, carefully staying out of reach as the guards tied Aments hands behind him.

"I think you are a spy," the scribe said, "but not a spy for Commander Merikare. You're a spy for the Sea Peoples, and we execute spies."

"That's not so," Ament muttered. "I just wanted to know where Zeben was...Commander Merikare wants to know."

"That was your mistake," the scribe said with a smile. "Commander Merikare knows exactly where this Zeben is. The man is the Commander's personal charioteer. Take him away," he ordered the guards. "I think the Commander Merikare will be most interested in what he has to say."

# Chapter 16
# Year 5 of Usermaatre Ramesses

Ament was thrown into a cell in the military headquarters to await the Commander's pleasure. Merikare arrived back around sunset, judging by the sounds that filtered through to him in the cell, but nobody came to fetch him. He slept fitfully, wondering what he could say that would not result in his immediate execution for spying. In the morning, the guards came for him and, binding him with ropes, hauled him before Merikare and threw him to the floor. Ament struggled to his knees and faced the commander.

"Who are you and where are you from?"

"My name is Mentak, sir. I am a Khabiru."

"You speak Kemetu very well."

"My father used to bring me down on his trading trips. I learnt the language so I could bargain."

"What trade?"

"Goats, sir. My father traded meat and hides, some cheese. I thought that maybe the army might buy my meat."

"You thought wrong. We have all the meat we need. Why were you asking questions in my name? A cunning ruse and worthy of a foreign spy, but why would you want to know the whereabouts of ordinary soldiers? Are they fellow spies?"

"Commander, forgive my subterfuge, but I am no spy. I was looking for this man Zeben but nobody would tell me anything, so I used your name to loosen tongues."

"Must I find a way to loosen your tongue? Tell me why you are really here. What did you hope to learn?"

"Oh sir, I am telling the truth. I am only a humble Khabiru goat herder looking to sell his meat. While I was down here I hoped to find this man Zeben who owed me a small sum from my last visit. I heard he had been pressed into the army, so I came looking for him. When nobody would tell me anything I used your name. I am sorry, sir, I meant no harm."

"And the other names?" Merikare looked at a scrap of paper. "Rath and Goloth?"

"His sons, sir. I thought if I could at least find them, they might know where their father was."

Merikare stared at the kneeling man and drummed his fingers on the arm of his chair. "At least you have your story straight, though that is no more than I would expect of a moderately competent spy. Perhaps unfortunately for you, I know these men, for I pressed them into service myself. What do you think they would say if I confronted you with them?"

Ament hesitated, thinking hard. Zeben would probably not recognise him, which was a danger; but equally dangerous, he might recognise him and blurt out his real name. "I don't know, sir."

"Fetch my charioteer," Merikare told one of the guards. To Ament, he added, "you are to say nothing, but let him greet you."

A few minutes passed, and then the guard returned with Zeben in tow.

"You see this man?" Merikare asked Zeben. "What is he to you?"

Zeben stared for a few minutes and then shook his head. "I don't know him, sir."

"You're sure? He claims to know you."

Zeben looked again, stooping to peer into Ament's face. Again he shook his head. "What is your name?"

"Ah... Mentak," Ament said, letting the last syllable fade into silence.

Zeben's eyebrows lifted. "Mentak?" he hesitated, and into the pause Ament offered up the slightest of nods. "I... I didn't recognise you."

"You know this man?" Merikare demanded.

"Yes, sir. His name is Mentak. He..." Zeben swallowed and looked away as if suddenly realising he knew nothing about Ament's circumstances and what story he had told.

"You see, sir?" Ament said quickly. "I came looking for him to pay his debt."

"Silence. Zeben, you were about to say?"

"Only that he is a long way from home, sir and I can only think he has come looking for repayment of the debt I owe him."

Merikare grunted. "What is this debt? How much?"

"A deben of copper sir, for a service he once did me," Ament said.

"How were you going to repay him, Zeben? You had nothing of any worth on you when my men arrested you."

"I... er, don't have it on me, of course, sir."

"Then where? Tell me, and I will send my men to fetch it."

"I had a vineyard, but it was confiscated."

Merikare regarded Ament closely. "Your friend has no means of paying you."

Ament shrugged. "No great matter, sir. I am willing to let Zeben have more time."

"Thank you," Zeben murmured.

"That is no longer for you to say," Commander Merikare said. "You are now my charioteer, pressed into my service. Whatever debt you owe this man is cancelled. Mentak, you now owe me a deben of copper. How will you pay?"

"The debt is Zeben's, sir...how is it now mine?"

"Because I say so. You have wasted my time and the time of my scribes when you should have just openly come and asked about your friend. For that I am fining you a deben of copper. How will you pay?"

"I... I cannot, sir. Not yet...but I will. Just give me a bit of time."

Merikare smiled. "Then you will work off your debt in my service." He summoned his guards. "Take this man to the Hapi corps and have him pressed into service." The commander smiled as Ament was hauled to his feet. "Who knows? If you survive the war and are suitably brave, maybe you will be released with all your debts paid."

Ament was hustled out of the room and down a long hallway, his guards hurrying him along with pushes and prods from their spears, but when they reached the courtyard, nobody seemed to know what to do with him.

"You," a guard officer said. "Go and find a Hapi officer, and you two, guard him until the officer claims him." He turned and strode off.

Ament shrugged and looked at his guards. "Think you could untie me now?"

"Not a chance," snarled one of the guards. The other just ignored him and picked at his teeth with a broken fingernail.

Zeben sauntered out into the courtyard and strolled across to Ament, nodding affably at his two guards. "Got myself out of that debt didn't I? Sorry you got caught up though."

One of the guards guffawed, and they both relaxed somewhat. Zeben moved a little closer and lowered his voice, murmuring in the Kaftor tongue.

"Do you know anything about my family?"

"Your wife and daughters are near here, and safe. Jerem is with them."

"Thank the gods. And my sons?"

"I know where they are."

"Can you get them free?"

"I'll try, but I should get you free first."

Zeben shook his head. "Forget about me. I'm safe enough as Merikare's charioteer. He won't go anywhere near the war if he can help it. Just get my boys out."

"I'll do what I can."

The two men stood in silence for a while. One of the guards cleared his throat and asked. "What were you talking about?"

"Just passing the time of day," Zeben said. "Mentak here comes from a place near where I used to live. He was telling me the news from home."

The guard nodded and looked away. "Well, hurry it up."

"Can you get my family to safety?" Zeben asked Ament.

He nodded. "I have a place far from Kemet."

"Take my wife there, then. My boys too, if you can. Tell her not to wait here for me."

Ament nodded again. "If you can escape, make for Urit and Dan-el the potter."

"I remember."

"Here, what do you think you're doing?" The junior guard officer reappeared, looking angrily at the guards he had left to watch Ament. "Why are you here, charioteer?"

Zeben grimaced and hunched his shoulders. "It's not fair that Mentak should have to pay the amount of my debt to the Commander," he said, putting a whine into his voice.

The officer laughed. "The Commander can do as he likes. It is no longer your concern, so be off with you. Ah, here are the Hapi men. About time."

An officer and small squad of the Hapi corps took Ament into custody and marched him away through the streets to the city outskirts where the main corps camp had been set up. He was handed over to an officer who was drilling a group of men, obviously not long out of prison, in the use of weapons.

"Another recruit for you, Hakor."

The drill officer looked Ament up and down and shook his head. "If it's not the scum from prisons they send me, it's farm boys and old men who reek of the animals they tend. What's your name, fellow, and what did you do in your former life?"

"Mentak. I herd goats."

"That's not all you do to them, I'll warrant." Hakor roared with laughter at his own joke. "Ever handled a weapon?"

Ament shrugged.

Hakor sighed. "Pick up one of those wooden axes and come at me. Let's see what you're made of."

Ament picked up an axe and hefted its light weight. He noticed the other recruits gathering round to watch and debated whether to show any skill or not. *If I'm too handy with weapons he might get suspicious.*

"Come on then. What are you waiting for?"

Hakor was standing there weaponless, so Ament swung hesitantly at the man's side with the wooden axe blade. The drill officer stepped forward quickly, inside the arc of the blow, and landed a blow of his own with his fist, sending Ament reeling back.

"Is that all you've got?" Hakor asked. "Even my infant daughter could fight better."

Ament grimaced and moved in again as the recruits started good-natured jeering. He swung, but as Hakor stepped out of the way, changed the angle of the cut, forcing him to step back.

Hakor nodded. "Better." He held out a hand to one of the recruits. "Give me your axe, and I'll make this more interesting."

The recruit pressed the handle of his own practice axe into Hakor's hand, and the instructor grinned, sweeping his axe left and right in broad arcs, the wooden blade whistling through the air as he advanced on Ament. Ament fell back, watching the instructor's eyes and then, as the man struck, blocked with his own axe. The shock jarred Ament's arm and he stepped back again, swapping the weapon to his left hand and flexing the muscles of his right arm. Hakor laughed and moved in again.

Suddenly, he tired of the game. He was better than the instructor, but Hakor's strength would overcome him if he kept delaying. The only way to overcome a stronger opponent was to move faster--turn the other man's strength against him.

He feinted left, ducked to the right, deflected Hakor's swing rather than blocking it, kicked the other man's shin and, as he stumbled, tossed the axe to his right hand and brought the wooden blade round to smack the back of the instructor's head with its side.

Hakor fell to his knees, shook his head and lurched to his feet again. He stared at Ament, anger warring with respect on his face. Then he nodded and tossed his own axe aside.

"You've fought before."

"On occasion," Ament confirmed.

"What other weapons can you handle?"

Ament shrugged. "Sword, spear, bow."

"A warrior indeed. Looks like you were a good catch. Can you obey orders?"

"If I have to."

"You have to." Hakor looked thoughtfully at Ament. "You look familiar. Have you been in the Kemetu army before?"

Ament shook his head. "I'm Khabiru."

Hakor nodded, but his expression was still thoughtful. "Welcome to the Hapi corps, soldier. What did you say your name was? Goat?"

"Mentak, sir. I herd goats."

Hakor grinned. "So you do. Well, now you're a soldier in the king's army, and that's a much nobler profession. Do your duty and survive and you'll find plenty of opportunities for advancement."

Ament continued with weapons training for another half day, but by the end, Hakor was treating him as if he was another instructor. He worried that he was attracting notice, but hoped that he would have found Goloth and be gone before anyone recognised him. The Hapi corps was a new one, but it was likely that officers had been brought in from other corps and Ament knew men of all ranks.

They were marched back to their camp after training, and Ament was assigned to a group of five soldiers under a junior officer and issued with a few basics in the way of equipment. He joined the others at the kitchens and received his daily allowance of bread and slightly wilted vegetables. Munching on these, he tried to deflect too many questions as to his origins, while asking a few of his own.

"What's your name?"

"Mentak."

"Where are you from?"

"Up north. I'm Khabiru. What Troop are we in?"

"Red. You speak with a Kemetu accent."

A shrug. "I've been here before. Where are the other Troops camped?"

"All around. Hakor said you were trained in weapons. Have you been a soldier before?"

A nod. "Where's the Blue Troop?"
"Why do you want to know?"
"I think someone I know might be in it."
"Who?"
"A lad called Goloth. The son of a friend."
"Strange name. Is he Khabiru too?"
Another nod.

In between drilling and training, the common soldiers sat around with little to do except talk, play games of Senet, carve charms out of wood or bone, or sleep, so after the meal, Ament set off in the direction of where the Blue Troop was supposedly camped. After a little bit of searching and cautious questioning, he found the group of five soldiers to which Goloth belonged, but the boy was not there.

"He's off getting extra weapons training," one of his group said. "The instructor says he's good."

"That's why you've gotta watch yourself and not be too good," said another man. "Who wants extra duty, eh?"

They pointed Ament toward the training ground, which was a different area from the one he had been on earlier, and eventually found a small group of young men peppering a series of straw targets with arrows. He stood off to one side with a group of other soldiers and watched, trying to work out which one was Goloth. It had been eight years since he had seen the youth, and Goloth had only been a boy then, but he identified one or two possibilities amongst the archers.

"Do you know which one is Goloth?" he asked quietly.

"The tall one...there...he's just hit the target."

Ament waited until the youth finished his set, and then sauntered over to where he stood watching the other archers.

"You have a good eye, Goloth," he murmured.

"Thank you, sir, I..." Goloth broke off and stared at the bearded man beside him. "Do I know you? Your voice is familiar."

"Your father asked me to find you."

"My father? You've seen him? And Rath?" Goloth's excited voice made heads turn in their direction.

"Calm down," Ament said. "You'll attract attention. Just watch the archers." He waited until heads turned back to the practice session before continuing. "Your father is well, but I haven't found Rath yet..."

"He went into the navy."

"I know, but I haven't found him yet. Your father tasked me with finding you both and getting you to safety."

"Why would you do that?" Goloth stared at the man beside him again. "Ament?"

"Softly. It's Mentak now and I'm a Khabiru goat herder."

"The beard's a good disguise."

"Not a disguise, lad. It's how I look now."

"What are you doing here? I mean, how is it you're here? Could you just wander through the camp?"

"Unfortunately, no. I had to join the corps. I'm in the Red Troop. But don't worry; I'll get you out of here somehow."

They stood and watched the archery for a while, being less conspicuous there than if they had wandered off somewhere to talk. Ament remarked on the low level of skill displayed by the other archers.

"If this is the standard of archery, we'd best escape before there's any fighting. The corps would be massacred by any reasonable unit of the enemy."

"The instructors say I'm rather good," Goloth said with a grin. "I used to hunt ducks in the reed beds, you see."

"Not many reed beds in the north," Ament commented, "but I dare say we can find something for you to hunt."

"We'd have to leave Kemet?" Goloth asked, dismay in his voice. "I thought..."

"Thought you'd just be able to go back to your old life?" Ament shook his head. "Your parents' vineyard was confiscated, so you'll all have to move up into Kanaan with me and my family." He saw the dejected look on the boy's face and clapped him on the shoulder. "It won't be so bad. You'll see."

A runner appeared from the direction of the camp and started yelling out as he got closer. At once, the archery instructor called an end to the proceedings and ordered everyone back to camp. As they ran back, Ament and Goloth listened to the rumours that flew like startled sparrows--the Sea Peoples were coming, and the Hapi corps had been ordered out to meet them.

# Chapter 17
# Year 5 of Usermaatre Ramesses

The court at Per-Ramesses was in an uproar. Messages poured in from all parts of the Kanaan coast and along the northern sea borders of Ta Mehu, telling of the appearance of ships of the Sea Peoples, and of armies advancing from all directions. The king hurried from the bed of his Queen Iset, straight to the Council chamber where his generals and scribes were gathered.

"Is it true?" Ramesses demanded. "The enemy is upon us?"

General Djehutemheb bowed. "Son of Re, it seems that first reports were exaggerated. The enemy is not yet sailing up the Great River, nor yet has set foot on the Way of Heru, but they are undoubtedly on the move."

"So what do we know for certain?"

"A fleet has debouched an army in the north and they are marching south. At the same time, another fleet has been seen sailing south along the coast toward the river mouths. I think we can expect an attack in both places."

"Show me."

A scribe brought out a large coloured parchment which showed the relative positions of Kanaan and Ta Mehu, and the approximate positions of the enemy army and navy. Ramesses perused it for a time, striving to turn the symbols into real features of landscape and of movements of men. He leaned back with a frown on his face.

"Is the army ready, General Djehutemheb?"

"Yes, Son of Re. We have four corps at full strength, waiting only for Your Majesty to join them. Supply wagons left days ago."

"And the navy, Admiral Hori?"

Hori hesitated a moment, but decided the risk of appearing overconfident outweighed the risk of appearing incompetent. "We are ready, Son of Re. Prince Khaemwaset commands the land forces of the Hapi corps, and I will lead the naval forces myself."

"Ah, yes, Prince Khaemwaset. He is ready for combat?"

"Ready and eager to get to grips with the enemy, Son of Re. He is a fine offshoot of a mighty king."

"Then give the orders. I will leave immediately for the northern corps and engage the enemy army. Admiral Hori, you will meet the fleet of the Sea Peoples and prevent them from setting foot on Kemet's sacred soil."

Ramesses swept from the city within the hour, at the head of a chariot squadron, General Djehutemheb close behind, and the remnants of the Ptah corps following him at the run. He passed supply wagons on the road that had left days before, the drivers urging their oxen off the road as the king thundered past. Onto the Way of Heru, racing north with a great billowing cloud of dust making his passage, and onto the coastal plains of south Kanaan where his corps awaited him.

The corps of Amun, Re, Set and Heru awaited him in ranks, their commanders out in front in chariots, having been warned of the king's approach. Ramesses' chariot separated from the rest of his squadron and drove past each corps, up and down and to and fro between the ranks of chariots, foot soldiers and archers, and as he passed they lifted up their voices in praise of the king and drummed spear shafts on leather shields. He kept his face stern but he rejoiced at his reception, his chest swelling with pride.

"How can I fail to make a name for myself like the Great Usermaatre?" he murmured.

Ramesses turned now to the corps commanders awaiting him in front of their men. He called them together beneath the hot sun and addressed them.

"The enemy has dared set foot upon the soil of Kanaan and marches south, intent on carrying destruction into the heart of Kemet. I tell you now that no man of the Sea Peoples and their allies will ever set foot on the black earth of Kemet, but will go down to utter destruction. I will trample them all beneath the hooves of my horses, beneath the wheels of my chariot, my bow will sing its song of praise as my arrows pierce every man who comes against me. Their limbs will be hewn from their bodies, their chests crushed, and their brains and blood will cover the ground. The enemy will find only death and their women will be carried into captivity and their children shall find themselves orphaned and wail their distress to their gods, but their gods will not answer.

"The Great Usermaatre smote the enemy in his day and brought peace to the land, and I shall do likewise, so that in years to come men will look upon my reign as the time when Kemet's power and glory was second to none."

The corps commanders applauded and bowed low before their king, praising him and calling him the Great Usermaatre. Ramesses stood and bathed in the warmth of their adulation for a time, and then signalled for silence.

"General Djehutemheb, you have a battle plan?"

"Son of Re, having just arrived in your entourage, I would like to confer with my commanders before deciding if any changes need to be met."

"Then do so."

Ramesses sat beneath a hurriedly erected awning and sipped watered wine while the General talked with his commanders and learned the latest intelligence from the scouts watching the army of the Sea Peoples.

"Your Majesty," Djehutemheb said after a short while. "My scouts and commanders confirm that the enemy are still advancing slowly along the coast road, and are being supplied by their fleet, part of which follows their progress. May I draw a map for you, Son of Re, so that I might better explain myself?"

Ramesses nodded his agreement, so the general took a spear in hand and traced out lines in the sand at his king's feet.

"The coast lies here, Son of Re, and the coast road here..." He drew two roughly parallel lines. "We are here...and the enemy--as of this morning--about here... If we advance immediately, in two days we should meet them in the region of this deep-gullied dry stream here..."

"I must be able to use my chariots," Ramesses interrupted.

"Of course, Son of Re. The gully will inconvenience the enemy, not our troops. There is a slightly sloping plain just this side of the gully that I believe would be advantageous for deploying our chariots. It slopes down toward the road, but gently, and our chariots would have no trouble moving across it. My thought was that we entice the enemy to move up the gully here...and then out onto the plain to meet us here...there is rocky ground close to the gully, so we must draw them away so our chariots can charge effectively." Djehutemheb drew several more lines as he spoke, and then stepped back to await his king's praises.

"If I was the enemy," Ramesses said. "I would not be drawn up that gully. I would push through and continue along the coast road. If my memory serves, there is broken country only a little further south that prevents chariot charges. That is where I would make my stand...if I was the enemy."

"If Your Majesty will permit me," Commander Senedje said. He waited for permission and then continued. "We must ensure that the enemy progresses no further than the gully before our army arrives. May I suggest that we send a corps quickly to block the road at that point?"

"One corps could not hold them," Ramesses pointed out. "If they could, I would not be using all four."

"No, Son of Re, but one could slow them enough. If they see the Amun corps in defensive position they will halt and scout out our defences before attacking."

Ramesses considered the rough map sketched in the sand at his feet. "And if they advance along the coast road here, we can attack down the slope, rather than across it."

"With the morning sun at your backs," Senedje said.

"I assume you want the Amun corps to block the road?" Ramesses asked. "You could be overwhelmed if the enemy attacks quickly."

"I would count it an honour, Your Majesty," Senedje said.

"Then let it be so. Take your Amun corps and hurry into position. The rest of the army will follow."

Senedje saluted and hurried away, calling out commands to his officers. Quickly, the men of Amun started to march, picking up their pace and setting off along the coast road. Ramesses watched them go and then called Djehutemheb to him again.

"Start the army on its way, General. I want them at the top of that slope, drawn up in battle formation, by nightfall, day after tomorrow."

Djehutemheb nodded and bowed. "Have you considered the details of the attack, Son of Re?"

"That will have to wait until I have seen the field of battle, so you'd better get the army in position with enough light to make an examination."

The army of Ramesses started on its way. Re corps led, with Set behind, and Ptah bringing up the rear. They marched fast, each man only carrying his weapons and a small bag containing grain, onions and dried meat, together with a flask of water--only enough provisions for three days. Those that reached the field of battle and then survived the attack on the enemy would be resupplied by the hundred ox-carts following on at a slow walk.

Ramesses led his army, his chariot squadrons advancing up the north road or, where the terrain allowed, fanning out on either side. They found evidence of the recent passage of the Amun corps, but the villages they passed were deserted, the inhabitants having fled both armies, seeking safety in the hills.

Djehutemheb pushed the army on past sunset until the pace slackened as they stumbled and wandered from the road in the darkness. The men camped where they found themselves, squatting on the ground or curling up with their weapons to hand, only to be roused shivering in the morning chill and urged into motion again. They ate on the march; a handful of grain chewed and swallowed, a bite of onion, a suck on a strip of dried meat and a swallow of tepid water. The road passed beneath their feet, and just after the second night they turned aside and started a slow climb into the hills, seeking the advantage of the upper edge of the battle plain.

Scouts now brought news of the enemy, still far to the north, and of the Amun corps dug in across the road and readying themselves for conflict. At noon on the second day, the army was in place, half hidden by a fold in the ground at the top of the open plain. Ramesses had the men prepare a meal and rest, while he and the three commanders scouted the place on foot. They paced across the length of it, noting the undulations and irregularities that might hinder or slow a chariot charge, and Ramesses declared himself satisfied.

By late afternoon, the setting sun was full in their eyes when they looked down the slope and below them and to the left they saw the fortifications of the Amun corps blocking the road south, while far to the right, to the north, they saw the dust cloud of the approaching army of the Sea Peoples.

"They will be here in the morning," Djehutemheb said.

"If they don't get here tonight," Commander Nakhtmin said.

"Their scouts will have noted the presence of the Amun corps, so they won't want to get too close with evening approaching. They'll camp to the north and advance in the morning."

"What is your plan for the battle, Son of Re?"

"The three corps and chariot squadrons wait out of sight in that fold of ground up here. When the enemy attempt to push against the Amun corps, we sweep down and take them on the flank with a massed chariot charge followed by foot soldiers."

The commanders digested this straightforward battle plan in silence. After a few moments, General Djehutemheb cleared his throat.

"Son of Re, there is a lip to the road below us and the ground beyond the road is more broken up. If chariots charge the enemy on the road, they may founder on that lip and will be limited by the rocky ground."

Ramesses glared at his general, but he could see the evidence lying before him. "What do you suggest then?"

"We must draw them out onto the plain where our chariots can be effective, Son of Re."

"And how do we do that?"

"A single corps facing their whole army will certainly seem suspicious and may make them cautious. They know we have spies, so why would we send a single corps to face them? So position another corps in full view up here. When the enemy sees Amun below and say, Re up here, they will believe that the Kemetu army faces them. As they will outnumber two corps, they should be confident enough to split their force and half of them at least will attack Re. Then, when they are fully committed and in the open on the plain, the chariots can smash them."

Ramesses thought about it and as much as he wanted his own plan to be the one they followed, he could see the sense of Djehutemheb's plan. He nodded his acceptance of it, but could not resist changing something, if only to let his general see who really was in command. "Not Re," he said. "I want Heru to face the enemy on the ridge top."

Nakhtmin bowed and extended his arms to his king. "I am honoured by your trust, Son of Re."

"Don't let me down."

Djehutemheb's prediction was correct, and as night fell, they could see a constellation of tiny camp fires spread out on the land to the north, where the army of the Sea Peoples readied themselves for the next day's assault. The Kemetu army ate cold rations that night and consumed everything they had. At least they would have full bellies and be well rested before the battle.

Scouts reported the enemy on the move before first light, and the first units were negotiating the deep gully as the eastern sky turned pink. The Sea Peoples gathered on the south side of the gully and drew up in battle formation on the road, while their own scouts spied on the Amun positions.

"Time for the Heru to show themselves," Ramesses murmured.

Nakhtmin saluted and hurried off, calling softly to his officers, who passed on the commands. The corps's foot soldiers stepped up onto the ridge crest and down the other side, allowing their comrades behind to join them. Re's face lifted above the eastern horizon, throwing their shadows forward toward the enemy, and the men raised a paean of challenge, beating spear shafts on their leather shields.

Below them, on the road, heads turned to view this new threat and rams' horns sounded. A shiver ran through the massed ranks of the Peloset and Tjeker units, the Sherden and Shekelesh raised bronze swords and roared back their response to the challenge, and the army splintered, perhaps two-thirds surging up over the lip of the road and onto the gently rising plain.

"We have them," Ramesses cried, unable to keep the excitement out of his voice.

"Not yet, Son of Re," Djehutemheb cautioned. "We must get them at least half way up the slope if our chariots are to be effective."

"Nakhtmin," Ramesses called out. "Show them your members."

A roar of laughter went through the ranks of the Heru corps at the king's suggestion, and the men lifted their kilts and waved their members at the enemy, a great insult in any culture. The Sherden in particular yelled angrily and started up the slope, followed by the bulk of the enemy army. Peloset archers loosed a ragged shower of arrows at the Kemetu, but misjudged the slope of the ground and the volley fell short. Then their charging comrades were too close to risk another, so they turned their bows on the fortified Amun position.

"Time, your Majesty?" Djehutemheb asked.

Ramesses grinned. "Let the slaughter begin."

"Majesty," Nakhtmin called, a note of urgency in his voice. "The enemy are upon us."

Ramesses ran to his chariot and leapt aboard, signalling the squadrons to follow him over the lip. The hooves and wheels thundered up and over in a breaking wave of death, the Heru corps ran to either side, allowing the chariots passage. A few slow soldiers were caught up and fell screaming below the wheels, but the majority followed the squadrons down the slope, the Re and Set corps close on their heels.

The Sea Peoples soldiers, charging up the slope toward the waiting Heru corps faltered as the chariots crested the ridge. Some of them formed up in tight groups with bristling spear points to discourage the horses, while other soldiers changed direction, scrambling to evade the spear point that was the Kemetu king. A few turned and ran.

Ramesses raised his bow and loosed shaft after shaft as his charioteer guided his chariot into the massed enemy, a hundred chariots thundering after them. They smashed through the loose enemy ranks, though several foundered on the tight spear points of the Sherden. Hard on the heels of the chariots came the foot soldiers of three corps in a disorganised rabble of soldiers, all yelling to encourage themselves and their fellows. They hacked and slashed with sword and axe, thrust with fire-hardened wooden spears, and fended off enemy retaliation with leather shields. The battle became a generalised conflict between pairs of soldiers, a confused melee of men intent on killing their opponent, while remaining alive to reap the fruits of victory.

The Sea Peoples outnumbered the Kemetu, but the Kemetu held the high ground and the slope of the field gave them the advantage as they pushed the enemy back. Chariot squadrons had carved a passage through the enemy ranks, but as they emerged close to the road, they came under attack by the Peloset archers. Ramesses charged the archers and his chariots followed as best they could--charioteers being struck down and losing control, horses plunging to their deaths, and several chariots tipping over the lip of the road and tumbling in a welter of broken limbs and smashed wood. Horses and men screamed their distress and pain, but enough of the chariots got through to scatter the archers. Then the Amun corps broke free from the enemy units besieging their position and streamed out onto the field, catching the most southerly Sea Peoples soldiers from behind.

A shudder ran through the enemy and they started streaming away to the north, down into the gully and up the other side. The soldiers fought as they ran, turning to inflict savage punishment on any Kemetu foolhardy enough to follow too closely. Rams' horns sounded, both from the Sea Peoples command, signalling a retreat, and from the Kemetu, encouraging pursuit.

Ramesses drew rein, his horses blowing hard, their flanks lathered in foam. An arrow had killed his charioteer, and he had been forced to take over in mid-battle, but he continued to lead his men from the front, encouraging them on even though he could no longer wield a weapon. He stared at the carnage on the battlefield, dead and dying men, and saw the enemy streaming away into the north, while a rabble of his own men pursued them. He beckoned to a dirty, blood-slimed General Djehutemheb and ordered him to sound the recall.

Djehutemheb hesitated. "Are you sure, Son of Re? We have them on the run."

"Look at them. They still outnumber us and when their officers get them under control, they'll turn and destroy any fragments of the corps pursuing them. Call them back and we still constitute an army capable of facing them again."

"Let it be as you say, Son of Re."

Horns sounded anew, and officers ran amongst the men with their whips, beating any man who was slow to obey orders. The corps formed up and a roll call was taken. Then the men fanned out over the battlefield, collecting right hands from the enemy fallen. These were piled in front of the king and the scribes took the tally.

"Six hundred and thirty-three of the enemy, Son of Re."

"And of our own men?"

Djehutemheb shrugged. "We do not have the final tally as many wounded will die, but fewer, your Majesty."

"A victory, then?"

"Indeed, Son of Re. The enemy has fled, leaving its life-blood on the field of battle. Truly you are like the Great Usermaatre."

Ramesses smiled and nodded. "And I have only started this campaign. I will crush the Sea Peoples entirely, so that all men may know that Kemet has a great king once more."

# Chapter 18
# Year 5 of Usermaatre Ramesses

The Sea Peoples did not in fact flee the field, but withdrew to their temporary base in northern Kanaan, there to lick their wounds and decide what to do next. They also sent scouts to determine the fate of the fleet they had sent to invade the river mouths of Kemet. Word was slow to return, and first reports told of the large fleet gathering outside the easternmost mouth of the river in preparation for invasion. The last report to come in told of the first ships sailing into the mouth under sail and oar, and of small numbers of Kemetu gathering to repel them.

Rath had proven to be quite skilled in handling a boat, having often taken a boat out onto the river at Per-Bast. In this way, he was useful to the commanders of Kemetu's new navy, and was made a junior officer almost immediately. He was sent upriver from Per-Ramesses, where the fleet was gathering, to instruct new batches of prisoners in basic river craft. This proved to be a frustrating assignment as most prisoners were townspeople with only a passing interest in the river and its ways. They were incapable of raising a sail or using an oar without splashing water everywhere, and showed a remarkable tendency to fall overboard. Rath persevered though, and gradually the new batch of men became, if not an asset to the fleet, at least not an overt liability.

A fishing boat sped upriver from Per-Ramesses; sail fully spread to catch the northerly breeze and a single man on the steering oar. Its bow wave spread out, the ripples rocking the reed beds and lily pads, the deep green waters swirling in its wake, as it closed with the little training fleet off Per-Bast.

"Under-officer Rath, where is he?" called the man in the boat. "Message for Under-officer Rath."

Rath stood up in his boat, the rocking motion making his students grab for the sides in alarm. "Here! Who seeks me?"

The fishing boat changed course and the man dropped the sail, using a small paddle to correct his boat's course as he came alongside.

"Message from Commander Khaemwaset, sir. You are to return to Per-Ramesses with all your boats and as many men as you can muster. Immediately, sir."

"Is it the enemy?"

The messenger nodded. "Off the easternmost mouth. A fleet."

Rath turned his little boat back toward Per-Bast as the messenger hauled his sail up again to carry the news further upriver. He immediately set his fellow junior officers the task of rounding up all the new sailors and embarking them on their voyage downstream to the northern capital and the fleet. Rath followed, making sure that his tiny fleet and his charges were as prepared as they could be for the coming battle.

The fleet covered the water near Per-Ramesses, hundreds of small craft as well as many larger ones equipped with fighting platforms and several barges crammed with soldiers. Rath reported to his superior officer and was issued with his instructions--he was to re-join the Heron squad and provide agile support for the larger vessels. They sailed almost immediately, after Admiral Hori and Prince Khaemwaset had boarded the largest barge.

Rath turned to the single archer assigned to his small fishing boat in surprise. "I didn't think our commanders would be in the thick of the fighting."

Siese, the archer, an almost toothless young man with stinking breath, guffawed, rocking the little boat as it left its mooring. "They won't see a scrap of action, mark my words. Soon as the enemy is sighted, they'll be dropped off to command from a safe place."

And so it was. It took the fleet half a day to reach their position, and by then the barge had touched the eastern shore and disembarked Admiral and Prince. Units of the Hapi corps were in place along the shore, and the Admiral consulted with its Commander Merikare as to the best placements of its archers and foot soldiers. A system of banners and horns were set up to convey signals over a distance as new commands could not readily be conveyed to the various units of the fleet in the midst of a fluid battle.

Scouts revealed the imminent presence of the enemy, though they were thought to be still offshore, negotiating the shifting channels between the mud and sandbanks of the river mouth. Night fell without the enemy coming in sight, so every boat pulled ashore, either on the east bank or west, and they settled down for an uncomfortable night. Camp fires were not allowed for fear of giving away positions and numbers to the enemy, and without the protective influence of smoke, they were besieged by mosquitoes and other biting insects.

Shivering in the pre-dawn darkness, Rath re-embarked along with a thousand of his comrades, and paddled out into the sluggish current to await the enemy. Wraiths of mist clung to the water's edge, lending the landscape the appearance of hovering between life and the afterlife. The sun rose, warming their cold bodies, and they offered up thanks to Khepri, the emerging sun, before eating the scraps of bread and cold cooked fish they still had in their pouches. River water slaked their thirst, scooped from the body of the god, and then they waited, holding rough position in the river by thrusting their oars into the green water.

"Come on," Rath muttered. "This waiting is worse than battle."

"Thus speaks the boy who has never been in a battle," Siese replied. "Just you wait; you'll be wishing you could take back those words before long."

The sun rose higher, burning off the mist, and still they waited, and then, just when Rath thought he could wait no longer, rams' horns sounded from the riverbank, and banners dipped.

"Enemy in sight," Siese said. He took his bowstring out from its waterproof pouch and strung his bow, testing the pull two or three times.

Another banner dipped.

"That's us," Rath muttered. He dug his oar blade in deep, propelling his tiny boat forward, while looking to check that the other boats in the Heron Squad were doing likewise. Other squads were performing other manoeuvres, each in response to their own banners being dipped or waved, and together, a hundred small boats broke free of the sluggish water near the western bank and headed downstream toward the mouth of the river.

The flotilla rounded the last broad curve of the river and Rath saw ahead some twenty large warships of the Sea Peoples, their many oars threshing the water into foam as they crept upriver. Horns sounded again, more urgently, banners dipped and fluttered in a confusion of messages, and the Kemetu formations fell apart as each captain steered his boat as he thought he was supposed to. Some of the enemy warships found themselves besieged by fifty small craft, while others were left alone to continue forging upriver.

One of the Kemetu barges, filled with soldiers, pulled toward a warship, its prow snapping through a dozen oars before it became wedged alongside. Soldiers poured over the side onto the enemy vessel and hand-to-hand fighting erupted. Another barge tried the same manoeuvre, but mistimed its approach and the beak of the Sea Peoples ship hit it amidships, stoving in its side and rolling it over, trampling it into the green water.

Rath heard the screams of dying men wash across the river, but he had his own worries. His boat was one of a dozen attacking another warship, but their efforts seemed more of an annoyance than a danger. He was reminded of flies buzzing around a grazing ox--the shake of a head or the swish of a tail, and the ox was left undisturbed. The little boats sailed as close as possible and peppered the larger craft with arrows, few archers missing their target. Arrows came back in profusion, and though the Kemetu boats were small and manoeuvrable, inevitably there were casualties.

Rath turned his boat away and sped out of range. "It's no good. Our few arrows are having no effect."

Siese shrugged and counted the few arrows he had left. "We're a distraction; no more. Only the barges can beat them and we have too few of those."

The ship they had been attacking thrashed its way past them, trying to join others in its fleet that were disgorging soldiers further upriver. Rath watched it pass, wondering how they could stop it, as all the barges were busy with their own opponents. He had an idea and paddled his craft over to another member of the Heron squad.

"Ho, Hannu, you are unhurt?" he called to the other boat.

"As is the enemy," Hannu replied. "This is pointless."

"I've got an idea. Do you have your axe?"

"Yes, but if your idea involves trying to board that beast, forget it. I'm in no hurry to die."

"Not board, my friend, but the ship is vulnerable in other ways." Rath quickly outlined his plan.

Moments later, both fishing boats started in pursuit of the warship, rapidly overhauling it. The enemy loosed volleys of arrows over the stern, but Siese and his counterpart in Hannu's boat, Mose by name, answered in kind, discouraging the archers. Together, the small craft crept up on the steering oars of the large vessel and bound themselves to it. They were now partly protected by the overhang of the warship, so Rath and Hannu immediately set to with their axes, hacking through the steering oars, while

Siese and Mose tried their best to keep the enemy archers from disturbing their attack.

Hannu cut through first, and his boat started to drift back, still bound to the heavy blade of the steering oar. It pulled his little boat over and green water rushed into it. Rath redoubled his efforts and his own steering oar fell with a splash, almost swamping his boat. He cut through the rope securing him to the oar and sculled back, away from the warship that was now floundering in the water. Hannu called out to Rath, who altered course to pick him up from the water. Mose clung to the swamped boat, and they had to prise him loose and haul him aboard.

The warship could still move as its main oars were intact, and could even steer after a fashion, but until they could rig another steering oar, they were out of the battle. Rath, his boat now heavily laden, made its way slowly back to where the rest of the flotilla had withdrawn. Two of the enemy warships had been damaged, seven had withdrawn to the mouth of the river and another six were still under attack. Five more had bypassed the battle altogether and had disgorged troops onto the marshy meadows upriver. The Hapi corps was hurrying to intercept them.

Ament had watched the river battle unfold with interest. As a fisherman and soldier, he could appreciate the movement of the multitude of boats, and the ways in which they fought or avoided battle. Water tactics were new to him, but he supposed that it was still a matter of bringing sufficient force to bear on vulnerable points of the enemy formations. It was just a bit harder to discern exactly who was winning in the battle on the river. He cheered with his comrades when an enemy warship was damaged, groaned in dismay when one of their own barges was sunk and watched gloomily as the warships slipped past the defences and started to disgorge soldiers further upriver.

"Why are we just standing here?" Ament muttered. "Don't our commanders know it's better to attack an enemy before he gains a foothold?"

As if they had heard him, the commander of the Hapi corps now issued his orders and the archers of the various Troops were ordered out. They ran past the foot soldiers to take up positions where they could harass the enemy.

Ament called out as he saw Goloth run past him. "Goloth, take no chances. No one doubts your bravery."

An officer near him upbraided him for inciting the men to be less than enthusiastic, and Ament explained the boy was his nephew.

"Then I shall look to you to make up for your nephew with acts of courage," replied the officer.

The archers released volleys of arrows into the enemy formations and though some fell, the rest withdrew out of range, while their own bowmen peppered the Kemetu archers. Ament saw several men fall, but Goloth appeared to be unhurt. Then orders were relayed to the foot soldiers and the Hapi corps started running to where the Sea Peoples were waiting.

There was little in the way of tactics--the Hapi corps was thrown at the enemy as a mass of armed men, yelling fiercely to keep their courage up, and the riverbank was soon covered in a multitude of individual fights, one man against another. Even the archers, now that they could no longer hurt the enemy, discarded their bows and rushed to join with their comrades battling the Sea Peoples. Ament caught a glimpse of Goloth just before he plunged into the mass of men and uttered a swift prayer to the gods for his safety.

Ament found himself fighting a tall bearded man with bronze armour and a plumed headdress. The man jabbered at him in a tongue that seemed reminiscent of Zeben's Kaftor language, and grinned as he thrust a bronze-pointed spear at him. Ament knocked it aside and closed, their shields clashing. He struck at the man's side with his axe, but the blade glanced off the armour, though the man winced at the force of the blow. Then the spear came round and hit Ament's shoulder, knocking him off balance. The man grinned again and stabbed at his kneeling foe, but Ament blocked the spear with his leather shield, entangling the point and ripping it away from the man's grasp. He slashed up and to the side and the blade slid behind the shin guard of the Sea Peoples warrior, slicing through muscle and tendon.

The man let out a bellow and slammed the edge of his shield down, just missing Ament's head. Ament leapt upward and knocked the man back, slashing at the now shieldless man with his axe. The man's leg, pouring blood, gave way under him and he fell to one knee as Ament's blade found an unprotected part on the man's right shoulder. The blade bit deep and the man grunted, pain and fear flaring in his eyes, but before he could do anything, Ament ripped the axe free and chopped into the man's neck. Blood sprayed out over him. He wiped his face with the back of his hand but only succeeded in smearing it.

Another man hacked at him, but his foot slipped in the gore spilled on the ground and Ament was able to dispatch him easily enough. He stood over the corpse of his enemy for a moment, catching his breath, but before he was ready, another enemy soldier attacked him. This one was young and inexperienced, and Ament simply batted away the man's sword and crushed his chest with a savage blow of his axe. A thump from behind made Ament stagger, but it was only one of his Red Troop comrades who had backed away from his own opponent and collided with him. He turned and helped his comrade, together rapidly dispatching the man.

Ament and his comrade, a man called Ptahmes, leant on each other and caught their breath. Both were liberally covered in blood and dirt, though neither was wounded. The main battle had edged away from their present position as the Sea People were driven back to their ships, so they watched for a while, though Ptahmes soon started fidgeting, wanting to rejoin the fight.

"We're winning," Ament told him, "and we've done our bit. Don't go seeking out death; it'll find you soon enough."

Ptahmes would not listen, and ran off to where the struggle was most intense. Ament cursed and followed him, but within minutes of rejoining the fight, Ptahmes was down, gutted by a spear thrust and Ament had his arm nicked by sword. The blood ran down his arm, making the axe handle slippery. His wound was one of the last suffered by the Hapi corps, as the Sea People soldiers swarmed back aboard their ships and cast off, leaving scores of dead and dying behind.

The men of the Hapi corps raised a great cry of triumph, though they had been mauled by the enemy. They watched as the warships retreated toward the river mouth, taking with them the other ships as they went. The Iteru fleet harassed them as they withdrew, but called off the attack as the enemy ships passed beyond the sandbanks at the mouth of the river. More cheering broke out on land and on the water, and men slapped Ament on the back, grinning through masks of fresh and dried blood.

"We won, we won!"

"But at what cost?" Ament asked soberly.

"What do you mean? The enemy has fled."

"Look around you," Ament replied. "We lost as many soldiers as the enemy, and while it is true that the ships have gone, they withdrew rather than fled. We sank none of their ships, but we lost two barges and scores of smaller boats."

"Yes, but they've gone. Kemet is safe from the Sea Peoples."

"For now," Ament agreed, "but they'll be back."

# Chapter 19
# Year 5 of Usermaatre Ramesses

The population of Ta Mehu was delirious with joy at having been saved from the scourge of the Sea Peoples, and threw open their homes to the victorious army and navy of Kemet. News had filtered down from the north of a great victory won by king Usermaatre, and now this was compounded closer to home by the enemy fleet being repulsed. The fact that none of the warships had been sunk was overlooked, and tales of the destruction wrought by the Hapi corps grew with each retelling of the story.

Prince Khaemwaset, proud of having led his men to victory in his first battle, ordered bread and meat be distributed to the citizens of Per-Ramesses, and gave permission for the men of the Hapi corps and the Iteru fleet to enjoy this largesse. They did so with enthusiasm, and the streets were soon filled with drunken men.

Ament took this opportunity of talking to Goloth in private. He prised the boy free of his comrades in the Blue Troop and led him off to a shadowed corner where they could talk. They sat down on the steps of one of the lesser temples and ate their free bread and meat, washed down with freshly brewed foaming beer from a single pot. After he had taken the edge off his hunger and thirst, Ament spoke.

"How's your arm?"

Goloth rubbed the shallow wound on his arm and grinned through a mouthful of meat. "Scabbed over already," he said. "I'm a fast healer. Hakor commended me to the commander, you know. Said I had the makings of a good soldier."

Ament nodded, but chose not to pursue this avenue of discourse. "Your father wants me to get you out of Kemet. I told him I'd get you back to your mother and sisters, and we'd all go north."

"What about Rath?"

"Him too. I came to get you both out."

"Where would we go?"

"You'd come home with me, to northern Kanaan. I fish in the Sea of Kinnereth and herd goats."

Goloth grimaced. "Doesn't sound very exciting."

"There's more to life than exciting," Ament commented. "By the time you get to my age you appreciate security and safety."

"What about father?"

"I'm going to try and persuade him to come too, but he says he'll be safe enough as Commander Merikare's charioteer. I think once I've got you boys out of it, he'll agree to come." Ament took another drink from the beer pot and stifled a belch. "Finish up and we'll see if we can't find Rath. I saw some sailors earlier, so he should be around somewhere."

They went searching in the dockside area where a score of taverns served more and stronger beer than was available for free on the street corners, and entertainment besides. The interior of the taverns were uniformly crowded and smelly, earthen floors and rough wooden benches and tables lit by sputtering oil lamps. Patrons stood or sat around swilling beer and ogling the naked girls dancing to the sounds of drums and sistra.

Ament had seen it all before, so just pushed through the throng, searching for Rath, while Goloth stumbled after him, his eyes wide. Nudity was commonplace in Kemetu society, but these girls were not chaste and demure girls like his sisters Instead, they were actively engaged in drumming up business. Every now and then a girl would run giggling into a back room with a drunken man in tow, and another would take her place on the dance floor to roars of approval.

They found Rath in the third tavern they visited. He was sitting with a group of sailors, paying little attention to the charms of the girls on display, but rather was engaged in friendly argument with his comrades. Goloth pushed through to the group and tapped him on the shoulder. Rath turned and his eyes lit up as he saw his younger brother.

"Goloth, by all the gods. Fancy seeing you. Join us."

Goloth shook his head. "I've got to talk to you." He looked over his shoulder at Ament. "There's a man over there that needs to see you."

Rath looked, but did not recognise anyone. "Who? Tell him to come over here if he wants to talk." He grinned at his comrades. "Little brothers, you know. Always trying to be mysterious."

Goloth leaned over and whispered in his brother's ear. "It's Ament, our uncle. He can't come over because if he's recognised it'll be death for him."

"What?" Rath stood up and stared across the room. He pushed his way through to where the unkempt bearded man waited for him. "You're..."

"Just call me Mentak. I'm a friend of your father, no more."

"What are you doing here?"

"He's come to rescue us," Goloth said. "Father sent him."

Rath stared and shook his head slightly. "Rescue us from what? I like it here."

"Your mother's worried sick, lad," Ament said. "She's alone with your sisters; her husband is in the army, and now you two boys have been taken from her. She needs you."

Rath grimaced. "What could we do anyway? Our vineyard's been confiscated, and anyway, if we just deserted they'd come after us. A flogging would be the least of it."

"I'll take you all up with me to Kanaan," Ament said.

"He's a fisherman and a goat herder," Goloth said.

"And that's what we'd be?"

"If you want...or something else. Either way, this is the best time to leave. It'll be days before the officers sort out who's just drunk somewhere and who's actually gone missing."

Rath looked back to where his new friends were drinking, and then at the dancing girls. He scraped his toe in the earthen floor and chewed his lip. "Look, take Goloth and get back to my mother. Tell her...well...I like it here. I want to stay."

"You'd rather enjoy the company of common soldiers and drunken louts than your family? Why?"

"I'm common too, Am... Mentak, and I like the navy. I got a commendation from my squad leader and...and there's a good chance I'll be promoted. That's a lot better than herding goats."

Ament shook his head. "I can't tell your mother that. You're coming back with me. You can tell her yourself."

"You can't make me, uncle. I don't want to say anything, but if you force me, I'll tell an officer who you really are."

Ament looked sadly at his nephew. "You'd really do that?"

"No, but please, uncle, don't make me go back. I'd only run away and I'd probably be flogged for my trouble when I returned."

Ament sighed. "If I thought I could just sling you over my shoulder and take you, I would, you know. All right, I'll tell your mother, but if you change your mind, go and see your father--he's Commander Merikare's charioteer. He knows how to reach me. Send the word and I'll come for you."

"I'll be all right."

Ament embraced his nephew and Goloth did the same, tears in his eyes at the thought of leaving his brother. They left the tavern and made their way through the city to the poorer streets where Ti-ament and her daughters had a room. Ti-ament was overjoyed to see them and cried, while Taui and Ini danced around and hugged their brother. Jerem hugged his father and Goloth, grinning delightedly to see them.

"What about Rath?" Ti-ament demanded. "And my husband?"

Ament had difficulty looking into her eyes. "Er... Zeben says he will remain as charioteer to Commander Merikare for the time being. He says he is in no danger and being there will help you too..."

"How? I need my husband with me."

"Well, he and the boys were taken because you would not give me up. If he was to disappear suddenly, Merikare would know exactly where to look for him and then you and the girls may suffer. The only way he can flee is knowing you are safe."

Ti-ament grunted. "And Rath? Where is my eldest boy?"

"He is safe...and, er...he wants to stay in the navy."

"What? That's ridiculous. Where is he? Tell him to come home immediately."

"I told him you'd say that, but he insisted. He wants to stay with his new friends. He says if I try to force him to come back, he'll run away and probably get flogged for being absent."

"That's right, mother," Goloth said. "I was there in the tavern when he said it."

"You were in a tavern? What were you thinking, brother, taking him to a place like that?"

"I had to keep him with me. He was in no danger and..."

"Never mind all that. You go back and tell him he's to come home immediately. Tell my husband too, while you're at it."

Ament sighed. "Have you not been listening to a word I say, sister? Zeben won't stir until he knows you're safe, and Rath has effectively left home. He likes it in the navy, and he wants to stay there--make a career of it." He looked at Ti-ament compassionately. "There are worse fates, you know."

Ti-ament continued to argue, but with less vigour and after a while she dried her tears and sniffed. "I suppose I'll have to do it then. At least I have one boy back."

"Uh, mother, I want to stay in the army," Goloth said.

"Don't be stupid."

"I'm an archer, mother. A good one too; Hakor says so. He's my instructor and officer in the Blue Troop. He says I've got the makings of an officer and..."

"You're only a boy."

"I'm fourteen."

"He's young," Ament admitted, "but I've seen him in action. He handles a bow well, and he's brave but not foolhardy. Nothing in life is guaranteed, but a skill should be fostered. If this is what he really wants to do, he should be allowed to do it." Ament cleared his throat and scuffed his foot on the dirt floor. "Just my opinion."

"I'm sure he's a skilled bowman," Jerem added quietly. "Even as a young boy he was gifted. I remember him bringing back ducks he'd killed, and he was only six then."

"So I am to be deserted by all my men? You'll just walk out on me and my girls just when we need you the most?" Ti-ament gathered her daughters to her and they picked up on her anguish, starting to cry softly.

"It is in the nature of children to leave their parents' house--especially boys. It's not as if there is anything to keep them here, now honestly, is there? You have to leave Kemet; your former life is over. I've already bought you a donkey for the trip and booked you passage with a small caravan. We can be by the Sea of Kinnereth in six months or less..."

"No."

Ament sighed again. "You have to go, sister, for the sake of your daughters if not for yourself..."

"Yes, we're going, but you're not." Ti-ament stared at her brother. "Do you honestly imagine I'd leave my young sons unprotected? You are staying with them to guard over them until they come to their senses. Then...and only then...can you return home."

"But who will look after you on the journey north? You can't expect Jerem to shoulder that responsibility. I'll come up with you and then return..."

"You are not leaving my sons unprotected for half a year or more. And who says I need looking after? You forget I've travelled with the army and know how to defend myself. Besides, Jerem is a lot more capable than you give him credit for."

"I'd trust Jerem with my life," Ament said, "But it's a big responsibility."

"I'd rather stay with you, father," Jerem said.

"No," Ti-ament said again. "My brother stays and you come with us, Jerem."

This time it was Ament that argued and Ti-ament that slowly wore him down. He gave up more quickly than she had though, because he could see the sense of her argument.

"All right," he said finally. "Once you're well out of Kemet I'll tell Zeben and he can arrange his own escape to Urit and Dan-el. I'll stay and keep an eye on the boys as long as I can. Just remember that I'm a wanted man here in Kemet. If anyone recognises me, I might be more of a danger to the boys than a protection. If that happens, I'll have to run."

The matter was settled, so Ament and Goloth stayed the night and then made the final arrangements for Ti-ament, Jerem, and the girls to join the caravan. It was leaving in three days' time and Ti-ament promised she would be with it.

"I'll try and get back to see you off," Ament said, "but being in the army myself, I'm not free to come and go. If I'm not there, go with the gods, sister, and I'll see you by the Sea of Kinnereth as soon as I can manage." He embraced his sister, Jerem, and the girls, and departed with Goloth.

He was unable to return to see them off but managed a quick visit to the city several days later. The room they had rented was now occupied by strangers and the caravan had departed. Careful enquiries revealed that a woman answering the description of Ti-ament had left with it, along with a young man and two small girls. Ament returned to his unit satisfied that at least some of his family was on the road to safety.

# Chapter 20
# Year 5 of Usermaatre Ramesses

Ramesses knew that though he claimed victory over the Sea Peoples at the Battle of the Gully, they were not yet defeated. His scouts brought in the news that they were gathering again in the north and that if he was to bring peace to Kanaan in preparation for wars of conquest; he would have to destroy these invaders completely. The news from the south was good. He had been concerned that a victory on land would mean little if the Sea Peoples used a fleet to invade Ta Mehu behind his back. Now word came from Admiral Hori and Prince Khaemwaset that the enemy fleet had been routed there in the mouth of the Great River.

"Kemet is in good hands," the king told his general and commanders. "Gather the corps together, for we march north to deliver a death blow to my enemies."

"We are weaker now than we were before the last battle," General Djehutemheb pointed out, "whereas the enemy has been resupplied from the sea."

"If you do not have the stomach for the fight, just say so, General. I can replace you easily enough."

Djehutemheb fell to his knees with arms outstretched. "Forgive me, Son of Re, I did not mean to imply I lacked courage; only that we face a more powerful enemy this time. I would willingly give my life for you and Kemet."

"You are forgiven, Djehutemheb. I am not ignoring the relative strengths of the armies, but there is no need for concern. Three things are on our side."

The general waited for a minute to see if his king would continue, but when he did not, ventured to ask, "What three things are those, Son of Re?"

"I'm surprised you need to ask. The first is that I am the Great Usermaatre reborn, and like him I cannot fail to lead my armies to victory.

The second is that the gods of Kemet are on our side. They are scarcely going to let foreign men with foreign gods rule over their sacred land."

"Of course, Son of Re. How could I not have seen those self-evident truths? And the third reason?"

"I will not allow them an escape next time. At the last battle, the field was limited by the road and the gully, and that gave the enemy the opportunity to withdraw. It will not be the case next time. I will engage them on a field that allows my chariots the ascendancy, and when they break and run, my corps will hunt them down to a man and slaughter them. The Sea Peoples have dared to invade Kemet, but their bones will decorate the borders of our lands. No foreigner will dare covet our rich lands, knowing that I, Usermaatre Ramesses, am there to defend them."

The general and his commanders applauded the words of their king and assured each other loudly that no enemy could possibly stand against this worthy successor of the Great Usermaatre. Ramesses let them praise him for longer than was necessary, as he needed their adulation. It rankled that he had let the enemy escape and he silently vowed that it would not happen again.

The corps of the northern army took two days to gather themselves together, to repair equipment and weapons, to strengthen their numbers with fresh recruits sent up to replace those that had fallen to the enemy. Then, with much ceremony, they turned their faces to the north and set off to destroy the army of the Sea Peoples.

On this first morning of the first day, Ramesses rode alone in his chariot at the head of his army, decked out in all his royal finery and wearing the blue leather war crown on his head. Behind him walked a hundred priests representing twenty major gods, lifting up hymns of praise and petition to their various deities, five hundred acolytes marching with them, blowing on rams' horns, beating on drums, shaking sistra and lifting up their voices to din the ears of the gods. Commander Nakhtmin led his Heru corps as the vanguard, having thoroughly redeemed himself in the previous battle. All the sins of his corps down in Per-Ramesses had been set aside, and he saw a glorious future opening up before him.

Jealous of his fellow commander's good fortune, Commander Senedje of the Amun corps came next, glaring at the backs of the Heru soldiers and forced to choke on the dust their feet kicked up. Commander Khay of Re followed, determined that he would be the one to gain glory in the next encounter; that he would find favour in the king's eyes. Commander Hori of the Set corps brought up the rear, but felt none of the jealousy of his fellow commanders. Being last in the line of march might seem like a lowly duty, but he knew that in enemy territory the attack could come from anywhere, and he took his responsibility seriously.

Further behind, and travelling at a slower rate, rumbled the cumbersome baggage train. Oxen pulled great wooden wagons with solid wheels, laden with equipment and rations for the army, while hundreds of servants trudged alongside. Every aspect of an army's needs was catered for, even down to the lowliest female camp follower who earned a pittance by cooking or washing or offering sexual solace.

The road north groaned under the foot and hoof and wheel, the length of the column so great that if the king had deigned to look behind him, the dust of the army's passing would have stretched to the horizon and beyond. Camp was made while the sun was still high in the western sky, and struck the next morning as Re ascended the eastern sky, so much time was needed to organise this huge army. Ramesses fretted at the slow pace, but Djehutemheb calmed him, saying his scouts had seen the Sea Peoples' army up ahead, waiting for them.

"They will not flee just yet, Son of Re, for they came to enslave our lands."

"I will trample them underfoot for their temerity," Ramesses said. "I should hurry north with my combined chariot squadrons and crush them utterly."

"Indeed, Majesty, but let us make sure that our victory is complete. If they should flee into rough ground where chariots cannot follow, we will need the corps. If the enemy stays where it is, we will be upon them in two days."

Ramesses took his General's advice, though it was obvious that he longed for the coming battle. When the enemy came in sight late on the second day, his impatience revealed itself. He issued orders for the corps to form into battle order immediately, and for the chariots to gather in the centre.

"Son of Re, the men are tired," Djehutemheb protested. "Let us wait until the morning."

"Who knows what they will do if we wait?" Ramesses retorted. He looked up at the sky where Re was sinking toward the western horizon. "Time enough to smash them."

Rams' horns sounded their message and the corps hurried into position, the men dragging their feet slightly as they had been looking forward to a hot meal and a bed. Whips rose and fell as the junior officers hurried their men along, and by the time all was in readiness, the king found that he had to shade his eyes from the sun's glare, so low had it fallen in the west.

"It is too late in the day," he murmured, though the only person to hear the king was his charioteer.

Ramesses could not bring himself to admit the mistake, however, so he told his charioteer to advance. Five hundred chariots followed, spreading out in a wide arrow formation with the king at its tip. They gathered speed, the dust of their passing billowing up into the still afternoon air, and the corps of foot soldiers started forward. The units rapidly lost cohesion as they ran, and it was a loose conglomeration of men who finally impacted the enemy line. Before then, the chariots had done their damage.

Five hundred chariots had speared into the enemy formations who had tried to fall back to let them through, but the front was too wide, and enemy soldiers fell like wheat before the harvester's sickle. Not as many as the Kemetu had hoped, though, and the ranks closed again after the chariots had passed, while archers peppered the chariots from behind as they strove to turn and charge again.

The main battle became a melee of struggling men, thousands of men hacking and slashing at one another. Kemetu fought in kilts with copper axes and swords, wooden spears and clubs, protected sometimes by small leather shields, while the conglomeration of Sea Peoples displayed a more varied appearance. Weapons were similar, but some of the warriors wore armour--small bronze plates stitched into leather tunics, or into sleeves that partly enclosed arms and legs. Some of the greatest warriors held large bronze shields that turned the points of almost every weapon.

The Sea Peoples fought in units made up of men from their own nations--Sherden in kilts with leather corselets, small round shields and broad-bladed swords, helmets with small horns and a disc that may have represented the sun. Shekelesh, bearded and fierce of countenance, fought in longer robes than their fellows, but were similarly armoured and armed. They wore cloth caps on their heads rather than helmets and often eschewed the use of shields.

The Peleset made up the bulk of the army. They were a tall race, clean-shaven and strong, and fought fiercely. Kilted, and wearing a corselet made of bronze-studded leather, they wielded wide-bladed swords, short stabbing spears, and round leather shields. Their heads were surmounted by a sort of crown made of feathers or horse hair, dyed red, and the sight of these plumes, nid-nodding above the line of shields as their units advanced on the Kemetu, filled hearts with terror and weakened limbs.

Despite the initial inroads made by the chariot charge, the Peleset now pressed the Kemetu corps back, maintaining impressive discipline. Swords stabbed and slashed, and short spears jabbed out from between the shields, forcing the Kemetu soldiers to retreat. The tide of the battle seemed about to turn, but Ramesses managed to turn his chariot squadrons and marshal them into some sort of order. A rain of arrows from the Sea Peoples' archers continued to find their targets, but Ramesses urged his force into motion once more, charging into the rear of the Peleset warriors.

The Sea Peoples' line shivered under the onslaught, opening to allow the chariots into the mass of fighting men. Charioteers grabbed weapons and joined the fighters in the chariots in a fight for survival. Ramesses loosed arrow after arrow at the enemy until his quiver was empty, and then took up a khepesh sword and laid about him. Other Kemetu gathered about their king, laying down their lives to protect him, and charging the enemy on foot, carving out a clear space around the royal chariot.

Ramesses leaned against the railing of his chariot, breathing hard. His right arm was slick with blood and his face and body spattered with gore, but he smiled as he surveyed the battlefield. A seething mass of men fought all around him, their feet churning up the dust in a great cloud which obscured his vision and clung to every surface. The shadows were long on the ground, and dimly seen through the haze, the eastern hills were lit by the setting sun.

"See there, Ahmes?" he said to his charioteer. "The enemy is being forced back."

"Indeed, Son or Re, and here comes General Djehutemheb with Commander Senedje." The charioteer pointed.

The General and Amun Commander approached, limping, and saluted the king.

"You are wounded, General?" Ramesses asked. "And you, Senedje?"

"Twisted my ankle on a cursed rock," Djehutemheb said.

"A club bruised my thigh, Son of Re," Senedje added. "It is nothing."

"The day hangs in the balance," Ramesses observed. "We must concentrate our forces to crack these Peleset."

"The day is spent, Majesty," Djehutemheb stated. "In an hour it will be too dark to fight the enemy. We must withdraw while our corps are still intact."

"No. I refuse to leave the field of battle until I have won."

"We cannot win in the hour we have left," the General said.

The two men glared at each other, Djehutemheb knowing he was right, and Ramesses angry with the General for being right. Then Senedje spoke, offering a salve to his king's pride.

"See, Son of Re. The enemy retreats."

Ramesses swung round and stared. The army of the Sea Peoples was breaking off the fight, though it was scarcely a retreat. The Peleset in particular had formed a rearguard as the Sherden and Shekelesh stumbled away to the north. Any Kemetu who pressed the seeming advantage too closely was sent reeling back, bloodied and bruised. The corps followed, but cautiously, allowing the Peleset to stream away as dusk fell to protect their withdrawal.

Night had fallen by the time the Kemetu army had advanced far enough to be clear of the battlefield. They camped and made fires from the timbers of the shattered chariots and whatever else they could gather from the land. Runners sent back to find the wagon train returned hours later with mules burdened by food and water, enough to give the corps some much needed sustenance. The men rested fitfully in turns, while large numbers remained on alert for any sign of the enemy's return.

The dawn brought the realisation that the Sea People were undefeated. They had camped within sight of the Kemetu, but made no effort to resume hostilities. Ramesses stood on a small hillock with his commanders and his general and debated his course of action.

"How many of the enemy fell yesterday?" Ramesses demanded.

"We have not yet counted them all, but it would seem that well over a thousand were killed, Majesty," Commander Nakhtmin said.

"And our own losses?"

"Nearly a thousand," Commander Hori reported. "And a hundred chariots destroyed or damaged."

"So many?"

"It is a victory, Son of Re," General Djehutemheb said. "We killed more than we lost and they withdrew from the field of battle."

"Yet they have not fled. They sit yonder and observe us as we do them. Counsel me, General. What do we do now?"

"Attack them at once, Son of Re," Djehutemheb said.

"I agree," Senedje and Nakhtmin said together.

Khay licked his lips before he spoke. "I counsel caution, Majesty, if only that our relative strengths are similar to yesterday, and we have lost many chariots."

"They do not have many chariots," Hori said. "We outnumber them in that regard and should exploit our advantage."

Ramesses nodded his general agreement, though spared a contemptuous look for Khay, who paled in the face of his king's displeasure.

"We will engage them once more. Djehutemheb, prepare the corps, but keep Re in reserve, it seems their commander is tired of fighting."

The other commanders drew back from Khay, who immediately fell to his knees with arms outstretched in supplication.

"Do not so dishonour me, Son of Re. I meant only that we should plan our next attack carefully. Put my corps in the forefront and let me prove to you our courage and devotion."

Ramesses stared and slowly nodded. "Let it be so."

Rams' horns sounded, and the officers started calling the soldiers into line, forming up opposite the distant enemy. Whips rose and fell as junior officers persuaded their men that battle was the desired outcome, and the commanders took their places. Before the signal to advance could be given, however, a shiver went through the enemy ranks and the line parted. Three chariots emerged and advanced slowly on the Kemetu position.

"What are they doing?" Ramesses demanded. "Is this some insane attack?"

"Doubtful, Majesty," Djehutemheb said. He stared at the advancing chariots, shading his eyes from the morning glare and squinting. "They hold spears, but reversed--with the spear points down."

"What is the significance?"

"I think they either want to surrender or to talk."

Ramesses smiled. "It would be churlish to refuse," he said. "Send Khay out to see what they want."

A messenger went running and presently a trio of chariots detached itself from the Re corps and raced out to meet the enemy chariots that had come to a halt halfway between the armies. Ramesses watched as the men in the two groups apparently talked, with much gesticulating, and eventually turned and raced back to their respective lines. Khay drove to where the king and Djehutemheb waited.

"Well, are they surrendering?" the general asked.

"Not exactly, sir." Khay bowed to the king. "Son of Re, the Peleset king Taita desires peace, but peace through strength. He says that his people have suffered famine and sickness in their native lands and seek other places to live. Some among the other tribes--the Sherden, Shekelesh, and Tjeker, seek to invade Kemet, desirous of claiming rich farmlands, but King Taita of the Peleset seeks only to settle in this land of Kanaan. He asks, one king to another, that you grant his people land on which to settle..."

"Does he, by the gods?" Ramesses growled. "I have just defeated him, but he now seeks to dictate terms. Who does he think he is?"

"Son of Re, King Taita said other things." Khay waited for permission to continue. "Majesty, in return for this grant of land, King Taita guarantees that the other tribes among the Sea Peoples will either sail away or reside in peace alongside him. Further, he guarantees that the Peleset will no longer raise up arms against the Kemetu, nor disturb the peace within the lands granted them. He is also willing to discuss the payment of an annual tribute."

"If he thinks I'm paying him for the sake of peace..."

"Not so, Majesty," Khay interposed quickly, daring to interrupt his king. "He will pay a tribute to you, and regard you as his overlord."

"I am suspicious," Ramesses said, gesturing toward the enemy. "His army is intact, so why does he sue for peace? I think he seeks to gain time, but time for what?"

"For reinforcements to arrive, perhaps?" Djehutemheb asked.

"You spoke to the enemy herald, Khay. What was your impression? Is this Taita a man of his word?"

"Alas, Son of Re, who can say? The herald spoke with an open face and an honest voice, and evidently believed the message he had been given, but if his king kept his own counsel from him, then he may have been deceived."

"What do you counsel, Djehutemheb?"

"He is afraid of something and seeks to delay us, Son of Re. I say we attack him immediately."

"And you, Commander Khay? How do you counsel your king?"

Khay was slow to reply, looking out over the plain toward the enemy before turning back to Ramesses. "Majesty, forgive me if I err in my understanding, but was it not your intention to defeat all your enemies before you looked to conquer the lands in the north? We have seen what a fierce enemy these people can be, and although I do not doubt that we can destroy them in battle, yet will we lose many fine men before we do. Fine men that your Majesty will need to conquer the north.

"I say that this Peleset king has offered you the key to the north. If you can reach an agreement with him, then you pacify Kanaan without losing men in battle. Further, you will gain a valuable vassal king and worthy tribute with which to enrich your treasury."

Ramesses considered Khay's words. "You are persuasive, Commander, and I am ever mindful of the lives of my people. Enter negotiations with the Sea Peoples, and I will send for my Tjaty to represent me before this king of theirs."

"I still think it would be better to hit them with everything we have," Djehutemheb grumbled. "Bargain then from a position of strength."

"I too wish for glory on the battlefield," Ramesses said, "and one day soon I will have it, but for now I would see this lands settled so that I can turn my eyes to the north."

# Chapter 21
# Year 6 of Usermaatre Ramesses

Ramesses' desire for peace in Kanaan so he could concentrate on his war of conquest in the north was not realised. Instead, he became aware that King Taita of the Peleset was wilier in peace than he had been in war. The negotiations between the two nations dragged on for over a year, and for every advantage the Kemetu gained, they lost two to the Peleset. It was quickly apparent that the Peleset were in Kanaan to stay, and that the seeming advantage Ramesses had held after the Battle of the Gully had been lost after the corps withdrew to the Way of Heru under the terms of the agreement.

The only good news was the subsequent destruction of the Sea Peoples' fleet. King Taita withdrew the Peleset from the naval confederation, seeking a separate peace with Kemet, but the other nations launched another attack on Ta Mehu, sailing up the river mouth to attack Per-Ramesses itself. They were repulsed in a bloody battle that saw several of the Sea Peoples ships sunk, others captured, and only a few shattered survivors managed to limp north along the coast to safety.

Admiral Hori and Prince Khaemwaset covered themselves in glory that day, as did a certain young man in the navy. Rath was promoted to the position of junior commander, and even his brother Goloth made a name for himself in the concomitant land battle, rising to become Overseer of archers in the Hapi corps. Their uncle Ament performed creditably as a common foot soldier, but managed to avoid undue notice by his superiors, preferring to remain unknown. Ramesses showered gold and honours on the commanders, and raised his other two grown sons--Meryamun and Prehirwenemef--to the rank of Troop Commander in the Amun and Set corps respectively.

The defeat of the remaining Sea Peoples was a great victory, and one which Ramesses made sure the people celebrated. He had inscriptions written everywhere, praising himself for removing this great threat to peace, but he remained silent on the compromises forced on him by his negotiations with King Taita. The details of the agreement were recorded and filed away by the royal scribes, but try as he might, Ramesses could not put the terms of that agreement from his mind.

"How will men remember me, Herwernef?" he groaned. "I was to have been the great Usermaatre in place of my grandfather, but now they will just remember me as the man who lost five cities to the enemy."

"Not so, Son of Re," the Tjaty responded. "For you have brought peace to Kanaan, and peace is a rare prize."

"You would say that, Tjaty, for you brokered this peace on my behalf, yet I am the one who will suffer because of it."

"If I may be so bold, Son of Re, how will you suffer? Your army and navy have destroyed the army and navy of the Sea Peoples, slaughtering them by the thousand and sending the others running like curs with their tails between their legs. Ta Mehu has been saved from their depredations and already Kanaan is benefitting. Trade has increased, and once more caravans are passing unhindered through to the northern lands. The people of Kemet will praise you for this."

"And the five cities who have passed under the yoke of the Peleset? What of them? Do they not represent a failure that will sit like a weight on my reign? Are they not a stain on my abilities?"

"Ah yes, the so-called cities. Majesty, only Ghazzat is a true city. Ashkelon and Ashdod are little more than fishing towns, and Ekron and Gath are mere farming villages. The ports were hard to defend and were under constant attack by pirates. I think we will have less trouble--and expense--guarding the north in future with the Peleset defending their homes."

"And when I want to invade the north, to expand Kemet's borders? Will the Peleset stand aside and let my armies through? And if they do, dare I leave their army behind me?"

Tjaty Herwernef regarded his king and thought carefully before he spoke. "If you were to take your corps north now, King Taita would be apprehensive, afraid that you were about to attack him, and then you would have trouble. His men are still under arms and could easily oppose you. But only wait a few years, giving him no cause to worry, and his men will turn to the purpose for which they came. Farming, Son of Re. I have it on the best authority that bad harvests drove them to seek new lands to cultivate. The Peleset are a farming people and desire to till the soil, plant crops and harvest them, so they can enjoy the fruits of their toil in peace.

Delay your war of conquest in the north and you will likely have Peleset warriors joining your corps rather than opposing them."

"How many years must I wait? I desire glory that men may praise my reign as the one where Kemet was at the height of its power."

"Five years, Son of Re, no more."

"Five years? What am I to do in the meantime?"

"Ah, Majesty, you toy with me," Herwernef said. "Have you not said before how you wish to make Kemet a land where every man and woman can be safe? Where every man can see the glory of the gods through great works in their temples and shrines?"

Ramesses nodded slowly. "That is so, but is it enough? The land is already at peace and my building work is carried out throughout the kingdoms."

"Kemet no longer wars with the Nine Bows, Majesty, it is true, but there are great enemies within that threaten the Ma'at of the land."

"Rebels? Surely no one still disputes my right to rule?" Ramesses stared at his Tjaty. "Followers of that woman Tausret and her general?"

"No, Majesty, for surely they are long dead, nor do I talk about any who openly defy you..."

"Who then?"

"Bandits, Son of Re. The kingdoms are rife with them, and common men cannot safely journey out of the cities for fear they will be set upon and robbed or beaten. Women too...for they are raped with impunity. Farmers fear to bring their produce to markets, and so hunger is common."

"You are Tjaty, Herwernef. Why have you not stamped this out? In Ta Mehu at least?"

Herwernef bowed low, sweating slightly. "I do not have the men, Majesty. I would need a corps, at least, and all the corps have been busy repelling the Sea Peoples. But now..." He looked up and shrugged delicately. "Give me the men I need and I will cleanse Ta Mehu of these wicked men, bringing peace to the northern kingdom in your name."

"You shall have them. Pick a corps, Tjaty."

"The Hapi corps, Son of Re."

"Not one of the frontline ones? Battle hardened and disciplined?"

"Such men are too valuable, and are necessary to guard Kemet from external enemies. The Hapi corps is drawn from the prisons of the north, and has proven its loyalty in battle. The men who were once criminals will help track down their erstwhile comrades."

"Then let it be so, Herwernef."

Herwernef summoned Commander Merikare of the Hapi corps and gave him his instructions.

"You are to scour Ta Mehu from south to north, from west to east, arresting or killing every bandit that preys upon the lifeblood of the kingdom. How you do it is up to you and your officers. You have six months."

Merikare thought carefully before answering. "What powers do I have?"

"Whatever you need. Ta Mehu is to be free of banditry. A man should be able to travel freely with gold upon his person and a woman should be safe from attempts upon her virtue."

"You said arrest or kill. Which is it?"

"Use your own judgment, Merikare, but remember that most bandits are just ordinary men led astray. Show no mercy to the ringleaders, consigning them to whatever death you think appropriate, and send the others to the mines and quarries. The prisons were emptied to form your corps instead of being sent to the mines, and so we need men working stone for the king's building program."

The Tjaty's scribes drew up documents outlining the corps's task and bidding all men pay heed to Merikare's demands, as they stemmed from the king. Merikare took the scrolls in hand and went to plan his campaign with his Troop Commanders and senior officers. He also sent for the royal spymaster and, using the scrolls for the first time, commanded him to track down every bandit gang in Ta Mehu.

"Every gang, Commander?" Djeti asked. "I know of fifty, and there are probably more."

"Let us start with those fifty then," Merikare said. "How many men are there in a gang?"

Djeti shrugged. "From five to twenty; typically less than ten. The stronger ones prey on travellers, the weaker ones extort farmers or rape women."

Merikare divided up his corps into groups of fifty men and sent a group to every sepat in Ta Mehu. Using the information supplied by Djeti, they were to track down each gang in their assigned sepat and systematically destroy them.

The corps rapidly caught and arrested or killed the bandits in twenty of the major gangs, at which point the others ran for cover. Crime dropped dramatically in the northern kingdom, and the morale of the common people improved. Investigations of the remaining gangs got harder, but Merikare and his Troop Commanders pushed their men, determined to finish what they started, and by the time the six months were up, had all but eliminated banditry within Ta Mehu. Merikare reported back to Tjaty Herwernef and was praised for his efforts, though the corps commander expressed annoyance at his inability to account for every single bandit.

"You might as well try to eliminate every rat and mouse in the city granaries," Herwernef said. "Your cats have done a magnificent job and you can be sure I will praise your name when I talk to the king."

"The job's unfinished," Merikare grumbled.

"Mopping up. That's all that is left, and I can finish the job with the local Medjay. I want you to tackle Ta Shemau next. I have been in contact with Tjaty Hori in Waset and he agrees you should carry on with your work in the south."

Merikare grimaced. "I am honoured by your confidence, but the southern kingdom will be harder. There are more hiding places in the cliffs and wilds than in the flat cultivated lands of the north."

"I am certain you will do as well, Merikare. Another six months?"

"Make it nine."

Both men were in fact being somewhat optimistic, as the bandit problem was more ingrained in the south. Gangs could rapidly disappear into the desert or flee into Kush when pressed hard by the men of the corps, often escaping completely. Then they would wait for the soldiers to go before venturing out to raid more farms or rob travellers on the roads. Merikare persevered, however, and although it took more than a year to pacify the south, the countryside of Ta Shemau was at last virtually free of crime.

The commander of the Hapi corps handed over the policing of the sepats to the Medjay, and reported back to Tjaty Herwernef in Men-nefer.

"You have performed creditably, Commander Merikare," Herwernef said. "All Kemet thanks you."

The Tjaty set sail for Per-Ramesses, where he waited until a full court session before seeking an audience with the king. He entered the throne room with his head held high and bowed before Ramesses, smiling as he announced his news.

"Son of Re, I have done as you commanded and rid the kingdoms of the scourge of bandits and lawless men. Once more a merchant may travel the roads of Kemet without fear of robbery, and a woman may venture outside without fear of rape."

"That pleases me mightily," Ramesses said. "Let all here in attendance praise Tjaty Herwernef, for he has pleased his king." He waited until the courtiers and nobles had applauded the Tjaty before continuing. "Tjaty Herwernef has already attained the highest rank within our kingdoms, but I will reward him for his services with gold and productive farms. Send for my scribe so that I may cause his deeds and their reward to be recorded for posterity."

Herwernef bowed and praised the king for his generosity, but never mentioned the great efforts Merikare and his corps had made to bring about this desired result. In fairness, the king did not ask, assuming only that his Tjaty had used the resources at his disposal. Just as one did not praise the copper chisel that was used by a skilled craftsman, only the finished product, so it was that the reward for ridding the kingdoms of their internal enemies fell to the man who had crafted the result.

# Chapter 22
# Year 6 of Usermaatre Ramesses

Ament managed to get word to Zeben that his wife and daughters had left Kemet and were heading north to the refuge he had mentioned before, but the Commander's personal charioteer refused to leave without his sons.

"They won't leave," Ament said. "Rath has decided he likes it in the navy, and Goloth is fast becoming a skilled archer in the army. Both have taken the first steps toward becoming officers."

"Can't you persuade them otherwise?"

"They are young men who have discovered their way in the world, Zeben. You must let them go, and join your wife and daughters."

"Dan-el the potter in Urit; right?"

Ament nodded. "Will you be able to get away?"

"Might be difficult. Merikare relies on me, but maybe I can feign illness."

"Travel fast and light, and avoid the roads."

"What about you? Come with me."

"I'll stay on a few months longer to make sure the boys are settled. Then I'll leave. I miss my wife and children too."

Ament heard the news a few days later. With the Hapi corps now back in their permanent station in Per-Ramesses, there was little for the men to do beyond the usual round of drill, so rumours were ever popular and the story of the flight of the Commander's personal charioteer was told around the camp fires with relish. Some men applauded his actions, though they were careful not to express those sentiments in the hearing of senior officers. The most likely place he had escaped to, men thought, was to his home in Per-Bast, though others thought him a fool if he tried something so predictable.

"He'll have to spend his life in exile," was the predominant opinion. "If he's not caught and flogged, that is."

Some, who were aware that Ament knew Zeben, though unsure of the relationship, asked his opinion. Ament just shrugged and muttered something noncommittal, steering conversation back to safer topics.

Ament had thought long and hard about his position within the Hapi corps. It was safer to remain a simple soldier, performing his duties without attracting attention, but being a junior officer offered a lot more freedom of movement. Such was his level of expertise that he found it easy to rise to become Leader of Fifty, though his Troop Commander--Nebit--had called him into his presence before awarding him that rank.

"So, Leader of Ten Mentak, I'm hearing good things about you."

"Thank you, sir."

"I intend making you a Leader of Fifty."

"Uh...thank you, sir."

"I did not think a Khabiru could fit into the army so well, but you've taken to the discipline well and you speak Kemetu like a native."

"Thank you, sir."

"The only thing about you I don't like is that odious beard and long hair. It makes you look dirty and unkempt and it has been suggested before that you get rid of it. Why have you not acted on that suggestion?"

"Sorry, sir, but it's the Khabiru religion, sir. We're supposed to let our hair and beards grow."

"Well, the time has come to make a choice, Mentak. Get rid of the beard and at least cut your hair short. Shaving it would be better. The Kemetu army will no longer allow such a slovenly appearance in its officers."

Ament chewed his lip. "If it's all the same to you, sir, I'll keep the beard and leave the army then."

"No, it's not all right," snapped Nebit. "Shave your head and face. That's an order."

"Uh...my religion, sir..."

"I don't care an addled egg for your heathen religion. Convert to the true gods of Kemet if it'll make you feel better, but get yourself shaved. Report back tomorrow morning. Dismissed."

Ament went away and thought it over, debating whether to run for it immediately. If he could avoid the patrols, he could be well away before his absence was noticed. Then he could get a dirty robe, join a caravan, and become just one more foreigner among a thousand others. He thought of Rath and Goloth, and though the boys had made their own choices, he did not want to leave without giving them one more chance to come to their senses.

"Curses," he muttered. "I'm going to have to stay a little longer."

The danger was that if he shaved, he might be recognised. None of the men knew Ament by sight, but he knew of at least three senior officers that were acquainted with the old General Ament, and he feared that even ten years later, a shaven Mentak might trigger a memory.

*How can I still disguise myself?*

Sighing, Ament sought out a bronze knife and sharpened it before taking hot water and coarse soap to one side. Without the aid of a mirror, he hacked away at his hair and beard, and then shaved his face until it was smooth and bleeding in only a few places. The nicks and cuts had long since stopped bleeding by the time he presented himself at the Troop Commander's tent the next morning.

Nebit stared and nodded, smiling. "Yes, that's a lot better. If you can now lose those filthy Khabiru robes of yours and adopt the Kemetu kilt and the headdress of an officer, you could pass for Kemetu anywhere."

"Thank you, sir."

"I'm making you a Leader of Fifty, effective immediately, but I'll have to move you out of my Red Troop. Any preferences for what Troop you'd like to join?" Nebit saw the look of surprise on Ament's face and explained. "It's a new ruling from on high. Officers of Fifty and above must serve in a different Troop from which they served as common soldiers. Limits the likelihood of favouritism or something, I'm told. So, what's it to be?"

"Blue, sir, if it's all the same to you?"

"Why?"

Ament hesitated. If the rule had been brought in to prevent favouritism, then Nebit would not look kindly on him wanting to be in the same Troop as Goloth. "They have a good archery unit, sir."

"So they do. Well, that's as good a reason as any. Blue troop it is. I'll have the note made in the corps files, but you can report over there immediately."

"Thank you, sir." Ament saluted and turned to go, but Nebit called him back.

"Funny thing, Mentak. When you were all bearded and dirty you looked just like any foreigner, and by the gods, they all look the same to me. But all shaved and clean, you look familiar. Do I know you from somewhere?"

"I don't think so, sir."

Nebit shook his head. "Somewhere. Your hair may not have been grey then, nor your skin so wrinkled, but... No, I can't place you. Well, never mind, it'll come to me if it's important. Dismissed."

Ament packed up his few belongings and made his way over to the Blue Troop, where he reported for duty and was assigned his quarters. The previous Leader of Fifty had died of snakebite a few days before, so Ament inherited his bedroll and a few clothes that were of higher quality than his own. He held the plain headdress of his rank and imagined himself in it, his gut twisting at the thought that he would more closely resemble the man he had been--the man he must not be--General Ament of King Tausret's army. The danger of being recognised was even greater now that he had been promoted. Some of the officers had belonged to other corps ten years before, even from the Set corps which had been his own.

He went looking for Goloth and found him sitting alone, binding new goose feathers to his arrows. Every archer worth the name tended his own equipment and allowed nobody to touch it. Even the arrows were personally marked so that after a battle he could claim jewellery from any of the enemy he had struck down. In Goloth's case, red and green thread were bound tightly round the shaft just below the feathers and gummed in place with resin. He looked up as Ament approached and grinned, leaping to his feet and saluting as he recognised his uncle's insignia of rank.

"Greetings, General Ament... I mean Leader of Fifty Mentak..."

"Hush, lad." Ament looked around but they seemed to be unobserved. "Not even as a joke. It's not something I wanted, but I was ordered to shave and accept my new rank. I'm just worried I look too much like I used to."

Goloth regarded his uncle thoughtfully. "You look older, uncle..."

"Don't call me uncle. Some people might know your uncle was General Ament."

"If they do, it hasn't affected anyone's attitude to me."

"Being the General is a little different from being his nephew. Aside from looking older then?"

"You do look like him a bit. If anyone knew you then, they might recognise you. You sort of...have an air of authority about you. More than you'd expect of a junior officer."

"I suspected as much," Ament said gloomily. "I suppose I'll have to desert then. Will you come with me? Your parents would be glad of it."

Goloth grimaced. "What would I do at home? Become a farmer or a fisherman..."

"Both worthy professions."

"But not for me. I want to be an archer of renown, to rise within the army and win the Gold of Valour from the hand of the king."

Ament nodded. "I feared as much, but I have to leave, I think. Will you be all right if I do? I promised your parents I'd look out for you and your brother."

"And you've done so, uncle. I'm rising through the army, and from what I hear, Rath is doing well in the navy. We have to step out and become men sometime. You know what it's like." Goloth grinned. "Who knows, maybe I'll meet my own Tausret someday, just like you."

Ament embraced his nephew with tears in his eyes and took his leave. He intended to approach Rath in the same way in the hope of giving him a last chance to leave too, but first he had to find him. Since the second battle outside of Per-Ramesses, the fleet could be anywhere, patrolling the lower reaches of the mouths of the river, or even braving the saltwater waves along the nearby coastline. Finding and contacting him might be difficult, and Ament was not sure he had that much time.

His fears of wearing the officer's headdress were soon put to the test. The whole corps was ordered out on parade and inspection, and Ament was in his place as Leader of Fifty, though he tried to avoid eye contact with other officers. Despite this, he still noted a few strange looks cast his way, and Troop Commander Nebit even stopped in front of him and stared into his face.

"I've seen you before, Mentak, but where?"

"Don't know, sir."

"You have the look of that traitor General of that Queen pretender, but he died."

"Everyone looks like someone, sir."

Nebit grunted and moved on, leaving Ament sweating. He knew he would have to leave Kemet quickly, but he hated to leave without giving Rath one last chance to return to his family. *If only I had never become an officer*, he thought. *As a common soldier I could wear my beard and long hair and nobody worried.* He considered a possible option. *Could I get demoted somehow?* The easiest way was through drink. Ament had demoted men himself for imbibing too much strong beer or wine and behaving in a manner unbecoming for an officer. *Problem with that is it attracts attention. I'd get demoted without question, but I'd be hauled in front of Nebit and given a dressing down first. Every time he sees my face gives him another opportunity to recognise me. He's already got the idea I look like who I really am, so how long before he brings in someone who really does know me?*

The inspection ended and the men were dismissed. Back in camp, Ament considered how he could slip away and decided the simplest solution was to go into Per-Ramesses with his old clothing bundled up and lose himself in the seething populace. Back in his old robes with a cloth drawn across his face he would be just another tribesman from the desert. Then if he joined a caravan...

"Leader of Fifty Mentak."

Ament looked up and saw a soldier looking at him. The man saluted and, now that he had attracted the officer's attention, continued.

"Troop Commander Nebit wants to see you in his command tent, sir."

"Did he say what it was about?"

The soldier shrugged. "Would he tell me, sir?"

Ament nodded and got to his feet, wondering whether Nebit had already remembered something. He started off in the direction of the command tent.

"Might be something to do with Troop Commander Mose of the Set corps, sir," the soldier called after him. "Commander Merikare too."

Ament hesitated, but continued walking as if he had not heard the man. Once out of sight, he sat down heavily on a bale of hay, his thoughts in turmoil. *Mose, the one man I can be certain will recognise me.* Mose had been his deputy commander ten years before in the final battle where the Set corps fought for Queen Tausret against the forces led by the present king and his father. *He wouldn't willingly betray me... I think...but Nebit must have called him in because he suspects my identity. He will be watching Mose for that flash of recognition. If he sees that, I'm dead.*

Ament considered whether he could return to his tent to pick up his old robes but decided against it. It was one thing to enter the city with a hundred others on leave and then slip away, quite another to walk through camp with a bundle of old clothes and fend off curious questions as to his purpose. Then there was Troop Commander Nebit. He was already suspicious and if Ament did not turn up soon, he would send other men out to look for him and bring him in.

*No, instant flight is the only thing that's going to save me. But where?*

The city of Per-Ramesses was no longer an option. He could steal clothes but that might attract other attention. Still, the risk might be acceptable if he could find a caravan heading north immediately. A month or two would see him well on his way back to his family by the Sea of

Kinnereth. *Nebit knows I'm Khabiru*, he realised. *I confirm his suspicion by fleeing, and he knows exactly where I'll go. I'm too great a prize to just let go, so he'll inform Merikare and he'll send the corps after me. If he tells the king, the whole Kemetu army will be pursuing me.*

Per-Ramesses was out, as was the road north along the Way of Heru by himself. Once the word got out, the north would be searched. The south was useless, as was west across Ta Mehu. Even if he managed to cross the cultivated lands unrecognised, there was only the western desert and the tribes of the Ribu to offer hospitality, and Ament thought that as unlikely as King Usermaatre Ramesses offering him his hand in friendship.

*No, the only possible route is east. East into the Land of Sin--a waterless, hostile desert where no man in his right mind would go. They'd never look for me there because they'd never imagine I'd be such a fool...am I a fool?* He remembered a trek he'd once made across the Sin, with his two young adopted sons and a man of the Shechem tribe. The Shechem had offered him sanctuary, and might do so again--*if I can find them in that trackless waste.*

# Chapter 23
# Year 6 of Usermaatre Ramesses

"I have heard it all before, Tjaty Herwernef, and it never amounts to anything. There must have been a hundred sightings of the General and his bitch Tausret in the several years following their defeat and almost certain death. Why do you bring me news of this one?"

"I believe this is something more, Son of Re," Herwernef said. "The witness thought he recognised him, and later was sure of it."

"And who is this uncertain witness?"

"Troop Commander Nebit of the Hapi Corps, Son of Re."

"Summon him. I would hear this tale from his own lips."

Herwernef sent for Troop Commander Nebit and a few other people whom he thought relevant to the story, and when they arrived in Men-nefer two days later, ushered them into the king's presence.

"Who are these men?" Ramesses demanded.

Herwernef introduced them one at a time, and as each man's name was called, the man dropped to his knees on the tiled floor and extended his arms in homage.

"Troop Commander Nebit of the Hapi Corps, Son of Re; Troop Commander Mose of the Set Corps; Commander Merikare of the Hapi Corps; Axeman Seneb of the Hapi Corps."

"Ah, yes, Nebit the uncertain witness. Stand and tell me your story."

"Son of Re, the man Mentak came to me as a raw recruit sent from Commander Merikare. He..."

"The first part of this story comes from you, Commander Merikare?" Ramesses asked.

Merikare stood also. "Yes, Son of Re. The man Mentak was asking questions of my scribes and aroused their suspicions. I arrested him and determined that he was a Khabiru searching for a man in my corps who owed him some small sum. I pressed him into service and handed him on to my officers."

Ramesses nodded. "Continue, Nebit."

"Yes, Son of Re. This Mentak was bearded and longhaired, dirty and unkempt, just like any uncivilised foreigner from Kanaan, but he proved skilled with sword, axe and spear."

"And this aroused your suspicion?"

"Not at the time, Son of Re. This was prior to the battles with the Sea Peoples and I welcomed any skilled soldier. I thought he looked somewhat familiar but could not put a name to the face. He fought within the Red Troop, and he was promoted first to Five and then to Ten, but when I desired to raise him to Leader of Fifty, I required him to shave and cut his hair, to dress and comport himself as a Kemetu officer."

"And?" Ramesses asked when Nebit paused.

"He was even more familiar, Son of Re, but it was not until we were on parade that I remembered who he looked like--General Ament."

"Where had you seen General Ament before?" Ramesses asked curiously.

"I was a Leader of Ten in the Khent-abt Corps, Son of Re. I happened to be standing near him on the day he walked into the desert with Queen Tausret."

"If you recognised him on parade, why did you not arrest him?"

"I... I could not be certain, Son of Re. I put it to him that he looked like Ament, but he denied it, saying..."

"You forewarned him?"

Nebit bowed his head and said nothing.

Ramesses sighed. "Go on with your tale."

"Yes, Son of Re. I thought upon his features after the parade and thought to myself that if there was one person who might recognise him it was Troop Commander Mose of the Set Corps, who had been Ament's deputy. I put my thoughts before Commander Merikare and asked him to request Mose's presence, knowing that the Set Corps was on leave in nearby Per-Ramesses."

"So, Mose, are you now loyal to my person as king of Kemet?"

Mose bowed. "I am loyal always to the king of Kemet, Son of Re."

"Was the man indeed General Ament?"

"Alas, I never saw him, Majesty. He fled the camp rather than confront me."

"So there is no real evidence either way?"

"Son of Re," Tjaty Herwernef said, "The man fled. Surely that is a sign of guilt."

"Perhaps. Why is this man here?" Ramesses asked, pointing at the trembling soldier.

"Seneb was the man I sent to fetch Ament," Troop Commander Nebit replied. "I thought that he could testify that the man was in the camp but fled upon being summoned."

"Get up, Seneb. Is that what happened?"

The soldier got to his feet but stood with eyes downcast, trembling at being in the presence of the king. "I... I... th...that is..."

"Answer the king," Herwernef snapped.

"Easy, Herwernef," Ramesses said. "Seneb, you are not in any trouble, nor will I lay any blame at your feet, but I must know the truth of this matter. Did you tell this man who may have been General Ament that Troop Commander Nebit wanted to see him? Just answer yes or no."

"Y...yes, sir... Son of Re."

"Good man. Now, did you say anything else to him? Anything that might have made him afraid?

"I, er... I said that Commander Merikare and Troop Commander Mose were with him, Son of Re."

"You see, Herwernef? Even if he innocent, being called in front of those commanders might have made him afraid. Being guilty of a lesser crime might also make him flee."

"Of course, Majesty," the Tjaty replied, "but if he was Ament, he would know that Mose could positively identify him. He was deputy and friend of Ament."

"Yes, a friend," Ramesses mused. "Too much of a friend to betray him, I wonder."

Mose stepped forward and stared at his king fiercely. "Son of Re, you do me an injustice. It is true that I was Ament's friend and was loyal to him and to the Lady Tausret, but I was bound by my oath to the crowned and anointed king of Kemet, and to my superior officer. I would have been without honour if I betrayed them then. Now, however, I am bound to Usermaatre Ramesses and my Commander Hori by oaths of loyalty and though it would grieve me to see General Ament go down into death, I would identify him in a moment if he stood before me."

Ramesses waved his hand as if dispelling a fly. "No one doubts your loyalty, Commander." Nobody commented on the fact that the king had been doing just that moments before. "So was it really Ament?" he asked.

"I never saw him, Majesty," Mose said.

Ramesses sat and thought for a while, weighing up the words of his commanders. At length he stirred and asked, "I am disturbed by his presence here in Kemet and within the army. What did he hope to achieve? Was it to stir up rebellion, or something more sinister? What if I had inspected his corps--would he have tried to kill me?" Ramesses flicked his hand again, signifying he was not actually looking to have those questions answered. "If we catch him, we can ask him, but if it was Ament, where would he go? What place would offer him refuge?"

"He had ties to Per-Bast," Herwernef said. "His sister owned a vineyard there."

"No longer," Merikare said. "His family was dispersed. His sister has disappeared, her husband fled."

"Their two sons are in the army and navy," Merikare added.

"What of their loyalty?" Ramesses asked.

"The son in the Hapi corps fought well, I'm told, and I've heard no complaints about the son in the navy."

"Have them watched, but Ament would be a fool to go to either. He'd be putting his head on a spike. Where else could he go?"

"He told me he was Khabiru," Merikare said. "Perhaps..."

"We know he isn't," Herwernef interrupted. "He's as Kemetu as you and I."

"I know that. All I'm saying is that if he gave Khabiru as his identity, perhaps he has been among them these last ten years. He has to have been somewhere, after all."

"Where do the Khabiru live?" Ramesses asked.

"Northern and eastern Kanaan, Son of Re."

"Search for him there, then. Send word to the corps to stop and identify all men seeking to travel north. Issue his description to everyone. I want him found and brought to me alive. He will tell me where that bitch Tausret is and then I will personally kill them both."

Commands were sent to every corps and every fort and guard post throughout the north and east, and for a few months the men who could identify Ament found themselves racing here and running there as men were apprehended and word sent back to the court. None of the arrested men proved to be Ament, however, and gradually the fervour of the searching men died away. If Tjaty Herwernef had been worried about reporting a failure to the king; that concern soon dissipated as news of a new revolt by the Ribu tribes in the west filtered through to the king's ears. Every other concern was thrust aside as Ramesses mobilised his corps to crush the rebellious tribesmen.

The Hapi corps was in the forefront of the punitive expedition, if only because it was the closest corps on hand when the news came through. Merikare immediately moved his men across the width of Ta Mehu and took up position near the city of Perire, where the main route from the west passed. Goloth, as a junior officer in the archers unit, found himself in a forward position with twenty men in his command, scouting out the territory from whence the enemy would come.

The navy took part also, though as the battles would be fought on land, their task was limited to supplying the army and guarding the river crossing points. Rath itched to fight the enemy, but realised he would likely only take a small part in the war. Nevertheless, he volunteered for any duty that would bring him closer to the excitement that was growing around Perire.

King Usermaatre Ramesses arrived, having met up with his experienced corps, leading two of them, Set and Ptah, across Ta Mehu. They were now encamped outside of Perire while the king examined the latest intelligence that had come in from the scouts. One of the reports had even come in from Goloth's tiny forward command.

'Enemy sighted,' it read. 'Half day west of forward position by the Hill of the Ram. Sighted several hundred Ribu tribesmen moving east in disarray with women, children and herds. Engaged about a hundred warriors and drove them off. They are now passing to the south of our position but moving slowly.'

Ramesses waited for the scribe to finish reading the message and then held out his hand for it. He read it through slowly and carefully, remarking, "The scribe has an atrocious hand." He handed it to his commanders who also perused it.

"The officer in charge has appended his name to it," Commander Merenre of Ptah said. "I doubt they took a scribe with them, so it will be in the officer's hand."

"It is Goloth," Commander Merikare said. "The man I told you about, Son of Re. The one associated with Ament."

"He can write? I thought him one of the dregs of prison."

"He is very young, Son of Re, but capable. His report will be accurate, so we must move quickly to contain the enemy."

The Set, Hapi and Ptah corps set out, taking little in the way of provisions. Ramesses meant to close with the enemy and destroy them quickly, before they could reach the well-watered lands near the Great River. They came upon them early on the second day, and were alerted of their presence by Goloth's small command falling back in front of overwhelming numbers. He reported immediately to Commander Merikare, who brought him into the presence of the king. As soon as he had been told to rise, he offered up his report and scratched a rough map into the dirt, showing where the enemy was, and where they were heading. The enemy knew of the presence of the Kemetu army, though evidently not its strength, and were now attempting to slip past them and move deeper into Ta Mehu.

"You have done well," Ramesses said. He turned to his commanders and started drawing up plans for meeting the Ribu.

Goloth stepped back and listened, tucking away the tactics and opinions into his memory for later examination. He felt excited being in the king's presence, and at least being able to listen as plans for victory were made.

The plans were quite simple really. Other scouts had brought in other useful information and the standard tactic of a chariot charge had to be put aside as the ground was too uneven for it to be effective. Instead, the three corps would overrun the Ribu, using superior numbers to overwhelm them and crush them. The Hapi corps would be in the forefront, and would meet the enemy head on, whereas the Set and Ptah corps would swing out to either side like the claws of a scorpion and hit the enemy from three sides. If they tried to escape, the only direction left to them was back the way they came, into the desert.

The corps moved out, manoeuvring into position, and scouts came into contact with them once more, later that day. They moved across the front of the Ribu and placed themselves firmly to the east. Night fell, and the corps camped, though they dozed around camp fires rather than setting up tents. Their slumber was disturbed by the continuous flicker of light on the western horizon and an occasional rumble washed across their ranks as if boulders fell from some impossibly high cliff. Toward dawn, a hot wind picked up, gusting out of the west, and the air took on the dry, acrid stink of desert dust.

"Storm coming," Hori said. "Hot and dry and dust laden."

"And in our faces," Merenre added. "It will make our job that much harder."

"Then we must win tomorrow's battle quickly," Merikare observed.

The Ribu had also noted the presence of the sandstorm and attempted to use it for their own purposes, hoping to stave off the Kemetu assault until it struck, and then to use the cover it provided to evade the army. Ramesses was equally determined that battle would be joined early on, and that victory would be his before the storm arrived.

In the event, neither army was entirely successful. The Ribu drew back as the corps attacked, Hapi pressing forward and harrying the retreating tribesmen, while Set swung wide and pushed in from the south as Ptah mirrored their movements to the north. Men started dying, and the Ribu gave up their attempts to avoid conflict and charged forward, yelling hoarsely. Soon the plain was filled with a struggling mass of men, making it difficult for the commanders to see what was happening, and almost impossible for them to respond to the vagaries of battle.

Goloth had rejoined his unit in the Hapi corps and to start with had, with the other archers, peppered the retreating Ribu with arrows; loosing two or three and then running to keep up with the advancing corps. As they advanced, they came upon arrows that had been used once already, and snatched them up to use again. When the Ribu went on to the attack and the fighting became general, Goloth put aside his bow and took his short-handled axe from his belt and started laying about him. He was soon covered in sweat and blood, and the dust kicked up by their feet became caked to his body and irritated his eyes.

All the while, the hot wind gusted in from the west and now a curtain appeared on the horizon, stretching further north-south than the eye could see, yellowish brown and roiling. Whenever Goloth lifted his eyes from the battle, the curtain was nearer, and soon it hung in the sky menacing friend and foe alike. The wind blew more fiercely and gusted dust into his face and sand grains stung his legs. Blue left the cloudless sky, fading to white and then yellowish and the roar of the approaching storm drowned out the clamour of battle.

Rams' horns sounded, faint above the howl of the wind and the corps pressed forward, eager to destroy the enemy while they still could. But Ramesses had left it too late. The swirling storm of sand and dust enveloped the Ribu, and moments later the Kemetu corps, and men no longer fought each other but instead fought the elements. Horns and banners became useless as means of communication, and men were forced to relay commands by touch. Groups of soldiers gathered together, each cut off from their fellows, and hunkered down, lifting shields over their heads. Kilts were removed and wound around faces to enable them to breathe, but bare backs and legs were stung by the blast of sand, and dust filled their eyes and ears, finding its way through the cloth to their mouths and nostrils.

Goloth sheltered with his archers and found himself on the leeward side of a cluster, where the sand did not sting his skin as much, though the billows of dust still found its way into his lungs. He coughed and spat and curled up tighter, thrusting his face into an armpit beside him, ignoring the stink of sweat. The wind howled louder and buffeted them from all directions now, drifting sand piling up around them. Somewhere above them they had to believe that Re still shone, but here in the storm it was almost as dark as night, what light there was filtered through layers of sand and dust into a twilight.

By degrees, the light faded as time passed, and it seemed like days had passed before a dim light crept around them once more. The wind dropped, and though they were still stung by sand and choked by dust, the light above them gathered strength. A little longer and the sun actually shone on them once more.

Goloth stood and looked about him at a changed landscape. He unwound his kilt from his face and spat dust from his mouth, standing naked as he looked around. Others stood now, searching for water flasks and calling out to companions, some of whom lay where they had fallen. Officers started shouting orders and gradually the corps drew themselves up in some semblance of order and moved eastward, away from the desert. There was no sign of the Ribu. They had either perished in the sandstorm or fled back to their own lands--no one much cared.

# Chapter 24
# Year 7 of Usermaatre Ramesses

If young Prince Ramesses was lonely now that his older brothers had left the palaces of Waset for the exciting north, he did not show it. He shared the echoing chambers and halls of the King's Per-Khemret and wider palace with a score of other children, a few older, most younger, but all progeny of the king's body borne to him by a dozen concubines. Only he could claim a queen as mother though, and while he did not thrust his station in the other children's faces, he made sure they all recognised it. More often than not, he decided what games they would all play, or if a game was already in progress, the older children would defer to him.

Once or twice, a boy a few months older than Ramesses had tried to bully him, but the nurses had leapt to the defence of the prince and the older boy had been hauled away and thrashed for his temerity by the scribe in charge of their education. No prince or child of the king's body was safe from this man, himself a son of Baenre Merenptah, but he took his duties seriously, diluting discipline with kindness. Ramesses had never suffered at his hands, and this favouritism had earned the young boy some resentment among the mothers of the other children, though they were at pains to hide it. The prince's mother, Queen Tyti, was not a woman to be taken lightly.

Most games were versions of hide-and-seek, played through the great expanse of the palace, or of chasing or fighting. The young girls favoured dolls made of cloth and wood or cuddled kittens and puppies, but the boys were guided toward more martial pursuits. Most of the boys were destined for administrative or priestly duties throughout the two kingdoms, but one never knew when they might be called upon to serve in the army. Thus, even from an early age, they trained with sticks instead of swords, little toy bows and blunted arrows, or ran and wrestled like real soldiers. They were guided in this by old soldiers, now too infirm for active duty, who could earn a little extra by tutoring the sons of the king in the veranda and gardens of the new palace.

"Come on, Nebenkharu, keep your shield up...that's right...watch out for the...never mind, try again."

Nebenkharu, no more than four years old, threw down his tiny wooden shield and sword and burst into tears, while his half-brother Amenemwia stood grinning. The victor looked to the old soldier for praise.

"That was right, wasn't it, Merenre?" he said.

"Yes it was," Merenre replied. "Now go over there and practice your strokes while I attend to Nebenkharu." He dried the young boy's tears with the edge of his kilt and touched the red welt on Nebenkharu's arm where his opponent's sword had hit him.

"You did well, young master. I can't think of anyone else who could have blocked that stroke."

Nebenkharu sniffed and wiped his nose with the back of his hand. "Even you?"

Merenre smiled. "When I was young and fit I could have, and when you have put on a few more years, you'll be able to as well. Now, that's enough swordplay for today, I think. Go and practice with a bow."

Nebenkharu wandered off across the veranda to where other children were trying to hit a straw animal with their arrows. Another old soldier, Huni, endeavoured to instruct four and five year olds in the use of bow and arrow. Judging by the pristine condition of the straw animal and the arrows littering the tiled floor, success had eluded him.

Elsewhere, yet another infirm warrior of past days watched as slightly older boys, including some of the young sons of court officials practiced with spears, launching them at another straw figure, this one of a man clothed as a foreigner. Whenever a spear struck home, boyish voices lifted in yells of victory, or jeers when a spear missed its target. Not all the boys were engaged in military pursuits, for under the shade of a nearby tree sat an old scribe, Siamen, and he had a solitary pupil.

"Are you certain you would not rather be practicing with sword of bow, young lord?" he asked of the boy sitting in front of him.

"I have mastered the bow already, Siamen, and I have no need of skill with a sword. When I am king, I will have others to do that for me."

Siamen smiled, though the boy's words troubled him. "You seem very sure that will happen, Prince Ramesses. You have older brothers, though, and one of them, Khaemwaset, is the king's heir."

The boy shrugged. "He is heir now, but when I am older the king my father will make me heir." Ramesses must have seen doubt in the old man's eyes. "It's true," he insisted. "My mother told me so."

"Then it must be so," Siamen said. Inwardly, he wondered whether this was just a childish fantasy, or whether the Queen was encouraging the boy to have unreal expectations. He decided to change the subject. "So what do you want to do? I fear I have no knowledge of weapons."

"I want to learn to read like you do, so I can read about the deeds of the kings on temple walls."

"You and the other boys will learn all you need to know a little later. You are only five, aren't you? Most boys start on this when they are seven."

"I want to start now." Ramesses stared at the old scribe and when he did not immediately reply, scowled. "I command you to teach me, Siamen. You are a servant and must do as you are told."

"I am a royal scribe in the household of the king, Prince Ramesses, not a common servant, but..." he held up one hand as the boy opened his mouth. "...I will show you some of the sacred writing and we will see whether you are ready to learn this most difficult of arts. But I warn you, not everyone can master the words of the gods."

Siamen sat in silence for a few moments, gathering his thoughts, and then he drew a wax tablet from his robes and a stylus with which to draw upon it. He made three marks upon the wax, taking care to render them accurately.

"What are these marks?" he asked.

Ramesses looked at them and frowned. "I have seen them... I think...but I don't know what they mean."

"I would be surprised if you did. They are the signs of protection. This one..." Siamen pointed to ☥ is the *ankh*. It represents life and its connection to that which has gone before. The gods infused life into the first man and they pass down this divine spark, this life force, from generation to generation. It is the descent of the eternal principle, the Atum, into the physical plane. Do you understand?"

"I... I think so..."

Siamen sighed. "It is a lot to comprehend. Look at the parts of it, young Ramesses. This horizontal bar represents the horizon, the plane of reality with everything above it being the sky, the abode of the gods...things of the spirit. The loop above the bar...and the tail hanging down...is a rope that binds the spiritual to the earthly. It offers the protection of the gods by passing down the divine spark into earthly man."

Ramesses did not look any the wiser, so Siamen passed on to the next symbol, 𓍱, pointing to it.

"This is the *sa*; very similar to the *ankh*, but without the horizontal bar. Do you know anything about it?"

Prince Ramesses fidgeted and shook his head.

"It too derives from a loop, but it is made of woven rushes. What do you think might be the significance of that?" Siamen waited, but when no answer was forthcoming, asked another question. "What are rushes used for?"

"I don't know...wait, yes. Servants put them on the floor in the kitchen sometimes and...and I've seen them on the roof of the hut with the outdoor ovens."

"Very good, and how might they be used by fishermen, do you think?"

"I don't know."

"Fishermen bind reeds together with rope and use them to stay afloat."

Ramesses yawned, not bothering to hide it. "I thought you were going to tell me about sacred writing."

"That is what I am doing, young Ramesses. Sacred writing is representational. That means that anything we see on earth is represented by something in the realm of the gods, and everything up there can be seen down here. The *ankh* is loop that binds the spiritual to the earthly and acts as a protection. You could say that the symbol of the ankh represents heavenly protection. When we draw it on Amun's temple wall or show the king holding an ankh, we are invoking the protection of the gods. Do you see?"

Ramesses looked over to where the other children were playing with their toy weapons and wondered if he would not rather be with them.

"Why not just say so?" he asked Siamen. "Why not just say 'Amun, please protect the king,'?"

"It is not how things are done. Now, do you want to hear some more or would you rather go and play?"

Ramesses thought he detected scorn in the old scribe's voice, and much as he wanted to play, he did not want any man to look down on him. "Go on," he said.

"Very well...the *sa* then. It is a bundle of reeds bound with a rope that prevents them from drowning, and is another earthly symbol of protection. That is the earthy representation of the plane of reality fastened by the divine spark, a cosmic cord if you will, forming a protective coil. This binds all things together and forms a centre, a mooring post, a place of stability anchoring heaven and earth."

"I know that one," Ramesses said, pointing to the third symbol. "It's a circle...but it's not well drawn. You've made it long and left both ends free."

"Ah, the child would seek to instruct the master, it seems. That is not a circle, young Ramesses, but the *shen*, a loop made of rope bound at the bottom with the ends forming a horizontal bar. It represents endless time bound to the earthly plane, protecting by enclosing life, surrounding it and defending it against hostile forces. Now, a question for you. Where do you see the *shen* most often in inscriptions?"

Ramesses shrugged.

Siamen shook his head and sighed again. "I do not think your heart is in this, young sir. The shen is most often seen as the cartouche, the protective loop around the royal name. It isolates the king from common men and protects him from all harm." The old scribe looked at the boy and shook his head again. "I think that is all I should say for now. Perhaps you are too young for such learning. Go and play, and return to this with the other boys when you are older." Siamen got to his feet slowly and tottered inside, leaving the young prince sitting on the ground beneath the tree.

Ramesses grimaced and got up too. "You're just a mean old man," he muttered at the scribe's back. The games the other boys were playing no longer attracted him, so he walked off into the palace, taking care to go in by a different door than Siamen. Without really guiding his own footsteps, he found himself in the Per-Khemret and decided to visit his mother.

"My darling Ramesses," Queen Tyti said when she caught sight of him. "Come here and give your mother a kiss."

He ran across the room and threw his arms around his mother as she bent over to embrace him, hugging her fiercely, and allowed her to plant a kiss on his cheek. Peering round her skirts, he saw his grandmother and smiled at her too.

"Hello grandmother."

"Hello grandson. Are you being a good boy?"

Ramesses nodded and transferred his attention back to his mother. "I want the scribe Siamen told off. He was rude to me."

Tyti sat on a cushioned couch and patted the seat next to her. "Sit with me and tell me all about it."

Ramesses sat, swinging his legs and scratching his belly while he considered what he should say. "He told me to go and play, but I asked him to teach me and he wouldn't."

"Start again, Ramesses. Speak as I have told you--start at the beginning and choose your words."

"I... I'll try, mother."

"Do not try. Do it."

"He's only five, daughter," Tiy-merenese said. "You expect too much of him."

"He's nearly six and who knows when he may be called to the throne. He must be ready for and always comport himself in a kingly manner."

"Will I really be king?"

"Never doubt it, my son, for you are doubly royal, being descended from kings on both your father's and mother's side."

"Daughter...be cautious. You are filling his head with things that may never happen."

"Do you deny his claim, mother?" Tyti demanded.

"He has a claim, but so do his brothers...especially his older brothers."

"Half-brothers only, mother. Spawned by that cow Tiye."

"They are my grandsons too, daughter."

"What? You would put a weak priest and army halfwits above my son?"

"They are older, and as long as the king upholds their rights, there is nothing you can do about it."

"We shall see about that. Many things might happen before my Ramesses is old enough to take the throne."

"Hush, child. Be cautious in how you express your thoughts."

"None overhear us, mother, and even if they did, they are my trusted servants."

"And what of...?" Tiy-merenese nodded her head toward the boy beside her. "He is too young to know when to keep his counsel."

Tyti regarded her son and slowly nodded. "Do not speak of what you hear, my son."

"But I will be king, won't I?"

"That is with...the gods. Learn what your tutors teach you; master the skills in war that a king needs, and trust in the gods...and those that love you. Now, what is this about the scribe Siamen?"

"He was rude."

"How was he rude?"

"I asked him to tell me about writing and all he would talk about was rope and loops and a lot of stuff like that."

"Do you remember any of the words he used?"

Ramesses thought hard. "*Ankh*, I think...and *shen*."

"The protective symbols that guard the king."

"You know about them?" Ramesses looked astonished.

"You think because I am a woman I am uneducated?"

"But that's what scribes are for and...and what use does a woman have for writing?"

Tyti smiled. "You would be surprised, my son. Now, you have told me that Siamen talked about protective symbols, but how was he rude to you?"

"He told me I was too young and to go and play."

"How is that being rude?"

"I am a prince and...and if I am going to be king, I will need to know. He should not have refused my commands."

"Perhaps you *are* too young to learn the secrets of the gods, my son." Tyti thought for a few moments and then put her arms around her young son, drawing him close. "Listen to me, Ramesses. Put my words in your heart and repeat them to no-one. You are not the king, nor even the heir, nor even close to being the heir, but things change. One day, the king may look upon you with favour, but on that day he will want to see more than just one of his sons. He will want to see a man who knows the laws of Kemet, who can read and write, who knows how to govern men, who can lead an army and conquer his enemies, who can inspire men. In short, a man who can be king."

"I can be all those things," Ramesses said excitedly.

"One day, perhaps, but I counsel you to be circumspect, to be mild and respectful to those who know more than you, for then they will teach you. You must learn every aspect of governance and do everything your father requires of you. Can you do that?"

"Yes, mother...but what does 'cumspect mean?"

"Do not be boastful, do not let others know what you are thinking."

"And gov'nance?"

"How to rule. When you are older I shall get tutors to teach you everything."

"Thank you, mother."

# Chapter 25
# Year 7 of Usermaatre Ramesses

The land of Kemet basked in peace. Peleset settlers now occupied five cities in Kanaan and surrounding farmlands, but they were content to make a living and did not raise up arms against the Kemetu. In the west, the threat of the Ribu had disappeared. Spies reported that the Ribu army had not been destroyed by the sandstorm but had fled back into their own lands. Ramesses put it about for public consumption that the god Set, deity of storms and warfare, had fought alongside the king to annihilate the enemy. Nobody contradicted the king, and the kingdoms settled down to enjoy the prosperity that Ramesses was determined to visit upon his people.

The Great Usermaatre Ramesses, the present king's grandfather, had clothed the land in temples and shrines, erecting monuments in praise of the gods in every city and town, spending a fortune, but employing thousands of masons, builders, artisans, scribes and ordinary labourers in his endeavours. The present Ramesses desired to emulate his grandfather in everything, but his treasury was a fraction the size. Wars and long years of unrest and uncertainty had depleted the wealth of his kingdoms, so he found himself unable to do everything he intended.

Two things needed to be built above all others though, and they were down in Ta Shemau, so as soon as affairs were settled in the north, he bid farewell to both Queen Iset in Per-Ramesses and Tiye in Men-nefer--both wives were with child again--and sailed upriver on the royal barge. The voyage was largely uneventful, though the business of the kingdoms continued unabated. Tjaty Herwernef had been left behind in Men-nefer to govern Ta Mehu in the king's absence, but this did not stop a regular fleet of small boats plying the waters between the northern capital and the ever-receding royal barge. Messengers brought petitions, reports, and sundry information to the king's attention and took his answers and responses back to the senders. As he got closer to Waset, the number of messages from Herwernef fell away, and those from the southern Tjaty, Hori, increased.

Tjaty Hori was there on the docks of Waset to greet the king as the royal barge, its red-painted oars threshing the water into foam, sped to its berth. The barge master rapped out orders and the oarsmen backed water skilfully, easing the barge's forward motion and bringing it gently to the dock. Ramesses strode down the gangplank in his regal finery and received the adulation of the crowds waiting to view their king. His Tjaty and the Commander of the local Mut corps, Panhesy, were also on hand. The king's greeting to the Commander was warm, even going so far as to clap the man on the shoulder and enquire as to his health. Panhesy had once taken a spear meant for either him or his father Setnakhte, years before they became the royal family, and Ramesses did not forget his debt of gratitude.

"You know why I have come, Hori?"

"I received your messages, Son of Re, and have prepared both sites for your inspection. Will you refresh yourself first at my residence?"

"I have had enough of enforced inactivity. I will visit the sites immediately."

The barge captain prepared to cast off as Ramesses went back on board, followed by Tjaty Hori, Commander Panhesy and a squad of soldiers.

Ramesses looked askance at the soldiers. "Are they really necessary, Panhesy? Do you imagine my life is in danger?"

Panhesy looked shocked at the suggestion. "Son of Re, no man in the kingdoms would raise a hand to you. The men are there to honour you. It is only seemly that you should be accompanied by a royal guard."

The trip across the river was a short one, and the barge was soon tied up on the western bank. Hori silently thanked the gods that he had had the foresight to arrange for chariots to be stationed there for the king's use. Ramesses mounted one, dispensing with the charioteer, and waited while Hori and Panhesy climbed into their own chariots. He led the way down the long straight road that passed between fields and orchards to the mortuary buildings and the greatest of these that was slowly rising from the plain. Although obviously unfinished, the royal palace and Mansion of Millions of Years of Usermaatre Ramesses at Tjamet was already imposing.

Ramesses dismounted and stood staring toward the front façade of the temple and palace. Although the walls were little more than twice the height of a man, they promised they would be an imposing spectacle when completed.

"I thought they would be further advanced."

"I regret, Son of Re, that there have been problems," Hori said.

"Your job is to fix problems."

"That is so, Majesty, but not all problems are easily solved. There is the problem of payment..."

Ramesses swung round to look at his Tjaty. "I gave orders that the Treasury was to supply as much gold as was needed. Do you deny that?"

"Of course not, Son of Re, but the gold has not been as forthcoming as it could be."

"Explain yourself."

"Majesty, the Treasury in Men-nefer certainly released funds, but only to the Temple of Amun here in Waset. Traditionally, they have had oversight of every building in Ta Shemau. They release gold only as it is needed..."

"That is as it should be," Ramesses said. "There must be proper accounting."

"Yes, Majesty, but..." Hori's voice trailed off and he allowed himself a small expressive shrug.

"But what?"

"The priests of Amun have not always been forthcoming."

"You are saying the temple priests have cheated me? Their king?"

"It would not be for me to say, Majesty, but the Great Temple of Amun and several smaller shrines have been extensively repaired and refurbished..."

"That was also my command."

"Indeed, Majesty, but I merely point out that work on the Temple has forged ahead, while your Mansion of Millions of Years languishes."

Ramesses scowled and turned back to regard the small workforce crawling over the site. "I will have a word with the First Prophet. It is seemly that Amun should live in a glorious house, but should not the king, himself a manifestation of Re on Earth, similarly enjoy such luxury?"

Hori could only murmur his assent.

"Gold will be released to further work on my Mansion and Palace, Tjaty Hori. You may be certain of that. You will ensure that that the buildings are erected without further delay."

"There are other problems, Majesty."

Ramesses glared at his Tjaty, and Hori lowered his head, unable to meet his king's scrutiny.

"Building stone, Majesty. Without gold to pay the teams of masons, we are running out of cut and dressed blocks."

"I have told you that gold will be provided."

"But in the meantime? It will be many days before new stone can be cut and fashioned. Even with gold, Majesty."

"Must I solve every little problem myself?" Ramesses appealed to the Commander of the Mut corps. "Panhesy, what would you do?"

"I am a simple soldier, Son of Re, but..." he gestured around the building site and the other temples and Mansions nearby, "I would look to other gods for assistance. Every temple and Mansion has a small supply of building material on hand in case minor repairs are necessary. I am sure the masons could avail themselves of these supplies...until fresh blocks could be cut."

"You would rob the gods themselves?" Hori asked, his eyes wide with dismay.

"Our king is also a god," Panhesy pointed out. "Would the other gods begrudge a small loan to one of their own?"

Ramesses laughed. "I like it, Panhesy. Hori, see that it is done."

Hori bowed. "As your Majesty commands." He hesitated and then sighed. "There is another matter."

"Go on."

"When the prisons were emptied to create the Hapi corps and the fleet, it had unforeseen repercussions. Without a steady stream of prisoners, the work gangs are severely understrength. We may have gold and stone, Majesty, but without men to work it, the buildings cannot be quickly erected."

"There are always prisoners," Ramesses said.

"Far fewer since the Hapi corps stamped on the bandits, Majesty. Your enlightened rule has reduced crime in the cities."

"Well, you will have to find more workers from somewhere. Offer higher wages. There must be thousands of farm workers eager to earn more copper carrying stones than tending the crops."

"Without crops there is no grain, meat or vegetables. Prices will go up."

"They will be earning higher wages. They won't starve."

"What of the city people, Majesty? They cannot afford higher prices."

Ramesses uttered an exasperated sigh. "It is not forever, Hori. Six months, a year perhaps, and the main work can be done. Then they can go back to their farms and their herds. I scarcely think people will starve in the meantime."

Hori glanced at Panhesy, but the Commander only shrugged as if to say, 'It is not my problem'. The Tjaty bowed again, knowing he would have to do something that would not endanger the Ma'at of the southern kingdom. "Let it be as you say, Majesty."

"Now, I want to see my tomb. I trust that has progressed further than my Mansion."

They mounted their chariots once more and headed away from the river, toward the dry desert valley that housed to rock-cut tombs of the kings and queens. The workmen's village lay in their path--Set Ma'at, The Place of Truth. Women and children, old and injured men gawked at the procession and some sank to their knees as they recognised the figure of the king in the leading chariot. The royal entourage did not stop, but swept past in a cloud of dust, heading deeper into the valley where the able-bodied men of the village toiled to fashion the resting place of their king. Stones clattered beneath hooves and wheels while dry white dust billowed in a choking cloud around them, drifting away like smoke as they drew up beside the only sign of activity in the barren waste.

The overseer of Ta-sekhet-ma'at, a thin man, walked hesitantly out to meet them from an awning spread between two boulders. A chair and small table with scattered papers lay in the shadows behind him as he greeted the Tjaty and Commander. He quickly noted the deference paid to the third man by these two exalted men and dropped to his knees in the dust, wincing as a stone fragment bit into one bony knee.

"Welcome, Son of Re, to the Great Field. I am Remaktef, Overseer of this place. You do us much honour by your presence."

"Get up, Remaktef, and tell me how the work is going. Is my tomb a worthy one?"

"It is progressing well, Son of Re," Remaktef said, rising to his feet. Blood oozed from a cut in his right knee, cutting a thin runnel through the caked dust on his shin. "We have encountered a small problem..." He hurried on as he saw the king frown. "Nothing insurmountable, I assure you, Son of Re."

"What is the nature of the problem?" Tjaty Hori asked. "And why was I not immediately informed?"

"It happened two days ago, Exalted One, and I waited to be sure that a solution could be found."

"You found a solution?" Ramesses asked.

"I did, Son of Re."

"Show me."

Remaktef bowed and turned toward his shaded papers, sorting through them swiftly and holding one up so the line drawing could be easily seen.

"This is a plan of the tomb...the entrance here...corridors...and here is the chamber where..."

Ramesses waved a hand dismissively. "I have no doubt those scribbles mean something to you, but I would rather see what they actually mean. Show me my tomb, Remaktef, and the nature of this problem that you say you have overcome."

"Of course, Son of Re. Forgive my presumption." Remaktef led the way to the opening in the ground and down the short flight of wooden stairs erected in the pit that had been excavated at the tomb entrance. He called to the men within to bring lamps and to kneel in the presence of their king. There was a flurry of activity and several men bowed and handed Remaktef oil lamps and hurried to remove scraps of rubble from the entranceway.

"If you would follow me, Son of Re, I will light the way, and my men can follow with other lamps for the Tjaty and Commander."

Ramesses nodded, and followed the tiny pool of buttery-yellow light cast by the little oil lamp in Remaktef's hand. Behind him, he heard the rasp of sandals on the grit of the floor and the heavy breathing of Hori in the confined space. The air was close and stale, filled with the fumes of burning oil, and sweat.

"Men work in these conditions, Remaktef?"

"Yes, Son of Re. The corridors are carved from the living stone as we descend through this first corridor...then less steeply in the second. There will be niches carved in the walls. You can see where they have been marked out."

Remaktef lifted the lamp so the light showed lines drawn on the smoothly carved rock walls.

"Just down here is the third corridor and where we ran into difficulty."

The Overseer led the king to the far end where a ragged hole yawned in the roughly cut floor of the corridor.

"A hole?" Ramesses leaned over and peered into the darkness. "What is down there?"

"A tomb, Son of Re."

"Whose?"

"The inscriptions on the walls are dedicated to Menmire Setepenre."

"The pretender? Amenmesse, brother of Userkheperure? That's impossible. He was never buried...was he, Panhesy?"

"He was buried somewhere, Majesty, but not in the tomb prepared for him."

"So who is in this one, Remaktef?"

"No one, Son of Re. The tomb is empty, containing only inscriptions relating toward its intended occupant."

Ramesses squatted beside the hole and stared down into the darkness. "The tomb is complete?"

"Yes, Son of Re."

"Have the inscriptions relating to the pretender erased. We can perhaps entomb another royal personage here in the future." He looked up at the Overseer. "In the meantime, what are you going to do about this hole?"

"It will be sealed with bricks and mortar, Son of Re, a simple procedure, but we cannot continue to excavate along this line. If we do so, we will break through into other parts of the tomb."

"I will not countenance a change in the orientation of my tomb," Ramesses said. "It must continue to run south."

"We can do that, Son of Re, but we must first move a few paces to the west." Remaktef moved over to the western wall and patted the rock. "Cut through here, angle slightly westward then again to the south. I had the scribes find the plans of Menmire's tomb, so I can calculate exactly how far west we have to move to avoid breaking through again."

"Not a step more than you have to, Remaktef."

"It shall be as you say, Son of Re."

# Chapter 26
# Year 7 of Usermaatre Ramesses

Usermaatre Ramesses was wise to keep the three women in his life apart, for each strove for power for their children, and if they had been housed together in one common Per-Khemret would no doubt have thoroughly unsettled the ma'at of king and palace. Queen Tyti ruled in Waset, the ancient capital of Ta Shemau, while Queen Iset presided over the northern military city of Per-Ramesses. While not an official queen, the oldest of the women, Tiye, all but reigned over the northern capital, Men-nefer. She had something more valuable than a title; for a title was something either Queen would have given up in an instant to grasp what Tiye possessed. Tiye was mother of the heir and, if she lived long enough, would one day be mother of the next king. Even now, as mother of the heir, she wielded considerable power and influence over the court.

Furthermore, she had sons. Queen Tyti had borne a son named Ramesses after his father, but since then only daughters, while Queen Iset had two sons, only one of which, Amunhirkhopeshef, still survived. Tiye, though, had borne the king's eldest three sons and now had delivered several more, her field being ever fertile whenever the king ploughed her. First she had borne a daughter, but a healthy boisterous child she called Tentopet, and then in quick succession, sons named Mentuhirkhopeshef, Meryatum, and Sethirkhopeshef. The Per-Khemret at Men-nefer rang to the sound of children's laughter, and Tiye herself was often to be found playing with her progeny.

At first, the nurses had looked askance at the king's wife intruding upon their duties, taking it as unfavourable comment on their abilities. Their discontent reached the ears of Tjaty Herwenemef and he, desiring a peaceful palace, made cautious enquiry. He was able to reassure the nurses.

"The king's wife does not hold your abilities in low regard," Herwenemef said. "Rather, it is because she has great love for her children and wishes to be part of their lives."

Tia, the head nurse, had ventured a reply. "Honoured sir, it is natural for a mother to love her children, but is it seemly that she displays it in such a...well...common manner? She is the king's wife, after all. And... I have it on good authority that neither the king's sister-wife in Waset, nor the Syrian wife in Per-ramesses, does such things."

"You would do well to remember that those ladies are Queens, Tia," Herwenemef said reprovingly.

"My apologies, honoured sir. I meant no disrespect."

The Tjaty nodded. "Your point is a good one, though perhaps not in the way you intend. The ladies in question are Queens, and as such stand far above other court ladies, outranking both wives and concubines. I agree that it would not be seemly for a Queen to take such a common interest in a child's upbringing, but for an ordinary wife and mother? I think such actions should be commended."

"But where does that put us?" Tia asked.

"As before, but when the king's wife is present, you will defer to her in all things."

The nurses grumbled but returned to their duties.

The children were too young to be learning much in their games. Sethirkhopeshef was barely walking and was sickly besides, and Meryatum did little else but push around little carved images of animals. Mentuhirkhopeshef had progressed to playing with little carved soldiers and his favourite possession was a little chariot drawn by two wooden horses. Into this he placed a carved archer and spent hours pretending he was the king leading his armies to triumph over the Sea Peoples.

Tentopet, Tiye's eldest surviving daughter was, of course, nowhere near the succession, but if she lived she would have a special fate carved out for her. Daughters of the king could be used to cement alliances with friendly nations, but if there were no suitable princes available, there was only one other possibility. In the same way that Tyti, daughter of Userkhaure-setepenre Setnakhte had married her brother Usermaatre Ramesses, so too would Tentopet marry the heir to the throne.

"You will marry your brother Khaemwaset in ten or twelve years," Tiye told her daughter. "Then when he becomes king, you will be a queen."

Tentopet frowned as she tried to make sense of her mother's words. "Can I have a new dolly?" she asked.

"As Queen you can have anything you want."

"Now?"

"Soon. I will have one made for you."

"Can I have a kitten then?"

Tiye made enquiries and found that three of the palace cats had recently had kittens. She found out where they were and took her daughter to view them. One cat, with newborn infants, hissed and spat at the visitors, while another ran and hid, abandoning its almost grown kittens. The third cat had alert bundles of fluff at her feet and purred when Tentopet put out her hand to stroke her. She selected a kitten that took her fancy--brown and grey with a single white paw--and clasped it to her breast. Soon, her dolls were forgotten as the princess played in the palace rooms with her kitten.

Tiye played with her boys in the palace gardens. They were too young to wield even wooden swords or toy bows, but they were fascinated by the menagerie and the ornamental ponds in the palace gardens. The menagerie was but a shadow of its former self in the days of Nebmaetre Amenhotep. In those days, the night air had reverberated with the roar of lions, the howling of desert wolves and the screech of owls, while monkeys chattered in the daylight, baboons lifted their arms to greet the rising sun, and songbirds whistled and warbled in the flowering trees.

Now cages stood empty, pits lay overgrown, and the animals that still existed scarcely raised a voice save at feeding time. A few monkeys still chattered and romped, begging passers-by for scraps of food, and small herds of gazelle, antelope, and striped horses wandered their earthen-floored enclosures disconsolately flicking tails at the ever-present flies. The flowering trees were untidy, and most of the songbirds had fled, but there was still a lot to interest undiscerning children.

Tiye would take a loaf of bread from the kitchen, or a basket of fruit, and her children would feed the monkeys, squealing with excitement or terror as food was snatched from their hands. Afterward, they would wander across the grass toward the ornamental ponds, as often as not pursued by flocks of ducks eager for the last crumbs of bread. Here, in the heavy shade by the water's edge, Tiye would open another basket and take out food for her own flock--milk and honey cakes, sweet figs and dates. The children would eat and then run and play beside the pools, almost more interested in the tiny creatures contained therein rather than the beasts in the faded menagerie.

The pools had started as pristine vessels of pure river water with artfully arranged pots of water lilies and small schools of silver-scaled fish. Over time, and under through neglect, the water had grown murkier, the edges of the ponds had dissolved into mud into which reeds had spread, and the lilies had outgrown their containers. Fish multiplied and frogs bred in the mud and reeds, herons stalked the far sides of the pools, and the whole thing became a place of wonder for small children.

Three or four children were too many for Tiye to control, so the nurses would be brought in once more to walk with each child, to cater to his or her whims, and to offer protection should the need arise. Most of these measures were minor.

"Tentopet, darling, stay clear of the reed beds...come back to me...oh, now look what you've done. You've spoilt your nice dress."

"Don't eat the mud, Sethir...no, no, no...ahh...let me wipe your mouth. Yes, spit out that nasty mud."

"That's a frog, Mentu. Yes, I suppose you could keep one as a pet, but I really think it would be much happier in the pond."

"Those are fish, Mery, and they live in the water. No, you can't go in after them. Oh, oh, quickly, Mery's fallen in."

Some protective measures were of a more serious nature. It had not been very many years since a royal child had died from snake bite in these same palace grounds, but the passage of time had lulled the anxieties of the palace inhabitants. Snakes, and particularly the hooded royal serpent of the goddess Wadjet, frequented marshy places and were partial to a plump frog, so the nurses maintained a watchful eye over their charges.

Every few days, men would be sent into the reed beds bordering the ornamental ponds with long sticks and wicker baskets. Their job was to flush out and capture any snakes that might have sought refuge there, then release them in the reeds outside the city. A simpler solution might have been to kill the snakes, but as the Wadjet serpent was the symbol of the gods' protection of the king, that was not considered appropriate.

Other times, the children would be taken to the markets within the city of Men-nefer, but Tiye did not often accompany her children there. She disliked the heat and dust and stink of the lower city, the bustling crowds, the staring eyes, and the ever-present swarms of flies attracted to the meat and fish on sale and the dung of domestic beasts that often littered the streets on market days. The children loved the noise and the colour though, and the older ones pestered their nurses to be taken. Soldiers were detailed to accompany the royal children, not because there was any real danger of harm being done to them, as Kemetu love children, but because a guard was a way of honouring them.

So soldiers from the palace guard accompanied every expedition into the city, made up of a small squad of men armed with staffs and a junior officer. This duty was a tiresome one, so it usually fell to the most junior officer, Ahtep, who happened to be a young man from the southern city of Waset. Ahtep was handsome, with dark features and a manly body, and one of the nurses, Neferbet, had fallen in love with him. Neferbet happened to be the nurse who looked after Princess Tentopet, so the young girl was often in the presence of these two lovers. Kemetu children are aware, from an early age, of what transpires between a man and a woman, so Tentopet was not shocked by what she saw, but rather exhibited a high degree of curiosity.

"Come child," Neferbet said to Tentopet. "We are going down to the market again. You like that, don't you?"

"'S'pose. Is 'Tep going?"

"I think so," Neferbet said with a smile. "Do you like him?"

Tentopet nodded. "Are you going to let him do that thing again, Nef?"

Neferbet was bustling around, gathering up the things she would need for their trip to the market. "What's that?" she asked.

"You know. Cuddle him 'gainst the wall. Lift your skirts...move funny."

"Uh...I thought you were watching the jugglers."

"Was, but I seen you." Tentopet cocked her head to one side and regarded her nurse solemnly. "Is you going to have a baby?"

"What? No, of course not."

"Tiah says that's how you make babies."

"Tiah should mind her own business," Neferbet said sharply.

"Are you going to marry him?"

"I... I'm not sure I'll be allowed. Nurses aren't supposed to."

"I think you should. Then you could have a baby." Tentopet frowned. "I want a baby, but mama says I'm going to marry Khaemwas' but he's old. I want to marry someone from Waset."

"It will be many years before you're ready to marry, child, but why someone from Waset?"

"'Cos 'Tep's from Waset. I want someone like him. He's nice, but my brothers are...are icky."

"I think he's nice too, but you mustn't tell anyone about him and me. You wouldn't want me to get into trouble, would you?"

Tentopet shook her head.

"It'll be our secret?" Neferbet asked.

Tentopet nodded.

# Chapter 27
# Year 7 of Usermaatre Ramesses

The women of the Waset Per-Khemret assembled to honour their lord and master when he returned from the Great Field. Despite this, the king kept them waiting as he was hot and dusty after inspecting his tomb and he had no thought in his head apart from refreshment. He stripped off and stood in the stone bath while servants poured cool river water over him, before patting his body dry with clean linen. A clean kilt and headdress, suitable jewellery in the form of golden armbands and rings, previously unworn sandals on his feet, all served to make him feel clean and presentable once more. Cosmetics followed, though as his visit to the Per-Khemret would be an informal occasion, the application of kohl and unguents was cursory, serving only to cover up the worst ravages of time on a middle-aged face.

Ramesses also summoned Pabekkamen, the Superintendent of the Royal Women to him and enquired after the health of the women in his charge. Pabekkamen, expecting his summons, produced a list detailing the status of every wife and concubine, especially as to her time of month and whether her hesmen flowed. He smiled when he heard of Queen Tyti's status.

Food and drink was served to the king in private. He ate on a shaded veranda, a light meal of fruit and honeyed cakes, washed down with cool river water. As he ate, he listened to Tjaty Hori recount the business of Ta Shemau. The Tjaty had washed the worst of the dust and sweat from his face and limbs, and accepted a cup of water to ease his throat as he talked about equally dry affairs of state.

In the absence of the king, the Tjaty was the highest authority and spoke in the king's name. He presided over the law courts daily and dispensed the king's justice to any who sought it. Nothing of any import had happened since the king left the southern kingdom, but he still had to be apprised of the tenor of the public mind. Grumblings, if left unattended, could flare into discontent and open rebellion, and it was the duty of the Tjaty and the local army garrison to keep the peace.

Hori was in full flow, reporting on a bad harvest that had partially drained the city granaries, when Ramesses winced and frowned. He stopped, concerned that the king was displeased with his report.

"There was no recourse but to release grain, Majesty. A lack of bread among the populace could lead to rioting and..."

Ramesses waved one hand dismissively, and spat into his other. He teased the bolus apart and picked out a fragment of tooth.

Hori leaned closer to examine the offending piece. "Stone fragments in the bread, Majesty? I am surprised. I though the bakers supplying bread for the palace took more care with their grinding."

"It wasn't the bread." Ramesses slipped the tip of his tongue into what seemed like a huge cavity in one of his back teeth. "There was no grit in anything I was eating. It just came out."

"Shall I send for the palace physician?"

"What can he do? No, it is not hurting me..." Ramesses bit into a honey cake and chewed tentatively. "There, it's... ahh..." He spat the food out and rinsed his mouth with water, swallowing. "The pain is easing, but perhaps I will eat no more. You were talking about grain riots, Hori?"

"No, Majesty, we avoided riots by releasing grain from the city granaries."

Ramesses nodded. "That was the correct response." He wiped his mouth with a linen cloth and stood. "We'll talk more later, Hori, but now I must visit the Per-Khemret. They will be expecting me."

"Of course, Majesty."

"You only have the one wife, don't you, Hori?"

"Yes, Majesty. I am not the Bull of Heru that can plough many fields."

Ramesses smiled. "You are, perhaps, fortunate in that. It is pleasurable to have many women available to meet my needs, but they can be tiresome. I think that is why we kings wage so many wars. It gives us an excuse to leave the confines of the palace." He stood looking pensive for a few moments. "Well, I suppose I'd better see what they all want. Jewels and new dresses, I suppose."

It was not what the women of the Per-Khemret wanted, though to be fair, several of them would not have refused such offerings. The king's mother, Queen Tiy-Merenese ruled the Per-Khemret with a firm hand, and after allowing the lesser women (a few wives and concubines) to fuss over her son, she clapped her hands and dismissed them all, with the exception of the king's sister-wife Tyti.

When they were alone, Tiy-Merenese dipped her head courteously. "Welcome, my son. May the gods always smile upon you."

"Thank you, mother. And you, Tyti? Have you no special welcome for me?"

The young woman inclined her head. "Of course, brother. I..." She saw the flash of annoyance in the king's eyes and remembered his earlier admonitions. "Of course, my lord," she corrected herself. "My heart is filled with gladness that you find the time to visit me and our son."

"He is well? Bring him to me."

Tyti called for a servant and told her to bring Prince Ramesses at once. As the servant left, she asked if the king would take some refreshment while they waited. "Some river-cooled wine perhaps?"

Ramesses sipped and uttered a cry of pain as the cold liquid sent a spike of pain into his jaw. Wine dribbled down his chin and he grabbed a cloth to wipe it away.

"What is it?" asked Tiy-Merenese. "Are you in pain?"

"My tooth. A piece broke off with my food earlier and for some reason it hurts more than previously." His tongue probed the hole and he grimaced.

"One of the women in the Per-Khemret suffers from toothache, my lord," Tyti said. "It happens to us all from time to time, but Timat is always in pain, so much so that the palace physician has to continually give her poppy."

"I can stand a bit of pain."

"Of course, my lord. You are a man and used to pain, unlike us women." Tyti glanced at her mother and Tiy-Merenese hid a smile behind her hand. Ramesses frowned, but said nothing.

"Timat is very fond of sweet things," the king's mother mused. "I wonder if that has something to do with her affliction."

"I cannot imagine why," Ramesses said. "Honey is used to preserve fruits, after all. If it was responsible for hurting teeth, it would rot the fruit instead of preserving them."

"Words of wisdom indeed, my lord," Tyti murmured.

A nurse entered the room with a five-year-old boy in tow. The little prince wore a plain white kilt though of high quality and his side lock had been oiled and ornamented with gold braid.

"Here is our son," Tyti said. "Greet your father the king, Prince Ramesses."

The little boy dragged his hand from his nurse's and stepped forward boldly. "Greetings, Son of Re. Life, Health..." he hesitated a moment and glanced toward his mother. "...and... and Posperity."

Ramesses stared at his son, his eyebrows raised in surprise. "Greetings to you too, my son. Who taught you to say that?"

"Mother. Was...was it not right?"

"It was very right. Come and embrace your father, child."

"Mother says I am no longer a child, but a prince."

"That is right too," Ramesses said with a smile. "Now come and embrace your father, Prince Ramesses."

The boy looked to his mother again, and when she nodded, walked up to the king and held out his arms. Ramesses picked him up and held him in the crook of one arm.

"He is a big boy, solid and well-muscled. Healthy too."

"He takes after his father," Tiy-Merenese said. "You were the same at his age."

"What games do you like to play?" the king asked.

The boy thought for a few moments. "Usernakhte made me a bow an'...an' a sword. I fight enemies."

"Usernakhte?"

"Captain of the palace guard, my lord," Tyti said. "The Prince readies himself for command."

"When I am king, I will kill all Kemet's enemies," the boy said.

Ramesses frowned, then stooped and set the boy on the floor. "You have not explained to him his place among the princes?"

"He is only five, my son," Tiy-Merenese said.

"If he is old enough to have the idea he will be king one day, he is old enough to know he is not my heir. Khaemwaset is Crown Prince. It does no good to fill his head full of vain hopes."

"Khaemwaset is too priestly to be a king," Tyti said. "And besides, you named him that so he would be a Sem-Priest of Ptah in the manner of the Great Usermaatre's son. Remember? My lord?"

"I have not forgotten...nor that Amunhirkhopeshef was taken from me. Khaemwaset is now my eldest son. He is Crown Prince."

"For now."

Ramesses stared at his sister-wife. "You dare wish ill on my son Khaemwaset?"

Tyti bit back her words, and lowered her head. "Never, my lord. You misunderstood my intention..."

"What my daughter meant to say, my son, was that the fate of all of us is with the gods. You are a young man still and your sons will be old men by the time you ascend to Re. Who can say which of your sons will survive that long? Look at the Great Usermaatre..."

"I am aware of what happened in those days, mother. I will accept that you misspoke, Tyti, but you need to instruct your son as to his proper station. He is more likely to be a priest than a king."

"You are still determined to make one of Tiye's sons the next king?"

"My eldest sons were born to Tiye," Ramesses said quietly. "That gives them certain rights."

"I want to be king," the boy piped up.

Ramesses squatted and took the boy by the shoulders, looking into his eyes. "I am sure you do, little prince, but I am the king and I decide who will succeed me. You have older brothers who will most likely sit on the throne of Kemet."

"But I want to."

"That is with the gods. When you are older, you will understand. Now, go with your nurse, learn your lessons well, practice with your toy weapons and become the best you can possibly be. That is all any of us can do."

Ramesses pulled his son close and kissed him, before beckoning to the nurse. He remained squatting until the door closed behind them, and then rose to face his sister-wife, the muscles of his jaw tight.

"Never do that to me again, Tyti. I decide the fate of my children, not you. Our son will grow up to be a soldier perhaps, or a priest, or an administrator of a sepat or province, but he is far removed from the succession."

"I am your sister as well as your wife," Tyti snapped. "And Queen. I am as royal as you, brother, and our son is thus doubly royal, unlike those sons of your common wife Tiye."

"Enough. You forget yourself, sister."

"My son, listen to your sister," Tiy-Merenese begged. "All she desires is that quality should be recognised. You are king; you can put aside any Prince and raise another up in his stead."

Ramesses turned to his mother with nostrils flared and visibly fought to control himself. "Mother, I love you and honour you, but do not seek to rule the kingdoms through me. I am King of Kemet, not you. My word is law, not yours. I will hear no more on this, upon pain of my displeasure. Is that understood?"

Tiy-Merenese sighed. "I only seek what is best for you my son...but yes, I understand."

"And you, Tyti."

"Yes, my lord."

"Good, then that is settled. Now, let us put all that behind us and turn to more pleasant matters. I have brought finely woven cloth and an array of jewellery and cosmetics to Waset with me. The chests containing these items will be delivered to your apartments, mother, for you to distribute among the women as you see fit. Tyti, I have had a beautiful golden bracelet made for you, a necklace of silver, turquoise and faience, and an onyx ring. It would please me to see you wearing these."

Tyti bowed stiffly. "Let it be as it pleases my lord to so order."

"It is not an order, Tyti, but it always pleases me to see you beautiful." Ramesses stepped forward and took Tyti's hands in his own. "You are looking most beautiful right now, and it would please me greatly to take you to bed. I have a desire to plough your field vigorously and who knows...maybe even sow another son for you."

"Another son for the king to neglect?"

"Do not sour this day, Tyti. Now come, let us seek pleasure together."

"I cannot, my lord. I am indisposed."

"What? That is nonsense. I particularly enquired of Pabekkamen as to your hesmen. He assured me it was not your time of month."

"Then he is wrong, my lord. I am unable to submit myself to you."

Ramesses glared at Tyti, and then at his mother. "Is this so, mother?"

Tiy-Merenese cast a troubled glance at her daughter. "I have no reason to doubt her word, my son. You must seek your pleasures elsewhere."

"Then I shall do so. There are many women in the Per-Khemret who will be only too delighted to spread their legs for their king and master."

"I am sure of it, my lord," Tyti said, anger blazing in her eyes. "Please do not think you have to stay and entertain us if you are overcome by lust."

"By the gods, you go too far, sister-wife." Ramesses kissed his mother but ignored Tyti, stalking from the room.

"Was that wise?" Tiy-Merenese asked.

Tyti shrugged. "Maybe, not, but it felt good."

"Are you really in hesmen?"

"No." Tyti stamped her foot. "He insulted me, mother, by preferring that common-born wife and her sons over my son. How could I open myself to him when I was bursting with anger? Let him find his pleasures elsewhere."

Tiy-Merenese sighed. "Ahh, daughter, you are too headstrong. Everything depends on the king's goodwill and you insist on making him angry. You can be sure that Tiye is sweet and willing in all her relationships with the king, so that when she asks something of him, he is likely to grant it."

"You heard him though. He prefers Tiye's sons to my own, despite the fact I am Queen and she is not."

"For now. They are youths while your son is but a child. Let Prince Ramesses grow a while, let him prove himself capable, and the king will see sense. Besides, anything may happen in the intervening years."

"What do you mean, mother?"

"Only that he once had four older brothers and now has three. I love my grandchildren--all of them, and I wish no harm to come to any of them, but who can know the will of the gods? Already Khaemwaset is interested in the priesthood, and Prehirwenemef and Meryamun show an eagerness to continue in the corps. Maybe little Ramesses will show an aptitude for governing men."

Tyti considered her mother's words and nodded slowly. "Perhaps you are right, and I have been foolish to anger the king." She looked toward the door. "But what of the anger he has raised in me? Must I forever bend my will to his?"

"He is the king. Leave him for now, daughter. Let him vent his anger on the body of a compliant concubine and come to him tomorrow or the day after, showing yourself penitent and loving. Let him plant another son in your belly, so when he returns to the north he will think of you fondly."

"I am not sure I can forgive him that easily." Tyti sighed. "It is hard to be a woman when men like my brother rule."

Tiy-Merenese smiled. "As long as men like your brother rule, a woman will always be able to get what she desires. Give him what he wants and he will give you what you want...whether he knows it or not."

# Chapter 28
# Year 7 of Usermaatre Ramesses

Ament knew the Land of Sin was as likely to kill him as the king's men, but he thought that if he could back-track the route he had taken with the Shechem tribesman Zephan, he might stand a chance. However, the only way he would be able to do that was to find the little unnamed village near where they had emerged from the stony desert. That had been somewhere south of the city of Iunu, and a day toward the east, on the border of the scrubland that fringed the desert. The village had had a well to supply water, the only reason for its existence so far from the river. That might make it hard to find, but to stay in the well-watered lands of Ta Mehu was to invite certain death at the hands of his fellow soldiers.

He left the river lands as soon as he could and spent days alone in the scrubland, looking for landmarks he might recognise. The village had changed little in the intervening years, though he recognised nobody when he made his cautious way into it; nor did anyone recognise him. A day later he left, making camp on the edge of the wilderness, where he cleared a patch of sand and sat and stared at it for a while, remembering. The journey from the Timna Valley across the Land of Sin to where he sat now had been long and hard, though there had not been any wells, there had been water seeps along the way to sustain life. Ament's problem was that he was a fisherman, used to the ways of the river and lake rather than a desert dweller at home among the parched sands. Unless he could find water at regular intervals, he would die a rather unpleasant death. He stood and stared into the east where the sun's heat rippled the air and made visions of water appear in the dry sands. His spirit quailed at the prospect of setting out blindly into that terrible place and he wondered whether he should risk the Way of Heru, and try to evade the troops searching for him.

"You'd never make it," he murmured to himself. "Now think."

Ament studied the patch of sand in front of him, racking his memory for the direction and distance of the nearest water source. The information eluded him.

"Think, Ament. Your life depends on it."

He sat and thought, remembering the rocky hills with the water seeping to the base where green things grew; where they had rested for a day before setting off for a well, and then the Shechem camp.

"North two days to a well...and then northwest another two..."

Ament reached out to place a rock to mark the spot on the cleared patch of sand and then stopped. He shook his head ruefully as a thought occurred to him.

"No wonder I cannot remember. I never travelled eastward in the Sin, only westward, coming out of it toward the Great River."

He moved around the sand patch until he faced the west, grinned, and flipped the rock he held in his hand onto the ground.

"There is the hill with the water soak..." He picked up another rock and placed it a short distance away to the north. "And here is the well; though it was scarcely more than a rock depression. That means the Shechem are about..." He measured out another distance to the northwest, "...here."

Ament frowned as he contemplated the large stretch of cleared sand between the Shechem camp and the cultivated lands of Kemet. He picked up a handful of pebbles and moved across to where the last rock sat.

"Southwest, a pace." He put a pebble down. "West, two paces, northwest three, a little bit north of northwest again, another three..." Ament continued to place pebbles until he had an uneven string of stones crossing the wide expanse of sand.

"No water seep is more than four day's travel from another, so I must carry sufficient water to last that long, at least. Provided I have it right." He grimaced. "If I am slightly off in direction or distance, I will die of thirst. The question is, do I dare risk it?"

"On the other hand, do I dare not? It is certain death for me if I am caught."

Ament thought about his planned route into the Wilderness of Sin, and made a few small adjustments to the pebbles marking his fate. At length, he stretched and turned back to the unnamed village to buy such supplies as the villagers could spare. He had copper with him, and if he died in the desert it would serve no one, so he spent it all. Water was the main consideration, so he bought several goatskin flasks--badly cured but better than nothing. No doubt the water would taste foul after days brewing in the skins, but foul water was better than no water. Food followed--a small bag of grain, some onions and a loaf of stale bread. He owned a knife already, so used the last of his copper buying a strong staff and a scrap of used papyrus and a charcoal stick from the person who came closest to being a scribe in the village.

"Do you want me to write something for you?" the scribe asked. "I know temple script and the common script."

"Thank you, but no. I will write what I need."

Ament would dearly love to have bought a donkey for the journey. A donkey would have carried all his food and water and, when its strength gave out, would have provided extra food, but he had no copper to spare and besides, the villagers owned no donkeys. So he filled the goatskins at the well and slung them around his shoulders, picked up his staff and sack of food, and left, walking resolutely into the scrubland.

Back at his starting point, he took the scrap of papyrus and charcoal stick, and carefully drew a map of the presumed distances and bearings of the water soaks he remembered, adding in other features he thought were present, like a low range of hills, stony and sandy desert, and one place where a chasm in the rock had forced them a day out of their way. The sun was low in the west when he finished, his shadow thrown almost over the whole of the sandy patch in front of him. He took that for a good omen, that Re had taken his likeness to his destination before he even started.

The heat was leaching from the day as he set off into the Land of Sin, his eyes fixed on a point on the horizon in the direction where he thought the first water seep lay. By his reckoning, if he walked by night and rested by day, he should be there by the time the sun rose the second time. Twilight came, deepening to night, and the first stars appeared on the overarching body of the goddess Nut. Ament held his course by the stars now, correcting his direction every now and then as the stars wheeled across the heavens. If he could have seen behind him, he would have seen his footsteps also taking a curved path across the desert, but he was spared this worrisome detail. Instead, he trudged onward, drinking sparingly the still-sweet well water.

He picked up the pace as the sun spilled light across the eastern horizon, wanting to make as much ground as possible before it got too hot to walk. At the same time he looked for a place that would afford him some shelter from the fierce midday sun, and found it just when he was starting to worry. A dry water course lay slightly to the north and in one place a flash flood had scoured out one bank, leaving a slight overhang that cast a sliver of shade. The sand beneath it was hot, dry and dusty, but it was slightly cooler than outside in the full sun. He poked around with his staff until he was certain there were no snakes or scorpions sheltering there, and then sat down with a groan of relief. Despite the heat he fell asleep quickly.

He awoke to find himself lying in the full sun, his skin dry and caked with dust where it had blown and stuck to the sweat-sheen on his exposed body. Ament groaned and tried to sit up, but his head pounded as if a mason was carving something into his skull. Rolling onto his belly, he managed to struggle onto all fours and shuffle into a tiny scrap of shade near a rock. With shaking hands he fumbled the stopper from a goatskin flask and gulped water. A moment later he choked and spat the water out, feeling as though he had drunk boiling water. The flask had lain in the sun for half a day and was uncomfortably hot. He sipped cautiously, regretting the action that had made him waste a precious mouthful. Lying back against the hot rock, he closed his eyes and tried to will away the headache that made his vision blur.

"Not used to the sun, are you?" he whispered. "Not like this in Kinnereth or on the river."

Ament drank again, draining that goatskin and starting another. The water seemed to soak into his body leaving his mouth as dry as ever, and he was tempted to drink more. He eyed the remaining skins glumly.

"Two and a bit gone, nearly four remaining. You'll need more before the day is over, so you'd better pray to all the gods you find that water seep tomorrow... and that there's water there."

He drank the rest of the third skin by the time the sun set and the temperature started to drop. His headache had receded to a mild throb and he contemplated the food he carried, but he felt thirsty still and the thought of dry bread revolted him. As soon as night fell and blessed coolness washed over him, he staggered to his feet and set off again to where he prayed the seep lay. An hour or two later, he remembered that he had departed from his previous course to utilise the shade in the dry stream bed and cursed.

"You're a fool, Ament. Which direction did you go when you sought the shade? Was it left or right? How far?"

He stopped and looked around, and then shrugged. "I doubt I'm keeping a straight course anyway and I really can't be certain the seep is there."

Ament set off again, drinking from the fourth skin, and chewing on an onion. The stars wheeled overhead, the ones that heralded the advent of the barque of Re appearing in the east. First light paled the horizon and Ament shivered, though not from the chill air.

"The second day and let's face it, you have no idea where you are."

He looked back the way he had come and shook the water skins he had left.

"It took you four skins to come this far and you only have two left. You just might make it back to the river if you turn around now and drink sparingly, or you can stay out here looking for water. If you don't find it, you're dead."

Ament sighed and looked around in the gathering light for the highest point in the landscape. Nothing looked familiar, but if water lay nearby, it was just possible there might be vegetation with it, and he would see further from an elevated position. He started toward a low hill before he even realised he had made his decision to stay and risk death.

The hill was higher than he thought and by the time he had dragged himself to the summit, the sun was high in the sky. Pools of shade lay between the jumbled rocks at the top and he sank gratefully into one without even bothering to check it for snakes or scorpions. He sipped water and started to scan the terrain below him for any sign of greenery or anything that might indicate the presence of water. There was nothing visible and his heart sank with the level of water in his fifth skin as he worked his way around the hill. Darkness fell at last and Ament curled up in a hollow facing the northeast and stared into the night.

"I might last tomorrow and tomorrow night, but the next day will kill me." Ament shook the last water skin and estimated it was only half full. "Even if I knew in which direction to walk, I couldn't reach the horizon before my water gave out. I am dead and I will never see my beloved Tausret again. Jerem and Ephrim are grown men and will make their way in the world, but what of little Adara? Zeben and my sister will look after them though...provided they reached Kinnereth safely."

Ament prayed to the gods of Kemet and even sketched a hesitant one to the 'El', the faceless god of the Khabiru, before falling into an uneasy sleep. His rest was disturbed by dreams of the red god Set coming for him with flaming eyes and he started awake with a cry, shrinking back against the rock with a whimper as the eyes followed him out of the dream. He stared out into the night and saw that the flaming eyes were really just one, and not even an eye, just a tiny point of orange light flickering in the distance. Despite the blackness of the desert, he could make out the horizon by the faint wash of starlight that suffused the night sky with a lesser intensity. For a long time he stared, trying to make sense of what he saw, and then he grinned.

"It's a camp fire--in the line of that spire of rock on the horizon. There's somebody else out here... somebody with water, or who knows where the seep lies."

Fixing the direction in his mind, relative to the stars, he climbed down from the hill and started picking his way through the stony desert in the direction of the fire. He lost sight of it quickly once he descended, but he was confident of the direction as he eagerly picked his way toward it. A twelfth part of the night passed...and another...and his confidence faltered. He considered calling out but decided against it.

"You don't know who they are. What if they are the king's men?"

Usermaatre Ramesses had already launched a great manhunt for the fugitive general and former Queen of Kemet, back in the days when his father had taken the throne by force. Ament did not doubt that his hate remained strong, and would spare no effort to capture or kill him.

"Still, what can I do? I can die of thirst alone in the desert, or I can risk contact with these travellers. Who knows, maybe they are Shechem?"

Ament checked his bearings against the slow drift of the stars, and tried to recall whether he had seen any landmarks near the orange flicker of flame. He remembered the spire of rock beyond the flame and looked for it against the lightening sky.

"There...by all the gods of Kemet and Khabiru...so close I might have tripped over them."

As if to mock him, he heard the braying call of a donkey echoing among the rocks, and then the sound of several as they raised their complaint about the chill pre-dawn. He made his way toward the sound, scrambling over the rocks. Now that he was so close, he became anxious that they might leave before he found them. Caution dissipated as the light of the new day grew, and rocks clattered beneath his feet. He stumbled out into a patch of sand and stopped. A robed man stood facing him with a curved sword in his hand.

The air gusted from Ament's lungs in relief that the stranger was not dressed in the garb of Kemet and he started to smile...until a noise behind him alerted him to the fact that the man was not alone. He glanced around, then returned his attention to the man in front of him. The second man said something unintelligible, bringing a short response from the first man.

"You speak Kemetu?" Ament asked. "Or Shechem?"

"Shechem?" The first man spat to one side. "You Shechem?" he asked in the dialect of the Sin tribesmen.

Ament remembered only a little of the Shechem tongue, but thought he knew enough to make his needs known. "I Kemetu, friend of Shechem. You know Jochim?" He named the chief of the tribe he had met years before, but the men gave no sign they recognised the name. "Zephan?" he tried, and saw the glimmer of recognition in the first man's eyes.

First Man grinned and slashed his sword back and forth. "Shechem dog, you die," he said and stepped forward, the blade swinging round.

Ament stepped back but heard the crunch of gravel as Second Man came up behind him. He leapt to one side, stumbled and fell, rolling over and springing to his feet, his hand dragging his short dagger from his belt. Second man was armed with a cudgel and the heavy wood thumped into the sand not far from Ament's leg. He stabbed out with his dagger, making the man pull back, but then First Man was upon him, the longer length of his bronze sword forcing Ament to retreat.

Cudgel advanced again, grinning toothlessly, but Ament paid him less heed than the man with the sword. First Man looked as if he had some familiarity with weapons, making him the more dangerous opponent, but Ament did not dismiss Second Man. A cudgel had no blade, but a blow from it could easily break bones and then the fight would be over.

The rising sun peeked over the horizon, and Ament ducked as First Man slashed at him, and then dodged the swing of the cudgel, edging around the clearing in an attempt to get the sun at his back. First Man saw what he was doing and tried to counter it by cutting Ament off. The movement separated the two men. Ament immediately leaped forward, his dagger stabbing at First Man so viciously, the man fell back a few paces. Second Man ran forward, swinging his cudgel. Ament heard the hiss of air, turned and threw himself toward Second Man so the club passed over his shoulder. His dagger swept round and slashed deep into Second Man's chest, and as the man staggered, rammed it home between the man's ribs.

Second Man reeled back with a cry of agony, wresting the dagger from Ament's grasp as the blade caught on bone. First Man shouted in anger and advanced swiftly, slashing with his sword. Ament was unarmed and knew he could not hope to long evade the sharp bronze, so ducked and weaved, and as the man extended himself, rushed in under the blade and grappled with the man. The two of them swayed to and fro, First Man trying to bring his sword blade round, and Ament grasping his right wrist with one hand and hit the man's body with his other fist.

First Man tangled his leg between Ament's and the two of them fell to the ground, but here the sword became an encumbrance, and all the tribesman could do was to pummel Ament's back with its base, while Ament freed up one hand to grasp at his opponent's throat. Neither man was particularly successful, but Ament could feel his age working against him. The tribesman was younger and more rested, and Ament felt the strength slowly drain from him. He had to end it quickly, but could not think of any action that might help.

Then the dying flurry of Second Man altered things. As Ament and First Man rolled across the sand, they bumped into Second Man who, groaning his last, flung out a hand and gripped the ankle nearest him in a death grip. It was the ankle of First Man, and the shock of this sudden unexpected assault, loosened his grip on Ament. Ament rolled free and, before First Man could raise his sword, Ament's hand found a jagged rock, raised it high, and brought it down on his opponent's head with as much force as he could muster. First Man grunted and lifted a hand to ward off Ament, but the rock descended again and again, battering through the man's defences and splintering his skull.

Ament lay on the dead body of First Man until the heat of the sun made him uncomfortable, and then rolled off with a groan. He prised the sword from the dead man's grip and pulled his dagger from between his companion's ribs before staggering into the shade of some large boulders and collapsing from exhaustion. As he lay there, he picked up the stink of animal dung and heard a faint chirrup.

"Their donkeys," he muttered. "And the water seep must be here. That was a bird I heard, I'd swear."

# Chapter 29
# Year 7 of Usermaatre Ramesses

Ramesses stayed in Waset longer than he had intended, spending his nights in dalliance with the lesser women of the Per-Khemret and his days attending to the building work on his Mansion of Millions of Years and its associated palace. Queen Tyti kept to herself not just for the next day or the day after, but for many days, even long after her supposed time of the hesmen had passed, still angry at the king's remarks and his subsequent behaviour. Her mother, Queen Tiy-Merenese, tried to reason with her, telling her that the king could do as he liked and that the only person she was hurting by her obstinate pride was herself.

"Do not alienate the king's affections, daughter. Smile for him, invite him to your bed, and he will soften his heart toward you."

"He holds that bitch Tiye in higher regard than he does his sister-wife by favouring her sons over mine. I cannot forgive that."

"Then she has won," Tiy-Merenese said.

Tyti stamped her foot, but her mother just smiled.

The next day, Tyti took especial care with her perfumes and selection of clothing, before sending a message to the king requesting a private audience. The reply was slow in coming, and Tyti ground her teeth in frustration. She refused to give any outward sign of her anger though, and sat meekly in the antechamber of the audience hall, awaiting the king's pleasure. When the summons came, she stood and entered the hall, kneeling before Ramesses.

"Thank you for seeing me, my lord."

Ramesses nodded, and examined his fingernails. "What concerns you, Tyti?"

"My lord, my heart breaks within me at the thought that you have turned your face from me."

"How have I turned from you, Tyti?"

"My lord, you spend time with the common women of the Per-Khemret and forsake your sister-wife who loves you."

"You think my other women do not love me?"

"I am sure they do, my lord, for how could any woman not love the Son of Re? But I love you more than any of your other women...here or throughout the kingdoms. Yet you do not spend your nights with me; the Bull of Heru does not take me to his bed."

"I seem to remember inviting you, but you turned me down."

"My hesmen..."

"We both know that was not the reason."

"My lord, I..."

"And now?"

Tyti held out her arms in supplication, though she kept her eyes downcast for fear her husband would see the fury in them. "I desire the Bull of Heru to plough my fertile field and give me another son."

"Willingly, but there is something I must know first."

"What?"

"I would know the real reason you denied your lord and master."

Tyti lowered her arms and took several deep breaths, composing herself before she lifted her head and looked up at her husband. "I was overcome with pride at the promise our young son Ramesses shows, and angered that you still refuse to make him your heir. My lord, I see now that I was at fault and beg your forgiveness."

"Did I not tell you that the elder sons of Tiye take precedence?"

"You did, my lord, and I blocked my ears to your words of wisdom."

Ramesses' eyebrows lifted and his lips twitched in surprise. "And did I not also say that Prince Ramesses is far too young for the responsibilities you would heap upon his shoulders?"

"As you say, my lord. I have since considered your words and found them good. I have also considered my actions and found them wanting, so I humbly ask forgiveness."

"You are forgiven, sister-wife. Rise and embrace me."

Tyti rose to her feet gracefully and moved into the king's embrace. After a suitable time of closeness, she drew back and asked, "May I visit my lord's bed tonight?"

Ramesses nodded his assent, and Tyti bowed and withdrew from the king's presence, but her movements and carriage once she was out of sight spoke of anger rather than love. She held her tongue until she was in the privacy of her own suite in the Per-Khemret, but then could contain herself no longer.

"You still deny me, brother, but I will win; you'll see. My son will sit on the throne after you, not one of Tiye's brood."

Ramesses forsook the lesser women of the Per-Khemret and took Tyti to his chamber now instead, but after a few days he found the presence of his sister-wife constricting, and announced that he would journey throughout Ta Shemau and visit the temples and shrines of the southern kingdom, seeking to make sure they were pleasing to the gods.

"You do not have to do this in person, Son of Re," Tjaty Hori said. "Send commands out to the Governors of the sepats and Mayors of the cities, and all will be accomplished."

"Do you think I don't know this, Hori? I want to go. I want to breathe the clean air of the river and the desert, I want to worship in the temples of the Ta Shemau, and sleep alone on a rush mat on the Royal Barge. I want to see the people of my kingdoms, to listen to their petitions, and to do what is right in the eyes of the common man."

Hori bowed to the inevitable and went off to arrange matters.

The next day, the city turned out to watch the king embark on the Royal Barge. With him went an honour guard of the Mut corps under the command of an officer picked by Panhesy, a nephew of his, Sanakht. One of the young priests of Amun went too, ostensibly to visit one of the temples of his god, but Ramesses suspected there was more to it than simple economy. He summoned Hori before they cast off and asked him direct.

"Why have you sent this priest with me?"

"They asked it of me, Majesty, and I hoped it would not inconvenience you. It is my understanding that he has business in Behdet."

"The real reason, Hori. Amun is rich enough that his priests can afford their own boat. They have no need of the king's barge."

"Usermaatranakht, Steward of the Estate of Amun, wishes an accounting of the temple lands in Behdet. He feels that the presence of the king will facilitate matters."

"I do not like to be used, Hori. Have the priest removed from my barge. Let him find his own way south."

Hori bowed. "As your Majesty pleases, but I beg you to reconsider. Amun is second only to the king in Ta Shemau in wealth and power. It could not hurt to listen to what the priest says."

"So Behdet was but a ruse to gain access to my person? I like this less and less, Hori. What is it he wants to say that could not be said by Amun's Hem-netjer in formal audience?"

"That I cannot say, Majesty."

"How much were you paid, Hori?"

"Majesty, I am shocked that you would think I would sell access to my king."

Ramesses looked at Hori and raised his eyebrows, while a small smile lifted the corners of his lips.

Hori had the grace to look contrite. "Five deben of fine gold, Majesty."

"That much? Are their words gilded too?" Ramesses nodded. "You may leave the priest aboard, Hori, and I will speak with him. What is his name?"

"Amenemopet, son of Tjanefer, Third Prophet of Amun, Majesty."

Ramesses started to board the barge, but turned back. "Naturally, you will pay ten deben of fine gold into my treasury."

Hori blanched, but bowed as he said, "Of course, Majesty."

The gangplank was withdrawn and the captain of the barge shouted out orders to the river men who pushed the barge away from the dock with long poles. Now the rowers took over. The scarlet-tipped oars bit deep into the green waters of the Great River and muscles on the backs and arms of the sailors stood out as they took the strain. For a few moments, it looked as if their efforts were insufficient to move the barge, but then it slid forward and the oars broke the surface of the river in a welter of droplets. To Ramesses, standing in the stern with the rising sun behind him, the drops suddenly blazed in a great arch of colour, and he gasped in wonder.

Amenemopet, standing a few paces away, saw it too, and offered the king a priestly interpretation. "Amun has put his seal of approval on your journey, Son of Re."

"I thought it was just something that happened when it rained."

"It is uncommon," Amenemopet conceded. "An omen of success nonetheless."

"We shall see," Ramesses replied. *I must find a way to draw his gilded words from him, to divine his purpose.*

The barge beat its way out into mid-river and turned into the current, the rowers now settling into their rhythm and sending the barge upriver at a slow but steady pace. Ramesses could see that the priest wanted to broach the subject of his reason for being aboard, but despite his curiosity, he turned away to where an awning had been set up to shade the deck. He signed for wine to be brought and sat on a stool, sipping his drink and relaxing as the city of Waset slipped slowly astern. Later in the day, a northerly wind sprang up and the captain raised the sail. The linen flapped and cracked in the gusts before filling out, making the heavy craft surge ahead. Muffled groans of relief were uttered by the rowers as they shipped their oars and took a well-earned rest.

Ta-senet lay two days' travel upriver. The barge could have managed it in less time with teams of rowers striving day and night, but Ramesses told the captain he was in no hurry, and to spare the men undue exertion. He spent the days relaxing in the shade of the awning, and at night, the captain pulled into shore and set up a camp for the king, guarded by both sailors and the honour guard from the Mut corps. They relied on stores from the barge, but supplemented with fresh fowl from the reed beds and fish from the river. Ramesses drank wine in the evenings, while the men made do with weak beer or cool water.

As they drew close to the southern city, the king forbade the capture of the giant perch as it was sacred to Ta-senet. Shoals of these fish could be seen in the clear waters, and often there would be flurries in the water as a crocodile drove into their midst, sending silvery-scaled fish leaping into the air. After one such occurrence, Ramesses beckoned to the priest of Amun, Amenemopet, and asked him why the perch was worshipped locally.

Amenemopet looked askance at Ramesses and delayed his answer, wondering why the king, as the principal priest of every god, should be asking such a basic question of a junior priest.

"Son of Re," he said cautiously, "this fish is found plentifully in these waters as a sign to the people that the god Hapi looks kindly upon them."

"A simplistic answer, priest. Is this what they teach in the temples now?"

"By no means, Son of Re. We are taught that the ways of the gods are many-layered and have lessons for both the simple peasant, and the erudite."

"You see me as a simple peasant then, if you offer up such an explanation."

Amenemopet saw his mistake and knelt before the king, his arms outstretched in appeasement. "Forgive me, Son of Re, if I misspoke. I felt certain that you must surely know more on this subject than I, a simple servant of Amun, and sought to teach me. I offered up a basic answer as if I was a child, learning of the gods for the first time."

Ramesses smiled. "An answer worthy of any of my courtiers, designed to display humility and turn away my wrath. Get up, Amenemopet, for you are forgiven. Now, indulge me and tell me of Ta-senet and its relationship with this fish."

"Son of Re, the city of Ta-senet is sacred to the goddess Neith, and the perch is among her symbols."

"Neith alone?"

"Also Khnum, her consort, and Heka, their offspring."

"I thought Atum was the consort of Neith?"

Amenemopet cast another nervous look at the king despite his reassurances. "Son of Re, none know better than you that Khnum, as creator of the Ba, is but an aspect of Atum, creator of all things." He saw the king nod and, emboldened, said, "likewise, although Heka or 'he who activates the Ka' is worshipped in Ta-senet as the offspring of Neith, other cities recognise her offspring as Sobek, Re, Apep, Het-hor, and Djehuti."

"You are bold indeed, priest, to mention the name of Apep in my presence. I am the Son or Re, and Re is the bringer of light and upholder of Ma'at. The serpent Apep is the opponent of Ma'at and light, embodying chaos."

"Indeed, Son of Re," Amenemopet said. "I only brought his name up in the interests of completeness. The god Amun similarly detests his name, so I will not mention it again."

"Good. Now, you associate Neith with Ta-senet because of her sacred fish, but that goddess has her centre of worship in Ta Mehu, doesn't she?"

"Yes, Son of Re. The city of Zau has long honoured her. She is the goddess of war and hunting, being represented often with a shield and crossed bows on her head. Some say the shield and curved bows also represent a fish, this imagery associating her with the sacred perch here in the south."

"There is another aspect that associates her with the fish too."

Amenemopet frowned and the nodded as he remembered. "She is the personification of the primeval waters of creation, the Cow of Heaven giving birth to the sun every day. As goddess of the waters, she is mother to all who lie within her, such as her son Sobek the crocodile god and the perch worshipped here in Ta-senet." He saw the king nodding and went on. "She is also the 'opener of ways' like Wepwawet the wolf god who guards the hidden entrance to the netherworld."

"A powerful goddess indeed."

"Yet she is overshadowed by her son Re, of whom my lord is in turn the son. Re and Heru of the Horizons are one, and both are but an aspect of Amun who, as you know, is worshipped as Amun-Re. All the gods of Kemet are but aspects of Amun."

"And you are a priest of Amun."

"Servant of the god and of the Son of Re."

"You have something you wish to say?"

"I would speak of the unity of the gods and of your purpose for Kemet, Son of Re."

Ramesses contemplated the young priest. *And so we come to it,* he thought. *It was for this that the Hem-netjer paid good gold to Hori that this priest might be close to my person. Do I let him speak now, or put him off?* He had almost decided to let the priest tell him of his purpose when the lookout at the prow of the barge called out that the city was in sight.

Ramesses looked away, and saw that the cliffs that hemmed the river on the western bank had receded, pushed back by the burgeoning fields of the city. "We will speak of this again, Amenemopet."

The priest could not hide his annoyance at the interruption, but bowed and backed away a pace or two, limited by the lack of room on the barge. "Let it be as you say, Son of Re."

The barge was met at the docks by the mayor and dignitaries of the city, and by many priests, all eager to gain the attention of their king. Ramesses allowed himself to be borne away to a feast where he listened to many long speeches of welcome. When all had been done in accordance with custom, the king took the mayor, councillors and leading priests aside and told them of his purpose.

"I mean to visit every temple and shrine and determine for myself the repairs needed to bring them up to the standard demanded by the gods."

"That is a noble enterprise, Son of Re," Mayor Khui said. "The gods will surely bless your Majesty and the city of Ta-senet." He hesitated a few moments and looked to the priests for support. "Er...several temples are in disrcpair, Son of Re. Reconstruction will take much gold."

"Do the temple coffers not hold enough?"

"No, Son of Re. The...er...harvests have been poor and er...taxes paid to the Temple of Amun in Waset have left little gold for the other gods."

"Even the temple of Neith? I understood her to be the titular deity of Ta-senet."

"Even that, Son of Re."

"Then I will make up the difference from the Treasury," Ramesses said.

"May you live a thousand years," Mayor Khui said.

"Now, what else concerns the good people of the city, Khui?"

"I, er...hesitate to mention such a small thing after the generosity shown by your Majesty, but the er...people of the city do have a request. I have tried to meet their desires from the meagre coffers of the city, but much remains to be done."

"Speak then, Khui. Tell me of these needs of the common people."

"They speak of leisure, Son of Re."

"I do not understand. Are they so rich they do not need to work?"

"Not that, Majesty." Khui looked at his councillors. "I do not have the words for this. Who will help me? Ahmes? Mose?"

"I can, Mayor Khui, for it is a subject close to my heart." An old man bowed to the king. "Son of Re, my name is Ahmes and until recently I was a craftsman and head of the Potter's Guild. I would work hard all day and was glad of the work for it meant I could feed my family, but in the heat of the day I longed for a shady tree to sit under and slake my thirst with cool river water. At the end of the day, when my limbs ached and weariness overcame me, I wished that I had somewhere I could sit and take my ease while my wife fried fish for my supper. When I was a younger man I would walk down to the river and sit on the grass, but I am an old man now and cannot make that journey easily."

"You are eloquent, old man, but what is it you want of me? I cannot turn back the years and make you young once more. Nor can I temper the sun's heat at midday."

"I would not want to disturb Ma'at by wishing for such things, Son of Re. It seems to me that there is something very simple that could be done. Only give the word, Majesty, and shade trees could be planted in the city so that hot and weary workers may take a few moments to sit and drink water out of the glare of the midday sun. In the evenings, men may sit under them and take their leisure, and on feast days and public holidays, families may take their repose beneath them."

"I have heard such proposals before, Son of Re," Khui said. "How many trees would be needed, and what cost would be involved?"

"That is something you will soon know, Mayor Khui," the king said. "I think this idea of Ahmes is a splendid one and should be implemented immediately. The cost will be very small compared to the gold I will be lavishing on your city to refurbish the temples and shrines."

Mayor Khui grimaced at the thought of the expense, but bowed in acquiescence. "Let it be as you say, Son of Re. I think perhaps...oh, ten trees planted on public land should suffice..."

"I was thinking a tree on every city block."

"Majesty, that...that would be impossible. The expense alone..."

"Let it be as I have said, Mayor Khui."

"Of course, Son of Re."

"Perhaps your Majesty could return in say...a year's time, to see how well your command has been implemented?" Ahmes asked.

Khui glared at his councillor, but dared say nothing beyond, "I am sure His Majesty is far too busy to visit our little town again, Ahmes."

"On the contrary, I will make time to see this project to fruition." Ramesses pursed his lips as he considered the idea. "In fact, I think I will broaden this out to every city, town and village throughout the kingdoms. I have long said that men will look back on my reign as a golden age when the kingdoms were at peace both externally and internally, and that all men and women could walk safely anywhere. The Nine Bows have been conquered and crime has been stamped out, so I can turn my attention to the welfare of the common man. Let trees and gardens be planted everywhere so that every man and every woman can take their rest in pleasant surroundings after a hard day's work."

The councillors and priests applauded, and Mayor Khui followed suit, though he was dismayed at the cost of the enterprise.

"Send for a senior scribe, Mayor Khui. I will dictate my command right now so copies may be made and sent out to the Governors of every sepat. Within a year, every city and town shall boast young trees in every city block and within five years men shall sit under them and take their well-earned rest."

# Chapter 30
# Year 7 of Usermaatre Ramesses

Ament was surprised to find that Second Man was still alive when he came to strip the tribesmen of their worldly goods and tip them into a shallow sandy grave. The man groaned and his eyelids flickered as Ament grasped his feet. He knelt beside the unconscious man and debated what to do.

*I cannot heal him, nor can I seek help for him.* He took out his dagger and contemplated the helpless man before him. "Explain to your gods that you attacked me, and your death cannot be laid at my feet."

Ament plunged the dagger into the man's throat and waited until the man stopped shuddering. Wiping the dagger clean on the man's loincloth, which he left on the corpse as a matter of decency, he resumed dragging Second Man to the grave he had prepared and dumped him in beside his erstwhile companion.

"I know no words to say over you, so you must put your trust in the mercy of your gods. I bear you no ill will as your deaths will mean I live."

He pushed sand over the bodies and placed several large rocks above them to spare them the ignominy of being dug up and eaten by scavengers. Then he returned to their small camp near the water seep and carefully took inventory of the tribesmen's belongings.

Five donkeys. One was laden with fodder and bundles of firewood, one with food and water, and three with an assortment of trade goods including copper ingots, bags of salt, dried fish and goat meat, and bronze arrowheads. A skin bag also held a tanned skin rolled up and tied with leather thongs. After making a meal from the food in the panniers and making sure the donkeys were fed and watered, Ament took out the scroll and unrolled it.

A series of burn marks joined by thin lines were arranged in a haphazard manner on the skin, along with some notations in an unknown language. He scratched his head over these, turning the skin this way and that, hoping to make some sense of the pattern. It was not until the next morning, after he had loaded up the donkeys and filled every skin with water from the seep that recognition dawned on him. He had taken out his own sketch map of the water sources of the Land of Sin to make sure of his course, and saw the similarity. Placed side by side, the two maps were by and large in agreement, though the skin included many strange shapes or symbols on it. It also omitted several of the water seeps closest to the Shechem village.

*Not surprising, I suppose, if they hated the Shechem. They wouldn't go anywhere near them.* He examined the skin more closely. *But how accurate is it? Do I place more reliance on my enemy's map or on my possibly faulty memory*?

Some of the marks on the tribesmen's map odd and looked like no symbols Ament had ever seen in written documents, and would have just dismissed them if he had not looked up at one point and seen the spire of rock close by that appeared to mark the position of the water seep. He looked at the map again and saw a mark that could be interpreted as a spire near one of the burnt marks. Ament grinned as he realised the tribesmen had seemingly included landmarks along the way. On that basis, their map was more reliable than his.

Setting out at last toward the nearest of the water seeps, he noticed hoof marks in the dust, which caused him some concern until he realised they had been made by his own donkeys. He was now reversing the course the tribesmen had taken. Feeling increasingly confident, he increased the pace, following the tracks back, though still checking on the presence of the marked landmarks. The journey to the next seep took two days, and although the seep was little more than a tiny pool in the shade of a small hill, he no longer felt anxious about his journey. His map worked, and if there was very little water at this seep, perhaps there would be more at the next one. He had enough in his skins to last another three or four days.

He slept well that night and rested his donkeys for most of the next day as well, in preparation for a forced march across an inhospitable stretch of stony desert. When he had crossed this stretch in the opposite direction so many years before, he had done so fortified by water and food obtained by a small oasis that was his next destination. In the distance, almost invisible in the dust haze, stood the low range of hills at whose base lay the oasis. Ament estimated it would take two or three days to cross the intervening ground. It would have been a daunting prospect if he had been attempting the crossing by himself, but he had sturdy donkeys to carry all the water he would need.

After the first night, he knew he would have to risk travelling by day. He had wondered about some of the cryptic notations on the map, and found that they referred to patches of ground covered by sharp rocks, or dust bowls that threatened to swallow up man and beast. It was difficult to negotiate these by star or moonlight, so he was forced to do it in the heat of the day.

"How did I manage this when I came this way years ago?" he asked the lead donkey, whom he had named Ramesses.

Ramesses paid no attention, intent only on negotiating a rocky patch safely.

"I suppose it was because Zephan knew the way," Ament mused. "He knew the safe trail and didn't have to pick his way through it like me."

There was no shade in the stony desert, so Ament pushed on until after sunset before making camp. He fed and watered the donkeys sparingly, determined to eke out his supplies in case the expected oasis did not provide much in the way of fresh fodder. Jackals howled in the darkness around him, making the donkeys nervous. They could no doubt smell the beasts and the water they carried, but the campfire and presence of a man made them cautious and they did no more than voicing their displeasure from a distance.

Ament wondered how the jackals could possibly live out in the hot and stony desert, without shelter, food or water, but as he sat by his small fire that night, he got an inkling of how they might manage it. As the rocks cooled, life stirred all around him. A scorpion crept out from under a rock, pincers held wide as it chased down and stung an incautious beetle. Moths flew in from the darkness, spiralling around the flames, and half-seen shapes flitted in the sky, uttering high-pitched squeaks as they snatched morsels from the air. An owl drifted silently by, wide eyes scanning the darkened rocks for rodents and insects, followed a few moments later by a shriek from some unfortunate as sharp claws extinguished its life. Lizards crept upon the rocks, staring at Ament with bright beady eyes, vanishing into the shadows if he moved. He took note of all these creatures and made a point of shaking out the robes he had taken from the tribesmen, and poking around with his staff before settling down to sleep.

He reached the low range of hills on the third day, when his water supplies were running low. Instead of the green oasis he expected, with pools of water and forage for his beasts, he discovered brown and sere vegetation, the pools dried to dusty bowls. His donkeys brayed mournfully and wandered through the dry grass seeking mouthfuls of such fodder as was to be had, while Ament sank down in the shade of a date palm and contemplated his future. The skins contained too little water to return across the stony waste, so his only hope was to try for the next water seep on his map. He spread it out on the sand and studied it. His own memory spoke of another seep two or three days to the south, but the map he had taken from the tribesmen hinted at a seep only a half day's travel away to the northeast, along the line of the hills.

*Do I risk it? I know...or I think I know...there is water to the south...if I can reach it. I have water for less than a day. Long enough to reach this other one if it exists, but I'll be thirsty by the time I reach it...and what about the donkeys? They need water too.*

He leaned back against the trunk of the palm tree and stared up at the green fronds waving gently against the blue sky. Something niggled at his mind, but slipped away as he tried to grasp it. After a few fruitless minutes, he got up to check on the donkeys. He had not unloaded them as he was as yet unsure as to whether he should leave immediately or rest them awhile. They had gathered under the shade of another palm and were scraping at the soil with their hooves, laying bare the roots of the dry grass and munching on them.

*I wish I could dig for roots. A succulent radish or two would be delicious, but there is only brown grass and palm trees.* He raised his eyes to the green fronds and stared at them. *Why are they green when the grass is brown and dry? Where are they getting water from?*

Ament swivelled on his heel and stared toward the shallow dust bowl that once held water.

*The water is still here, but it has seeped under the sand. If palms can get it, so can I.*

He strode to the lowest point in the bowl and dropped to his knees in the hot sand. For a moment, doubt assailed him and then he bent forward, scooping the sand away and pushing it behind him. Gradually the hole grew deeper, though every now and again he had to stop digging deeper and clear away sand from the edges that cascaded down upon him.

*It's not here. There's nothing...*

A hand struck cooler sand. He pulled it out and saw that a few grains stuck to his skin. Ament grinned and started scrabbling frantically in the depths of his shallow pit. The sand grew darker and now was definitely damp. He could smell the water, and so could the donkeys. They ambled over and stood around the edges, braying. A few more scoops and water pooled in the bottom for a few moments before falling sand filled in the tiny pool.

Ament redoubled his efforts and was at last able to lower his face into a puddle of cool water and gulp mouthfuls of the gritty liquid. He drank until he was satisfied, but as he rose to his knees, his donkeys crowded round, eager to get their share of the water. The edges of the pit started to fall in, so Ament took a switch and beat back the beasts. Then he took every water skin he had and filled them before leading the donkeys down one at a time.

"You first, Ramesses, for you are the king of the donkeys. Now you, Tiye, drink until your belly grows fat. Tyti, drink your fill too, but leave some for little 'Khopeshef. Oh, bad donkey...you have collapsed the sand walls."

He drove the beasts back and dug out the pit again before allowing Setnakhte to drink and then 'Khopeshef who had wrecked the pit. Eventually, the seep was little more than a muddy wallow and he let the donkeys do as they desired with it, hooves digging to find another mouthful of water, while he went back to the shade and slept until evening.

Ament woke when the shadows were long, and found his donkeys peacefully grazing nearby. He drank from a skin; the donkeys having muddied up the water in the pit too much for it to be potable, and consulted the map once more. Whichever route he took, he would be able to travel at night at least part of the way, following the foot of the low hills. He decided on the new seep to the northeast, for although it was new territory, it was close enough for him to return to his present location if it proved worthless. As the sun dipped below the western horizon, he bullied the reluctant donkeys into line and set off along the line of the hills.

Well rested and watered, the trek along the base of the hills in the cool of the night was pleasant, and Ament felt his spirits rise for the first time since he had run from the Army. He now seriously thought that he would find refuge among the Shechem, be able to stay with them for a few months until all pursuit died away, and then make his way home to Kinnereth. The donkeys too, reacted to the water and forage in their bellies by ambling along without complaint. Stars wheeled overhead as the hours of the night passed, and Ament started to wonder if he would recognise the seep if he found it. The map had given no landmarks as a clue save for the line of low hills, and they still marched along on his right-hand side, black against the starlit body of the goddess Nut.

Dawn was not far off, a greying of the eastern sky though not yet washing the easternmost stars from the sky, when he saw a brighter star than most, low on the horizon and seemingly close by. He stopped to stare at it.

*That is not a star...it's a fire. Men are here, at the seep no doubt.* Hard on the heels of this realisation came the thought that he should immediately retrace his steps to the dry oasis and from there strike south. *I don't want to meet up with friends of the men I killed...but what if they are Shechemites? That would be the answer to my prayers.*

Ament resolved to creep closer and establish the identity of the strangers before deciding. He placed a large rock on the bridle rope of Ramesses, and started forward, but he was scarcely out of sight before the donkeys, feeling themselves abandoned, started braying. Hurrying back, he quieted them, gave them some fodder and water and tried again. Ramesses took his desertion as a personal affront and started braying again. Cursing, Ament calmed them once more and took them with him.

*I've got to find out who they are. If I'm careful, I can get close enough to them to identify them and then I'll sneak away.*

Ament could almost feel the presence of the sun just below the hills when he stumbled over a low bush. He was close to the seep now, and there was water here as evidenced by plant growth. Sniffing, he thought he could detect smoke and that stink that comes from a body of men and their wastes when they have remained in one place for a few days. The donkeys showed interest in the foliage, cropping the leaves from nearby bushes, so he secured the bridle rope to a larger one and slipped away while their attention was otherwise engaged.

Although the light was rapidly increasing, Ament made his way swiftly to where the camp was situated - close by a small pool of water nestled underneath a rocky outcrop. Men had erected six tents near the pool and a single large camp fire blazed as a man with his back to Ament threw wood onto it, the heat of the fire dispelling the chill of the early morning. Other men emerged from the tents and Ament saw to his dismay that they were Kemetu--shaven and dressed in standard army issue kilts and sandals.

*Time to withdraw and get as far from here as I can.*

A man walked off into the bushes and Ament saw movement as if animals were tethered there. His suspicions were confirmed a moment later as a donkey brayed, answered immediately by his own beasts. The Kemetu soldiers swung round at the sound and grabbed weapons, one man barking out a series of commands. Several men started in his direction, and Ament wriggled back and then, bent double, ran for it.

If the plant cover had been denser, he might have been able to make his escape, but he had scarcely reached his donkeys than three men burst out of the bushes, one with a drawn bow and the others with spears. For a breath or two, Ament thought of dragging the tribesmen's sword from beneath his robe, but he realised he would be dead a moment later. Other men appeared, disarmed him and led him back to the camp, while his beasts were led off. Ament was forced to his knees in front of the officer, who demanded to know who he was. He pretended not to understand the Kemetu words.

"Shechem," he said, pointing to himself. "Honest trader," he added in what he thought was the Shechemite tongue. "You let me go?"

"Was there anyone with him?" the officer demanded of his men. "Another man? Or even a woman perhaps?"

"We saw no one, sir. Nor any sign."

"What shall we do with him?" another man asked. "Kill him?"

The officer was staring at Ament. "Do I know you?"

Ament shrugged and pointed to himself again. "Shechem."

"By the gods," the officer breathed. "Take away the filthy robes and the beard and you could almost be..." He hauled Ament to his feet and stared into his eyes more closely. "It is you, isn't it? General Ament."

# Chapter 31
# Year 7 of Usermaatre Ramesses

The king never made it down to Ta-senet to see whether trees had been planted on every city block to give shade to workers in the midday heat, but he received a report from Mayor Khui assuring him it had been carried out according to the king's wishes. Ramesses had no reason to doubt his word and if it matched the results from other cities and towns that he did visit, it was a praiseworthy achievement. Crowds cheered the king whenever he appeared in public, and every report that came to him from the Governors of the sepats up and down the length of the kingdoms was likewise a reflection of the adulation of the masses.

Ramesses boasted to both Tjaties, his Queens and principal wives, and his sons that now he could claim to have matched the triumphs of the Great Usermaatre.

"Under my rulership, Kemet is at peace with all the nations, crime is almost stamped out so even a woman with gold bangles on her wrists may walk the roads of city and country without fear of molestation, and now the cities and towns are shaded for the good of my people."

"The gods too are grateful, Son of Amun-Re," Anememopet said. "Temples and shrines throughout the kingdoms bear witness to your generosity and piety."

Ramesses now kept the junior priest of Amun close at hand, having taken a liking to him. Amenemopet, for his part, cultivated this relationship and lost no opportunity to further the ambitions of his superiors.

"Remember that Amun-Re is supreme in Kemet, and as creator and sustainer of every aspect of life, he speaks for every god."

"So you have often told me, Amenemopet."

"It is the god's truth, for Amun-Re looks down with favour upon your every endeavour. I know because the god speaks to me in dreams."

"He does? Tell me of these dreams."

Amenemopet took several deep breaths and calmed himself, assuming a pose that reflected a calm acceptance of the god's will. "The god appears to me as I lie asleep on my pallet in the temple, taking the form of a strong man with a ram's head surmounted by the feathers of truth and the golden disc of the sun blazing upon his head. In my dream, I fall at his feet and offer up worship, calling upon him to command me, his servant on earth."

Wonder and awe traced paths across the king's face. "Does he speak?"

"Yes." Amenemopet stood with his head bowed as if overcome by emotion.

"Go on. What does he say?"

"He says, 'Tell my son who shall henceforth be known as the Great Usermaatre...'"

"He said that?"

"Yes, Majesty. Shall I continue?"

"Yes, yes. Go on. Tell me what Amun-Re said about me."

"Tell my son who shall henceforth be known as the Great Usermaatre that I am well pleased with him. He honours the gods and brings every good thing to his people, from highest to lowest. The name of Usermaatre Ramesses shall be on every man's lips for eternity and all nations shall praise his wisdom and strength." Amenemopet fell silent, but his face held a troubled expression.

"Did the god say anything else?"

Amenemopet waved his hands about and moved his lips as if he was having trouble expressing himself. "Amun-Re spoke further, Majesty, but I hesitate to repeat his words lest you think the words my own."

"Speak, Amenemopet. I would know these words from the god."

"Know that I would never say anything that criticised your actions, Majesty. I would die first."

"So noted," Ramesses said impatiently. "Now tell me what Amun-Re said."

Amenemopet bowed. "Let it be as you command, Son of Amun-Re. The god said... 'Tell my son that in one respect only will men hold his name in less than perfect regard. He allows the priests of every god to take gold from his treasury without a proper accounting. Dishonest men threaten to stain your good name.'" The priest wrung his hands. "Majesty, I beg you to remember that these are the god's words, not mine. He went on to say that you should channel all funds to all temples through the only priest you could truly trust--the Hem-netjer tepy en Amun in Waset, Bakenkhons."

Ramesses frowned. "The only priest?"

"The god's words, not mine."

"There is something of a paradox here, Amenemopet. If Bakenkhons is the only trustworthy priest, why should I trust you?"

"You must judge me as you see fit, Son of Amun-Re, but I might draw your attention to the fact that Hem-netjer Bakenkhons appointed me to represent him and the god at your court. If he is trustworthy, then surely his decisions and appointments are similarly trustworthy."

"And yet...every other priest?"

"So says the god, Majesty, yet the solution is simple. Channel all the gold needed for refurbishing the temples through the Great Temple of Amun in Waset. Let Bakenkhons then demand of every temple a detailed accounting and disburse funds according to need."

"It will look as if I distrust them."

"Better that than to let others bring your name into disrepute, Majesty."

"That is true," Ramesses mused.

"It will also lessen the demands on your time, Son of Amun-Re. As it is, priests of every town or city you visit din your ears with petitions for this temple or that shrine. To listen to their pleas and judge which ones are worthy of attention distracts your Majesty. Let Bakenkhons assume this burden--as the god recommends--and priests everywhere will leave you alone."

Ramesses nodded slowly. "Those are the words of Amun-Re," he agreed. "Thank you, Amenemopet, I shall consider this idea closely."

# Chapter 32
# Year 7 of Usermaatre Ramesses

Ament stared at the Kemetu officer who now turned to his men with a broad smile on his face.

"On your knees, men of Set corps. General Ament has come among us once more."

All around him, men looked at one another and then first one and then another sank to their knees in the sandy soil of the oasis, dropped their weapons and held out their arms in praise. The officer now dropped to his knees.

"Greetings, General. You won't remember me, but I was a Leader of Fifty in your loyal Set corps. My men here were common soldiers who survived the last battle and others who found themselves persecuted by the usurper Ramesses and fled for their lives into the desert."

Ament hesitated, wondering if this was some trick to make him reveal his identity, but as he looked around at the smiling faces of the kneeling soldiers, the notion was ridiculous. They already knew who he was. "Arise...what is your name, Leader of Fifty?"

"Perneb, sir." The man got to his feet and beckoned to his men. "This is Leader of Ten Nehi and this Leader of Ten Meru. Here is Leader of Five Ankhu."

"Almost as many officers as men, it seems."

Perneb laughed. "We have more men, sir, at our main base. Nehi and Meru have detailed knowledge of this area, so I brought them with me." His expression became serious. "Er...is the Queen with you, sir? Did Sitre Tausret survive?"

"She lives, and is safe. You do not need to know more, and the fewer people who know, the better."

"But she...you...will lead us once more? We will overthrow the usurper and restore her to the throne of Kemet?"

*If he imagines that even a corps of hardened and experienced men could overthrow Ramesses then he is a fool...but I can't tell him that.*

"I am not at liberty to divulge the royal plans, but your presence here in the Land of Sin will be welcome news to Her Majesty."

"May I er...ask what you are doing here, sir? Dressed as a tribesman in those stained robes and er...with that filthy beard?"

*I cannot risk telling him I am fleeing from Usermaatre's army. Any of these men could be a spy and inform on me. The truth I think...but not all the truth.*

"I wander these lands from time to time. The Queen needs to know what happens in her kingdoms."

"But here in the desert?"

"I was looking for the Shechemite tribe. They helped me before, and I thought they might do so again."

"There is no such tribe near here, sir. Maybe further east?"

"That is what I thought. I have a map that shows water seeps. I took it off the same tribesman that gave me his robes."

"Unwillingly, I'll warrant," Perneb said with a laugh.

"There was some argument over it," Ament conceded. "Anyway, if the Shechemites are not to be found around here, I must seek them elsewhere. South maybe."

"You think they will join you...us?"

"Possibly."

"I think your presence would be more useful with the loyal Set corps, sir. You could strengthen our resolve and give us new heart."

"Perhaps after I find the Shechemites."

Perneb shifted his weight and looked at his fellow officers. "We...er, must insist, sir."

"You mean to kidnap your general? Where is the sense in that?"

"Not kidnap, sir. You would be our honoured guest."

"Thank you, but I must decline. As I said, maybe later."

Perneb sighed and nodded to his men who stepped up behind Ament. "It is for your own protection, so I must insist you accompany us."

Ament turned and looked at the soldiers, noting their determined expressions. "It seems I have no choice in the matter."

The Set corps squad broke camp within the hour and set off along the line of the hills toward the northeast. Despite his anxiety over his enforced participation, Ament was impressed by Perneb's control over his men. The men moved off briskly, leading laden donkeys, the bulk of the men trotting along in double file with scouts sent out in all directions. There was none of the usual Kemetu grumbling or use of whips by the officers. Instead, the men responded willingly and cheerfully to orders, though the men talked as they ran and told jokes, behaviour which would be frowned upon in the normal corps. Ament, with his beard trimmed, and clothed in army kilt and headdress, made his way along the column to where Perneb strode.

"You maintain good discipline over your men," he said.

Perneb nodded. "They are good men, steadfast and loyal, and we have a common goal."

"How many men do you have under your command?"

Perneb flicked a glance at Ament. "I am Leader of Fifty, if you remember."

"So you have only fifty men?"

"I do, but I am only one of many."

"That is what I mean. How many men are in the loyal Set corps?"

"Nearly six hundred, organised into two Troops. Your presence will bring others to us I am sure."

"Who commands?"

"Harkhuf."

"The one who was a Troop Commander in the old Set corps?"

"The same. Meryre and Shere are Troop Commanders now, who used to be Leaders of Fifty."

"But not you, who was also a Leader of Fifty?"

Perneb grinned. "The next Troop will be mine."

"Harkhuf was something of a martinet, I seem to remember," Ament said.

"Is that meant as a criticism, sir?"

"Not necessarily. A corps, particularly one facing great odds, needs a strong disciplinarian in charge."

Perneb nodded. "He looks after us, sir."

"But you now expect me to take over?"

"That is not for me to say."

"But I was your General."

"Indeed, but..." Perneb ran along in silence for a time, then, "You have changed, sir."

"In what way?"

"The General Ament I remember was fiercely loyal to Sitre Tausret, prepared to face any danger, take any risk, yet you seem reluctant to accept the loyal Set corps."

"Until this morning, I did not even realise it existed. I still don't know if it is a serious fighting unit or just a collection of fugitives hiding from the new rulers of the kingdoms."

"Fair enough," Perneb said. "You'll find out soon enough, and then we'll likely want a commitment from you in return."

The men ran on through the heat of the day, but Perneb allowed them several periods of rest and was liberal with the water. They camped as dusk washed over the desert, and the next day struck northward away from the range of hills.

Ament no longer had access to his map, but sketched the outlines in the sand during one of their rest breaks, adding in their route of the day before and their present course. He frowned as he worked out directions and distances, and then took his questions to the Leader of Fifty.

"We are close to the inhabited lands of Ta Mehu. Do you mean to take me back into the kingdoms?"

"Afraid we will turn you over to the usurper? I saw you scribbling in the sand, but you misjudged distances. We are still many days travelling from the nearest village, let alone a military fort."

"Where are we going then?"

Perneb smiled, but would say no more, and with that Ament had to be satisfied.

They ran northward three more days, outdistancing the donkeys that followed on more slowly. Perneb drove his men hard, now that they were nearing their destination. On the morning of the fourth day, he halted his men and beckoned Ament to join him on a slight hillock.

"We are within sight of home," Perneb said.

Ament stared out into the desolate desert, but could see no signs of habitation, only a rocky landscape that harboured not even a hint of green growing things.

"I see nothing."

"Good. If you see nothing, who know there is something there; how much less will our enemies see if they pass by."

"But there is nothing there."

"Look again, sir." Perneb pointed. "There...that slight shadow...a line..."

Ament stared until his eyes hurt. He saw what Perneb described as the shadow and the line, but could not imagine what those vague features had to do with a camp for several hundred men. He said so.

Perneb chuckled. "There's nothing for it then, we'll have to go closer."

The Leader of Fifty led the men down off the hillock and into the boulder-strewn land, angling to one side to bring his little party into line with the shadow. As they neared it, Ament gaped in astonishment. From out of nowhere, it seemed, a ravine appeared, as if the gods themselves had wielded an axe and cut into the rock. The closer they got, the larger it loomed, and now guards challenged them, swiftly passing them through when they recognised Perneb.

The ravine became a trench and widened out into a deep but narrow valley, the floor of which actually boasted a small stream of flowing water. It was cooler once they descended to the floor, and the air more humid. Ament felt as if he was coming home and mentioned his feeling to Perneb.

"A home away from home for most of us," Perneb replied. He gestured at the stream which in this part of the ravine was flanked by grass and date palms. "We call it 'Little River' and think of it as one of the branches of Iteru. Even here, the gods of Kemet sustain us."

"I would never have guessed this...this whole valley was here. Where does the water come from?"

Perneb pointed back the way they had come. "There's a spring back there. Water just gushes from the rock. It is said that a woman prophet conjured it in a time of need." He grinned. "I know. What's a woman doing being a prophet in the wilderness? It's just a story."

"And where does the water go?" Ament asked. "Does it join up with Iteru?"

"There's a small lake at the far end, right by the cliff wall. It never seems to get any larger, so it probably just soaks into the sand. Either way, it's a gift from the gods."

More men appeared as Perneb's little group moved down the ravine, gathering and crowding round, pointing, whispering and then erupting in cheers as they recognised Ament.

"It's General Ament."

"Praise the gods; now we'll thrash the usurper."

"Gold and women to be had in Ta Mehu."

"Where did you find him?"

"And where's the Queen?"

Perneb raised his arms to calm the crowd. "All in good time, brothers. The General needs to consult with our commanders first, then we'll celebrate his coming."

"What about the Queen?"

"She is well...and safe. Now make way, brothers. Our commanders will be eager to welcome our old general."

The crowd parted, letting Perneb and Ament through, and then followed behind as they walked further down the valley to where tents had been erected beneath an overhang in the cliff face. Several men stood outside the tents, hands on hips as they waited for the approaching crowd. Perneb stopped a few paces away and saluted the waiting men.

"Corps Commander Harkhuf, Troop Commanders Meryre and Shere, may I present General Ament."

Harkhuf stared hard at Ament. "Is it really you? I thought you were dead. You walked into the desert with the Queen and everyone said you died there."

"We decided to live, but it was not safe to let certain people know we were still alive."

"The Queen lives too?"

"She does."

"Where?"

"Somewhere safe."

Harkhuf continued to stare, drinking in the sight of his old commander. "By the gods," he said at last, "it's good to see you. How is it you are here, though? Did you know of us? Has someone talked of our presence here in our refuge?"

"Chance," Perneb said. "Or the gods. We stumbled upon him at the southern oasis. He said he was looking for the Shechemite tribe."

"Who are they?" Meryre asked.

"Friends," Ament said. "I thought they could help me."

Harkhuf smiled. "I think we will be able to help you more. Gods, it is good to see you, General." He saluted and then stepped forward to grasp Ament's arms. "Let us offer you refreshment. No wine, I'm afraid, but we have some passable beer."

The Loyal Set Corps had more than passable beer to offer. Supplies were brought in from Ta Mehu and supplemented by beef and vegetables grown locally. One of the former soldiers had even been a brewer of beer, and had gained more fame as that than he ever had as a warrior. The soldiers were not even celibate, many having brought along wives when they fled the kingdoms, and many other women followed, catering to all aspects of the men's needs. Consequently, the celebration of Ament's arrival swiftly became a general orgy of drunkenness and licentiousness.

Ament was appalled at the lack of control exercised by the Commander. Harkhuf sat and drank, smiling as men rioted around him. Music and dancing degenerated into couples copulating on the ground near the fire pits, and drunken fights broke out over some of the women. Ament leaned across and spoke to Meryre.

"This is not behaviour I would expect of Kemetu soldiers."

Meryre shrugged. "They have cause to celebrate tonight. It is not every day General Ament comes to lead us all to victory."

"I have no army to lead against Usermaatre Ramesses even if I desired to do so, and you are only two Troops against eight corps or more."

"More will join our ranks when they know that General Ament leads us once more. The common people always loved Queen Sitre Tausret and they will flock to her banner again."

"How long since you walked the streets of Kemet's cities, Meryre?"

"Five years, thereabouts, and I long to do so again. We will, soon, as victors."

"The people love Ramesses now," Ament said gently. "He has made their lives safe, is rebuilding temples and shrines up and down the Great River, and the kingdoms are at peace. The common man loves peace and prosperity above all else."

"You worry too much, General. They will rise up and overthrow the usurper, you'll see." Meryre got up to get himself another pot of beer, and Ament slipped away into the darkness, finding himself a quiet place near the stream where he could think.

*They are deluded one and all. The gods know I honour their steadfastness and loyalty to Tausret's cause all these years, but their efforts are doomed to failure. Kemet has changed in the last ten years.*

Ament leaned back against the palm tree, seeking peace in the silence broken only the splash and gurgle of the water over the rocky streambed. Looking up beyond the feathery palm fronds that were like shadows across the slash of sky bound by canyon walls, he breathed deep of the cool, moist air.

*If only it was the Shechem in this valley. I could stay here six months or a year and then make my way home. With these people though? What do they expect of me?*

Tiny bats flitted in the air above the stream, hawking for insects. Ament knew they made small cries as they hunted, but it had been many years since his ears had heard them. Somewhere far downstream, something splashed, but the darkness hid its identity.

*What do I do? Would they let me leave if I said I wanted to? I am their general after all; they'd obey me, wouldn't they?*

A burst of drunken obscenity from the camp broke into his solitude. Sparks floated into the sky, the tiny red lights competing for a few moments with the starry body of Nut. Then the camp fell into comparative silence once more and Ament returned to his thoughts.

*They are poorly disciplined and though they say they are loyal to Tausret they will die or surrender in their first battle with seasoned troops. They will want me to stay and lead them, but that way lies death. I should leave and seek out the Shechemites, where at least I'd feel safe, but will they let me?*

"General Ament, where are you?"

It was Harkhuf, with Meryre beside him, who came down to the stream.

"You wandered off, General. I was concerned for your safety."

"For my safety?" Ament asked, getting to his feet. "I thought I was safe enough with the Loyal Sets."

"So you are," Harkhuf replied, unsmiling. "But there are cobras in this valley, and we would not want to lose our General so soon after finding him. I will provide some men to look after you."

*Ah, so that is the way of it. I am useful, so I am an honoured guest but I must remain under guard.* "Whatever you deem to be right, Commander." Ament yawned and stretched. "I am tired. Perhaps you could direct me to my tent."

# Chapter 33
# Year 8 of Usermaatre Ramesses

The king was in Per-Ramesses, enjoying his Queen Iset, when a messenger drove a chariot, horses lathered and dust-covered, into the military barracks there with an urgent letter from the Governor of Perire. Courtiers passed the message and messenger up the hierarchy until it reached Chamberlain Nefermaat. He hesitated to interrupt the king in his pleasures, but decided the news warranted incurring the royal displeasure. Nevertheless, he hesitated once more outside the bedroom as it was evident from the cries emanating from behind the doors that the king and queen were both caught up in the throes of passion. He waited until they seemed to have finished, before knocking on the door frame. When his tapping drew no response, he cleared his throat and called out.

"Son of Re, it is I, Chamberlain Nefermaat. May I approach your Majesty?"

"What is it, Nefermaat? I am otherwise occupied."

"Son of Re, I would not dream of interrupting you, but the matter is urgent."

"Enter then."

Nefermaat slipped through the door and bowed toward the naked figure of the king standing beside the bed. He saw, but tried to ignore, the naked Queen still lying in rumpled linen. Forcing the image of the queen from his mind, Nefermaat bowed again and addressed Ramesses.

"Son of Re, a messenger has arrived from the Governor of Perire, with word that the Ribu are invading the lands in the west."

"The Ribu? That's nonsense; he must be mistaken. I destroyed the Ribu."

"That is what the messenger said, Son of Re. Perhaps the Governor is mistaken."

Ramesses frowned but nodded. "I will hear his message in the small audience hall. Let him take refreshment and a bath if he desires, and I will see him in..." he looked down at Iset, "...about an hour. Leave us now."

Nefermaat backed out and closed the door behind him, listening for a few moments until the sounds of renewed passion broke out. He smiled and walked away, murmuring to himself that as the king was not worrying about the Ribu, then neither would he. The Chamberlain made sure the needs of the messenger were attended to and then went about his other palace duties.

Ramesses, after ploughing his Queen's field vigorously for the second time, bathed and dressed in new linen, let the Overseers of the bedchamber apply makeup and jewellery as befitted the king of Kemet, so it was closer to three hours before he entered the small audience hall. The messenger, who had been straddling a stool by the wall and picking his teeth, leapt to his feet and then dropped to his knees as he recognised the man who walked in.

"Son of Re; Life! Health! Prosperity!"

Several men followed the king into the hall--Chamberlain Nefermaat, the Commander of the then-resident corps, Natsefamen of the Shu corps, and one of his Troop Commanders, Prince Meryamun. Guards ran in and took up positions along the walls.

Ramesses had looked up briefly as the guards entered, but now turned his attention back to the kneeling messenger.

"What is your name?"

"Meni, Son of Re. I bring a letter from Governor Khabekhmet of Perire."

"So I understand. Where is it?"

Prince Meryamun approached, saying, "I have it here, Father."

"Approach, Prince Meryamun. It is good that you are here." Ramesses held out his hand for the scroll. He unrolled it and scanned the writing, then rolled it back up and handed it back to his son.

"Do you know what is in the letter, Meni?"

The messenger licked his lips nervously, terrified to be addressed by the king. "N... no, Son of Re. I cannot read."

Ramesses nodded. "I did not think you would read a message addressed to me, but are you aware of its contents?"

"No, Son of Re."

"The Ribu. Governor Khabekhmet writes of the arrival of the Ribu. He must be mistaken for the Ribu were destroyed. Can you shed light on this, Meni?"

"Light, Son of Re? I... I don't understand."

"Please, Majesty, allow me," Nefermaat said. "Meni, the Governor says the Ribu are coming. Do you know if this is true?"

Meni frowned, apparently thinking hard. "I've not seen them myself, sir, but I spoke with men who have. They're Ribu, right enough. This man what has seen them, fought them two years ago. He knows Ribu, sir."

"This means war again, doesn't it, Father?"

Ramesses nodded. "I had thought them destroyed by the hands of Set when the sandstorm claimed them, but it seems I must finish the job myself."

"You'll take me with you, Father?" Meryamun asked. "I am more than old enough to face Kemet's enemies."

"Yes, though you shall face them as a Troop Commander in the Shu corps. Tjaty Herwernef is in Men-nefer, so he will have to be told. Nefermaat, have a scribe draw up instructions to fortify the city. You will attach my seal and Meni... will you deliver it for me?"

"I would be honoured, Son of Re."

"Go then with Nefermaat. I want you to leave within the hour."

"And me, Father? What shall I do?"

"Natsefamen, you will mobilise the Shu corps at once. We march west at dawn the day after tomorrow. Meryamun, organise messengers to bring the fleet to Per-Ramesses and also the Hapi corps."

"Yes, Father...er, where is the fleet?"

"Find out, boy," Ramesses said sharply. "You're a Troop Commander now. Find out and get them here on time. You have a day and a half."

Prince Meryamun saluted and ran from the audience hall, while Natsefamen followed at a more sedate pace.

Nefermaat had a scribe draw up the necessary instructions for Tjaty Herwernef in Men-nefer, had it tied up with the king's seal on fresh clay, and gave it into the keeping of Meni, who at once left for the northern capital. Natsefamen at once called his remaining Troop Commanders and ordered them to bring the corps to a state of readiness. Prince Meryamun dispatched chariots and small messenger vessels up and down the branch of the Great River, with copies of the king's commands to be carried to the Fleet and any units of the Hapi corps they happened upon.

The Shu corps was ready that evening and Ramesses inspected the men, professing himself satisfied with their state of preparedness. There was one aspect that concerned the king though.

"I want more chariots. The best way to roll up relatively undisciplined troops is with a strong chariot assault. You have two hundred, the Hapi corps has about the same. I want another hundred ready two dawns from now."

"Where from, Son of Re? I mean, I could send north for more from the northern corps but they would take a month to arrive."

"Scour the city, Natsefamen. Ransack the storerooms. Turn the armoury upside-down. Find me parts of chariots, spare wheels, timber that can be fitted, and construct me more chariots. Send for the Master of Horse and tell him to supply enough horses for all the chariots you will find. Every horse that is fit for even light duties must be ready on time, together with charioteers, stablemen, feed, harness." Ramesses regarded his Commander sternly. "Do not let me down, Natsefamen."

The Commander paled, but saluted and hurried off shouting commands to his officers, and soon the city and surrounding countryside was like a kicked ants' nest. Over the course of the next day, equipment started to accumulate, broken pieces, rotted leather, fresh-cut reeds, and craftsmen descended on the jumble, assembling them as best they could into working chariots.

"I fear it will not be enough, Son of Re," Chamberlain Nefermaat confided. "I have seen the chariots they are making--heavy, awkward vehicles, and the horses, Majesty...they are largely untrained."

Ramesses nodded his agreement. "I have seen them, Nefermaat, but anything Natsefamen can produce will help. I doubt if any of those chariots will take part in the main assault, but every one that is made releases another fast chariot from scouting and guard duty."

"Does the Shu Commander know this, Majesty? I only ask because I have seen him vomiting in anxiety."

"No, and you are not to tell him. I want his every effort until we depart. Whatever he produces will earn my praise."

Elements of the Hapi corps filtered into the city over the course of the day, under the command of Troop Commanders or Leaders of lesser numbers. The corps had been on training exercises in eastern Ta Mehu and was widely dispersed. Fast riders had been sent out to round up the remaining Troops and Commander Merikare, who had turned up at midday, was confident they would all be there by dawn the next day.

Less certain was the arrival of the Fleet. Merikare thought they were exercising near the easternmost mouth of Iteru. Fast boats had been sent scudding northward, but no one could guarantee that the barges, which alone could carry the corps and their chariots, would be there in time.

"Start us off today, Son of Re. I have twenty chariots and twice as many archers ready to go."

"But no boats to carry them, Merikare. That is why we need the Fleet."

"Send us overland, Majesty. We can cut across Ta Mehu from east to west and with luck be at Perire a day before your barges."

"What good would that do? Twenty chariots and forty archers will not stop the Ribu. Besides, their presence will give them warning of our approach."

Merikare bowed low and took a deep breath. "Son of Re, I mean no disrespect, but the Ribu knows your Majesty will oppose them. Our presence may make them cautious and give you time to approach. At the very least, you will have reliable information on their numbers and disposition."

"And a sharp response by the Ribu could annihilate your little force. Who would command this dangerous enterprise?"

"There is an able young archer, newly promoted, who thirsts for such duty. His name is Goloth."

"What sort of an uncouth name is that?"

"His father was Kaftor, I believe, but he is loyal and brave."

Ramesses considered and then nodded. "Send this Goloth then, and let us see what he is made of."

The Hapi detachment left that day, boats transporting the chariots, horses and men across the water, whereupon they raced off across the broad, flat meadows.

A flotilla of the Fleet arrived, including three barges, and every available chariot was disassembled and stowed aboard, together with as much equipment as had been assembled. Ramesses met with his corps Commanders and Prince Meryamun to discuss the departure.

"We need the rest of the barges before we can embark the men," the king said. "How long before they are here?"

"Messengers have been sent out, Majesty," Natsefamen replied. "There is nothing we can do now but wait."

"I wanted to leave at dawn tomorrow. Even so, it will likely take another three days to get to Perire. Who knows where the Ribu will be by then."

"My lord Father," Meryamun said quietly. "I know that I am young and inexperienced in the ways of war, but might I make a suggestion?"

"Might as well," Ramesses grumbled. "We could be here for days waiting for the barges."

"That is what I mean, Father. You have three barges loaded with chariots and supplies. Send them to Perire at once... this very day. They will disembark in the west long before the men arrive, but craftsmen can reassemble every chariot ready to receive the men by the time they arrive. It would save some time."

"The Prince is right," Merikare said. "No matter when we left Per-Ramesses, we would disembark in the west three days later. It would then take the best part of another day to reconstruct the chariots. How much better would it be if they were ready and waiting for the troops when they arrived?"

Ramesses considered this advice and nodded. "Send the loaded barges immediately, together with a Troop of the Shu corps to guard them. Also send more fast ships to the estuary to find my barges and hurry them up."

The Fleet arrived later that day and Admiral Hori, together with Prince Khaemwaset, hurried into the presence of the king. They made obeisance and reported that all vessels were ready to carry out the king's wishes.

"The messenger said the Ribu have invaded," Khaemwaset said.

"Yes, my son. That is why I need the fleet. I must carry the Shu and Hapi corps to Perire to meet the enemy."

"The Fleet stands ready, Son of Re," Hori said.

"Then load the barges and any other vessels that can carry men. The chariots are already half a day ahead of you. I want them ready to sail at dawn tomorrow."

"And the course, Son of Re?"

Ramesses stared at his admiral. "Upriver of course, to the junction with the western branch, then down that one. It should take three days."

"More perhaps, Majesty. The river is low and some parts of the branches are choked with weed."

"Why was this allowed to happen? Who is responsible?"

"The rivermen of each village are responsible, Majesty, but so many have been called up into the Fleet there are insufficient to control the waterways properly."

"I am displeased, Hori. Send men immediately to clear the river ahead of the Fleet."

"Yes, Majesty."

"Father, there is another solution," Khaemwaset said.

"To what, my son?"

"To getting the men there faster."

"How? There is no straight road across Ta Mehu. Other than crossing the river branches several times, the only way is to use the river."

"Or the sea, Father. Rather than send the Fleet far upriver to the junction, we could send them to the mouth of this branch, across to the west over the sea, and then up a short way to Perire."

"Show me."

Khaemwaset called for a sketch map of Ta Mehu to be brought and then outlined his plan quickly.

"Can this work?" Ramesses asked his admiral.

"Well...er..."

"Forget that he is my son and that I am king. I want an honest answer."

"Yes, Son of Re." Admiral Hori licked his lips and shot a quick glance at the Prince. "Since you demand it of me, Majesty, I would say no. There are too many uncertainties. We know the river mouths push out mud and sand and these become shoals. The Fleet could easily get stuck on these."

"Is this true, my son?"

"It is possible," Khaemwaset conceded. "But we could avoid the shoals by sailing further offshore."

"Making it a longer voyage and saving no time," Hori pointed out.

"Even so, the Fleet could be there in two days."

"And if we did, how would we navigate? Kemetu ships always steer close to land. If we sailed out of sight of land, the Fleet could get lost."

"Ridiculous," Khaemwaset snorted. "Kemet lies south of the Great Sea. All we would have to do is steer south."

Admiral Hori flushed, and he opened his mouth for a barbed retort before remembering he addressed the king's son and heir. Instead, he controlled his anger and spoke to the king.

"I have offered my opinion, Son of Re. I think the northern route would be a mistake."

"So do I," Ramesses said. He held up a hand to cut off his son's outcry. "Nevertheless, I am minded to offer Khaemwaset a chance to prove us both wrong. My son, there are eight barges to fill with men. When all are aboard at dawn tomorrow, you will sail north with two of them, and Admiral Hori will take the southern route."

Neither Hori nor Khaemwaset were happy with this decision and both protested that dividing the forces was unwise.

"Six out of eight, Son of Re," Hori grumbled. "You won't have enough men."

"I will have all my chariots and most of my archers. More than enough for the Ribu."

"And if...when...I get there first?" Khaemwaset protested. "How can I contain the Ribu with half a corps?"

"You will wait for the main force to arrive, my son. Now let it be as I have said."

# Chapter 34
# Year 8 of Usermaatre Ramesses

Goloth and his little force of twenty chariots and forty archers made good time across the flat farmlands of Ta Mehu, despite being loaded down. The two-man chariots carried three people each--a charioteer and two archers--so perforce travelled slower than they wanted. There were five branches of the Great River at this time (it varied from year to year), and at each branch they had to find a village from which they could commandeer boats to ferry them across. One main road linked the sides of the northern kingdom and flourishing villages or towns grew up where road and water met. Travellers would always need a ferry, so ferrymen earned a good living.

The king's writ bought them a crossing at each branch, though passage across the river was always slow. It was a matter of either breaking down each chariot to fit on small craft, swimming the horses across; or utilising larger craft that could take, at most, three or four chariots at a time. They crossed the first branch within sight of Per-Ramesses, and the second close to nightfall on that first day, demanding board from the inhabitants of the village on the far side.

On the second day, they crossed rich, dark soil that gripped the narrow wheels of the overburdened chariots and slowed their progress to walking pace. Goloth fumed, knowing that his reputation with his Corps Commander hinged on the success of his mission. If he took longer to reach Perire than the king's barges, he would be shamed before his peers.

"It's not going to happen, by all the gods of Kaftor and Kemet."

Goloth ordered a halt and redistributed his men, explaining why he was taking this drastic step.

"At this rate we will be the laughing stock of Hapi if not the whole army. Intef, I am promoting you to Overseer of the Bow. You will..."

"Forgive me, Overseer Goloth, but that is your rank. How can you raise me to the same level?"

"I am Acting Commander, Intef and still outrank you. As such, I can give you a temporary promotion. Now, you will take twenty men, on foot, and cross Ta Mehu on foot. The others will come with me in lightened chariots, and we shall make every effort to fulfil our duty by getting to Perire well ahead of the army and scouting out the enemy positions."

The chariots, now bearing a driver and a single archer each, did not sink into the moist soil and despite Intef leading his men westward at a run, were soon out of sight. Goloth drove them on, crossing two more branches of the river that day. On the second day after leaving Per-Ramesses, his tiny force landed on the westernmost part of Ta Mehu, and started inland toward Perire.

Goloth sent three chariots racing ahead of his others to scout out the presence of the Ribu, with instructions to report back at regular intervals whether or not they discovered the enemy. They did so, and as time passed, the road flying by under the chariot wheels, reports came back saying the enemy was nowhere in sight. Chariots issued forth from Perire, demanding to know what they were doing there, but Goloth refused to turn aside, saying he was under orders from the king himself.

The main road petered out after Perire, devolving into little more than farm tracks, and Goloth moved more slowly, sending more chariots out in a wide arc. A day past Perire, and a chariot raced out of the northwest with news of the Ribu.

"The enemy, sir, perhaps half an iteru to the northwest."

"What direction are they moving?"

"East, sir. Armed men, very few women or wagons that we could see."

"How many?"

"Thousands, sir. Too many to count."

"Did they see you?"

"Yes, sir. They sent a column out toward us, but they had no chariots, thank the gods. We could have killed a few...sped in and loosed arrows...but we thought it best to get back and warn you."

Goloth nodded, his mind working as he processed the news of the thousands of Ribu and his twenty chariots and twenty archers.

"Take another chariot and go back to the river. Hurry along Intef and the others if they have arrived, then stay and wait for the army. It is vital that the king learns of this."

"Yes, sir. Er...what will you be doing? In case the king asks, sir?"

"We're going to engage the enemy."

As soon as the two chariots raced off to the east, Goloth gathered his remaining chariots and turned them northward, into the presumed path of the Ribu army. He kept fast chariots to the front, scouting the way, and half a day later crossed in front of the advancing horde. Immediately, he peeled his chariots away, racing alongside the enemy columns as he assessed the threat.

"Note this," he said to his charioteer as they bounced over the ground. "No chariots, about two...three thousand men, some armour...mostly spears and axes..."

The charioteer twitched the reins and their chariot veered away from the column, a shower of arrows descending on their former path.

"...and archers. How many would you say? One in ten?"

Goloth retreated and gathered his men together, outlining his plan.

"We cannot hope to stop them or even do them more than superficial harm, so we won't even try. Instead, we shadow them and if we get the chance, we sweep in close and pick a few men off before retreating. I want no losses, so don't take chances." Goloth looked around his circle of men, noting their grim faces. "Twice a day, I will send a chariot back to the river to tell the king the situation, but the king decides the plan of attack."

Goloth's little force put his plan into action, darting in from the sides, loosing a torrent of arrows that disrupted a small portion of the Ribu column, and then racing away in the face of any retaliation. Time and again they stung the enemy, until the Ribu command lost their temper and sent a column of swift runners after them, splitting their forces to counter this Kemetu attack. Goloth smiled as his chariots easily outdistanced the pursuit before doubling back and hitting them again.

The Ribu halted and waited for the next attack, massing archers against the threat. Goloth retreated in the face of the arrow swarm, losing two men and a team of horses. He pulled back to wait for the Ribu advance before once more peppering the marching men. At midday, he sent one chariot back to the east to carry word of the enemy's progress, leaving him only sixteen chariots to continue harassing them.

Goloth rested men and horses in the midday heat, but renewed his attacks as the sun slid down the western sky. Again the Ribu halted after the first sortie, bringing their own archers to the fore, and again Goloth withdrew out of range until the Ribu started forward again. Dusk saw another chariot dispatched to find the king, and Goloth withdrew half an iteru to make camp. He did not think the Ribu would come looking for him at night, but he set out guards just in case. These guards would lose sleep, but Goloth marked them down to carry news back the next day. They ran short of supplies. There was forage on the plains, but no water except the meagre supplies they carried and the bulk of this went to the horses.

"Be strong," Goloth exhorted his men. "Another day and the army must surely be upon us." No man complained as they knew Goloth suffered alongside them.

The chariot force closed with the Ribu army slowly the next morning, preserving the strength of the horses. They found them breaking camp not far from where they had left them the previous night, sweeping in over the guard posts and slashing their way through the edges of the camp. For many minutes, the scene was one of chaos, with much yelling of commands and screaming, and then the Kemetu chariots broke free, but left five men and two chariots behind. Goloth gathered his thirteen remaining chariots and withdrew, watching as the Ribu started forward once more.

"We can't stop them," Goloth muttered. "Only slow them a little bit. Will it be enough, though?"

Twice more Goloth and his men halted the advance, but twice more he lost men and chariots as the Ribu countered his attacks more efficiently, and by dusk he was down to eight chariots. This time he withdrew half an iteru toward the river before sending off one last messenger to the king.

"We are no longer an effective fighting force," Goloth told his men. "Our attacks will be as sparrows mobbing a hawk. An annoyance perhaps, but I hardly think the Ribu will halt their advance again because of us."

The night passed slowly, with both men and horses suffering from thirst. With the first rays of dawn, Goloth sacrificed a mouthful of water he had been saving, invoking both the Kaftor sun god Belus and the Kemetu Khepri of the rising sun. One or two of his men groaned aloud as the precious water spilled from his flask onto the dry earth and was immediately soaked up.

"Khepri, kindly aspect of Re, known as Belus in other parts of the nations under you; take pity on us this day as we fight to keep the enemies of Kemet from despoiling this land of the gods."

Dry-mouthed, Goloth looked round at his men and grinned. "Mount up, men of the Hapi corps. We go to face the enemy once more."

"Sir, may I speak with you before we depart?" The leader of the charioteers looked grim and two or three of his men stood with him, as if lending him their support.

"What is it, Siese?"

"The horses, sir. We checked them first thing and their heartbeat is fast, their breaths shallow and their gums remain white too long when pressed."

"Meaning?"

"They suffer from a lack of water, sir."

"We are all in need of water, Siese."

"I know, sir, but a man can push himself beyond his limits in the king's name. A horse cannot. They will reach their limits and collapse."

Goloth considered what this meant. "Can the horses pull the chariots?"

"For a time...for a short time. They could collapse in mid-charge though, dooming their men."

"So what are you saying?"

"We cannot engage the enemy, sir. We must pull back toward the river if we are to save the horses. Perhaps the king is almost upon us..."

"And perhaps he is not," Goloth cut in. He scowled and paced back and forth for several moments. "All right. I have no wish to squander my men unnecessarily, but we will not retreat without doing our utmost to delay the Ribu. Send your weakest horses back toward the river, telling the king we will hold the enemy until he can bring the army up."

"Sir...we cannot hold the enemy. They are thousands and we are but a handful."

"Then you have leave to tell the king how we are outnumbered, but know our duty. Do it, Siese."

Siese saluted and rejoined his men. They talked, examining the horses again while Goloth and his archers awaited the result of their deliberations. Finally, a chariot was dispatched to the east and Siese returned to Goloth and saluted once more.

"The weakest team has been sent back, sir. The rest of us will do our duty though it means our deaths."

"Let's hope it won't come to that," Goloth said quietly. "Can your men handle a bow?"

"Yes, sir, though not very well." Siese smiled. "Otherwise, we'd be archers."

"Good man. So here's what we're going to do..."

The chariots moved slowly that morning, heading toward the presumed path of the enemy. As they drove, Goloth searched the landscape but saw nothing that would help them. Dust billowed into the sky from the passage of the enemy, and as soon as they came in sight, Goloth's little force dropped back, keeping ahead of the Ribu. The sun rose in the sky, and the horses slowed, plodding dispiritedly. Goloth knew they could not last much longer, so pointed to a small hillock a little to the north.

"Head for there," he said, pointing. "We'll make our stand."

"They'll roll right over us and crush us," Siese said.

"Then we'll die knowing we did our duty." He saw the fear in some eyes, so he added, "We're not in their main path, so they might just pass us by."

At the hillock, they turned the horses loose and overturned the chariots, gathering together every arrow they could find and arming some of the charioteers with spare bows. Then they waited, mouths dry, watching as the Ribu host marched closer, drew alongside, and halted. An hour passed, and then another.

"What are they doing?" Siese asked.

"I don't know," Goloth replied, "but look beyond them. There's a dust cloud on the horizon. I'm inclined to think the king's army has arrived."

A cheer went up from his men, but Goloth quickly quashed it. "Don't draw attention to them." He pushed between two of the chariots and strode out a few paces, then lifted his kilt and urinated in the direction of the Ribu. A growl arose, a wordless humming like a hive of bees kicked by a careless boy.

Goloth turned and bent over; flipping his kilt up to bare his buttocks at the enemy, and the growl rose to a roar. Siese joined him, then the other men, yelling and taunting the Ribu and displaying their nether parts.

"Arrows coming!" yelled one of the men, and they scrambled for the meagre cover of the overturned chariots as a storm of arrows descended on them. Cries of warning turned to screams of pain. Others snatched up the fallen arrows and sent them straight back, inflicting deaths and injuries of their own. Some of the Ribu charged their position, hacking at the overturned chariots with axes, stabbing between them with spears. Goloth's men released arrow after arrow, the tips almost touching their attackers and then, as the supply of arrows dwindled, seized spears and axes from the fallen and laid about them. Both Ribu and Kemetu died.

The pressure from the enemy increased and the few surviving Kemetu were pressed back into a tight circle. Goloth took a spear thrust to his arm, while Siese knelt, nursing a wounded belly, while every man surviving bore his own blood as well as that of others.

"We have served Kemet well, brothers," Goloth croaked. "We will meet in the underworld."

The Ribu drew back and Goloth prepared himself for the final thrust--for death. Instead a shudder went through the enemy host and he heard rams' horns sounding, felt the earth tremble beneath his feet. Then the Ribu host broke apart under the onslaught of five hundred Kemetu chariots with the Shu and Hapi corps hard on their heels. The enemy formations shattered and started to flee toward the west, but the chariots overtook them, trampling them beneath hooves and dealing out all manner of death. Goloth and his handful of survivors stood and cheered as the corps swept by them. Men stopped and offered water, and physicians moved about the field of battle, offering up what help they could.

The sun was well on its way toward the western horizon when the king returned, sweaty and dust-covered, and he almost drove past the little hillock with its shattered chariots, but Commander Merikare, in another chariot, called out to the king, pointing. Ramesses turned his chariot and stood looking down at the wounded and bandaged men, as his horses fidgeted and stamped.

"You are the archer with the uncouth name?" Ramesses asked.

"I am Goloth, Son of Re." He bowed awkwardly.

"You have done well, Goloth. Come and see me at Men-nefer." Ramesses twitched the reins and wheeled his chariot away, leaving the men to make their own way to camp.

# Chapter 35
# Year 8 of Usermaatre Ramesses

"Ah, you should have seen me, mother. The king, my father, chose me to fight by his side. I drove my own chariot as we destroyed the Ribu and I must have killed a hundred of the enemy."

"Thus speaks youth, ever boastful."

"You are just jealous, Khaemwaset, because I fought at the king's side and you didn't."

"I had duties of my own, you arrogant boy..."

"Enough of this, Khaemwaset. Your brother Meryamun is justifiably proud of his exploits in war, and I am proud of both of my sons. Come, Khaemwaset...Meryamun...embrace your mother and then sit down and tell me everything."

Both young men dutifully embraced their mother Tiye, and sat beside her on benches in the cool and shaded gardens of the Men-nefer Per-Khemret. Blossoming trees released a delicate perfume into the still air, songbirds called pleasingly from the boughs, and shoals of silver fish darted in the cool depths of the ponds. Servants brought them river-cooled wine and honey cakes, and then withdrew out of earshot.

"Tell me everything," Tiye said.

"I trampled the enemy beneath my chariot..."

"I was responsible for getting the corps to Perire..."

"But I won the battle itself..."

"There would have been no battle to win if I hadn't..."

"Enough, both of you," Tiye snapped. "I expect you to behave like Princes, not like quarrelsome little boys."

"Sorry, mother," Khaemwaset said, abashed.

"He started it," Meryamun muttered.

"I don't care who started it; I want it to stop. I'd like to hear what you both did, but if I cannot hear it from your lips in peace, I'll ask the scribes for the official account, and you know what that will be. The king will take credit for everything."

"He is the king," Khaemwaset said. "It is his right."

"Yes it is," Tiye agreed, "but I want to hear what my sons did. So you first, Khaemwaset. You are the heir."

Khaemwaset puffed up his chest with pride. "Yes, I am. Well, mother, the king was in Per-Ramesses, with two corps..."

"The Shu and Hapi."

"I know, Meryamun, I was there."

"Yes, but our mother wasn't."

"Hush, my son, you will get your turn. Let your brother tell his tale."

"As I was saying, the king was in Per-Ramesses with two corps and waiting for the Fleet to arrive. Well, as soon as we received word of the Ribu threat we had set out for Per-Ramesses and arrived there quickly. The king called me into conference where we debated the best means of meeting the threat. Most of the others wanted to send the corps on the barges southward and then up the westernmost branch, but I disagreed."

"I have no military training," Tiye said, "but even I know that the only other way to cross Ta Mehu from east to west is to cut straight across by land."

"We'd already sent a few men that way," Meryamun said. "A few chariots and archers. Not that there was much they could do except spy on the enemy."

"They ended up doing a bit more than that," Khaemwaset said. "Or weren't you going to mention that? Anyway, I'm talking now." He turned back to his mother with an annoyed expression on his face. "Where was I?"

"You had just disagreed with the route the corps were going to take."

"That is when I suggested the sea route. I said that it would be faster going downriver to the sea, then up the western branch. And the king agreed with me, mother..."

"Only partly," put in Meryamun. "Admiral Hori disagreed, so the king only sent two barges by that route."

"But it worked," Khaemwaset said triumphantly.

"You sailed on the Great Sea?" Tiye asked. "Not just where the river meets the sea? What was it like?"

"Like nothing you can imagine. The river is more or less calm, even when the current catches your boat or the north wind blows fiercely, but the sea is in constant motion. You look north and west and east, and as far as you can see, there is no land...much as I imagine it must be on the fabled Outer Ocean. The motion of the barges was most curious too, up and down as the water was raised into hillocks by the wind, then twisting and rolling as if we rode on the back of a horse. We used the oars to get us offshore, away from the shoals, but the wind tried to push us back. It was as if the gods of Kemet did not want us to stray too far from them."

"Astonishing," Tiye said. "I wish I could ride upon the sea too, though I think I would be frightened."

"You would not enjoy it, mother. The motion is not the only strange thing; there is the smell too. Salt and fish and rotting weed...but somehow the fresh wind off the water lifts your spirits. I found myself wanting to turn northward and sail out of sight of land. Imagine what it would be like to look in every direction and see only water."

"Disturbing," Meryamun commented. "And unnatural. Men were made by the gods to live on land with no more water than is found in the Great River. If we were meant to go out on the sea, the gods would have given us fins like a fish instead of legs."

"Yet the Sea Peoples cross the sea. They don't just follow the coast, but strike out across open water, out of sight of land. They are just men too, not fish."

"Well, I still think it is unnatural."

"So what happened?" Tiye asked. "You successfully navigated the open water and came to the western branch of the river?"

"Yes, I guided my two barges and every man aboard them safe to their destination, though several men said they wished to die." Khaemwaset smiled. "You would think those men drunk on strong wine. They vomited until I thought they would void their very bowels...but they survived, though weak, and I brought them back to land."

"And was the sea route faster, my son?"

"It was, mother. Two days, I told the king, and two days it was. We arrived just as the barge with all the chariots arrived, so with the extra men we had the chariots all reassembled much faster. Then I took my men westward toward Perire and happened upon a chariot bearing news of the Ribu."

"The chariots and archers the king sent across land," Meryamun said.

"Yes, their commander's name was Goloth, a Kaftor name I believe. Anyway, he sent chariots and messengers back twice a day, telling us where the enemy was and in which direction he marched. I was able to set up a string of men and chariots that would lead the king straight to the enemy."

"I hope the king appreciated your efforts, my son. It sounds like great honours should be coming your way."

"I am happy to have done my duty, mother. The greatest honour I could possibly have--to be the heir--is mine already."

"But you didn't actually do any fighting," Meryamun said. "You just got the men to Perire, along with Admiral Hori and the corps commanders."

"That was an achievement in itself," Tiye pointed out. "The king needs capable men around him to do his bidding."

"The king fought the enemy, as did I. Why is that counted as less than Khaemwaset's effort?"

"Go on then," Khaemwaset said with an indulgent smile. "Tell us of your great feats of arms. Tell us how you single-handedly defeated the Ribu."

Meryamun scowled. "You know very well that's not what I am saying, but I was there, in my chariot, and I killed many men."

"Of course you did."

"Set take you, brother. If I had been born before you instead of after, I would be heir and I'd make a better one than you. Ships will never guard Kemet's border; only armies will do that, and I am an army commander. If I was king, Kemet would be safe forever."

"But you are not, little brother, and never will be. I am heir and you are not, so an army commander is all you will ever be."

"You are not king yet," Meryamun yelled, "and a lot can happen before our father joins Re in the underworld."

"Is that a threat?" Khaemwaset demanded.

"Sons, enough!" Tiye said. "Khaemwaset, you are heir so I expect more from you than childish bickering. Meryamun, you are the younger son, so you will apologise to your brother."

Meryamun got to his feet and glared down at his brother and mother. "I will not apologise for the truth. I would make a better king than him, and one day our father will see that." He turned and stalked off through the garden.

Tiye called to her younger son to come back, but he would not return, disappearing into the palace.

"Never mind, mother," Khaemwaset said. "He is young and full of his own importance. He hates to see anyone ranked above him."

"He is sixteen floods and should be acting like a man."

Khaemwaset nodded. "He fought valiantly in the battle against the Ribu and probably thought he would be honoured above all others at the victory feast in Perire."

"He really did well? That was not just empty boasting on his part?"

"It was the truth, mother. Well...almost the truth. I wasn't there as I had to take the fleet north to guard the river should the Ribu break through, but Commander Merikare was there and he told me."

"What did he tell you?"

"My brother did not drive his own chariot any more than the king did. They both had charioteers, while they dealt out death with the bow. Meryamun was on the king's right hand as they charged the enemy ranks, taking them in the rear for the most part. They smashed the ranks of the Ribu and my brother did indeed kill Ribu, though perhaps not as many as he would claim."

"I wish I had seen it...no, perhaps I do not, but it must have been an exciting thing to see. The king and my son at the head of the army, destroying the Ribu enemy. They were destroyed, weren't they?"

"Utterly. They were close to three thousand strong and we took nearly two thousand right hands as trophies, as well as many spears, axes and arrows. The Ribu are finished this time. No sandstorm appeared to rescue them."

Tiye ran over her son's words in her mind, weighing them and savouring them. "You say the chariots took the Ribu in the rear. How is it that they managed that? Were they already in flight?"

"Ah, that is the other thing that gnaws at Meryamun's pride. The Ribu were in disarray because they had been goaded into attacking a tiny force of archers. Many saw the chariots coming and turned to face them, but the enemy ranks were disorganised and easy to shatter. You could say the king owes his victory to those few archers..." Khaemwaset broke off and looked toward the servants, making sure they were out of earshot. "...though it would not be wise to hint at such a thing in the king's hearing."

"I love your father," Tiye said with a smile, "but he will not hear it from me. So who commanded these brave men?"

"A man called Goloth whom I mentioned before. He is brother of a certain Rath who is in the Kemetu Navy."

"What strange names. You said this Goloth was a Kaftor?"

"Their father was...or is...Kaftor, and their mother Kemetu. Completely loyal though, it seems. Certainly I have no complaints about Rath, and by all accounts Goloth aided the king's victory."

"Tell me how."

"He had twenty chariots and as many archers, but he did not hesitate to attack the Ribu, inflicting many casualties over a few days. He sent men back to keep the king's army informed of the enemy's position and route, and delayed them until the king could destroy them."

"I hope the king will reward him for his bravery."

"It has already happened, mother, and that is in part why Meryamun is so upset. At the feast in Perire, the king bestowed the Gold of Valour on Goloth and confirmed him as Commander of Archers in the Hapi corps. He then bestowed a vineyard on him, and...oh, you'll love this irony, mother...the vineyard is in Per-Bast, and it turns out to be the one that Goloth's father owned before it was confiscated."

"Why was it confiscated?"

"Goloth's mother was sister to General Ament who served Queen Tausret."

"That bitch? It's a wonder the family was allowed to live."

"I think the king left them alone in the hope that Ament would return to see his sister. By the time that proved to be hopeless, the fire had gone from his belly and he merely turned them off their vineyard."

"And now it is back in the family. Was that by chance or by design, do you think?"

"I think by chance, though who can say? Whatever the reason, it hardly matters. Goloth is loyal to Usermaatre Ramesses. I have no doubt of that."

"And his brother...who was it? In the Navy."

"Rath. I have no reason to doubt his loyalty."

"Will he be rewarded too?"

"If he deserves it. He has done nothing of note yet, but I shall keep my eye on him."

# Chapter 36
# Year 8 of Usermaatre Ramesses

Hard on the heels of the victory over the Ribu came news of the Sea Peoples. Two years before, the Peleset had sued for a separate peace after Ramesses had fought the combined Sea Peoples confederation to a standstill, and when the news was conveyed to Men-nefer of the new uprising, Ramesses raged against the perfidious foreigners.

"It is your fault, Tjaty Herwernef. You persuaded me that this Peleset dog truly desired peace. Now he has betrayed me, as I knew he would."

"Son of Re, King Taita of the Peleset has kept faith with you. The Sea Peoples petitioned him to let them march through their lands, but he refused. Now, they are preparing to sail a fleet down the coast to enter the river mouths and deliver their army into the heart of Ta Mehu."

"How could you possibly know this?"

"King Taita has declared it so...and my own spies confirm it."

"When?"

"That is less certain, Son of Re. A month perhaps?"

"Then we must act quickly. Where is the Fleet?"

"Some is still in the western branch near Perire, other units here in Men-nefer..."

"Send it all to Per-Ramesses and have Admiral Hori and Prince Khaemwaset attend on me here. What about the corps?"

"Hapi continues the mopping up of Ribu units in the west, Shu is in Men-nefer. Re came down to Per-Ramesses when you took Shu out."

Ramesses nodded. "Shu goes up to Per-Ramesses and send north for Heru. Three corps should be enough if the Sea Peoples land, but I intend to destroy them before that."

When the Admiral and the Prince attended upon the king, he told them the exact same thing--that the Sea Peoples would be destroyed before they could ever land upon the soil of Ta Mehu.

Admiral Hori struggled to keep his concern off his face. "Son of Re, I... I am not sure I can guarantee that. Kemet is not a seafaring nation, whereas the Sea Peoples are...well, just that. Their skill is greater than ours on the water, so we should prepare to meet them on land where our might is greater."

"If they land upon our shores I will smite them with my corps, Hori, but I will still hold you accountable for your failure."

"And I, father?" Khaemwaset asked.

"You are my heir and you showed yourself imaginative and determined in taking the sea route to Perire. Do so again by destroying the Sea Peoples fleet."

Khaemwaset bowed and said, "As my lord commands," and Hori had no choice but to follow suit.

Admiral Hori left for Per-Ramesses immediately, taking with him the boats that were in the northern capital, while Khaemwaset took a fast boat down the western branch to bring the part of the fleet that was still there. Mindful of the words he had had with his mother, he took the junior officer Rath with him, meaning to find out more about the young man. Also mindful of Admiral Hori's instructions, he sent all but one barge threshing its way upriver, while he took a lightly laden one out to sea.

"Do you know why I'm doing this, Rath?"

"I would not presume to question you, my lord."

"I am told you are a young man who thinks, so presume," Khaemwaset said. "Tell me why I am disobeying the admiral's orders."

Rath looked north to where the western branch met the Great Sea. A fresh wind almost negated the pull of the current, so the barge's oars were out, threshing the green water into foam. Ahead of them lay a line of breakers where salt water met fresh, and where they would meet rougher conditions.

"You are Son of the King's Body. Your status..."

"Wrong. Do you truly imagine I am so vainglorious I would put myself ahead of the safety of the kingdoms? Try again."

Rath considered the Prince and stumbled as the barge crested the line of breakers, forging its way out into the muddy waters offshore.

"Kemet's future lies with a strong Navy. You welcome any opportunity to take ships out to sea, because only by doing so can you know how Kemet's enemies view us."

"Better. Kemet will always be a land power, though. We will never match the expertise of the seafaring nations. You are closer when you talk of how they view us."

Rath turned to look back the way they had come. The barge plunged its way out to sea and then turned parallel to the shore, heading eastward. He stared at the land slipping past and imagined himself one of the Sea Peoples.

"You want to put yourself into the mind of a sea captain coming to invade Kemet. You think that by doing so you can find a way to counter the threat."

"Very good, Rath. Admiral Hori thinks only of the success we had last time and does not consider the failure."

"Was it a failure, my lord? The Sea Peoples were driven off."

"They failed to land an army, but their fleet escaped almost unscathed. As often as we allow that, they will return. If Kemet is to be safe and secure, the Sea People's ships must be destroyed."

"The admiral tried to do that. I know, my lord, I was there."

"Tried...and failed."

"So what will you do that is different?"

"Perhaps we just need more boats, more barges."

Khaemwaset kept silent so long, Rath wondered if the discussion was over and whether he should bow and withdraw, and then he caught a glimpse of the Prince watching him.

"More boats are not the answer, my lord."

"Why not? If we matched their strength..." Khaemwaset let his voice trail off, hoping that Rath would utter an insightful observation.

"Kemet needs another twenty years to match their strength, my lord, and that will be very expensive so is effectively never. The enemy ships are larger, carry more men, and are faster. They can offer battle and overwhelm us unless the corps back us up, or flee our every effort and return when our backs are turned. We cannot watch every khet of coastline all the time."

"What would you do then?"

"I am only a very junior officer, my lord. It is not my place to advise you."

"Then I make you a barge commander. Now you can advise me."

"My lord..." Rath dropped to his knees on the spray-swept deck. "You do me too much honour."

"I'll decide if it is too much. You can start by advising me. If your advice is useless I'll demote you again. Now get up and speak your mind."

Rath got to his feet and licked his lips. "The Sea Peoples have two great advantages over our navy, my lord--strength and speed. Both must be countered to achieve a victory over them."

"Our corps, working in conjunction with the Fleet, match their strength, but few of our boats match theirs for speed," Khaemwaset said. "If they do not desire it, we can never engage them in battle."

"So we must prevent them from running away."

The Prince laughed. "Do not imagine we can present our backsides to the enemy and enrage them like your brother did with the Ribu. Yes, I heard the stories. Try that with the Sea Peoples, and I think you can expect an arrow in your buttocks."

"No, my lord, I did not contemplate such an action."

"Then how?"

"I don't know, my lord. Not yet anyway. I have an idea, but I don't know if it will work. Will you grant me time to think about it?"

"You have until we dock in Per-Ramesses. Then you can retain command of this barge or revert to the little fishing boat you once commanded."

Rath bowed and excused himself, walking up to the bow and braving the plunging motion of the barge as it forged its way across the mouths of the Great River and started its turn into the eastern branch. He saw nothing that gave him an insight into how to defeat the Sea Peoples.

The turn into the river mouth was tricky, the waves pushing the barge from behind and the river current impeding its progress. They crossed the tumultuous line of breakers and moved into calmer waters where the meadows along the seafront drew in to guide the barge upriver. Signs of civilisation appeared, ruins and a standing statue of an ancient king sinking into the moist and fertile earth. An idea glimmered in Rath's mind, but as he looked to the empty meadows opposite, the idea disappeared. An inlet appeared on one side, its narrow channel almost choked by reeds and waterlilies, and he wondered whether ships could be hidden therein to emerge and cut off the enemy's retreat.

"They'd see us, and anyway, we couldn't hide enough in there to make a difference," he muttered.

One of the nearby sailors looked up at his words, but then went back to coiling rope. The rope kinked and he called another man across to help him straighten it out. They laid it across the deck, and one of them winked at the other, calling out to yet another man to quickly fetch something from the bow. The third man hurried forward and as he stepped over the rope, the other two men lifted it suddenly, tangling the man's legs so he crashed to the deck with a yell. Most of the crew erupted in laughter, but the captain upbraided their levity and got them back to work. Rath stood and stared at the rope and the man who had fallen, the idea that had germinated in his mind earlier now pushing out tendrils as it grew.

They docked at Per-Ramesses ahead of the main fleet still working its way downriver from the junction, and as Admiral Hori was not on hand to take the young Prince to task, Khaemwaset called Rath to him before they disembarked.

"You have a solution?"

"I believe I do, my lord," Rath said cautiously. "However, I would like to make a few enquiries before I reveal it."

"Admiral Hori will be here in two days or less. Once he gets here he will assume command of the fleet and organise matters according to his own ideas of attack and defence. I would like to have an alternative to offer him."

"May I have a letter of authorisation from you, my lord? To encourage men to talk to me."

"As long as it is only talk. I cannot authorise expenditure without knowing exactly what it is for."

"Talk is all that is needed at the moment. Er...perhaps the use of a scribe too?"

"I want results, Rath."

"I shall do my utmost, my lord."

Rath took himself off to the ship-builders yards and started talking earnestly to the rope-makers there. He inspected their stores and asked questions, had lengths of rope weighed, both wet and dry, and had a junior scribe make some calculations for him which took the better part of a day. From there, Rath viewed the masts of barges and the tools available to the builders, having the scribe make lists for him. As Rath could not read the scribal writing, he had him append some of the basic script he had seen his father use when he managed the accounts of his vineyard.

"I could read it for you," the scribe said.

"I know, but I will be presenting this to Prince Khaemwaset and Admiral Hori...perhaps even the king...and I must be prepared to do it alone."

Rath still had not brought his figures to Khaemwaset after Admiral Hori arrived with the Fleet. Hori immediately called a meeting of his commanders, which Khaemwaset had to attend without knowing if Rath had come up with a reasonable alternative. He listened in silence to the usual plans being made of meeting the Sea Peoples ships on the river, engaging them in battle as best they could and hopefully driving them off.

"Drive them away and they will return," Khaemwaset said. "We must destroy their fleet completely."

"That much is obvious," Hori retorted. "The problem, as always, is how to achieve it. Do you, perhaps, have a solution to this problem, Prince Khaemwaset?"

Khaemwaset grimaced, thinking furious thoughts about his junior officer who had promised so much and delivered so little. He kept silent for a time in the face of his admiral's scorn and the mirth of his fellow officers, but finally could take no more.

"I have a solution, Admiral Hori, but the officer I sent to gather information has not yet returned."

"No doubt it involved engaging the enemy out to sea instead of in the river?" Hori asked. "You seem to have a love for the dangers of salt water."

"No, my lord Admiral, but I will present my plan to you as soon as my tardy officer returns."

A messenger ran in and proffered a letter to the admiral. He scanned it and dismissed the man.

"Your man had better hurry then, Prince Khaemwaset, for the enemy have been seen north of here. On the present course and speed, they will be here in three days."

Admiral Hori immediately started issuing orders to ready the Fleet for action, sending officers scurrying to carry out his desires. Khaemwaset withdrew quietly and went in search of Rath, eventually finding him in the rope makers' yards examining some thick cables.

"You are aware Hori has arrived?" Khaemwaset demanded.

"Yes, my lord, and also that the enemy is near. That is why I thought I had better make sure I had all the things we would need."

"It's too late, Rath. The time for making plans has passed. Hori is already putting the defence in motion. The same defence as last time."

Rath looked up from where he was poring over some diagrams. "You are a Prince and the heir, though. You have some forces at your command?"

"Some," Khaemwaset agreed, "but not enough to mount a different defence."

"How many men?"

"Five hundred."

"Not enough." Rath frowned. "You could get more? From the Hapi corps perhaps? Another five hundred? They don't need to be skilled, but they need to be strong."

"Will your plan succeed? If I disobey my admiral and fail, the king my father will not look kindly on me."

"It will...if the gods smile on us."

"What else do you need beside a thousand men?"

Rath smiled and looked down at the diagram. "Six barge masts, an expert bowman, several khet of very fine rope, several more of fine rope and barge mooring cable and three times as much of the heaviest cable in the rope yards. Luckily, Samu here was just assuring me they have it all."

"Show me what you intend."

Rath showed him.

Two days later, Rath and Khaemwaset stood in the grassy meadows on the eastern side of the river branch, where the river ran at its narrowest and the current rippled the water. Beside them, three barge masts had been hammered into the ground for most of their lengths, two leaning away from the river and one toward, and the tops lashed together firmly. Behind them, half an hour distant and out of sight of the river, a thousand men waited. Across on the western shore, another almost identical structure stood, with only a small knot of men beside it.

"Is it going to work?" Khaemwaset asked.

"That is with the gods," Rath replied.

"Shouldn't we put it in place now? Rather than wait until the enemy is upon us?"

"No." Rath sensed rather than saw the irritation on the Prince's face. "No, my lord. If we move too soon, we risk discovery."

"It'd better work," Khaemwaset muttered.

A runner jogged up to them and saluted the Prince. "The enemy is in sight, my lord. They are just crossing from the sea to the river."

Rath made a swift calculation of the distances involved, and how long it had taken the messenger to reach them.

"Go to the men camped inland and tell them to start moving up..." he glanced at the position of the morning sun, "...at midday. No sooner."

The messenger stared at Rath and then looked at Khaemwaset. "My lord?"

"Do as he says."

The messenger ran off, and the two men by the hammered-in masts stood in their meagre shade and waited while the sun slowly crept up the sky.

"There..." Rath said, pointing.

To the north, first one, then another, and then several scraps of sail seemed to scud along the tops of the long grass and reed beds, drawing nearer and becoming larger. Soon, wooden hulls could be discerned, and banks of oars threshing the waters of the river as the warships of the Sea Peoples came in sight.

Rath and Khaemwaset crouched low and watched as the ships thrashed their way upriver, the men counting them as they passed.

"Twenty-three," Rath said.

"This plan of yours had better work. That many ships will overcome our fleet and if they escape to the sea, they'll return at will, devastating our lands."

The last of the ships disappeared round a bend in the river, once more becoming scraps of sail blowing across the reed beds. Rath stood up and waved his hands over his head, and the men on the far side of the river ran out and busied themselves with their own preparations. Presently, one of them picked up a bow and fitted an arrow carefully, taking aim at Rath. The archer loosed and the arrow arced into the sky, trailing a thin thread behind it. It faltered in its flight, dragged back by the weight of the thread, and fell into the river half a khet from the eastern shore.

"It's not going to work," Khaemwaset groaned. "Didn't you even test this first?"

The men on the far side dragged the arrow from the river, and the archer moved down to the water's edge before trying again. Again the arrow fell short, as the extra distance gained by moving closer was negated by the extra weight of the wet cord. The arrow was retrieved once more and this time the archer waded out into the water until he stood waist deep. He loosed and although the arrow came closer, it still splashed into the water. The men on the far side grabbed the cord to drag it back, but Rath yelled to them to wait, and dived into the river, striking out strongly for the drifting arrow.

Rath reached the arrow and grabbed it, but the current carried him downriver. He was in danger of being carried away, but the first of the thousand men arrived and a few of the stronger swimmers plunged in and hauled him onto the bank. Coughing and spluttering, he stumbled back to the mast tripod, clutching the cord in his fist.

"Pull it across," he told the men. "Carefully. If it snaps we have to start again."

The men took care and drew the cord across the river. Tied to its end was a thicker, stronger cord, and a few khet later, they grasped a heavier mooring cable. Now more men lent a hand, hauling it across the river, and as it dragged the final cable across, hundreds of men took their place on the rope, drawing toward them a braided cable as thick as a man's waist. This was hauled, with much cursing and sweating, to the tripod and wound around it, securing it firmly. The cable stretched across the river, bowing in the middle to almost brush the water and rising to half a man's height by the shore. Water, squeezed from its fibres by the pressure put upon them, rained down as a drizzle on the surface of the river.

"It will never hold," Khaemwaset said. "The moment a ship strikes that, the rope will part and all this will have been for nothing."

Rath thought he might well be right, but was not going to say anything. Time would tell, and all they could do now was wait. In the distance, a faint smudge of smoke staining the blue sky told of some conflict, of a battle hard fought.

Khaemwaset sent off a runner upriver to find out what was going on, and then another after an hour. The second one returned, saying he had met the first upon the road, and that the combined Shu and Hapi corps onshore, and the Fleet, had met the enemy almost within sight of the walls of Per-Ramesses and defeated them. Now the Sea Peoples were withdrawing toward safety.

"How many ships were sunk by the Fleet?" Khaemwaset asked.

"Two, my lord. Also one burned and one captured."

"More than I thought," the Prince said. "The rope had better work, Rath, or I'll be mocked by the admiral and you really don't want that to happen."

Rath did not bother to reply, but started shouting orders to the officers of the thousand men. They picked up their weapons--bows and spears for the most part--and took up positions near the river's edge.

The first of the Sea Peoples' ships came in sight, using oars and the current to speed their way, but they backed water when they caught sight of the rope strung between the tripods. Rath could see the enemy officers gathered in the bow, staring downriver, and he guessed they were trying to judge the dangers it might present. Evidently, it failed to impress as the oars dug deep once more, propelling the ship forward. In its wake, another two ships came in sight, and more masts could be seen beyond them, swaying above the reed beds.

The first ship hit the suspended rope, shuddering to a stop, though the rope creaked and Rath thought he could see the sunken masts of the tripod shift in their earthy sockets. It held and several oars in the enemy ship snapped and the mast toppled forward from the strain. The ship slowly turned sideways, putting more pressure on the rope, but the current pushed hard on the side of the vessel, swamping the sides. Screams and shouts arose as the ship ponderously turned over, rolling under the rope and splitting apart. Suddenly the river was full of struggling men and the Kemetu archers picked them off, while any who reached the near shore were dispatched by the spearmen.

The second and third ships saw what was happening, but it was too late to avoid the rope. One hit it and started turning broadside on, while the other turned side on, hoping to beat away, but its oars got tangled in those of the boat in front and the stern of the second stove in the side of the third. Both ships went down in a welter of broken timbers and screaming men, the river below now covered with debris and dead men.

More ships of the Sea Peoples appeared. Some drove hard for the rope, hoping to break through, while others headed for the banks. One ship was pushed under by the force of the current, and another drove up over the rope, bearing it down below the surface, but the ship could no longer move by its own power and the river pushed the stern under water and swamped it.

Two boats disgorged their men onto the eastern bank and rushed the tripod, but the thousand Kemetu men fought back and gradually overwhelmed them. One of the ships managed to push off from the shore again, but without a full complement of oarsmen it drifted down to the rope and held. Archers now picked off the remaining crew members. The other ship was overrun and captured by Kemetu.

The Sea Peoples tried again as their remaining ships now crowded the stretch of river above the rope barrier. Two ships collided, snapping oars, and another one tried to ram the rope, and although it creaked loudly, the rope held. The crew members fought to prevent their ship from turning side on and swamping, but to no avail. Another ship drove up onto the western pastures and its crew overwhelmed and killed the few men guarding the tripod there. Axes were brought out and they set to work chopping through the thick rope cable.

"That's it," Rath said, pointing it out to Khaemwaset. "We can't stop them."

"You should have put more men there. What were you thinking?"

Rath decided not to point out that the Prince had been aware of the details of the plan and had not thought to put men there either, but decided that could constitute a criticism of his betters. Instead, he just watched as the rope was hacked through and the barrier fell into the river with a splash.

At once, the remaining ships of the Sea Peoples resumed their flight to the sea amidst the wreckage of several of their vessels. The Kemetu men ran alongside for a while, shouting and mocking their enemies, but eventually gave up as one after another, they crossed the river bar and escaped.

"If only we had more men in the west to protect the rope," Khaemwaset said.

"I'd still call that a resounding victory, my lord," Rath said. "Seven ships sunk, one captured, and at least three others damaged. Better than Admiral Hori achieved with the whole Fleet, if the messenger is to be believed."

Khaemwaset nodded. "True. And altogether, half their ships destroyed. They will not return in a hurry."

"I will set the rope makers to weaving another, stronger rope just in case, my lord."

"Leave that for somebody else. That is no job for one of my commanders."

"You are confirming me in that position, my lord?"

"Yes; you have proven your worth today. It is subject to the Admiral's approval, of course, but after today he will not dare contradict me."

# Chapter 37
# Year 9 of Usermaatre Ramesses

**Usermaatre Ramesses speaks**

Now I shall take the measure of my son and heir, Khaemwaset. I have observed him in battle, when it is easy for one with the blood of kings flowing within him to achieve greatness. Pride, if nothing else, would prevent him from disgracing himself and indeed, I saw no signs of weakness. He performed his duties well, achieving a great victory over the fleet of the Sea Peoples, and already the people acclaim him as a worthy son of the father. That being said, he must now prove himself in other ways now that peace has settled over the borders of Kemet. It is one thing to order men into battle, quite another to maintain order over oneself.

He came to see me not long after the Sea People sued for peace and in my gracious magnanimity I had granted them what they sought. All things were done correctly. My son, who might have expected to walk in unannounced on his father, petitioned the Tjaty for an audience, and the request was brought to me along with a host of other petitions from lesser men. I smiled and readily granted him audience, honouring him before the court by receiving him in the Great Throne Room. He advanced through the throng of courtiers, tall and slim and young, but displaying a maturity and presence beyond his years. Drawing near to the throne, he bowed low and greeted me.

"Life! Health! Prosperity! Usermaatre Ramesses, Son of Re, Lord of the Two Kingdoms."

"You are welcome indeed, my son and heir." I gestured to the assembled courtiers. "Praise Crown Prince Khaemwaset, victor over the fleet of the Sea Peoples."

The court cheered dutifully, having heard his praises sung before, but then I honoured him by rising from my throne and descending from the dais to embrace him and kiss him on the cheek, and the applause softened and warmed. I could tell that the court was delighted to see such love and affection openly displayed between king and heir.

"Father, may I speak with you in private?"

"Of course. Dine with me at noon."

I took my place on the throne once more, and Khaemwaset made a graceful exit. I carried on the business of the kingdoms for another hour or so, until pangs of hunger rumbled in my belly. Tjaty Herwernef immediately stepped forward and drew proceedings to a close, allowing me to withdraw to a side room. It had a wide window with a view of the palace gardens, and the fragrance of a blossoming tree and the twittering of birds calmed me after the stresses of the court.

I divested myself of the Double Crown, of the heka and nekhakha of kingly authority, of my goat's hair false beard, and scratched my chin and my shaved head while the servants brought in food and drink. Khaemwaset walked in and greeted me once more, but this time informally, and we sat to partake of a light midday meal.

For a time we spoke of nothing of any consequence, all the while accepting food and drink from the servants, remarking on the taste of the sliced goose, of the crispness of radishes and onions, the sweetness of the figs, and the tartness of the beer. I ate sparingly, favouring the left side of my mouth as my teeth hurt on the right side, but Khaemwaset, secure in his youth, ate enough for both of us. I sat and watched him eat when I had finished, until at last he drained his cup, pushed away his plate and wiped his mouth with clean linen.

"That was good," he said, and stifled a belch.

"I am glad that food still holds attractions for you, my son. I would be interested in knowing what else does."

Khaemwaset raised an eyebrow. "You have heard something, father?"

"Herwernef keeps me informed of most things that happen within the kingdoms."

Khaemwaset nodded. "Nothing is hidden from the eyes of the king."

"I would rather hear it from your lips, my son."

He sat in silence for a short time, as if collecting his thoughts, before he spoke. "You have won great victories over the Sea Peoples and the Ribu, father. It will be many years before the enemies of Kemet dare to trespass upon our borders, and this is all because of the force of your arms."

"You have had a share in this victory," I said modestly. "Your fleet all but destroyed the Sea Peoples."

"You are generous, father. Kemet's strength lies in the army, and you wielded it in a masterful fashion." Khaemwaset hesitated and then plunged ahead. "Kemet's navy has been fashioned and is handled well by Admiral Hori. He has able commanders, some of whom I have raised to that position. My presence is no longer required, and I ask that I be relieved of my duties."

"The king traditionally leads the armies of Kemet against the foe," I said, and I could feel by forehead wrinkling into a frown as I spoke. "As heir, you have rights, but are you asking to lead the army in my stead? Or do you seek a lesser position? General of the Armies, perhaps...or if you would rather stay within the navy, you can replace Hori..."

"That is not what I seek, father."

Now I did frown, for a dutiful son should not interrupt his father--especially if the father was also the king. He saw my frown and hastened to make amends.

"My apologies, father. I meant no disrespect, but you misunderstand me."

"Really? Then tell me how I have been so ignorant to have done so."

"I misspoke, father...forgive me. I only meant to say that I desire to leave all military pursuits behind, both in the navy and the army, and concentrate on the priesthood."

I have to admit I stared at my son as if he had lost his mind. "The king leads the army against his foes," I reiterated after a few moments. "How will you do so if you have no experience?"

Khaemwaset shrugged. "I will always have generals and able corps commanders to lead the army."

"That is not the same thing at all. Kemet has only had one king in recent memory who did not lead his army--the heretic--and look how he turned out." The thought disturbed me so much I got to my feet and started pacing. "Every other king has done so...even that bitch Tausret led her army."

"I know, father, and I do not willingly shirk my duties. If I am called upon to do so, I will lead the army into battle, even if I have to rely on my commanders for advice."

"No."

"No?"

"I do not accept such an idea. The king commands...always. To do otherwise is to weaken the monarchy. I will not countenance my heir being a man who would expect others to fight in his place."

Khaemwaset looked away and took several long, deep breaths before facing me again. "Then replace me as heir, father."

"What? No. You are my eldest living son."

"But not your only son. Meryamun..."

"Meryamun is a fool," I broke in. "And before you say it, Prehirwenemef is not suited for high office either."

"Ramesses then..."

"Your half-brother Ramesses is a child."

"But promising, I hear."

"Will you be the one to explain to your mother why I would pass over three of her grown sons to make the child of my sister-wife my heir?"

Khaemwaset grunted.

"I thought not. Khaemwaset, you are the best of my sons and even had you not been the eldest, you are the one I would now pick to succeed me."

"You are kind; father, but we all know what your plan was for me...why you named me Khaemwaset. I was to be a priest like the son of the Great Usermaatre. That was my future...that is my future...and I am content that it should be so."

I frowned and stopped my pacing beside the table that still held the remnants of the meal. The servants had been clearing it away, but withdrew from my immediate proximity, waiting for me to pass by. Instead, I broke off a small piece of bread and rolled it in my fingers while I considered my son's words.

"I was a young man when I made those decisions, more concerned with modelling myself on a great man rather than carving out a name of my own."

Khaemwaset nodded. "Even to adopting the throne name Usermaatre. I understand, father, but there is nothing wrong with doing things as our revered ancestors did them. You named me Khaemwaset and declared that I would be a Sem-priest of Ptah...and I am happy to be that. I welcome a future where I am a priest of Ptah--maybe I will rise even to the office of the Hem-netjer of Ptah."

"As king, you will be the High Priest of every god."

"I think a special relationship with Ptah will be enough for me."

"And what of the kingdoms?"

"What do you mean, father?"

"Your decision affects others as well as you. You want to shut yourself away in the temple of Ptah, but the kingdoms need stability; they need Ma'at. How can they achieve this without an heir? What will become of the kingdoms and every person within them if there is no designated king after me? There will be rioting and civil war as every general with an army or nobleman with the faintest claim to royalty tries to take the throne. Is that what you want for Kemet?"

"Of course not, father."

"Then accept your fate. You are my heir, the Crown Prince, and my successor."

"It...it is a burden..."

His words sparked anger and I turned on him, my voice raised. "By all the gods, do you think I don't know that? Of course it is a burden, a weight upon your shoulders, but it is also the greatest honour the gods can bestow. Why else were you born as my son if not to take up this burden when it was handed to you and fulfil the destiny the gods have written in the heavens for you? You will remain my heir and by the gods you will act like my heir."

I turned away from him, clenching my fists and breathing hard. When I had calmed, I continued in a voice that I think...I hope...conveyed my disappointment.

"You will continue as my heir but I will, because you ask it of me, relieve you of your military duties. Go and play at being priest until you come to your senses."

Khaemwaset was silent for perhaps ten measured breaths and then, "I am sorry, father, but I think it for the best."

I did not reply, and resolutely kept my back to him. After a time, I heard the sounds of his sandals on the tiles as he withdrew from my presence. I turned then and dismissed the servants, waiting until they had closed the door and left me alone.

I was furious, but what could I do? I could hardly punish him, or force him to continue in the navy. This is what I meant when I said that peacetime activities would measure my son. His actions now, here, far from the battlefield, would prove his worth. And in truth, there are many other aspects to the kingship that an heir must master. Leading an army is but one of them; and almost as important is being able to govern in peacetime is another. I shall have Tjaty Herwernef take him in hand; guide him in the intricacies of government and the laws of Kemet and thus prepare him for when he must rule.

Another thought occurs to me. He should have a hand in decision making. I must look for something important concerning the kingdoms and have him decide what to do about it. Leave it up to him entirely. If he makes a mistake, let him correct it. Responsibility for his actions is an important lesson. I don't know what exactly, so I shall give it some thought. An appointment perhaps...though I cannot think of a suitable one right at this moment.

I am still a young man--well, not young exactly, but not old either. There is time. And if in five or ten or thirty years I find Khaemwaset really is not suited to succeed me, then I shall elevate one of my other sons. While I may not have as many sons as the Great Usermaatre, unless you could the many children of my concubines, I believe I have ample choice. The king who succeeds me will lead Kemet to greatness once more.

# Chapter 38
# Year 9 of Usermaatre Ramesses

Ramesses basked in the glory of twin victories over Kemet's enemies. The Ribu had been destroyed in the west, and then the Sea Peoples fleet had suffered an ignominious defeat in the waters near Per-Ramesses. His spies reported that the crippled fleet had withdrawn well to the north of King Taita's territory and were now licking their wounds. However, another report came in from closer at hand, one that caused the king some disquiet.

"The traitor Ament? Are you certain?"

"Nothing is certain, Majesty," Tjaty Herwernef replied. "My spies report a man going by that name, but whether that is indeed so, is unconfirmed."

"Tell me what is known."

Herwernef bowed and marshalled his thoughts. "Son of Re, ever since your glorious father Userkhaure-setepenre overthrew the usurper and mounted the Double Throne, men have looked for the traitor known as General Ament and the usurper herself known as Tausret. For many years they were believed dead, lost in the western deserts, but every now and then someone would claim to have seen them. No one has reported Tausret for at least five years, but it is claimed Ament still wanders the land."

"Is it possible?" Ramesses demanded. "Who in Kemet would give them shelter?"

"It is possible," Herwernef conceded, "though unlikely they are in Kemet. Outside is another matter." The Tjaty looked pensive. "Your Majesty knows that in the earliest days of your father's reign there were still soldiers loyal to the usurper? Many of these fled into the deserts, particularly in the Land of Sin. There are perhaps three hundred of them now."

"That many? Why were they not stamped out?"

"They were judged to be leaderless and harmless. In fact, they served a useful purpose."

"Indeed? I can think of no useful purpose for allowing traitors to flourish."

"Son of Re, a few traitors together can easily hide but a hundred together cannot. We know where they are, and I have left them alone so that any disaffected elements in Kemet may be drawn to them instead of causing trouble within the kingdoms. For ten years or more, they have done nothing beyond raid a few villages and steal a few crops and herds."

"They are stealing from me, Herwernef. Do you condone this?"

"No, Son of Re, but their depredations are minor. In fact, they are more like bandits than soldiers. It would cost the treasury more to root them out than to allow them their petty thefts."

"I have sworn to stamp out bandits within the kingdoms and allow men and women to walk safely where they will."

"Strictly, they are not within the kingdoms."

"So you recommend leaving them alone?"

"Until the last few days, yes, Son of Re. Now, however...well, things have changed."

"Because of this report of Ament?"

"Yes, Son of Re. The man may or may not actually be Ament, but people believe he is. Already, disaffected men are flocking to his banner. I think that now we must eradicate them."

"Where are these traitors?"

"In the Land of Sin. If you will allow me, Majesty..." Herwernef called a scribe over, who unrolled a papyrus map showing a sketch of Ta Mehu and adjacent lands. The Tjaty pointed to a crescent-shaped mark in the desert. "There is a valley here...a ravine...with a stream and date palms. Nearly five hundred men live here, together with the man known as Ament."

"You are certain of this?"

"I have a spy who has lived among them for nearly two years."

Ramesses studied the map and asked about a few of the features marked on it. "Send word to General Djehutemheb that he is to bring two corps south, the Re and Set I think, and eradicate this nest of traitors."

"Two corps, Majesty? There are only five hundred men."

"Five hundred men who presumably know the desert well. I want every man killed." The king looked thoughtful. "Except the man they call Ament," he added. "I will find out who he is before I kill him."

Ament had come to regard his sojourn in the desert of Sin as a prison sentence. He longed to return north to his beloved wife Tausret and his family, but his wishes were not regarded by his captors. Ostensibly, Ament was a guest--an honoured guest--but in reality he was a prisoner. The commander of the loyal Set corps, Harkhuf, made a show of consulting him in every decision, and paraded him whenever new recruits filtered through the desert to their ravine, but any attempt he made to leave the immediate confines of the camp were politely but firmly stopped. Harkhuf had bestowed an honour guard on Ament, but as few people among the loyal Sets wished him harm, their primary purpose was to prevent his escape.

The months of his captivity passed slowly, with nothing to occupy his time but wandering the floor of the valley and watching the soldiers being put through their paces. For all that Harkhuf called them a corps, they were a far cry from the men who had once stood behind him and faced the army of Setnakhte and Ramesses. These men went through the forms, but they were slovenly and lazy for the most part, and Ament considered they made better bandits than soldiers. In the early days, when he still thought he was a guest, Ament had made various suggestions and had even tried to instigate a few changes, but to no effect.

Now he just looked for an opportunity to escape.

There were few opportunities. Every time Ament showed any sign of wanting to leave the valley, or even approach the few entrances, he was turned back. After a few attempts, he spoke to Harkhuf. The commander greeted him without getting up and pointed to a stool in the corner of his tent.

"General Ament, always a pleasure to see you. May I offer you refreshment?" He picked up the jug of beer beside his chair and held it out. "Freshly brewed," he added, belching loudly.

Ament sat, but carefully kept a neutral expression on his face as he declined the beer. "I want to know your intentions," he said.

"Concerning what?"

"Me. Your corps. Kemet."

Harkhuf laughed and took another drink from the beer jug. "Easily answered. You are our honoured guest. My corps grows in strength. Kemet awaits us."

"That is no answer. You say I am an honoured guest, but I cannot even take a piss without your men watching."

Harkhuf looked beyond Ament to where his guard stood carefully watching him, as he had instructed. He waved them back casually. "My men love you and desire that no harm come to you. There are snakes and scorpions in the valley."

"I have lived with snakes and scorpions all my life, Harkhuf. I know how to look after myself. I am not a child to need nurses."

"I shall tell my men to offer you more privacy, if that is your wish."

"It is. And they will also allow me to leave the valley?"

"Why would you wish to leave?"

"Others leave the valley; why shouldn't I?"

"Others leave the valley for a purpose--to trade for food or weapons, to spy on our enemies, to raid farms."

"I could do those things too. I am tired of seeing nothing but the sheer walls of this rocky prison."

"I am sorry you see it that way, Ament. You are precious to us and we only want to keep you safe."

Ament could see that Harkhuf was unlikely to let him just walk out of the valley, so he decided to try another avenue to achieve the same result.

"How am I precious to you? I was once your General, but those times have passed."

"By no means," Harkhuf replied. "The names of General Ament and Queen Tausret are well known in Kemet, and thousands of the common people desire your return. Even to hint at your presence brings much attention, and the numbers flocking to our cause has increased ten-fold since you arrived. Very soon, we will be able to challenge the corps of Ramesses and overcome them."

"You do not seriously imagine these men can challenge the might of Kemet's corps? I see them daily and know them for what they are. If you have five times this number they could scarcely overcome the newest and least experienced of the corps, and Ramesses has many to call upon."

"What you see is but a fraction of our strength," Harkhuf said.

"You have other groups?"

"When we march on Kemet with you and Queen Tausret at our head, men will flock to our banners. Men will desert the corps and join us against the usurper."

Ament turned away so Harkhuf would not see the contempt in his eyes. "How can you possibly believe that?"

"We have spies in all the corps. They tell us of the grumbling and discontent among the men, and when the spies talk of the old days, everybody says they long for them to return."

"All soldiers grumble, Harkhuf. It doesn't mean they will desert their officers."

Harkhuf stared at Ament and then shook his head. "I am tired of your lack of faith. Leave me."

"At least let me help," Ament said. "Let me train the men."

"They have officers already."

"And I am supposedly their General. If that is true, then let me gauge their readiness for battle by taking them out on an exercise in the desert. You say only men with a purpose are allowed out of the valley; but isn't training the highest purpose of all?"

Harkhuf grimaced and waved his hand dismissively. "I will think on it. Now, leave me, I have work to do."

Ament left the tent but as he did so he glanced back. It appeared that Harkhuf's work was to drain the jug of beer.

His guards joined him again as he walked away from the commander's tent. He made his way to his own tent and lay down, knowing that this was the only place he did not feel the stares of the men upon him. The conversation with Harkhuf had depressed his spirit, but had also told him that there was no future in staying with these men. They would not release him, but neither did they have the slightest chance of ultimate victory.

*How can I leave? The main path at the end of the valley is well guarded, as are the three lesser paths. That only leaves the cliffs themselves. They are climbable, but not if I am seen. That means I could only succeed if my guards are absent, and they only leave me alone when I'm in this tent. I could sneak out at night, but I need daylight to climb those cliffs. Still, it's possible.*

The possibility energised him, and he left the tent, walking up the valley a hundred paces or so, his guard rousing themselves and trotting along behind him. He stopped and sat down near the stream, leaning back against a date palm and casually regarded the other side of the valley. Half closing his eyes, he appeared to be resting, but he searched the rock wall for possible routes to the top. After a bit, he moved another hundred paces on and repeated his exercise. Over the course of the day, he moved the length of the valley, examining first one and then the other cliff for climbable surfaces.

*I think it can be done...there are a dozen ways out, but how do I lose my escort?*

He tried pretending to fall asleep in the heat of the day, waiting motionless for his guards to doze off or lose interest, but there was always at least one vigilant enough to notice when he moved. They were vigilant too at night when he slipped under the back of the tent, meaning to hide somewhere and try to scale the cliffs at first light, but they challenged him, and he had to pretend a call of nature. Then, when he was considering a brazen attempt to get past the guards at one of the entrances, Harkhuf came to his aid. The corps commander called Ament to his tent.

"I have considered your request and decided it would benefit the corps."

"Which request is that?" Ament asked cautiously.

"To leave the valley and help train my soldiers...our soldiers. We will, of course, do our utmost to protect you, so I am assigning ten fit young men to never leave your side."

The exercises started the next day. Ament, excited at the prospect, led a hundred men up the track and onto the stony desert floor above the crescent ravine. Here, he divided the men into two groups, giving them scraps of red or blue cloth to tie around their upper arms. He explained some basic tactics of attack and defence, and put them through their paces. It was hot, thirsty work, and by midday the men were grumbling so much, Ament had no option but to let them return to the protection of the valley. He had a few choice words to say to them that evening, and ordered them out again the next day, this time with water skins as well as weapons.

Ament was a little surprised to find he actually had an interest in how these men performed, but put that down to his residual duty of care for men who had once been under his command. They might now be little more than bandits, but sooner or later they would come up against properly trained soldiers, and he wanted them to at least have a chance of survival.

His primary aim was still escape though, so he surreptitiously watched the men who watched him, but was dismayed to find they took their duties seriously, clinging to him tighter than ticks on a bull's neck. They went everywhere with him, and if he tried sending one or more off on some errand, resisted.

*I'll have to allay their fears. Give them no reason to doubt my loyalty to their cause and perhaps they'll relax their vigilance.*

So he poured himself into his duties, putting the men through a variety of exercises, having them plan and execute attacks on each other, analysing their mistakes and creating counter-tactics. He organised ambushes, set the men battling one another with staves, and impressed on them the need to maintain discipline and to work together as a team.

"Remember, if you look after the men closest to you, they will look after you too."

After a few days, he put the men of each team under a Leader of Fifty and let them work out their own plans while he ran everywhere, observing and advising. The heat and exertion taxed him greatly, but he was pleased to see that his guards felt it more. They had become lazy, tucked away in their little valley, and started to resent Ament's continued activity. He now had to goad them to keep up and often outdistanced them in his sprints across the rocky ground in pursuit of the teams' running battles.

On one such occasion, he slipped behind some large rocks and hid as they stumbled past, cursing. He allowed them a few moments of panic at having lost him, and then strolled out into the open, grinning at their discomfiture. Ament had momentarily considered slipping away into the desert, but decided against it, knowing he was ill-prepared for a spur of the moment departure.

*I can live without food for a few days, but I'll need water.*

Harkhuf had taken his water map off him, but Ament thought he might be able to remember one or two of the nearer water seeps. The lack of knowledge severely limited his options.

*I'll have to give up finding the Shechem, which means north is my only chance. There are wells along the Way of Heru...and soldiers...but if I'm careful I can find my way home. First things first, though...how do I get a water supply?*

Ament thought about the problem that night and had an idea. It would depend on how observant his guards were, and also whether he could give them the slip for a short while on a regular basis. The next morning, he took two water skins with him before he led his men out. If anyone noticed he was carrying two, they did not remark on the fact and indeed, a few of the men also carried extra water. At one point during the hottest part of the day, he raced off as he often did, with his guards dispiritedly following. He slipped away and headed north toward a rock he had noted as a landmark. Reaching it unobserved, the buried the skin at its base and headed back, making his presence known before his guards raised the alarm. He repeated this over the next several days though was not always able to slip away, and only once did someone remark that he had left with two water skins and was returning with only one.

He shrugged and walked on. "I must have put it down somewhere. Do you want to go and look for it?"

Ament knew the water would not last long in the skins, so if he was going to run for it, he would have to leave soon. He had eight skins buried at the base of the rock, and if he took another two on the last day, he thought he would have enough. Food was another matter, as was a weapon. Both would look suspicious if he openly took them, so he decided he would just eat as much as he could the night before, and hope to secrete a small knife about his person.

The day came when Ament decided he would run. He had eaten well the night before and at first light had devoured as much bread as he could, washed down with weak beer. A small copper knife went unseen in the waist folds of his kilt, and he slung two bulging skins of water about him. As he set off for the entrance with his men, Harkhuf came out of his tent and beckoned to him. He went over, trying to hide his sudden apprehension that he had been found out.

"Two water skins?" Harkhuf asked.

"Thirsty work," Ament replied.

Harkhuf looked at him in silence as the men trooped past, some of them looking at their commander and their General with curiosity.

"You've done well training the men, Ament. I think I might come out with you and observe."

Ament strove to keep his face impassive. "You are, of course, welcome, Harkhuf."

Another long look by the corps commander, then Harkhuf nodded. "Perhaps later today."

Ament looked back as he started the ascent and saw that Harkhuf was still watching him. He raised a hand in a half salute.

*He suspects. If I don't leave today, he may act to curtail my freedom once more.*

Ament decided on a wide-ranging exercise that day, instructing the red group to lose themselves in the rocks to the west and south, and the blue group to hunt them down. This gave him the opportunity to run his little group ragged, and by midday had reduced his guards down to two of the fitter individuals. He caught his breath and looked around him, noting some activity to the south, which he pointed out to his two guards.

"I think the reds have been caught in an ambush. We'd better hurry over there and see what they did wrong."

One of the guards groaned, but the other stared into the northeast and asked, "If that's the reds in the south, with the blues ambushing them, then who is that?"

"What? Where?" Ament stared at a thin plume of dust in the distance, where a file of men with sunlight glinting off bronze spear tips grew steadily closer. "They're not our men; they only have training staves."

"And there," said the other guard, pointing to the north where another thin dust cloud rose in the still, hot air. "And more to the west."

"The corps have found us," Ament said. "You, quick as you can; back to camp. Warn Commander Harkhuf we're going to need every man up here. And you..." he pointed to the other man. "Run to our men in the south and warn them."

"What about you, General?"

"I'll stay here and keep an eye on their movements. Now go. Hurry."

Ament found a tall rock and balanced on it, scanning the horizon for signs of armed men--and found them. Dust now rose from files of men closing in on his position from every point from the east to the southwest, and if his calculations were correct, at least one whole corps faced them.

*They haven't got a hope...we haven't got a hope...but who are they looking for? For everyone, or just for me? Do I run now? This might be my best chance of escape, before the corps completely surrounds us.*

As much as Ament wanted to leave, he felt strangely reluctant, and came to realise that he still owed some duty of care to these men who had once put their trust in them. He scrambled down from the rock and started running toward the ravine. The red and blue groups joined him before he got there, and as he was informing them of the threat advancing upon them, Harkhuf emerged from the valley at the head of the remaining men.

"So you've led the corps to us, General Ament."

Ament dismissed the notion with an impatient gesture. "One corps at least, though I couldn't see any banners. They're advancing from the north, spread out to east and west, thin on the ground now but will concentrate as they get closer. I think we should strike out to the north and east and break through before they're organised."

"Nonsense," Harkhuf said. "This is our chance to show them what we're made of. We stand and make a fight of it."

"We're outnumbered at least two to one," Ament protested. "More if there's more than one corps. These are experienced troops too..."

"Troops who will desert when they know who they face."

Ament stared at Harkhuf, and then at the Troop Commanders standing near him. "It is madness to face them here, outnumbered as we are. Break out quickly, before we are overwhelmed."

"You are too cautious, General Ament," Meryre said.

"We are braver than you give us credit for," Shere added.

"I know you are brave," Ament replied, "but I have greater experience than any of you. A wise man picks his fights and this is one battle you cannot win. Escape now and live to fight another time."

"There are soldiers to the south of us too," called one of the men.

"You see? Already we are surrounded, but it is still not too late to break out."

"And then what?" Harkhuf asked. "Who would join us if they knew we had fled before the corps. Better to fight here and die if the gods will it. At least we would die with honour."

Ament cursed, but could see no way out of it. "Then we had better choose a defensive position and form our lines."

"We, General Ament?"

"If we are to die, I will die as I have lived, fighting my Queen's enemies."

"Queen Tausret still lives? Truly?"

"Yes."

"Then go to her if you can," Harkhuf said. "She needs you by her side."

"Tell her the loyal Sets knew their duty," Meryre added.

"Come with me," Ament said. "If you believe the Queen needs me, then she needs her loyal army too."

"Too late, General." Troop Commander Shere pointed to the south where men were already engaged in battle.

"Go with the gods," Harkhuf said. "North and east two days and you may find a well. If not..." he shrugged and handed his own water skin to Ament. "Maybe this will suffice."

Ament stood and watched as Harkhuf led his men south to join his men already fighting the corps, and then turned to the north. He knew that the oncoming squads of men were drawing together as the encirclement shrank, but that if he got close to them quickly, they might be far enough apart to slip through their ranks unseen. A small copper knife would not be of much use against a trained soldier.

As he approached the oncoming soldiers, he hid behind rocks, slipping from cover to cover in the jumbled landscape. He was helped by the sounds of fighting behind him as the soldiers picked up their speed, convinced that the enemy lay ahead of them. A squad passed some twenty paces away, none of them looking round as they ran past, and Ament was able to resume his northward journey. He dug up his extra water skins where he had cached them, and looked back toward the ravine where already the sounds of battle were dying away.

*What a waste. Hundreds of men sacrificed for a lost cause.*

Ament shook his head wearily and set his feet on the path he hoped would lead him home.

# Chapter 39
# Year 9 of Usermaatre Ramesses

The corps guarding the northern borders had little to do now that peace had broken out in Kanaan. King Taita of the Peloset refused to be drawn into any conspiracy to attack Kemet and dutifully reported such attempts to Ramesses. As a result, the northern corps were rotated south more often, and given useful work to keep them busy in Ta Mehu. The Shu corps, commanded by Natsefamen was currently employed repairing roads in the northeast, while the Set corps, commanded by Hori, was resting up in Per-Ramesses before returning to border patrol. Natsefamen and Hori both enjoyed a game of Senet with their wine when not on duty, and often sought out one of the higher class taverns in the city. Here they could relax in salubrious surroundings without being disturbed by the drunken antics of common soldiers.

Natsefamen pushed the Senet board to one side and leaned back, stretching. He had lost three straight games and was a little annoyed at the smug expression on his fellow commander's face.

"What did you promise Sai, Hori? You know I'm the better player."

Hori laughed and lifted his wine cup in a mock salute. "Not today, my friend, and not because I sacrificed to Sai. You've had too much to drink, so that's three kite of silver you owe me." He looked quizzically at the other commander. "I presume you're good for it?"

"Set take you. You know I am." Natsefamen suddenly grinned at the words he had uttered. The god Set was the titular deity of Hori's corps, so wishing for that god's intervention was somewhat unnecessary. "More wine?"

"Don't mind if I do, as long as you're paying."

Natsefamen called over the pot-boy and ordered another jug of his best wine. "And none of that slop you served us last time," he called after the boy's back. "I'll have you know we are two of the king's best commanders...ah, he's gone."

"Another game?" Hori indicated the Senet board and the scattered pieces.

Natsefamen shook his head. "I feel like some more energetic entertainment. Let's have some music," he called out. A few of the other patrons looked up from their cups with interest. "Dancing girls too."

The tavern owner looked up from his seat near the kitchen entrance. "Music I can provide...for a price."

"And girls?"

"Perhaps, but it'll cost you."

"Bring them on." Natsefamen took off a copper bracelet and tossed it to the tavern keeper. The man grunted and slipped it beneath his tunic. "I'll see to it, sirs."

The pot-boy returned with the wine--as sour and thin as before--and two musicians tottered out. They were old women, toothless and wrinkled, and Natsefamen grimaced at the sight. There was no doubting their skill at the lute and the flute, however, and soon every foot in the tavern was tapping out the beat. After a few minutes, a young girl started dancing; wearing little except jewellery, and the clientele cheered her on. Both musicians and dancers were applauded at the end and gathered up a small shower of rings and bangles, some wood, some copper. Natsefamen hoped to buy the girl a drink and find out what else she could do, but she quickly disappeared.

"Never mind," Hori said. "We'll find you someone later."

"I wanted her," Natsefamen grumbled. "I liked the look of her. She reminds me of someone up at the palace."

"The palace, eh? Getting ideas above your station, old friend? You stick to the maids and serving girls."

Natsefamen laughed wryly and poured them both another cup of wine. "I won't always be an army officer, you know. I mean to get a position in the palace guard, rise to a court position and find myself a high-born wife. Then anything's possible."

"Sounds like it involves a lot of grovelling to servants who have never faced a man looking to kill them," Hori said. "Give me the army way any day. You know where you stand with a soldier."

Natsefamen waved his cup around while he searched for a convincing argument, succeeding only in spattering his friend with wine. "I'm going to be both," he said at last. "Soldier first, then courtier."

"Better than the other way round, at least. I've got a good example of that in my corps right now. The king's son, Prehirwenemef." Hori retained enough good sense to lower his voice and look around for eavesdroppers before continuing. "The gods help Kemet if he ever rises further than Troop Commander."

"Not likely to though, is he? Might make corps commander, but he's fourth son... third surviving. My own burden is more likely. I've got Meryamun, remember?"

Hori nodded and slurped some more wine. "We have both been burdened with high-born donkeys."

"Shh!" Natsefamen looked round now, and then hiccupped. "Is he really that bad? I thought Prehirwenemef was a quiet lad."

"So he is," Hori agreed. "To the point of sulkiness. He doesn't like to take orders, and while he won't argue the point to your face, he goes off in a huff and grumbles to anyone who will listen. And there are plenty of soldiers willing to do that."

"Bad for morale, but what can you do?"

"I could put up with that, even, if he was any good at soldiering. That's the problem with having to accept high-born boys. They think they know better than anyone else, even experienced officers."

"All he needs is blooding," Natsefamen said, pouring wine again. "Put him through a battle or two and he'll see sense."

"He doesn't exactly put himself forward if there's any danger."

"A coward?"

"I wouldn't put it that strongly. Cautious to a fault, though."

"He comes from good stock. Once he's led men into battle, he'll improve."

"I doubt it. Not if last month's debacle was anything to go by."

"What happened?"

"We'd had some trouble from one of the eastern tribes...Essenites or some such. So I sent Prehirwenemef out with his Troop to teach them a short, sharp lesson. Sent a good man with him--Ramose--to advise him and show him the ropes. Well, they stumble upon a scouting party of Essenites. Best thing is to move fast then...be onto them before they can prepare a defence. Ramose said as much, but our little prince wouldn't listen. He camped instead, and then dithered around debating whether to retreat and call for reinforcements. When Ramose finally talked him into taking action, Prehirwenemef insisted the men advance slowly in a tight column, without scouts, and came upon a deserted village. Then he leads his men straight into it, and of course it's an ambush. The Troop was a good one; fought its way out and saved the life of the prince, but lost some good men...including Ramose."

His voice had risen as he talked, so Hori looked around again to make sure they were not overheard.

"Look, don't get me wrong; Usermaatre is a good general, and I'm not complaining except to you, but the king's skill has not been passed onto his sons. Not Prehirwenemef anyway. As far as I'm concerned, that young man is a danger to his men and to the corps as a whole."

Natsefamen nodded. "What can you do, though?"

"I'm thinking about how to put in a quiet word to the king. Through the Tjaty maybe."

"I'd advise against it."

"What? Why?"

"The king doesn't take criticism very well."

"But if his son is endangering the corps..."

"I know from experience," Natsefamen said. "You forget, I have another prince in the Shu corps."

"Yes, but I can't remember anyone has ever said Meryamun lacked courage."

"Exactly the opposite, but that's just as dangerous."

"How so?"

Natsefamen considered the question for a while. He dipped a finger in a puddle of wine on the scarred wooden surface of the table and drew patterns--the eye of Heru, the symbolic ostrich feather of the god Shu, the was-sceptre of the god Set.

"Well?" Hori prompted.

"Two instances," Natsefamen said. "I was wondering whether to tell you about the second. The first was when a couple of bandits made off with a mule from the corps's lines. Meryamun was duty officer that night when the theft was reported. Now he should have reported it to me and let me make the dispositions for recovery, but no...he hitched up his personal chariot, ordered five men to follow him and tore off into the darkness like a madman. Returned just before dawn with the heads of the two bandits and the stolen mule trotting behind."

"A good result then."

"Until his men returned. One dead and another wounded so badly he died a few days later. I called Meryamun into my tent and asked him whether he thought the recovery of a mule was worth two men's lives. He told me that the mule was the property of the king and so were the men. He said any soldier in the corps was expendable."

Hori shook his head in disbelief. "And the second instance?"

"That was when we were repairing roads in the south. It is good practice to engage the men's enthusiasm, so I made a competition of it, Troop against Troop, with an extra day's leave for the team that repaired the most road. Usuf's Troop won and unfortunately he boasted about it in Meryamun's hearing." Natsefamen grimaced and took another gulp of wine. "That young man does not like to be bested in anything."

"What happened?"

"Meryamun attacked Usuf, luckily just with his fists, but that was enough. Usuf had the good sense not to fight back, but even so, he suffered a broken nose, a split lip and three teeth knocked out before his fellow officers could hurry him away."

"Gods...what did you do?"

"If any other of my commanders so forgot himself, I'd have him broken to the ranks and thrashed...but the king's son? How could I? Even a reprimand could be injudicious."

"A difficult situation."

Natsefamen nodded. "Luckily I was close enough to the king to go and see him within a day. I told him what had happened and he laughed. He praised Meryamun for standing up to Usuf and asked if I remembered what it was like to be a young man. I persevered in my condemnation of such behaviour, and I was told in no uncertain terms that I was to take no punitive action against Meryamun.

"Usuf's family will take it amiss if I do nothing," I said. "They are minor nobility from Behdet."

"Give them five kite of gold from the corps funds," the king replied. "And Natsefamen, I want to hear nothing further on this matter. Understand? Make it right."

"And so, of course, you did," Hori said.

"And so, of course, I did. What else could I do? The king made it plain he was proud of his son rather than otherwise. I paid off Usuf and transferred him out of the corps. Then I sent Meryamun off on detached duty until tempers had cooled. He'll be reporting back in a few days' time, and the corps will be returning to patrol duty. He can't get in as much trouble on the border, but the gods only know what he'd be like as a king."

"He's not the heir though," Hori pointed out.

"He's only a breath away. Not that I wish Khaemwaset ill, of course."

"One could wish the younger brothers were more like the older."

"I'd be happy if collectively they were half the man Khaemwaset is."

"Then pray to the gods they keep the heir in good health."

"Indeed. More wine?"

"I think I've had enough. All this talk of princes has soured my belly."

"A girl then? Something to take your mind off your troubles and leave you in a good mood? Perhaps the tavern owner would send that dancing girl back."

"I know where there are some livelier ones."

"Lead on then, my friend."

# Chapter 40
# Year 10 of Usermaatre Ramesses

Ramesses was in the north again, having led his corps through the territories controlled by King Taita, and forced the Sherden and Tjeker tribes of the Sea Peoples to sue for peace. He had attacked them by land and sea, catching them in pincers of hardened bronze and inflicting a series of defeats upon them. Taking the success of the treaty with the Peleset as his example, he granted the Sherden and Tjeker kings lands in the north of Kanaan and exacted tribute from them.

Now he marched south again, content that the kingdoms were once more at peace. In the wake of the previous attacks by the Ribu and Sea Peoples, unrest had stirred within the kingdoms, crime had increased, and bandit gangs had been encouraged by the inattention of local corps. The Hapi corps was unleashed once more and they swiftly stamped out the last vestiges of crime, enabling men and women to walk the roads of Kemet in complete safety again. Even the erstwhile rebellion uncovered by the spies of Tjaty Herwernef had come to nothing. The corps had marched out into the desert and attacked a rebel force, putting them all to the sword. General Ament had not been found, and the king was of the opinion that he had never been there. He had surely perished years before.

Leaving the northern corps behind to guard the borders, Ramesses drove his chariot down the Way of Heru at the head of a token force, toward the northern capital of Per-Ramesses. The city had been built by his predecessor and namesake, the Great Usermaatre, but he had never warmed to it, preferring the more congenial surrounds of white-walled Men-nefer or ancient Waset. Per-Ramesses stood too close to the border and was a constant reminder of the northern nations and the constant threat they posed to the peace of the kingdoms.

It was also the home of Queen Iset. She ruled the Per-Khemret with a heavy hand, drawing strength from her Syrian mother and introducing foreign ways that stirred unrest among the other women of the king. Ramesses had overlooked these peculiarities in the early days, being enamoured of her beauty and the wild nature of their coupling, but had slowly drifted away from her, preferring the stable company of his other main wives. Returning now from the north, he knew he would have to pay her a courtesy call at least. His member stirred at the thought of her still-young body and he smiled. Perhaps it would not be so bad.

Iset was more often than not in a bad temper. Her marriage to the King of Kemet had not gone as she had hoped, had been led to believe by her mother. Far from being the centre of attention she was stuck in this northern city that the king only visited on the way to or way back from, war. Every time he graced her with his presence, she got the feeling that he wanted to be elsewhere.

"It's not good enough, mother. I want to be Queen in fact as well as name. He's on his way here again, sweaty and dusty from his war, and he expects me to just open my legs like any common woman and welcome him in."

Habadjilat adjusted the folds of her long-sleeved dress and regarded her daughter coolly in the shadowed courtyard of the Women's Quarter. "I thought Ramesses was a competent lover."

Iset stamped her foot with annoyance. "Oh, mother, stop it. You know that is not what I'm complaining about. Yes, he is competent enough, and though like most men he seeks his own pleasure first, I enjoy our coupling."

"He is a typical man, for all he is a king," Habadjilat said. "But you knew that when he took you for his Queen."

"I just thought...oh, I don't know what I thought."

"You had some romantic nonsense that he would put away all his other wives and concubines, and love you alone, I suppose."

"Something like that," Iset said grudgingly. "Oh, I'm not a fool, mother. I know a man's eyes wander and he feels any shortcoming fiercely, and a king more so. He bolsters his pride by mounting many women. I understand that, but...oh, mother...I wish he would regard me as more than just a vessel for his lust."

"You are also the mother of two of his sons."

Iset sat down beside her mother on the stone bench beside the fish pool. "Not the heir though."

"That was hardly going to happen. Before he married you he had four sons to Tiye and another on the way from his sister Tyti. One is dead, at least, so there are still only four ahead of your Amunhirkhopeshef."

"That ill-omened name! Ramesses says he loves me, but then foists the name of his dead son upon mine. It is barbaric."

"It is not something I would expect of a civilised man, I agree," Habadjilat said, "but it is the custom here. And as for naming, what is the king going to say when you tell him the name of your youngest son?"

"What is wrong with the name Mursil? My grandfather was a good man. So was my father Amalek for that matter, but I had enough respect not to use his name."

"Nothing is wrong with using my father's name. It is our custom. All I'm saying is that the king may not see it that way. Kemetu men are strange."

"I could have told you that, mother. On our first night together, he professed himself shocked that I had hair between my legs. Do you know what he did? He told me to pluck it all out, or at the least shave it."

Habadjilat hissed, her eyes narrowing. "He dared say that? Why did you not tell me the king was calling you a whore?"

"What would you have done, mother? The king can do no wrong within the Per-Khemret, and you know that most Kemetu women, certainly the palace women, are as naked as young girls."

"They are shameful whores," Habadjilat agreed, "but I thought they did it from choice, knowing no better. The king told you to do it? What...what did you do? Tell me you didn't..."

"Of course not. You raised me better than that. On the other hand I did not want to refuse him outright and lose his favour, so I dissembled. I put off the decision and enticed him with my womanly wiles, and in time he came to like how I was different down there."

"So apart from the naming of your younger son, all is right between you?"

Iset shrugged delicately and trailed her fingers in the cool water. A silver fish nuzzled her hand and she laughed delightedly, sending it flicking into the depths. "He will take me to his bed and assuage his needs most assiduously, but as soon as his lust is spent he finds some excuse to go. If it is not the northern corps and war, it is the southern cities where no doubt he slakes his lust on Tyti and Tiye. Per-Ramesses is too far removed from where his heart lies."

"What do you mean to do about it, daughter?"

"What can I do? I try to satisfy his needs, and petition him every day to favour my son above his brothers."

"He will not do that," Habadjilat said. "Still, Amunhirkhopeshef is only seven years old and the king may live another thirty years. A lot can happen between now and then."

"What do you mean?"

Habadjilat looked around carefully, but there was only an old gardener and a handful of other palace women in view. None of them were close enough to overhear their quiet conversation.

"The king's eldest son died of some water demon picked up while he was hunting. The other sons are in the navy and army--both dangerous professions. Who is to say what might happen to them?"

"That is with the gods."

"Perhaps in this case the gods need assistance."

"You would dare?" Iset whispered, her eyes wide.

"I? I can do nothing. I am merely the mother of one of the queens and am almost without power or influence in the court. You, on the other hand..."

"I...I couldn't...you would tell me to kill?"

"If you want your son to succeed to the throne."

"Of course I do, but...how? I am not proficient with weapons and they are grown men, army officers."

"There are other ways," Habadjilat said. "Magic is very efficacious at a distance, I am told."

"I don't know any sorcerers."

Habadjilat sighed. "Neither do I, but they can probably be found in the larger cities, Waset especially. You must ensure the king takes you south with him."

Iset chewed her bottom lip and considered her mother's words. "I might be able to do that, but to take the lives of the king's sons..."

"They are sons of Tiye, a mere wife of the king, not the sons of a Queen."

"That is true. But what of Tyti's son Ramesses?"

"He is only a boy. Deal with the men first."

Usermaatre Ramesses arrived in Per-Ramesses amid great jubilation. News of his victories and the brokered peace had preceded him and the Governor of the city made sure that the population turned out to welcome their king. In the king's name, he ordered beef and bread and beer distributed to the populace, and musicians gathered at strategic points along the route of his triumphal entry to the city. Priests of all the deities of the city offered up prayers of thanks for the king's safety and scribes set about recording the details of his campaign so that the builders could later inscribe his deeds on temple walls everywhere.

At the palace, Ramesses went first to his suite where he bathed and dressed in fresh linens before partaking of a light meal. He knew that the ladies of the Per-Khemret awaited him, and that Queen Iset in particular desired his presence, but despite the lust he felt rising within him, he was determined to remain in control. When he was good and ready, he sent word to the Superintendent of the Per-Khemret that he would visit the Women's Quarters.

The women were gathered together in the portico of the great courtyard, where the perfumes from blossoming trees, the sounds of songbirds, and the dappled light through the trees, made a pleasing background for the king's pleasure. Queen Iset was the highest ranked woman, though there were others older and more experienced on hand to welcome their lord and master.

Several old women bowed gracefully and withdrew. They were wives and concubines of previous kings and though Ramesses treated them with the utmost courtesy, they never graced his bed. Similarly, the Queen's mother, Habadjilat, made her obeisance and excused herself, leaving her daughter Iset to rule over some twenty lesser women. One by one, these women approached the king and received a brief royal embrace and dismissal, though three of them presented the king with babies born since his last visit. He glanced at the baby girls, and deigned to look closely at the only boy, murmuring words of praise to the simpering mother. At last, all the women had withdrawn, and Queen Iset was left alone with her husband. She smiled and dipped her body gracefully in the manner of the court of Hatti.

"Welcome, my lord. I have longed for your presence these many months."

Ramesses nodded and looked around at the empty room. "Where is your youngest son, Montuherwenemef?"

"Our son is well, my lord, and I will present him to you soon. First, though, I desire to welcome my husband. You will take wine?"

Ramesses nodded his assent and a servant, all but hidden in the shadows, ran out with a jug of wine and a silver cup, pouring for the king before withdrawing to the edge of the room. Neither king nor queen took any notice of him, or of the other servants present. As far as the royal personages were concerned, they were alone.

Ramesses drank from the cup. "You do not drink with me?"

"All I desire is to drink of my husband's presence, my lord."

"I would readily slake my thirst with you." He held out the cup to one side as if to place it on a non-existent table, and a servant darted out a grabbed it before it could fall.

Kemetu women often dressed in sheer linens that exposed the body while making a pretence of covering it, often showing bare breasts, but Iset had never embraced this fashion. Reared in the conservative halls of the court of Hatti, she retained her modesty and revealed her naked body only to the king and the ladies of her bedchamber. Now, she dipped courteously to the king and drifted off toward her chamber, loosening the clasps of her dress as she went. Ramesses followed, already tumescent.

Ignoring the ever-present servants, they coupled vigorously, the ageing king once more proving he was a worthy Bull of Heru. Afterward, the sheen of sweat still upon their bodies, they sat naked beside the wide window overlooking the courtyard and sipped honeyed milk to revive their energies. Women passing by in the gardens averted their eyes from the royal couple, and Iset ignored them in turn. Ramesses, though, followed them with his eyes.

"I would ask a favour of my lord," Iset said quietly.

"Ask, and it shall be yours," Ramesses replied. His gaze drifted over the naked body of his Queen and he stirred once more.

"Take me with you down to Waset."

Ramesses dragged his eyes up to meet Iset's steady gaze. "Waset? What is wrong with Per-Ramesses? Are you not adequately provided for here?"

"I have everything I could possibly desire through your generosity, my lord, save for one thing. That is to know more of Kemet and its people. I am stuck up here in what is little more than a garrison town which you visit from time to time, while you spend your days in white-walled Men-nefer or ancient Waset. Take me to these cities, my lord, so that I might see the wonders of glorious Kemet, experience your divine presence every day and..." Iset smiled provocatively, "welcome you to my bed more often."

For a time there was little more talk as the king and queen coupled once more.

Ramesses lay back gasping for breath and smiled at Iset. "It pleases me to grant your wish. You shall come with me to visit Men-nefer and then upriver to Waset."

"You mean it? You won't change your mind?"

"Have I not said it? A king does not go back on his word. You shall bring our sons Amunhirkhopeshef and Montuherwenemef too. It is time they met their brothers. It is time I met Montu'mef too. He is two years old and I have never even held him in my arms. Tonight we shall all feast together."

Iset swung her legs over the side of the bed and threw her linen dress around her shoulders. She took a deep breath but could not bring herself to look at Ramesses. "My lord...there is something you should know. About Montu...about our youngest son."

Ramesses sat up, concerned at the apprehension in her voice. "Is he sick? Suffering from some malady? A demon? What?"

"He is in good health, but I...I did not name him as you wished, my lord."

"Of course you did...why would you not?"

"I was angered, my lord."

Ramesses stared at Iset, his brow furrowed in perplexity. "Angered over what?"

"My lord, I am a daughter of Hatti and in my land it is great misfortune to name a child after a person who has not made a name for himself. When you insisted on naming our first child Amunhirkhopeshef, it...it was an act of disrespect..."

"Disrespect to whom? Amunhirkhopeshef was my first-born son and heir, and his name is an honourable one."

"Disrespect to the gods of Hatti, my lord. He was an untried boy of fourteen summers. Our son should have been given the name of a redoubtable warrior or king. Such a name would draw down upon him the bravery and strength of his namesake."

"That may be the custom in your land, but it is not that of Kemet. His name means 'Amun is with his Strong Arm' and that is all the name he needs." Ramesses got up off the bed and came round to face his wife. "What have you done, Iset? What name have you given our young son?"

"Mursil, my lord."

"Mursil? A Hatti name for the son of the King of Kemet?"

"Yes, my lord."

"You disobeyed me? Despite my express command to call him Montuherwenemef?"

"My grandfather's name was Mursil. He was a mighty warrior and..."

"I don't care if he was a goat or one of your pagan gods. You had no right to name our son that when I had told you what to name him. By all the gods of Kemet, I have never heard such nonsense. He is going to have to be renamed at once."

"My lord, no. That is very unlucky."

"For a Hatti maybe, but not for a Kemetu. I will see to it before I leave."

"Before *we* leave, my lord?"

"I am minded to take my sons with me and leave you behind."

"My lord gave his word. Does my lord go back on it?"

Ramesses scowled and signed to a servant to bring his kilt. As it was fitted about his waist, he nodded. "I have said it, and so shall it be. But know this, Iset daughter of Habadjilat, you have forfeited my trust. You shall remain Queen, but do not think to rule in my bed again."

"But my lord, you are the Bull of Heru and I am your willing cow."

"I will find other fields in which to sow my seed."

"And...and my sons?"

"The act was yours, not theirs. They are still my sons and though they are far from the succession, I will find them positions worthy of their rank."

# Chapter 41
# Year 10 of Usermaatre Ramesses

The king left Per-Ramesses and the arms of Queen Iset and made his way to Men-nefer. Despite his anger with his Syrian Queen, he had not denied her passage to Men-nefer and onward to Waset--just not on the royal barge. She would follow him to the northern capital and at once progress upriver without him. Thus the king kept his promise and also showed his displeasure. Iset and her mother wept at the decision, but gave no outward sign of the anger and resentment they really felt. Iset would bring Amunhirkhopeshef to Men-nefer and leave him there to be raised by Tiye, while her younger son, once Mursil but now renamed Montuherwenemef, remained in Per-Ramesses under the care of the queen's mother Habadjilat.

"Let them both learn good Kemetu ways," Ramesses said. "If they do so, I shall restore them to places of honour in my court; if not, they shall be cast aside and be as if they never lived."

So, some five days after the king, Iset and her elder son arrived at Men-nefer and within another two days the Queen moved on to the southern capital.

Tiye gave the king a warm welcome and, within two months of his arrival, was pleased to announce she was with child again.

"Another son to add to my lord's quiver full of royal arrows," she declared.

"Or another daughter," Ramesses said. "Your last three children have been girls."

"That is how I know it will be a boy. What shall we name him?"

"Let us wait for the egg to hatch before we pluck the goose."

"I thought a name of strength like your own, my lord. The name Ramesses--born of Re--would remind everyone who his father is."

"I already have a son called Ramesses."

"You can have another. After all, you named the Syrian's brat after my beloved Amunhirkhopeshef."

"That was different. Amunhirk..." Ramesses broke off and frowned. "Do you wish ill on my son Ramesses? He still lives and you seek to give another child his name. That is it, isn't it? You want him dead so your precious sons can inherit everything."

"No, my lord. Such evil thoughts are far from my mind. Why should I begrudge your sister-wife's son life when I have three strong sons older than him and already serving you and Kemet well?" Tiye lowered herself to her knees and clasped the king's legs in abject supplication.

"Get up, Tiye. I believe you. I know that you would never jeopardise the future positions of your sons with such a terrible act."

Tiye rose to her feet and embraced the king.

"Returning to the subject of a name," the king went on, "I will not call our child, should he be male, Ramesses, but rather Paramessu, after the warrior king who was grandfather to the Great Usermaatre."

"A wonderful name, my lord, and one that will reflect your glory in the future."

Ramesses left his wife in the Per-Khemret and once more immersed himself in the ongoing processes of governance. His main duties involved liaising with his fellow gods as their universal high priest, but he also represented Kemet at the highest level. As the Double Kingdom was pre-eminent among the nations, there were always ambassadors and lesser representatives of foreign kings at the court, each seeking the ear of Kemet's king to seek an advantage. The king welcomed each ambassador and feasted them, listening to the words of other monarchs through them, accepting tribute and sending gifts in return. In this way, peace was kept and trade fostered.

Governance occurred on many levels below this, a complex hierarchy of interlocking responsibility. The Tjaties of each kingdom ranked one step below the king, handling problems of the law and disputes that could not be resolved at a lower level. Governors of the sepats handled lower level disputes and Mayors of cities and towns represented the common people on a local level. Mixed into these levels were judges--a relatively new position--of responsible men with a knowledge of the law that could adjudicate where higher level judges might have personal involvement.

All these levels intermeshed and worked to achieve a much sought-after commodity--that of balance, or Ma'at. Thus anything that disturbed Ma'at was regarded with horror and the problem was dealt with immediately. In the tenth year of Usermaatre's reign, an internal problem presented itself that required immediate royal attention.

"Son of Re," Tjaty Herwernef said, "My counterpart in the south, Tjaty Hori, has died."

"I sorrow to hear that," Ramesses replied after a few moments. "This must be rectified immediately."

"There are several suitable replacements, Majesty. May I be permitted to share these names with you?"

"Have a list drawn up, together with arguments for and against each name. Then give it to Crown Prince Khaemwaset. I shall let him make the selection."

Herwernef pursed his lips and hesitated before giving voice to his thoughts. "Is that wise, Son of Re? The position of Tjaty is extremely important, and Prince Khaemwaset has little experience in such matters."

"Then it is high time he learned. I want him to learn responsibility."

"Perhaps I might discuss the names with him first? Guide him in what to look for?"

"Influence him, you mean?"

"No, Son of Re, but...he is young and will need guidance."

"Prepare the list, and then send him to me."

Tjaty Herwernef dutifully prepared a list of possible candidates for the high post, together with the advantages and disadvantages of each. If he wrote in glowing terms of friends or the scion of families of men to whom he owed political favour, this was to be expected, and both he and the king were aware the other knew. Ramesses took the scroll and perused it without comment before admitting the heir to his presence.

"Tjaty Hori in Waset has died," he told him.

"I know, father. I heard."

"I want you to travel there and select the new Tjaty."

Khaemwaset gaped at his father for a few moments. "You want me to...I don't have any experience..."

"Just so. This is what you need."

"But I...er, don't know who would be suitable."

"Herwernef has prepared a list of possible candidates." The king handed his son the scroll.

Khaemwaset unrolled it and looked at the names. "I don't know any of these men. They...they look like they might be...but no...this says he..." He looked up at his father, bewilderment on his face. "How can I make an important decision like this? What if I make a mistake?"

"Mistakes can always be corrected," Ramesses pointed out. "But I don't want you to use that as an excuse. Take your time over the selection and remember that if the man you select is relatively young, he might well outlive me. He'll be your Tjaty then, so make sure it is someone you trust."

"I am honoured by the trust you put in me, father."

"You have to start somewhere, Khaemwaset. As long as you are heir, you need to know how these things are done. Now take the scroll and board the vessel Herwernef has prepared for you. You will leave immediately."

"May I take a companion?"

"Female? Some woman you can't live without?"

"No, father. I can find women anywhere. I mean a friend. Pere, son of Ruma, Overseer of the Treasury."

Ramesses thought for a few moments and then nodded. "Very well."

The barge left that afternoon under orders to deliver the heir to Waset without delay. Khaemwaset and his friend Pere spent much of the ten day voyage beneath an awning at the rear of the vessel, discussing the relative merits of the names on the scroll. There were seven names on the parchment and the prince quickly ruled out four of them for reasons that were more personal than relating to their expertise at governance.

"The minor nobles first, my lord. Djer, son of Djedmose?"

"Never liked him. Full of his own importance and always trying to curry favour at the palace."

"Khety, son of Ahhotep?"

"A miser. Used to spend his days at the palace eating the king's food and ordering the servants around. He'd line his purse with the king's gold."

"Minmontu, son of Rames?"

"Shifty eyes."

"Really? You'd rule him out because of that?"

"The king said I could choose whom I liked. Besides, Minmontu once beat a servant to death."

"Was he prosecuted?"

Khaemwaset shrugged. "I don't know. It was just something I heard."

"Pihuri, son of Kahori then?"

"Too thin."

"You don't like thin people?"

"He looks too hungry. And he used to watch me all the time. Stare at me. I just don't like him."

"Well, you're getting through the list quickly. There are only three left, though they are men who already hold positions of trust."

"Who are they?"

"Ramessesnakht, the King's Son of Kush, for one."

"King's Son of Kush? That's an important position. Why would he want to be Tjaty?"

"I think his term of office is coming to an end. Tjaty of the South would be a much more lucrative prospect than just retiring to his family estates."

"He's a possibility then, I suppose. Who else?"

"Ptahmose, the Royal Scribe of Memoranda. He'd have experience, having worked under the old Tjaty."

"Hmm, I'll consider him, but he doesn't excite my enthusiasm. And the last one?"

"Siemnut, First Charioteer of the Royal Stables."

"What? All he knows is horses. How is that at all relevant?"

Now Pere shrugged. "Perhaps Herwernef owes him a favour."

"In that case I'll rule him out of contention right now."

"Seriously?"

"The king said the decision was mine."

"So that leaves us with just Ramessesnakht and Ptahmose. What else do you know about them?"

"Nothing. I'll have to wait until we get to Waset to find out more."

"You lived in Waset for years. Is there somebody you'd prefer?" Pere asked.

"How would you like to do it?"

"Me? No, my lord, never. I'll follow my father into the Treasury, with the king's permission, but that's as high as my ambition reaches."

Khaemwaset laughed. "They say a wise man knows his limitations."

"So apart from me, do you know of anyone else suitable?"

"No. Under normal circumstances, I'd ask Hori for his advice, but of course with him being dead...aah...there is possibly someone else I could ask."

"Oh? Who?"

"Let me think on that a while," Khaemwaset said. "It may not be appropriate, so I'll have to give it some consideration. In the meantime, let us consider every person we can think of. It may be that even if we do not come up with someone suitable, we can at least decide on what attributes are important for the position of Tjaty."

Although there was no Tjaty to organise a welcome for the Crown Prince upon his arrival in Waset, the city Governor, To, performed those duties, turning out the populace to line the streets and cheer him on his way to the old palace. The streets were swept and the refuse cleared, walls along the route white-washed and colourful banners unfurled. Soldiers of the city corps turned out and marched proudly as an honour guard for the heir, delivering him without incident to his quarters in the palace.

Khaemwaset and Pere bathed and dined, talking with Governor To over wine and honey cakes. They discussed the state of the city and region, before touching on the matter which had brought them south.

"Do you have candidates in mind, my lord?" Governor To asked.

"I have a short list of two. Ramessesnakht, King's Son of Kush, and Ptahmose, Royal Scribe of Memoranda."

"Both good men, my lord, but I regret to say Ptahmose is not in good health. He is about to retire."

"That makes selection a bit easier then," Pere said. "It has to be Ramessesnakht."

"Unless you know of anyone more suitable, To?" Khaemwaset asked.

"I will give it some thought, my lord, but may I suggest you talk to Bakenkhons?"

"The Hem-netjer of Amun?" Pere asked.

"I knew him from when I lived in Waset as a youth," Khaemwaset said. "He struck me then as a knowledgeable and wise man."

"But a priest?" Pere said. "What can a priest know of men suitable for governing a kingdom?"

Governor To smiled. "The realm of Amun is like a kingdom within the kingdoms of Ta Mehu and Ta Shemau. Bakenkhons has ruled that kingdom well for many years, and I believe he will be able to advise you well, my lord."

"It was in my mind to ask Bakenkhons before I arrived," Khaemwaset revealed. "Now your words have made my thoughts take form. I will ask him for advice."

Khaemwaset dismissed the Governor and at once sent a messenger to the Hem-netjer of Amun to ask for a meeting. The messenger returned less than an hour later bidding Khaemwaset attend upon him in the Great Temple at sunset.

"What?" Pere cried. "The priest summons the Crown Prince? Who does he think he is? I will instruct the palace guard to drag him into your presence."

"You will do no such thing, Pere. He speaks for the god Amun on earth, and I am but a son of the king. I will go to him."

Despite Pere's protestations, Khaemwaset went to the Great Temple at sunset, walking over with only two men as guards. Even the Captain of the Palace Guard had wanted to send more men, but the prince had refused.

"Amun has sent for me and will protect me," he said.

An acolyte was waiting for him at the northern gate and accompanied him across the darkening courtyard and into the temple, lit now with flickering light of rush torches. The dancing flames made the shadows sway and leap, and despite knowing he was under the protection of Amun, Khaemwaset felt fear. He found it was one thing to have a healthy respect for the gods in the bright sunlight, but quite another to brave the shadowed presence of the god in the darkness of his own precinct.

They mounted stairs at the rear of the temple and slowly climbed, stumbling on uneven stones, into the heights of the eastern pylon where the Hem-netjer's rooms were situated. The acolyte knocked on the door and murmured in low tones before opening the door and ushering the prince inside.

Khaemwaset stepped through into a dimly lit long room, and saw a figure at the far end, head bowed and back turned to him. He coughed gently and moved forward, but the figure did not move or acknowledge his presence in any way.

"Bakenkhons? Hem-netjer?"

The figure turned slowly and raised his head. Khaemwaset gasped and took a step back, limbs trembling, for atop the shoulders of the figure, a golden ram's head faced him, great ruby eyes reflecting back flashes of flame from the torchlight.

Khaemwaset's hand flew to his mouth and he bit back a cry of terror, for this figure was undoubtedly the god Amun.

The golden head dipped and the figure spoke. "You are welcome, Prince Khaemwaset."

The voice was muffled but human and Khaemwaset felt faint with relief. "I... I came as...as you..." Khaemwaset staggered; his knees suddenly weak. The figure gestured toward a cushioned chair.

"Sit, sit..." Hands rose to the golden head and lifted the mask clear. Beneath it was Bakenkhons's sweaty face. He placed the head on a low table and advanced toward the trembling prince.

"Forgive me, my boy. I did not mean to frighten you, but it was necessary."

Khaemwaset swallowed and cleared his throat. "Wh...why?" he stuttered.

"I would have come to the palace to talk, as you requested, but I was forbidden to do that."

"Forbidden? Who forbids the Hem-netjer of Amun?"

"The god," Bakenkhons said simply.

Khaemwaset could only stare at the priest in silence.

"Does that surprise you?" Bakenkhons asked. "I am the Hem-netjer of Amun, and I alone converse with the god. I did not mean to frighten you, but the god bade me greet you in that way. It was to impress upon you the awe and majesty of the god."

Khaemwaset took a deep breath and exhaled loudly, calming himself. "Why did the god want that?"

"The god knows why you are in Waset, and desires that you should listen to his voice before you make a decision."

"Of course I will hearken to the voice of Amun."

"Your willingness pleases Amun."

"Speak then, Bakenkhons. Tell me what Amun wants of me."

"These are the words of the god Amun. 'Two paths stretch before the king of Kemet. One leads to peace and prosperity, a long life and everlasting fame. The other leads to unrest and dissatisfaction, to troubled times and a forgotten tomb.'"

"H...how can the king avoid the other path?"

"That choice has been given into your hands, Khaemwaset, son of Usermaatre."

"My hands? How?"

"The man you choose will lead Ta Shemau down one path, and where he leads, Ta Mehu will follow."

"But the king...surely the king can lead Kemet down the good path?"

"If it was left to my understanding," Bakenkhons said, "I would trust solely in the king's actions, but Amun tells me otherwise. So you tell me, Khaemwaset, do I ignore the words of Amun or not? It is your choice."

Khaemwaset sat in silence, thinking on the words of the priest.

"It is a weighty matter to put one's trust in anyone but the king," he said slowly, feeling his way through the dilemma. "But even kings listen to the words of the gods." Khaemwaset thought some more and reached a decision. "I must obey Amun."

"It is well," Bakenkhons said, "But do not think you are running counter to the king's wishes. He put the matter in your hands and you may be certain that Amun wants what is good for both Kemet and Usermaatre Ramesses."

"Then I will have no doubts. Tell me Amun's wishes and I shall implement them."

"The god Amun bids you appoint Governor To to the position of Tjaty of the southern kingdom."

"Governor To? But he...he is already Governor of the City."

"It is your choice, of course, Prince Khaemwaset. I am merely the mouthpiece through whom the god speaks."

"I have only just met him and know nothing about him."

"He is an experienced administrator and is related to me."

"Ah."

"Amun has not told me why he chose To, but I imagine it has something to do with the fact that the new Tjaty must rule from the City of Amun, and having ties with the Temple and priests will only strengthen his authority."

Khaemwaset nodded slowly. "Someone must serve and if Amun wants To to be Tjaty, then that is good enough for me."

# Chapter 42
# Year 12 of Usermaatre Ramesses

Life moved slowly around the Sea of Kinnereth in northern Kanaan, and one day was much the same as any other. Certainly, the events of the world largely bypassed the lives of fishermen, farmers, herders and minor tradesmen, impinging only where taxes were concerned, or if soldiers of one king or another passed through.

Ament and his extended family lived quietly, and not even his nearest neighbours and closest friends suspected that he had once been a General of Kemet, or that the ageing woman who was his wife had once ruled the Double Kingdoms, albeit briefly. The years are seldom kind to men and women scraping a living by hard, back-breaking work, and both ex-General and ex-Queen were feeling their age. Skin wrinkled and sagged, hair lost its colour, joints seized up and muscles ached continually, but neither complained. They had their lives, each other, and a young daughter, as well as adopted sons. Ament's sister Ti-ament lived with them, together with her Kaftor husband Zeben, and their two young daughters.

Ament fished the Sea of Kinnereth and made a good living, while his adopted sons Jerem and Ephrim managed their flocks of goats. Zeben grew olives and vines, while the women and their daughters did a variety of home-oriented activities such as the production of vegetables, spinning and weaving, and basic pottery. The two families, occupying one house, grew, reaped or produced everything they needed except for grain and the occasional luxury item like spices, salt or dyes for their cloth. These were bartered for meat, wool and fish with surrounding communities or taken down to the trading ports on the Great Sea.

Of the nine people in Ament's household, eight were more or less contented with their lot. Ti-ament was not. She felt keenly the absence of her sons Rath and Goloth, and had never accepted that their continued life in Kemet was their own decision.

"They are only boys," she whined, for neither the tenth nor the hundredth time. "How could you leave them there, brother?"

As usual, Ament could only sigh and mutter words along the lines of "What was I to do, drag them kicking and yelling from their comrades? I barely made it out alive myself."

"Go back and get them."

"There is no point. They know how to get to the town of Urit and ask for me at the shop of Dan-el the potter. If they want to leave, they will."

None of these arguments swayed Ti-ament, who was sure her sons were in great danger, and she continued to pester her brother. This brought Tausret's ire down on her for trying to send her husband into danger once more.

"He has already risked his life to bring you, your husband, and your daughters out of Kemet. Would you send him to his death trying to bring out two young men who have decided of their own free will to stay there?"

And this in turn upset Zeben who, although a mild and soft-spoken man, loved his wife deeply.

"You should not upbraid your sister so, when she is only worried for her children."

More to keep the peace than with any hope of a successful resolution, Ament took Tausret aside and suggested that perhaps he could make a quick visit to Kemet once more.

"Peace has returned to Kemet and young men, once excited by the prospect of war and advancement, may now be inclined toward a quieter life."

"And if they are not?" Tausret retorted. "They will refuse you again and your sister will not believe it. No, you are the head of this household..." Tausret glowered at the quickly extinguished smile on her husband's face, "...so you must forbid any further discussion of it."

"She is my sister," Ament said, "and hard to refuse. Besides, they are my nephews."

"And they are Zeben's sons. Let him go and look for them."

"Zeben does not know his way around. He is a fine orchardist, but knows nothing of the army."

"You are not to go," Tausret said. "I forbid it."

"I thought I was head of the household," Ament said, grinning.

Tausret's response was to burst into tears. Ament immediately embraced her and soothed her, knowing that her tears had little to do with an emotional outburst, and more with ensuring his cooperation. They said little more, Tausret because she believed she had made her point and Ament because he knew he would eventually have to go.

Ti-ament continued to pester her brother though, and Ament gave in.

"I will go down to Kemet once more and ask them to return with me. Ask, mind you. I cannot force them to return and if they do not accompany me, you must accept it, sister."

"Thank you, brother. I know my boys will come home with you."

Tausret was less polite and yelled at her husband, and when he did not respond, beat him with her fists and then wept.

"How many more times must you put yourself in danger in Kemet? Your place is here with me and our daughter Adara. She is nearly of marriageable age and she needs you to give her to her husband."

"What husband? Who are you talking about? Has Adara..."

"Adara has been entirely appropriate in all her dealings, husband, though she looks upon Dov ben Yeshua with favour. Anyway, that is beside the point. We are talking about the lack of love you show me and Adara."

"I love you more than life itself, Tau; and Adara as well; but you know I must do this. One last time I must go down into Kemet and see my nephews. My sister believes they will return with me, but you know and I know they will not. I shall be there no longer than it takes to speak to them both and then I will come home. I will...I..."

Ament staggered and put one hand up to his face. Tausret put an arm about him and helped him to a chair.

"What is it, husband? What is wrong?"

"I...don'...'no'..."

"Do you feel ill? Do you want water?"

Ament nodded weakly. "'Es..."

Tausret dipped a cup into the water jar and handed it dripping to her husband. Ament reached for it with his left hand but could not grasp it. It fell to the floor and shattered.

"I sho...ree..."

Tausret stared at Ament, eyes wide and her hand crept to her mouth. "Husband, what is wrong with your face?"

"Wha'?" Ament tried to lift his left arm again and failed. He groaned and slumped sideways onto the table.

"Adara, come quickly," Tausret called. "Ti-ament, Ini, Taui." Together, the women of the household lifted Ament onto his bed. Then Taui ran to fetch her father from the olive orchard, while Ini ran to the lakeshore to find her cousin Ephrim. Adara had the hardest task--that of finding her brother Jerem. The youngest adopted son was a shepherd and took the family's flocks of sheep and goats up into the hills, grazing them on distant pastures.

Adara knew it would be hard to find her brother, so she ran to the house of Yeshua and called to Dov, his son, bidding him come help her. Dov came readily enough and accompanied her up into the low hills, asking of small boys guarding handfuls of goats if they had seen Jerem. The boys pointed and within the hour found Adara and Dov found the flocks and Jerem sitting in the shade of a rock, tending to an injured lamb.

"Jerem, come at once," Adara gasped. "Father has been struck down by a demon."

Jerem started to his feet. "What is the manner of his affliction?"

"He has lost the use of his left arm, his face is misshapen and his speech is slurred," Adara said.

The three of them hurried down from the hill, and as they reached one of the boys guarding a few goats, Jerem told him to mind the flocks he had left behind.

Dov and Adara had been discussing the demon attack on her father as they ran, and Jerem interrupted. "I...I saw this as a boy, I think...in the Timna mines. A man fell and lost the use of an arm and a leg. The physician said it was an illness, not a demon."

"It can be cured?" Adara asked.

"I don't know."

"But the man in Timna? He recovered?"

Jerem said nothing and Adara did not press him for an answer, no longer wanting to know.

They found everyone gathered about Ament's bed. The women had made him as comfortable as possible, but Ament looked pale and his breathing was harsh and forced. Tausret and Ti-ament tried to make all the children leave the room, but Adara refused.

"He is my father. I am staying."

There was little any of them could do, however, but watch over Ament as he struggled against the demon. They prayed to what gods they thought might help, and Dov ben Yeshua went to make a sacrifice on the altar of his El. Perhaps it even worked, because Ament was still alive the next day and resting. He still had no use of the left side of his body, and his face looked like potters clay into which too much water had been mixed. The water even ran out as drool, and Tausret dabbed it away with a cloth.

"Well, that settles it," Tausret said. "My man is going nowhere."

"You can't imagine this was brought on by his decision to go back to Kemet," Ti-ament protested. "I would never put my brother in danger."

"Except that is exactly what you were asking of him--to go into Kemet's corps. Your boys didn't want to leave a few years ago. Why should they have changed their minds?"

"Why should they not have? Besides, I am a mother," Ti-ament said. "If our situations were reversed you would ask Zeben to go and look for Adara."

Tausret sighed. "You may be right, but Ament is in no fit condition to go anywhere."

"I could go," Zeben volunteered. "They are my sons, after all."

"Too dangerous."

"I am not afraid."

"No one doubts your bravery, Zeben," Tausret said, "or your love for your sons, but you would stand out in the corps. You look like a Kaftor, and men would notice you. Besides, you fled the corps commander and he may remember you."

"I'll go," Jerem said.

"Nonsense."

"No it's not, mother. In fact, it is the logical choice. Father is a marked man, as is uncle Zeben. I know Kemet, and I know Rath and Goloth. I can slip in and out without anyone noticing and be back here in a few months."

"All true," Ephrim said, "but it should be me. I am the elder."

"Well, neither of you are going," Tausret said.

"It makes more sense that I go," Jerem said. "You are the fisherman of the family while father recovers, whereas I am the shepherd." He smiled ruefully. "It will be easier to get boys to look after the flocks than to find another man to sail the boat."

"You could sail the boat," Ephrim objected. "You've done it before."

"Yes, I could, but you'd be better."

"Neither of you are going," Tausret repeated.

"I'm sorry, mother, but I am," Jerem said firmly. "I am a man now and make my own decisions. I have obligations to this family."

"I won't let you go."

"Give me your blessing, mother. It would mean a lot."

Tausret argued for a little longer, but in the end relented and gave Jerem her blessing. "Straight down and straight back," she said. "No more than three months."

By the time Jerem was ready to leave, Ament had recovered enough to sit in the sun and watch the children play, though his speech was still slurred and his left leg and arm refused to obey his will. Jerem came to him on the eve of his departure and asked for his blessing, kneeling before him.

"May go's go wif 'oo," Ament slurred.

Jerem embraced his father's knees and then rose to leave, unable to look as tears spilled down the old man's cheeks.

Ephrim and Dov accompanied Jerem as far as the town of Urit, and helped him find a suitable caravan heading south. Northern Kanaan now swarmed with Sea Peoples from the tribes of the Sherden and Shekelesh. Recently settled in this area by the treaty between Ramesses and their kings, they had spread through the area, taking over a large part of the local trading. Dan-el the potter grumbled mightily at this, though he allowed that as long as you allowed the Sea peoples their gods, they were peaceable enough.

"I can see trouble coming, though," he muttered. "The Khabiru think their pagan gods are threats to the El. Wouldn't surprise me if the Khabiru broke the peace."

"We will not be the first to break the peace," Dov said stiffly.

"You're Khabiru?" Dan-el asked. "If I have given offence..."

"None taken, though I thought with your name..."

"My mother's wish," Dan-el said. "I worship the hilltop Ba'als like most people round here."

"El is a jealous god," Dov conceded, "but fighting over precedence benefits no one. We won't start anything unless we're pushed to it."

"Trouble is," Dan-el commented, "once somebody pushes, everyone gets caught up in the dispute." He took a deep breath and blew it out noisily. "Let's just put it to one side. Live and let live, I say. Now, Jerem found a decent caravan?"

Ephrim nodded. "A spice caravan with a side of exotic woods. They've taken him on as a general labourer and guard, and even guaranteed him a return passage if he can wrap up his business quickly."

"Well, I won't ask what it is. The less I know the better. I'm surprised you let him go on his own, though. I thought you were inseparable."

"I wish I was going too," Ephrim said. "Kinnereth gets awfully dull. I'd like to see Kemet again."

"I'd like to see it one day too," Dov added, "but Kinnereth holds enough interest for me for now."

"You mean Adara, don't you?"

Dov nodded.

"Marriage?"

Dov coloured and looked at his feet. "One day soon, maybe. She's thirteen already."

"Next year then," Ephrim said. "Wait until my father is a bit better before you ask him formally, but I think he suspects your intentions already."

"And er...does he...er..."

Ephrim grinned. "I think you can safely say you'll be welcomed into the family. Now, I really think we should make a move. We need to be well on our way before nightfall. Thank you for all your help, Dan-el."

The old potter shrugged. "Me an' your father are friends, aren't we? You just give him my regards and bring me some more dried fish when you next come back this way."

# Chapter 43
# Year 12 of Usermaatre Ramesses

Following upon Usermaatre's displeasure with Queen Iset, he sent her upriver to Waset alone while he dallied in Men-nefer with Tiye. When at last he decided to make the trip south to his new palace, he boarded the royal barge and set off in solitary splendour. He expected to find both queens waiting for him on the docks of Waset, but when the barge put in at Abdju, Queen Iset came down to greet him, along with the Governor of the sepat. She fell to her knees there at the waterside in full view of the populace and implored his forgiveness.

"Son of Re, I abase myself before you, and implore you to forgive my transgressions."

Ramesses raised her up and held her at arms' length. "I sent you to Waset. Why are you here?"

"My lord, I could not face being in your southern capital without you. I vowed to wait for you here in Abdju, and throw myself on your mercy so we might enter the city together."

The king saw that tears had streaked her face with kohl and his heart warmed toward her. "You are forgiven," he said, and embraced her.

The king and the queen continued on to Waset, a voyage that took them another eight days as the north winds failed them. As they approached the city docks, Ramesses stood beneath an awning on the deck of the royal barge, dressed in all his finery and wearing the double crown. The blades of the oars, red-tipped and glistening from the water, beat like the wings of the ibis as the barge made its way to the dock. Crowds were on hand to welcome them, led by Tjaty To. The old Tjaty, Hori, had died two years before, and To was proving to be a just and able administrator.

To had turned out the population of Waset to welcome the king, providing bread and beer for everyone. Consequently, the people of the city cheered the arrival of the king. To bowed before his king on the dock, together with the Hem-netjers of every god, and then Ramesses walked through to the Great Temple of Amun, where he offered up praise to the god. He entered the innermost part of the temple where the god resided and spent time alone with him. The queen did not accompany him, but remained aboard the barge.

When the king emerged from the temple, he briefly conferred with his Tjaty before boarding his barge again for the short trip across the river to the western bank and his new palace. Ramesses left Iset to make her own way with her servants and baggage, and sped ahead by chariot. He briefly inspected the progress that had been made on his Mansion of Millions of Years, and then repaired to the palace, where he took refreshment.

The Per-Khemret still had an unlived-in feel about it, with rooms that still boasted freshly smoothed stone with rock dust in the fine crevices at floor level. Efforts had been made to soften the hard lines with furnishings and dyed linen drapes, but it still lacked the homeliness of the older suites in Men-nefer, or even Per-Ramesses. The courtyard garden was similarly stark, the trees that had been dug up and transplanted still struggling to feel comfortable in their new surroundings, the shrubberies still sparse, and the fish ponds lacking the burgeoning comfort of reed beds and lotus.

The king was greeted by his mother Tiy-merenese and sister-wife Tyti, and welcomed into the coolest part of the rooms. He greeted them effusively and presented small gifts of jewellery he had had made especially for them. The lesser women of the Per-Khemret received less thoughtful items of jewellery or furnishings, but were still loud in their thanks, thereafter excusing themselves to afford the king some privacy.

"You had to bring the Syrian here?" Tyti asked, her expression curdled by distaste.

"She desires to see more of Kemet and its customs. I think, too, she is still foreign in her ways, but I am confident some time spent here will correct that."

"Am I now to contest with this woman for your favour? Will you install her in my rooms perhaps?"

"I leave such matters to you and my mother. Find Iset a position as befits her status, but Tyti, you are my principal Queen. Now, send for little Ramesses. I desire to look upon him."

The prince was sent for and presented to his father. At ten years old, he displayed a good understanding of his position in Kemetu society and gave thoughtful responses to the questions posed him.

"Mother says I should prepare to be king..."

This comment earned Tyti a sharp look from the king.

"...but I think that unlikely. The gods grant you a long life, father, and one of your sons to succeed you."

"Khaemwaset is my heir."

"He will make a good king, I think," Prince Ramesses said. "A king stands between the gods and men, and Khaemwaset is priestly. He will need generals though, if Kemet is to remain strong."

"You see yourself as a general?"

"I want to serve you and the next king in the best way I can, father. I enjoy military training, of course, but I also like the law."

"Well, there is a wide range of occupations available to you, my son. You may find the army calls to you, or even our fledgling navy. If not, then there is important work to be done in the law courts, the treasury...maybe even as Governor of a sepat, or a scribe. A younger son, even if far from the line of succession, may lead a productive and honourable life."

"Yes father." Prince Ramesses bowed. "I shall try to make you proud of me."

"I already am, my son. Go now, your mother and I have things to discuss."

Ramesses was silent for a time after his son left. He stood looking out at the gardens faltering under the harsh sunlight, and at the chains of servants bringing jars of water to the transplanted trees and wilting shrubberies.

"He is a good boy," he said at last, "and one destined for a life of service."

"He could be so much more," Tyti said. "Ramesses is nearly a man and already shows promise in many ways."

"Not as a king, though."

"Why not?"

"I have an heir. Khaemwaset is a competent general and has a good relationship with the gods. Then I have Meryamun and Prehirwenemef, who are also good commanders. I have no need of other heirs, but I do need good men to loyally serve under them."

Tyti so forgot herself as to snort. "Khaemwaset will make a better priest than a king, and the other two lack the...the dignity needed to be a king worthy of respect. Ramesses, for all he is yet a boy, has all of that and more..."

Tiy-merenese put her hand on her daughter's arm, attempting to cut her off before she said something to offend the king.

"I know all this," Ramesses said, surprising both women with his mild response. "Yet they are elder sons and I will not dispossess them of their birthright. If they are not yet kingly material, they will grow into it. After all..." he added with a smile, "I plan to remain on the throne for a long time yet. Whichever son succeeds me will be an old man by the time he does."

"May that day be long delayed," Tiy-merenese murmured.

Ramesses spent no more than two months in his southern capital, occupying his days with visits to his tomb and inspections of every aspect of his Mansion as well as sitting in the law courts. The nights he spent with Tyti, and when she was indisposed, with the lesser women of the Per-Khemret. When he finally quit the city, a number of the women, Tyti included, were with child. Iset was not. The king was polite and spent time with her, but seldom took her to his bed.

"Next year, maybe," he said.

"At least take me north with you, that I might be with my sons."

"Your sons are learning how to be good Kemetu princes in your absence. Do you likewise learn to be a Kemetu queen here in Waset, and I will reunite you."

"Tyti hates me."

"Tyti does not hate you. Learn to get on with her. She and my mother rule the Per-Khemret so you would be wise to heed their wishes."

After two months of administration and palace life, Ramesses was feeling restless and decided he would forego passage back to Men-nefer by royal barge. Instead, he sent it downriver without him and took a small contingent with him on the overland route. He was quickly aware that he was no longer a young man as the unfurling tens of khet brought sore muscles and joints. At dusk on that first night, he dismounted from his chariot and it was all he could do to stifle a groan of discomfort and pain. They were travelling light, so there was no tent for privacy, no cot to rest weary bones on, no slave to rub away aching muscles, or water to wash away the dust. Instead, he rolled up in a mat near one of the fires and slept fitfully.

The next day, his aching limbs made it an agony to even stand in a chariot as it bounced over the rough road that led northward. He refused to show pain in front of his men, so pushed the pace, forcing them to follow in his dust. Another fitful night followed, but as the days slowly passed, his body became accustomed to the stresses placed upon it and he started to enjoy himself.

There was a lot to enjoy, despite the heat and aridity of the eastern desert. Once he got past the aches and pains, even the dust and heat brought him joy. The hot wind blew in his face, the hooves and wheels of the chariot kicking up a haze of dust that billowed behind him, coating his body with a pale layer, and left an acrid but not unpleasant stink in his nostrils. It was evocative of the lonely places, of the red deshret that balanced the black Kemet of the river lands. And high above, arcing overhead was the pale blue shell of the sky, across which the barque of the sun god made his stately procession. The heat beat down at him, drawing sweat from his body and limbs, but reminding him of the special relationship he bore to the sun god.

The nights, too, brought pleasure. Rocks and sand that the sun baked so hot one could not walk barefoot on, cooled rapidly after sunset. Heat leached rapidly from the desert air, making man and beast shiver. The king refused any special treatment, determined to be one with his men, and shared their camp fires, ate their plain rations, and drank no more water than they. He would lie back on his mat and stare up at the star-strewn body of the goddess Nut, marvelling at the familiar patterns the stars (whatever they were) traced on the blackness.

The nights were not silent. Apart from the murmur from the men on guard and the whickers and snorts of the horses, the desert itself provided its own song. Wind whispered around the rocks and hissed over sand beds, while animals (and possibly demons) called in the darkness. Jackals howled as if crying out their praises to Anapa, tiny bats flittered overhead, their shrill cries barely audible, and the screech of a hunting owl and the shriek of its prey reminded Ramesses that in life dwelt death.

As the days passed, Ramesses relaxed and took pleasure in the simple things of life. He had once enjoyed going on campaign, sharing the hardships of his soldiers and proving to himself that he was a man. With this, too, came the deep satisfaction of destroying the enemy. Now his bones and joints told him he was no longer a young man.

Somewhere north of the crescent land where the ruined city of the old heretic spoke of the vengeance of Amun, he called an early halt and camped on the clifftops above the river, withdrawing from his men by a few khet. He sat and watched the full moon rise above the sculptured rocks and dunes of the eastern desert, even as Atum-Re dipped below the western horizon. The solitude and the silence weighed upon his heart as he contemplated the great expanse of desert now vanishing into shadow. Except for the outline of a road and his chariot and patient horses standing a few paces off, there was nothing to say that the kingdoms of Kemetu even existed.

"What have I done that will make me remembered?" he asked the night. "I have peace with the Nine Bows and the laws of the land are enforced throughout the kingdoms. I have built temples and shrines throughout the land, repairing others, and I am building a magnificent palace. Also, I have a sheaf of sons and an heir to rule after me...but is it enough?"

The rising moon cast a silvery light over the desert, accentuating the shadows, but no answer came from the night except the soft sigh of the breeze.

"And what of my wives, great Khonsu?" he asked the moon's disc. "Why must they contend amongst themselves and ruin the peace that should be mine at home? Tiye is the wife of my youth and mother of my heir, but she cannot be queen and this angers her. Tyti my sister is queen as is her due, but she demands the prince Ramesses be heir in defiance of my will; and now Iset the Syrian demands her son be raised up. I should never have married her and made her queen. I should have just bedded her as a palace woman instead of honouring her so." He shook his head and gazed up at the disc of the moon and wondered, as he had before, why Khonsu's face was so marked, whereas the face of Re was unblemished.

"It is fitting that the face of Re should be perfect, but Khonsu is also a god. How can a god be less than perfect? Do the markings mean something?"

Ramesses sighed and got up, leading his horses on foot back to the camp. Khonsu had left his questions unanswered, but he put doubts from his mind and prepared himself for the next day when they would descend from the plateau of the eastern desert onto the rich flat plains across the river from Men-nefer. It had been pleasant to escape the duties and cares of being king for the half month it had taken to travel north, but the work of the king must now resume.

The king entered white-walled Men-nefer on foot, having left his chariot on the east bank and taken a ferry over to the city. Although word had been sent ahead of his arrival, little fuss had been made of the king's presence. Tjaty Herwernef was busy in the law courts, but sent the palace guard to escort the king through the dusty streets. The populace scattered before the spearmen of the guard, and watched the royal procession pass with great eruptions of cheers.

"The people are glad to see their king," Ramesses observed. "I am gladdened."

"The people have cause to be happy, Son of Re," Djau, Captain of the Palace Guard said. "Everyone loves a good betrothal."

Ramesses stopped dead in the street and stared at Djau. "What betrothal is this?"

"Why...er...the betrothal of...er...forgive me, Majesty, I...I...assumed you knew."

"Assume I don't. Tell me."

"The heir and his sister Tentopet."

Ramesses started toward the palace again, his face grim.

Chamberlain Meryre knew more of the situation and was less nervous in divulging the details to his king. He explained that the betrothal had only been mooted at that point, and was the idea of Tiye, as mother to both the heir and girl concerned. Ramesses grunted, and decided that in that case he would delay discussing the point further until after he had refreshed himself. Giving instructions to the Chamberlain to notify Tiye of his intention, he walked through to the royal suite.

An hour later he was bathed, perfumed and dressed, but he was still a little agitated that Tiye would even consider such an important step as a betrothal without seeking permission first. He took himself off to the temple of Ptah and offered up a sacrifice and hymns of praise to the creator god, calming himself down as he communed with the god. Then he directed his footsteps toward the Per-Khemret where, as per his instructions, Tiye and his daughter Tentopet awaited him. The son in question, Khaemwaset, was not present, currently being with the fleet in the lower reaches of the Great River.

"Greetings, husband," Tiye said, bowing gracefully to the king. "I pray to the gods incessantly for your continued health and prosperity."

"You are well?"

"I am, my lord, thank you."

There was a pause as each person considered the reason for the meeting, yet hesitated to initiate what could develop into an acrimonious argument.

"Tentopet is nine years old," Ramesses observed. "A little young to be betrothed."

"A formal betrothal would be three years away, my lord, but it never hurts to be prepared."

"But Khaemwaset?"

Tiye lifted her head and stared at the king. "What is wrong with Khaemwaset?" she demanded. "He is your heir, and as such should marry his sister."

"He is twenty-three."

"Only fourteen years older than Tentopet. You are twenty years older than your sister-wife Tyti."

Ramesses made a dismissive gesture with his hand. "That is not the point. I had no brothers and one sister; there was no other choice. Tentopet has numerous brothers, and I think there are better choices for a husband."

"Who? Meryamun? He's a good lad, but I fail to see how he would be better than Khaemwaset. Tentopet could be Queen one day, rather than just the wife of an army general."

"Not Meryamun."

"Prehirwenemef? He is closer to her in age, but the argument is the same."

"Not him either."

"My lord? The other princes are younger than Tentopet. Sethirkhopeshef is weak and sickly, whereas Meryatum and Mentuhirkhopeshef are mere children. I would not offer them my daughter until they had proved themselves worthy."

"I agree, Tiye. All that you have said is accurate. None of your sons are a better match for Tentopet than Khaemwaset."

Tiye frowned. "Then...then what do you mean? Who?"

"Prince Ramesses."

"Your sister's son?"

"Queen Tyti's firstborn."

"You would marry your daughter Tentopet to a child who will never sit on the throne? Why, when she could marry Khaemwaset...or any of her full brothers?"

"Tentopet is the best of my daughters. I would have her make a good marriage."

"What better marriage than your heir?"

"Khaemwaset is not for her. Nor are your other sons."

"But Ramesses?"

"He is a good lad; intelligent and devout."

"You mean to make him your heir," Tiye said. "That's what all this is about, isn't it? You will supplant my sons with your sister's son...and what then? The sons of that Syrian whore?"

"Have a care, Tiye. Iset is my Queen and I will not have her slandered."

Tiye bowed her head, knowing she had gone too far. "It is true though, isn't it, my lord? You mean to supplant my sons."

"Nothing could be further from the truth," Ramesses said gently. "Your eldest three sons will always stand in front of Prince Ramesses. But Tentopet will marry Ramesses. I have spoken."

# Chapter 44
# Year 13 of Usermaatre Ramesses

Queen Iset remained in Waset for a year, hating every day of it. Used to being the most important woman in the Per-Ramesses palace, her subordinate position to the king's mother Tiy-merenese and his sister-wife Queen Tyti, rankled. Tyti did not go out of her way to humiliate Iset, but rather ignored her, and that inaction was harder to bear than active dislike. If there was an important ceremony, Iset would be assigned a minor role; if a visiting dignitary called on the Tjaty, Tyti and her mother would be invited to meet with him, but Iset's invitation, issued through the Per-Khemret, would invariably go astray. The other women of the Per-Khemret avoided the Syrian Queen where possible, and never volunteered a comment or a kind look. Iset was certain this was on the instigation of the other queen, but any accusation she made was met with polite, disinterested denial. Even the servants avoided her.

Faced with her sentence of banishment from the king, she resolved to do everything the king required of her, hoping that he would relent. She cultivated Tjaty To and inveigled him into explaining the laws of Kemet. They were complex and far outside her experience, so he assigned her an old scribe and let her sit in on the law courts, with the scribe muttering explanations whenever she asked questions. Through To's connections, she had a senior priest of Amun attend upon her, initiating her into the lesser mysteries of the god. When he tired of his duties, he brought in priests from other gods to enlarge her knowledge.

In the first month of Akhet, she publicly renounced her Syrian gods, declaring that henceforth she would put her trust in all things Kemetu. She had no confidants within the palace, so nobody knew her true feelings on the matter, but she smiled and made sure the king would hear about her announcement. If she had hoped for a speedy end to her exile, she was disappointed, but she put a brave face on it and resumed her studies.

And then in the second month of Peret came the message she had longed for. Tjaty To called upon her in the Per-Khemret and told her that the king commanded her back to Per-Ramesses.

"Not the court in Men-nefer?" she asked.

"The letter says Per-Ramesses." Tjaty To felt for the young queen and, knowing of her recent travails, took pity on her. "Queen Iset, perhaps this might be regarded as good news that the king does not order you into his presence."

"How so?"

"It has not escaped my notice that your relations with Queen Tyti are less than cordial. She and the king's mother must give their formal approval for you to leave the Per-Khemret, even though the king commands it, and I think they would delay your departure if they felt you were commanded into his presence. It is also within their power to deny you comforts for the voyage north. If, however, they saw it as the exchange of exile in Waset for exile in Per-Ramesses, they might be glad to see you go."

"I hate them," Iset cried. "I hate them and I will see my son crowned king of Kemet if it is the last thing I do."

"If you insist on trying for that, Queen Iset, it may well be the last thing you do. Besides, Prince Ramesses is but one of the princes that stand between your son and the throne. I beg you; put such thoughts from your mind. Your son will achieve a high position in Kemetu society anyway."

Iset took To's advice as regards Tyti and her mother, even if she still harboured a burning desire to see her son on the throne. She humbled herself in the Per-Khemret and asked permission to obey the king's command and take herself back to Per-Ramesses. Queen Tyti examined the king's message and gave her permission. She even ordered a decent vessel to be made ready, and allowed her rival some measure of luxury for the voyage.

"You came to us a foreigner, a Syrian, but you leave us with at least the semblance of a civilised demeanour," Tyti said. "One could almost imagine you to be Kemetu."

Iset bowed her head. "I have always tried to do as my lord the king desired."

Tyti dismissed Iset and turned to her mother, speaking loudly enough to be heard by Iset as she left the room. "One may wash a pig and dress it up in finery but one should not expect it to remain so when it returns to the sty."

Iset ground her teeth, but pretended she had not heard the insult, or the laughter that followed it. Outside Tyti's room, she composed herself and went to ready herself for the voyage north. She was commanded to Per-Ramesses, but she intended to stop off in Men-nefer anyway, and see the king and her son Amunhirkhopeshef.

The vessel at Iset's disposal was not one of the royal barges, but a smaller craft relying on only five oars to a side. Decking covered only the rear section, and makeshift reed huts had been erected on it to house Iset and two of her servants, and the captain of the vessel. The oarsmen worked and slept and ate in the body of the boat, seldom more than ten paces from the queen, and urinated and defecated over the side, often in full view. If she had needed a reminder of the lack of regard in which she was held, that long voyage north supplied it.

The only thing that made her days pleasurable was to turn away from the boat and view the river valley as it slowly slipped past. Iset had only been sixteen when she and her mother fled the court of Hatti, and she could barely remember the hills and mountains of her birth country. Most of her adult life had been spent either in the flat and featureless farmlands of the river's delta, or along the broad ribbon of water that gave life to Kemet.

Although she had publicly adopted the ways of Kemet, she still regarded herself as a princess of Hatti, and now that she was out of the sight of the Waset court and the ladies of the Per-Khemret, she returned to wearing the voluminous folds of dress favoured by Syrians rather than the revealing garments of Kemetu society. It may have made her a little hotter, but she felt more comfortable with her body concealed from the gaze of the sailors.

Iset's spirits lifted at the sight of the high white walls of Men-nefer, and she ordered the vessel put into the docks. The captain tried to argue that his orders were to take her to Per-Ramesses, but she would have none of it.

"The king, and my eldest son, is in Men-nefer, and I mean to see them, even if I have to throw myself into the river and swim ashore. Now you can either take me in or explain to the king why his queen was eaten by a crocodile." Iset saw the captain's uncertainty and smiled encouragingly. "Your orders were only to deliver me to Per-Ramesses and that is exactly what you will do. They do not prohibit you from stopping off along the way."

"That is so, my lady," the captain agreed. He shouted out the orders and the vessel turned toward the city docks.

Nobody was expecting the arrival of a queen of Kemet on the docks of Men-nefer, so Iset found herself walking almost unaccompanied through the dusty streets to the palace. The captain, seeing her predicament, took three of his burliest men and guarded her and her two servants until he could hand over his duty to the palace guard. Court officials are nothing if not resilient, so despite their initial shock at her appearance, the Chamberlain quickly organised rooms to be made ready in the Per-Khemret and sent servants hurrying to inform the king and Tiye.

"I want to see my son Amunhirkhopeshef as soon as I have paid my respects to the king," she said.

"I will have it done, Majesty," the Chamberlain replied. He oversaw the settling of Iset in her rooms and as he stood watching the servants bustling around, one ran up to him and whispered.

"The king will see you now," he said, and perforce, Iset had to leave immediately without having a chance to refresh herself or change her travel-soiled clothing.

She had not thought beyond seeing her husband and son, but as she was ushered into the audience room, Iset realised she was still wearing the clothing more suited to a Syrian princess than a Kemetu queen. The expression on the face of the king told her she had made a mistake, and Tiye's sneer made her quail inside. Putting a brave face on it, she greeted Ramesses as befitted a wife and queen.

"I had not thought to see you here, Iset. My instructions were for you to return to Per-Ramesses."

"Forgive me, my lord. I have not looked upon your face for so long I could not pass by the city without greeting you...and my son Amunhirkhopeshef."

Anger and sorrow flitted across the face of Tiye. She stood beside the king with one hand resting on his arm.

"I thought Queen Iset was learning Kemetu ways, Son of Re," Tiye murmured. "Yet here she is looking like a woman just arrived from Hatti. Is this how she obeys you, my lord?"

Ramesses patted Tiye's hand gently and stared hard at Iset. "That is a valid question, Iset. I had hoped you would have fully embraced Kemetu ways by now, even as our son Amunhirkhopeshef has, yet those garments you wear tell me otherwise."

Iset bowed her head, furious that Tiye should shame her before the king. "When in Kemetu society, I am fully Kemetu, but on the long and arduous journey north, I sought to dress more comfortably. If I have erred, I beg my lord's forgiveness."

"It seems I have erred in thinking you were now a Kemetu Queen. I think you should continue on to Per-Ramesses and resume your life there."

"As my lord wishes, but...may I greet my son Amunhirkhopeshef before I leave?"

"You may, but change into something more becoming. Our son has embraced Kemetu ways fully and I would not see his mother's origins flung in his face."

Her face burning from embarrassment and anger, Iset stormed off to her rooms in the palace. She snapped at the servants and smashed a pot of unguent in a fit of temper before calming down and changing into more conventional clothing. Amunhirkhopeshef was sent for, and he appeared shortly, every part of him proclaiming himself a prince of Kemet.

He greeted his mother coolly, polite and utterly correct in his language and actions, standing stiffly as she embraced him and soaked his cheek and shoulder with her tears.

"I am pleased to see you in good health, mother."

"Ah, my little boy...so grown up and manly. I have missed you so much. Have you missed me?"

"I have been busy learning to be a proper prince, mother."

"Yes, I can see you are a prince of Kemet, but you should not forget the blood of Hatti also flows within you."

"I am Kemetu now...only Kemetu."

Tears broke out afresh in Iset's eyes, and she wiped them away with the back of her hands. "Will you come and see me in Per-Ramesses? I am sure your brother would like to see you too."

"I have many brothers now, but if my duties permit I will pay my respects to my father's Queen as custom dictates."

Iset sobbed, but nodded. "I will always love you, my darling boy. Come to me when you can."

Amunhirkhopeshef bowed and took his leave of his mother, leaving Iset to throw herself on her bed and weep. Half a day later, servants came to tell her that her vessel had been readied and the king had ordered an honour guard to convey her to the docks. She bundled up her Syrian clothes and left the palace, her face veiled to hide her tear-reddened eyes.

The boat left Men-nefer and swiftly made its way down the easternmost branch of the river to Per-Ramesses. Until they were out of sight of the white walls, Iset stood in the stern of the boat next to the steersman, staring back at the city and weeping for her lost son.

"I will have my revenge," she told her mother Habadjilat, once they were safely alone in the privacy of the Per-Khemret. And to be certain they were not overheard, the two women spoke in the language of Hatti.

"Revenge for what?" Habadjilat asked.

"For turning my son against me; for the insults thrown at me by Tiye; for my lord turning his face from me." Iset thought for a few moments. "And for Tyti's insults this last year."

"You plan to revenge yourself on all these people? How?"

Iset looked thoughtful and walked over to an ornamental fishpond in the Per-Khemret courtyard. She sat on a stone bench and trailed her fingers in the cool water. Silver fish flicked up from the depths to investigate the disturbance, and away again.

"There have been times when I would gladly have spilled blood to wash away their insults."

"A dangerous course, daughter."

"Yes."

"You no longer desire this?"

"There would be a measure of satisfaction if Tyti and Tiye were removed, but it would not really improve my situation," Iset said. "A king's wife, even a queen, cannot rule in Kemet, so I cannot look to rule in their absence. The king would rule me, and after him, his heir. The sons of Tiye and Tyti would still outrank mine and the king would continue to show them favour."

"So it comes down to Amunhirkhopeshef, does it? Any revenge you take must benefit him." Habadjilat sat beside her daughter and took her hands in her own. "Daughter, if you are to see your eldest son on the throne of Kemet, you must remove those who stand in his way. Not Tyti, not Tiye, but the older princes. We are all but a breath away from the afterlife; four breaths and Amunhirkhopeshef is the heir."

"Could it be done? Without suspicion falling on me and my son?"

"I have considered this since you went to Waset," Habadjilat said, "And I think it could, providing the proper precautions are taken."

"Tell me how."

"You can rule out open violence, and we have no control over warfare, where death walks beside every man. But there are other avenues. Some of the princes like hunting. If they were out of sight, a resolute archer could strike them down. Then there is disease..."

"Disease is with the gods."

"Perhaps; yet I have heard it said by physicians that sickness spreads between people in ways that are nor easily understood. Anyway, that is but one avenue. Poison is another; the venom of a snake or scorpion yet another. Then there is magic. This last may be the safest, for the spells can be carried out at a distance."

"You have indeed thought of these things, mother." Iset sat in thought for a time. "We cannot do these things alone. We need the help of others--trustworthy others."

# Chapter 45
# Year 13 of Usermaatre Ramesses

Usermaatre Ramesses believed he was the ruler of Kemet, but the real power now lay elsewhere. He had fought foreign wars to defeat the Sea Peoples and the Ribu from the West, he had stamped out most of the criminals that preyed upon travellers within the kingdoms, and he had provided shade trees and gardens in many of the cities where common people might rest and take their ease after a hard day's work. Desirous of catering to the spiritual welfare of the people, he embarked on a massive program of repairing, rebuilding and creating shrines and temples up and down the length of the Great River.

All this cost gold, of course, and the treasury swiftly became depleted, despite earnest efforts to replenish stocks from the gold mines of Kush. As the gold declined, so did the power of the king, but instead of the country descending into turmoil and crime, another force grew in ascendancy during these years. Several years before, the honeyed words of the priest of Amun, Amenemopet, had convinced the king that he should trust only the Hem-netjer of Amun, Bakenkhons. Believing that the god Amun himself spoke through the young priest, Usermaatre Ramesses had acceded to the god's wishes and allowed Amun to liaise between the treasury and everyone who demanded gold. A lot of the metal that was the congealed tears of the sun found its way into the coffers of Amun, and the strength and influence of the priests of that god grew.

Then Tjaty Hori died and was replaced by Tjaty To, of the family of Bakenkhons, and the river of gold flowing through the hands of Amun became a flood. Family members were appointed to influential positions--Amenmose became Overseer of the Treasury of Amun, Chief Steward of the Western River, and Overseer of Works in the Mansion of Millions of Years. Amenemopet, the priest who had first set the king's feet on the path that led to the dominance of Amun was given, in recognition of his services to the god, the post of Overseer of Recruits of the Temple, and Ramessesnakht (not the King's Son of Kush, but another of the same name) became Fourth Prophet of Amun and his son Usermaatrenakht was elevated to become Steward of the Estate of Amun. The younger son of Ramessesnakht, Amenhotep, also became a priest of Amun, and his father started grooming him for higher office.

Tjaty To worked closely with Hem-netjer Bakenkhons and newly-appointed Fourth Prophet Ramessesnakht, bringing together the secular and priestly arms of government in the south. Whenever court officials, junior priests or servants were present, they were careful to guard their tongues, to be circumspect as regards their opinions, and never to even hint at disloyalty to the king. In private, however, they allowed their speech free rein.

They walked along the western riverbank--three of the most powerful men in Ta Shemau--and spoke of the future. Guarding them was one of the few men Bakenkhons truly trusted, a hulking brute of a man who hailed from darkest Kush. He had never been able to tell anyone his name for he had been mute from birth and he was illiterate. However, it amused Bakenkhons to name him Saba after one of the ancient kings of Kush. His glossy dark purple skin was scarred by cicatrices, and his face had been horribly mutilated, but his heart beat true for his master. Any secrets he learned while guarding the Hem-netjer could not easily be transmitted to anyone else, even had he chosen to do so. With Saba guarding them, the three men were as safe as they could reasonably be.

"How long must we wait?" Ramessesnakht demanded. "There are many suitable candidates for the priesthood. We could have men loyal to us in every city, not just Waset."

"Patience," To murmured.

"Youth always demands instant answers," Bakenkhons added.

"You of all people should see the need for speed, Hem-netjer. How much longer can you reasonably expect to hold office?"

"Do not look to advance through my demise," Bakenkhons reproved. "You will get there soon enough. Third Prophet Thonefer is ill and will soon relinquish his position."

"Surely his son Amenemopet..."

"He is Overseer of Recruits and not yet ready for such responsibility."

"I did not really mean..."

"Perhaps not, but we must put Amun before our personal ambitions."

"Of course," Ramessesnakht said. "Tjaty, where does your interest lie in this? We priests serve the god, but you are appointed by the king to serve the interests of the southern kingdom."

"A man can serve two masters, as long as the aims of both concur."

"And do they?"

"I believe so. The king seeks a settled and peaceful kingdom, as does Amun. I am the king's voice in Ta Shemau and I am also kin to the Prophets of Amun. Our interests often coincide."

"Kemet is greater than just Ta Shemau, though," Ramessesnakht said. "Amun reigns throughout the land, but you only rule in the south."

"For now."

Bakenkhons stopped and stared at the Tjaty. "What are you saying, To?"

Saba caught an undercurrent of the tension between his master and the other men and though he did not understand it, he prepared to defend him, edging closer. The Hem-netjer of Amun saw the movement and unobtrusively waved him back.

To shrugged. "I am saying nothing. Merely observing that none of us know what the future holds."

"I would remind you that we serve Amun above ourselves."

"I am aware of that, Bakenkhons, but let me ask you a question. Who serves Amun better...Tjaty To or Tjaty Herwernef?"

"You, of course."

"And between me and the king?"

Bakenkhons hesitated, and despite the fact that they were alone on the riverbank, looked around. "The king has always given Amun his due."

"Can you swear that that will always be true?"

"Could we even swear that of you?" Ramessesnakht asked.

"Ah, but you know me. I am related to you both and family counts, doesn't it?"

"That is true.""

"So in the matter of the king and me?"

"You are family," Bakenkhons said.

"Just so."

"So what did you mean when you said, 'for now'?" Ramessesnakht asked.

Tjaty To smiled and resumed his stroll along the riverbank. "You serve Amun and already the Estate of Amun is like a kingdom inside the kingdoms. I foresee it growing until it becomes more powerful than either Ta Mehu or Ta Shemau. You, Bakenkhons, if you live long enough, will be as a king ruling over Amun's Estate. You too, Ramessesnakht, if that day is delayed. But what of me? Am I destined to be only the Tjaty of a single kingdom? Or even of both? May I not aspire to more?"

"How can you be more?" the young priest asked. "Above you is only..."

"By the gods," Bakenkhons breathed. "I will not say it out loud, even for just our ears, but you really aim that high?"

"It has happened before," To observed.

"When?" Ramessesnakht asked.

Bakenkhons nodded slowly. "He speaks of Tjaty Ay, who became Kheperkheperure Irimaat in the days following the Heretic."

"The Heretic? You would bring back those days? Amun would oppose you."

"Don't be a fool, Ramessesnakht. I'm not talking of the Heretic himself, may his name be cursed forever, but of his uncle. Irimaat Ay served four kings faithfully, and when the line of Nebmaatre Amenhotep failed, took the reins of government for himself and ruled Kemet well. Amun prospered under him."

"I don't know the story," Ramessesnakht said. "What happened to him?"

"He died, as all men must, but he attained greatness when it was thrust upon him."

"And you would do the same?"

"Why not? Am I any less deserving of greatness?"

"That would depend," Bakenkhons said.

"On what?"

"On how Amun fared under your rule."

Tjaty To kicked at a pebble with his foot. "One hand holds another," he said.

"Meaning?" Ramessesnakht asked.

"How Amun fares depends on how I fare under Amun."

"Amun supports the king...whoever is the king," Bakenkhons murmured. "You need have no fear in that regard."

To stared out over the expanse of Iteru, where fishing boats plied their trade. "The Estate of Amun is exceedingly rich; richer even than the king's Treasury. In theory, all lands belong to the king, but the king would not dare confiscate Temple lands, so in practice the Estate is the largest landowner in the kingdoms. With wealth comes power and the wealth of Kemet flows through the hands of Amun. I am concerned that Amun--and of course I am speaking of the Temple Estate, not the god--may grow so powerful it no longer needs the king." The Tjaty turned to look at the priests. "Then where would I be?"

Bakenkhons looked To in the eyes and put a hand on his shoulder. "Amun does not forget those who serve him, and neither do his priests. When the time comes, Amun will offer you the throne. Until then, be circumspect and consolidate power. Usermaatre is still too strong to supplant, but he is growing old, and his heir Khaemwaset will be as wet clay in the hands of the potter when his time comes."

# Chapter 46
# Year 13 of Usermaatre Ramesses

I have sat now on the throne of my father for thirteen years, and done everything in my power to emulate the deeds of the Great Usermaatre, my grandfather, but my very real achievements feel as hollow as the grains of wheat in the temple granaries after an infestation of weevils--all wholesome and good on the surface, but lacking substance beneath.

I had such lofty ambitions when first I sat on the throne. I would be one with the Great Usermaatre and indeed, had that in my mind even before then. Why else would I name my eldest sons after his eldest sons even though I had not yet entertained the notion that I might one day be king? I was a soldier and worshipped the name of the Great Usermaatre, for he made Kemet first among the nations, and I could envisage nothing nobler than to be like him.

Usermaatre fought and defeated foreign foes, smashing the Hatti utterly and restoring Kemet to its preordained and preeminent place among the nations. Peace at home and abroad typified the golden age of his reign, and I hoped to do likewise. I defeated my enemies, destroying the Ribu and throwing back the Sea Peoples from the borders of Kemet; I stamped out crime and dissension within the kingdoms, making the land a place where men and women can walk in safety.

I have not forgotten the gods either, building many temples and shrines, and refurbishing many others up and down the length of the Great River. People everywhere praise my name. This piety and devotion have cost me dearly though; the treasury is depleted and I am forced to watch as temples and monuments crumble. I order them to be repaired, of course, and you could say that my continual efforts are praiseworthy, but how much more magnificent it would be if the buildings were erected properly in the first place.

It all comes down to the amount of gold in the treasury. Kings who have gone before me have had so much more wealth to draw upon, from the great golden Nebmaatre Amenhotep, to my namesake Usermaatre

Ramesses. They could achieve lasting fame and monuments that extol their glory down the years because they had gold in abundance, whereas I do not. The mines of Kush have been less productive of late, and what gold is drawn from their rocky depths has a thousand uses before ever it amasses in the royal treasury.

I have heard it said that the gold within the treasury of the Temple of Amun far exceeds that of the royal coffers, but those who say that have little understanding of the complexities of governance. When I first started my great program of building and repair, a thousand priests would pester me at every opportunity, importuning me for gold for this temple, or gold for that shrine, and so the wealth of the kingdoms was frittered away. The accounting was complex, and it was difficult to see whether progress was being made. Then one of the priests of Amun came to me with wisdom that he said came straight from the god dwelling within his innermost sanctuary in the Great Temple of Waset.

"Hear, O Great Usermaatre Ramesses, Son of Amun-Re," he said. "Hearken to the words of your divine Father who dwells within, vouchsafed through a dream to his servant Amenemopet. Know that though Usermaatre Ramesses has defeated all his enemies great and small, both outside and inside the kingdoms, yet is he beset by biting flies and mangy dogs that prey upon his generosity and goodness."

When I asked what he meant by these ill-omened words, he replied that these were not the words of a man but the words of the supreme god of Kemet.

"O Great Usermaatre, hear then and hearken to the words of Amun-Re. The biting flies that suck at the lifeblood of Kemet, and the mangy dogs that eat of the flesh of the kingdoms are those very priests that feed on the generosity of the Son of Amun-Re."

"How can that be, Amenemopet, priest of Amun-Re? Do you accuse yourself?"

"The god says that I can be trusted."

"Only you?"

"Also the Hem-netjer tepy en Amun in Waset, Bakenkhons, Son of Amun-Re. The god bids you pay no more gold to the importuning priests of every god."

"How then will temples and shrines be built? How will they be repaired?"

"You will pay the gold to the Temple of Amun-Re in Waset. Your faithful priests there will disburse gold as it is needed to the priests of every god and provide a detailed and exact accounting."

And so it came to be, for even a king, divine in his own right, must pay heed to Amun-Re. I could hardly ignore the words of the god, coming as they did through the holy channel of dreams. If this was what the god wanted, then that was how it must be. In truth, I felt a tiny tickle of doubt in my mind, for it is possible for a man, even a priest, to lie to a king, but I put that doubt down to the whispers of the giant serpent Apep, who seeks to destroy ma'at and battle the god Re daily.

As it happens, it must have been a true dream, for although gold flows out of my treasury as fast as before, the priests of every god leave me alone. If I see that shrines and temples are in disrepair throughout the kingdoms, it must be that the priests of that god have failed to put a good case to the Temple of Amun in Waset. Bakenkhons all but rules Waset, and the Temple owns more land around the southern capital even than I, the king. But no matter; all land in Kemet ultimately belongs to the king. I only choose to let others govern it for me.

Men look at me and think me favoured by the gods--and that is true. Such gold as escapes the notice of the Temple is spent on my great Mansion of Millions of Years on the west bank of Waset, and its attendant palace. Twelve years have passed since work started on it, and the walls and pylons have arisen like mountain cliffs, the halls are forests of tall swollen pillars, carved and painted, joined by shadowed passages that blaze with colour as hundreds of artists decorate walls and ceilings with text and artwork. The rooms of the palace proceed apace too, and the Per-Khemret is now second only in magnificence and luxury to the one in Men-nefer. When the last of the trees and flowering shrubs are planted, when the fishponds are fully stocked and the menagerie completed, it will be like no other place in the kingdoms. I long for that day.

I must seriously consider which of my women will live there. At the moment, my mother and my sister-wife Tyti are in residence, along with Iset, my Syrian wife. The wife of my youth Tiye resides in Men-nefer, but I think it is not right that the mother of my heir should be separated from this magnificent new palace, and I think I will bring her here. What to do with Tyti and Iset though? There is no love lost between my wives, though the reasons for this are petty and demeaning to all of them. Tiye resents my later wives, though surely she must see that the Bull of Heru must plough many fields. She is still mother of my heir and loses no precedence by the presence of the others.

I know my failure to make her Queen rankles, but I have explained this to her. She is a commoner, whereas Tyti my sister is daughter of a king, and even Iset is a Syrian princess. It is right and honourable that they be made queens. As for Tyti, she resents the fact that Prince Ramesses is not the heir, but I have explained that too. Am I to cast off my older sons just because she desires it? No; never. Iset resents both wives, wanting her own son Amunhirkhopeshef to be heir, but he is younger even than Prince Ramesses, who has a better claim. Nothing I do or say seems to have any effect on these women, and they din my ears continually with their complaints, so I must separate them. If Tiye comes to Waset, the others must leave and take up residence in the north. They won't like it though. I think I can leave my mother Tiy-merenese in Waset. She and Tiye always got on well, and my mother is too old to move far from the city she grew up in and loves.

Such is life...and death.

Therein lies another expense I had not considered. When a man becomes king...or even heir...he must think of what comes after, when our term on earth ends and we face eternity. If we are to enjoy the afterlife in a manner befitting our status in life, then we must make provision for it. A tomb is the most important of these tasks, so as soon as I became heir I initiated my tomb in that stark valley where so many of my predecessors are buried--Ta-sekhet-ma'at or The Great Field.

If my own tomb was all I had to be concerned with, I could relax, for I have a good team of builders employed in the valley, but as king I have responsibilities for so much more. I have royal wives and it is only proper that they have tombs matching their status. Then there are my sons and daughters, each of them needs their niche in which to spend eternity. I can reasonably leave my heir to take care of his own as he will be king after me, but the others need some provision, whether it is separate tombs or just rooms off my own grand structure.

The Great Usermaatre buried many of his own sons within his own tomb, but I have employed another solution. Near Ta-sekhet-ma'at is another dry valley, Ta-Set-neferu, The Place of Beauty, wherein the queens and principal wives of former kings are buried. My own wives will lie here eventually, and I have constructed tombs for my children here also. Nothing too elaborate; but sufficient for their status as sons of the King's Body.

It should, of course, have been many years before any of them were needed, but the sudden death of my beloved eldest son Amunhirkhopeshef, necessitated a rapid readying of his tomb. It was incomplete, with paintings and reliefs on only some of the walls, but I had other paintings rapidly rendered on wooden panels within the other chambers of the tomb. The gods will forgive him his hasty burial; I am sure, as the titles placed in the tomb identify him beyond doubt. 'Hereditary Prince' shows him to be my heir, and 'Royal Scribe' and 'Master of the Horse' speak of his high status. They will see these titles and welcome him as my son, even though he did not have enough time to carve out a name for himself.

In one way I am more fortunate than the Great Usermaatre. He had many sons, but one after another they died, leaving his thirteenth son, Baenre Merenptah to succeed him. I, on the other hand, have only lost one son. All the others are strong and healthy...except little Sethirkhopeshef, of course. Still, Usermaatre's later years must have eaten at him as one son after another died; as heir after heir was buried before him. I cannot imagine the heartache he must have felt. I felt my Amunhirkhopeshef's loss keenly enough, but Khaemwaset is strong and well-favoured by the gods, so there will be time enough to complete all preparations for their afterlives.

So here I sit, in the seventeenth year of my reign, an ageing man but not yet old. My joints hurt in the mornings, my teeth ache and twinge and my bowels often do not give me peace. All men suffer from these maladies, I know, many worse than I, and still manage to live into old age. My grandfather Usermaatre lived to be ninety, and my father lived to be seventy, so the gods may well grant me another thirty or forty years.

"Ahh... another thirty of forty years of increasing pain?"

I must consider where I go from here. Kemet is at peace with the nations and relatively free of crime, my tomb and Mansion of Millions of Years are nearing completion, so what is there left to do?

The temples are an ever-present drain on the treasury, but what can I do to alleviate that? Another foreign war perhaps, reinstating Kemet's unequivocal hegemony over Kanaan and the Hatti? If successful, that could yield gold and slaves, but I now have the Sea Peoples settled through Kanaan and if I strike northward with my corps, can I fully trust them in my rear?

Can I seek riches by more peaceful means then? I have already sent off an expedition to Pwene to bring back gold, incense, ivory, rare woods and exotic animals, but they have been gone nearly three years without word. Do they still survive? Will they ever bring back riches to swell my treasury? What if they do not? Can I send out gold-seekers into Kush and find new mines to replenish the treasury? But to find gold, I must spend gold...gold I do not have. Perhaps I shall have to wait a little longer for the riches of Pwene to come to me before I consider other sources.

Outwardly, my reign is one of peace and plenty, filled with sons and the love of the common people, yet my heart is not glad within my breast. I feel I have been raised up only to be cast down. What can I do?

Well, I will tell you what I will not do. I will not sit here in my palace and bemoan my fate. I have many blessings and my family is foremost among them. I have sons who are grown men, and a daughter who is already married to her brother Ramesses. Why did I marry Tentopet to Ramesses? What god whispered in my ear? Tiye is right--my eldest daughter should have married my heir, yet I bypassed Khaemwaset and settled on a younger son. Why? What made me do it?

I don't suppose it matters, though. There have been royal weddings and a new generation of royal children will soon arrive to secure this new House of Ramesses on the everlasting throne of Kemet.

My princes are my legacy, and I will be remembered not only for my conquests and my pious buildings, but also for the strength and durability of those that come after me.

The story of Usermaatre Ramesses with continue in:
Strong is Ma'at of Re: The Heirs

# Thoughts on Writing Historical Fiction

A work of historical fiction comes from the mind of the writer, but it is dependent on historical facts. When I write about relatively modern times I have not only the bare bones of history to hang my story on, but also the personal writings of the characters and their contemporaries, and a host of relevant facts and opinions to flesh out the story. The further back you go in time, the less is available to draw upon, and by the time you reach Ancient Egypt, even the facts are disputed. Egyptologists have pored through the ruins of a past civilisation, examined the colourful walls of rock tombs and their contents, studied temple hieroglyphics and self-serving inscriptions of the kings, and deciphered fragments of papyrus to paint us a picture of what society was like three thousand years ago and more. It is necessarily incomplete, for much has been lost and what has not been lost is not always understood. The history of Ancient Egypt is a work in progress. When I, as a writer of historical fiction, attempt to tell a tale from the distant past, I work with what is given me by serious researchers.

Ramesses III is a relatively well known king, mainly from his early years on the throne and the manner of his death, but there are large gaps in his life story. We can piece together some of it by referencing his wives and sons, and the known voyage to Punt that occurred midway through his reign, but some parts are just not known. However, by studying the known facts, laying them out and linking one with the other, we can fashion a tale that builds upon the framework of the house that is his reign. If I might pursue that analogy a bit further, my research adds floors and cladding in likely places, roofing it over with reasoned conjecture, and adding invented dialogue, to create a story of what might have been.

Many of the characters are real people that existed in Egypt at the time--wives, sons and daughters, court officials--and others are made up. If I tried to limit myself to the known facts, this story would be like looking down a microscope and seeing the tiny organisms in a drop of pond water swim in and out of focus. Instead, I have added possibilities that slow down the action and allow us to examine what happened and postulate reasons for their actions.

*Strong is the Ma'at of Re* is a novel based on the known life of Ramesses III and incorporates as many of the facts of his reign as I can, in the proper order, but it is still a work of fiction. The first book dwells mostly on the king himself, the second on his heirs and would-be heirs, and the third on the conspirators that plotted the death of their king.

Even Egyptologists cannot agree on which of the wives of Ramesses III gave birth to which son. To my mind, some of those theories make sense, others don't. For instance, the sister of Ramesses III, Tyti, is credited by some researchers as the mother of the elder princes who were born while Ramesses was still a commoner. I reasoned that was unlikely as brother-sister marriage only occurred within the royal family. The marriage of Ramesses and Tyti could only happen after he became king--or at least heir. Thus another woman was the mother of these elder princes and was likely a commoner, as was Ramesses at the time. That made Tyti the mother of Prince Ramesses, who went on to become Ramesses IV. Long hours were spent disentangling the blood lines and making reasoned assumptions of relationships and motives. Some of my decisions can be seen at a glance in the *Simplified Family Tree of Strong is the Ma'at of Re* (below), and others appear in the pages of this book. You may disagree with my decisions; that is your prerogative, but I believe my choices make sense.

And so it goes on. The bones of history make the framework of my story and I must decide which opinions will clothe the bones in flesh and skin. If I choose well, my story takes on a life of its own.

I have researched this period extensively, and while I cannot claim to have read everything, I believe I have weighed up sufficient evidence to make an informed decision.

My main sources have been:

**Anglim, Simon et al**, 2002, *Fighting Techniques of the Ancient World*, Thomas Dunne Books

**Budge, EA Wallis**, 1959, *Egyptian Religion: Ideas of the Afterlife in Ancient Egypt*, University Books

**Budge, EA Wallis**, 1967, *The Egyptian Book of the Dead*, Dover Publications

**Cline, Eric H. & O'Connor, David**, editors, 2012, *Ramesses III: the Life and Times of Egypt's Last Hero*, University of Michigan Press.

**Dodson, Aidan**, 2000, *Monarchs of the Nile*, The American University in Cairo Press

**Dodson, Aidan**, 2010, *Poisoned Legacy: The Decline and Fall of the Nineteenth Egyptian Dynasty*, The American University in Cairo Press

**Dodson, Aidan & Hilton, Dyan**, 2004, *The Complete Royal Families of Ancient Egypt,* Thames & Hudson

**Frood, Elizabeth**, 2007, *Biographical Texts from Ramessid Egypt*, Society of Biblical Literature

**Petrie, William Matthew Flinders**, 2005, *A History of Egypt: Vol III. From the XIXth to the XXXth Dynasties*, Adamant Media Corporation

**Redford, Susan**, 2008, *The Harem Conspiracy: The Murder of Ramesses III*, Northern Illinois University Press

**Romer, John**, 1984, *Ancient Lives: The Story of the Pharaoh's Tombmakers*, Guild Publishing

**Shaw, Garry J**, 2012, *The Pharaoh: Life at Court and on Campaign*, Thames & Hudson

**Vernus, Pascal**, 2003, translated from the French by David Lorton, *Affairs and Scandals in Ancient Egypt*, Cornell University Press.

**Wilkinson, Richard H**, 2000, *The Complete Temples of Ancient Egypt*, Thames & Hudson

I would like to offer up special thanks to Colleen Darnell, the William K. and Marilyn M. Simpson Associate Professor of Egyptology at Yale University, for helping me with a translation that made sense of a particular aspect of the story.

Sara Jane Sesay became my 'First Reader' for this trilogy and I am indebted to her attention to my storytelling. She is a woman with a great deal of experience in Egypt and matters Egyptian, and is a good friend.

Julie Napier is my cover artist. A skilled photographer and experienced artist, she has created all of my book covers, some of which have been nominated for awards.

I would like to thank my many readers too. Some of them wrote to me when they reached the end of my Amarnan Kings series, asking if I would write another Egyptian series. I wrote the *Fall of the House of Ramesses* trilogy, but was asked again for more. It seemed to me that although the 19th dynasty had fallen, aspects of it continued on into the 20th, so I researched the early kings and started the *Strong is the Ma'at of Re* trilogy on the reign of Ramesses III. Readers of the previous trilogy will no doubt recognise some of the characters, fictional and non-fictional, and I hope will come to invest in their 'lives' once more.

# Some notes on Strong is the Ma'at of Re

Readers of my previous novels on Ancient Egypt will recognise many of these notes, but I think they are sufficiently relevant to repeat them, with some modifications.

In any novel about ancient cultures and races, some of the hardest things to get used to are the names of people and places. Often these names are unfamiliar in spelling and pronunciation. It does not help that for reasons dealt with below, the spelling, and hence the pronunciation is sometimes arbitrary. To help readers keep track of the characters in this book I have included some notes on names in the ancient Egyptian language. I hope they will be useful.

In Ancient Egypt a person's name was much more than just an identifying label. A name meant something, it was descriptive, and a part of a person's being. For instance, Ramesses means 'Re has fashioned him', and Khaemwaset means 'He who appeared in Waset'. Knowledge of the true name of something gave one power over it, and in primitive societies a person's real name is not revealed to any save the chief or immediate family. A myth tells of the creator god Atum speaking the name of a thing and it would spring fully formed into existence. Another myth says the god Re had a secret name and went to extraordinary lengths to keep it secret.

The Egyptian language, like written Arabic and Hebrew, was without vowels. This produces some confusion when ancient Egyptian words are transliterated. The god of Waset in Egyptian reads *mn*, but in English this can be represented as Amen, Amon, Ammon or Amun. The form one chooses for proper names is largely arbitrary, but I have tried to keep to accepted forms where possible. King Ramesse III's name can have various spellings depending on the author's choice, such as Ramesses (used in this book), Rameses, or Ramses.

The names of the kings have been simplified. Egyptian pharaohs had five names, known as the Horus name, the Nebti name, the Golden Falcon name, the Prenomen and the Nomen. Only the Nomen was given at birth, the other names being coronation names. The Horus name dates from pre-dynastic times and was given to a king upon his coronation. All kings had a Horus name, but by the eighteenth dynasty it was seldom used. The Nebti name dates from the time of the unification of Egypt and shows the special relationship the king had to the vulture-goddess Nekhbet of Upper Egypt and the cobra-goddess Wadjet of Lower Egypt. The Golden Falcon name conveys the idea of eternity, as gold neither rusts nor tarnishes, and dates from the Old Kingdom. It perhaps symbolises the reconciliation of Horus and Set, rather than the victory of Horus over Set as the titles are usually non-aggressive in nature.

By the time of the eighteenth dynasty, the prenomen, or throne name, had become the most important coronation name, replacing the Horus name in many inscriptions. Since the eleventh dynasty, the prenomen has always contained the name of Re or Ra.

The nomen was the birth name, and this is the name by which the kings in this book are commonly known. The birth names most common in the nineteenth and twentieth dynasty were Ramesses and Seti. Successive kings with the same birth name did not use the method we use to distinguish between them - namely numbers (Ramesses III and Ramesses IV). In fact, the birth name often ceased to be used once they became king and the coronation prenomen distinguished them. Ramesses III became Usermaatre Meryamun, and Ramesses IV became Usermaatre Setapenamun to start with and then Heqamaatre Setapenamun, while Ramesses V became Usermaatre Sekheperenre, and Ramesses VI became Nebmaatre Meryamun. Potentially very confusing, so I have generally used the birth names on informal occasions and limited the use of the prenomen to more formal occasions or when referring to past kings. Birth names were still used by family members on informal occasions and I have often used prenomen and nomen together, just so the reader is absolutely sure of the person's identity.

Another simplification has occurred with place names and titles. In the twelfth century B.C.E., Egypt as a name for the country did not exist. The land around the Nile Valley and Delta was called Kemet or The Black Land by its inhabitants, and the desert Deshret or The Red Land. Much later, Greeks called it Aigyptos from which we get Egypt. Other common terms for the country were The Two Lands (Upper and Lower Kemet), and the Land of Nine Bows (the nine traditional enemies). Likewise Lower Egypt (to the north) was known as Ta Mehu, and Upper Egypt (to the south) was known as Ta Shemau. The name 'Nile' is also from the Greek, so I have used the usual designation of the time - Great River, or Iteru.

Similarly, the king of Egypt or Kemet was later known as 'Pharaoh', but this term derives from the phrase Per-aa which originally meant the Great House or royal palace. Over the years the meaning changed to encompass the idea of the central government, and later the person of the king himself. The Greeks changed Per-Aa to Pharaoh. I have decided to remain with the ubiquitous title of 'king'.

During the eighteenth dynasty, the kings ruled from a city known variously as Apet, No-Amun or Waset in the Fourth province or sepat of Ta Shemau, which itself was also called Waset; or just 'niwt' which meant 'city'. This capital city the Greeks called Thebes. The worship of Amun was centred here and the city was sometimes referred to as the City of Amun. I have called this great city by its old name of Waset.

Ramesses II built a new capital city in the eastern delta and called it Per-Ramesses, meaning literally 'House of Ramesses'. Merenptah moved the capital to the ancient city of Men-nefer, known to the Greeks as Memphis, as this city belonged to the god Ptah and Merenptah was literally 'Beloved of Ptah'. The kings of the twentieth dynasty used all three cities but started gravitating back to the southern city of Waset, especially as the power of the priests of Amun grew. Ramesses III built his new palace on the West Bank opposite Waset.

The gods of Egypt are largely known to modern readers by their Greek names; for instance, Osiris, Thoth and Horus. I have decided to keep the names as they were originally known to the inhabitants of Kemet - Asar, Djehuti and Heru. The Greek names for unfamiliar gods can be found in the section *Places, People, Gods & Things* at the end of this book.

Mention should be made of the incidence of writing amongst the characters in this book. It is generally accepted that no more than 1% of ancient Egyptians were literate and that knowledge of the complex hieroglyphic writing was the purview of the scribes and priests. Hieroglyphics are commonly seen in the formal inscriptions on temple and tomb walls. However, there was also another form of writing in ancient Egypt. This is called hieratic writing and is a form of cursive script used for writing administrative documents, accounts, legal texts, and letters, as well as medical, literary, and religious texts. This form of writing is commonly found on papyrus scraps, painted on wood or stone, or scratched onto pottery ostraca (shards). Thousands of these have been found, often closely associated with the lower strata of society, and it is believed that many more people were at least marginally literate than is commonly accepted. There is every reason to believe that people for whom some form of notation was essential to their everyday lives were capable of some level of writing.

When I refer to a person writing in *Strong is the Ma'at of Re,* it should not be assumed that the person is fully literate, but instead has knowledge of writing consistent with their place in Egyptian society.

# Places, People, Gods & Things in *Strong is the Ma'at of Re*

**Abdju**
city of Abydos, near modern day el-'Araba el Madfuna

**Abu**
(1) city of Elephantine, near modern day Aswan
(2) elephant

**Adara**
only daughter of Ament and Tausret

**Ahmes**
(1) charioteer of Ramesses III
(2) head of the Potters' Guild in Ta-senet

**Amenhotep**
ship's captain on the Pwene expedition.

**Amenemopet**
young priest of Amun

**Amennakht**
High Priest of Amun in Men-nefer

**Ament**
Former General of Egypt, husband to former Queen Tausret

**Amentep**
apprentice physician, son of Rahmes

**Amun**
creator deity, local god of Thebes (Waset), often worshipped as Amun-Re (Amun-Ra)

**Amunhirkhopershef**
(1) eldest son of Ramesses III & Tiye
(2) first son of Ramesses III and Queen Iset

**Amurri**
the Amorites

**Anapa**
the god Anubis

**Aniba**
administrative capital of Wawat (Northern Kush)

**Ankhu**
Leader of Five in the rebel Set corps

**Asar**
Osiris, god of the underworld and resurrection

**Ashkelon**
a Philistine city

**Atum**
the creator god

**Auset**
the goddess Isis. Sometimes called Aset or Iset

**Aya**
concubine of Ramesses III

**Bak**
a hunter in Per-Ramesses

**Bakenkhons**
Second Prophet of Amun in Waset

**Bebi**
a spy in Per-Bast

**Behdet**
city south of Waset, modern day Edfu

**Belus**
the Kaftor sun god

**Bes**
god worshipped as protector of mothers, children, childbirth

**Dagon**
a god of the Philistines

**Dan-el**
a potter of Urit, friend of Ament

**Den**
a hunter in Per-Ramesses

**Divine Adoratrice**
Duat Netjer, priestess ranking slightly below God's Wife

**Djanet**
city in the north-east of Ta Mehu, Tanis

**Djau**
Captain of the Palace Guard in Men-nefer

**Djehutemheb**
General of the Northern Armies

**Djeti**
spymaster of Ramesses III

**Djutep**
commander of the Sept corps

**Dov**
husband of Adara, son of Yeshua and Ziphah

**Duamutef**
a protection god of the Canopic jars, son of Heru

**Elior**
son of Dov & Adara

**Ephrim**
eldest adopted son of Ament and Tausret

**Geb**
god of the earth

**Gebtu**
Coptos, modern day town of Qift

**Gezer**
a Philistine city

**God's Wife**
Hemet Netjer

**Goloth**
younger son of Ti-ament and Zeben the Kaftor

**Great Sea**
Mediterranean Sea
**Hakor**
instructor in the Hapi corps

**Hannu**
a sailor in the Heron Squad

**Hapi**
a protection god of the Canopic jars, son of Heru, the river god

**Harkhuf**
Commander of the Loyal Set corps

**Hatti**
the Hittites

**Heka**
the Crook, a symbol of kingly authority

**Hemdjert**
(Habadjilat) Syrian princess, mother of Iset

**Hemet Netjer**
God's Wife

**Hem-netjer**
High Priest

**Henen-nesut**
Herakleopolis, city near modern day Beni Suef

**Heqa Khaseshet**
Hyksos, an Asiatic people who invaded northern Egypt ending the 13th dynasty

**Heru**
the god Horus

**Herwernef**
Tjaty in the North

**Hesmen**
a woman's menses

**Het-Hor**
(Hathor) goddess of joy, feminine love and motherhood

**Hori**
(1) Commander of the Set corps
(2) Tjaty in the South
(3) Great General of the Lord of the Two Lands, Admiral

**Huni**
overseer of bakers in the Heru corps

**Hut-Repyt**
city in Ta Shemau, near modern day village of Wannina

**Ini**
youngest daughter of Ti-ament and Zeben the Kaftor

**Intef**
Overseer of the Bow in the Hapi corps

**Iset**
daughter of Hemdjert the Syrian, Queen of Ramesses III

**Iteru**
(1) the Great River, the Nile
(2) a unit of length, 20,000 cubits or 10.5 kilometres

**Itet**
concubine of Ramesses III

**Iunu**
a northern city, Heliopolis, now at the north-east edge of Cairo

**Jerem**
younger adopted son of Ament & Tausret

**Jochim**
chief of the Shechem tribe

**Kaftor**
one of the Sea Peoples, the Philistines

**Kamose**
Governor of Per-Ramesses

**Kanaan**
modern-day Palestine and Israel

**Kasir**
fishing village on the Red Sea

**Kebir**
a group of islands in the Red Sea, the Dahlak Archipelago

**Kemet**
the land of Egypt

**Khabekhmet**
Governor of Perire

**Khabiru**
a tribe of Kanaan who became the Hebrew

**Khaemwaset**
second son of Ramesses III & Tiye, Sem-priest of Ptah

**Khay**
Commander of the Re corps

**Khenbet Council**
the king's legal and administrative advisors

**Khent-Min**
city north of Waset, modern day Akhmim
**Khepre**
Khepri, an aspect of the sun god Re

**Khet**
a unit of length, 100 cubits or 52.5 metres

**Khmun**
Hermopolis, city in Ta Shemau near modern day El Ashmunein

**Khnumhotep**
Overseer of the Treasury Year 4 to 20 of Ramesses III

**Khonsu**
god of the moon

**Khui**
mayor of Ta-senet, modern-day Esna

**King's Son of Kush**
Viceroy of Nubia

**Kinnereth, Sea of**
the Sea of Galilee in Kanaan

**Kush**
Nubia

**Lipit-Ulmash**
an Akkadian caravan owner

**Long Sea**
the Red Sea

**Matia**
a washerwoman of Per-Bast

**Medjay**
an elite paramilitary police force

**Meni**
messenger from Perire

**Men-nefer**
ancient capital of Lower Egypt, Memphis

**Mentak**
adopted name of Ament in exile

**Mentemtowe**
Assistant to the Assistant Overseer of the Treasury

**Mentuhirkhopeshef**
seventh son of Ramesses III and Tiye

**Merenre**
Commander of Ptah corps

**Merikare**
Commander of Hapi corps

**Meru**
Leader of Ten, rebel Set corps

**Meryamun**
third son of Ramesses III and Tiye, Troop Commander in Shu

**Meryatum**
sixth son of Ramesses III and Tiye

**Meryre**
(1) Butler at Waset palace (aka Mesedure)
(2) Chamberlain at Men-nefer
(3) Troop Commander Loyal Set corps

**Min**
god of fertility

**Montuherwenemef**
younger son of Ramesses III and Iset, named Mursil by Iset

**Mose**
(1) a sailor in the Heron Squad
(2) Troop Commander of the Loyal Set corps

**Mut**
the mother goddess

**Nakhtmin**
Commander of Heru corps
**Napata**
capital of Kush

**Natsefamen**
Commander of Shu corps

**Nebit**
Troop Commander of the Red, Hapi corps

**Nefermaat**
Chamberlain at Per-Ramesses

**Nehi**
Leader of Ten, rebel Set corps

**Neith**
goddess of war and hunting

**Nekhakha**
the Flail, a symbol of kingly authority

**Nekhen**
Hierakonpolis, city of Hawks, south of Waset, opposite modern-day El Kab

**Nubt**
city in Ta Shemau, modern day town of Kom Ombo

**Nut**
goddess of the night

**Pabekkamen**
Superintendent of the Royal Women in Waset

**Panhesy**
Commander of Mut corps

**Paramessu**
official name of Pentaweret

**Pasenhor**
one of Goloth's officers

**Pehe-mau**
Hippopotamus

**Peleset**
one of the tribes of the Sea Peoples

**Pentaweret**
youngest son of Ramesses III

**Per-Asar**
a city in Ta Mehu

**Perahu**
king, city, and people of Pwene

**Per-Bast**
Bubastis, a city in Ta Mehu

**Per-Duat**
House of the Adoratrice

**Pere**
junior scribe of Per-Khemret in Men-nefer

**Perire**
a city on the western border of Ta Mehu

**Per-Khemret**
House of Women, the 'Harem'

**Perneb**
Leader of Fifty, rebel Set corps

**Per-Ramesses**
the capital city of Ramesses II

**Per-Wadjet**
city in Ta Mehu near modern day Desouk

**Peyferewy**
Assistant Overseer of the Treasury

**Piankhi**
a physician on the Pwene expedition

**Pontu**
First Servant of King Perahu of Pwene

**Prehirwenemef**
fourth son of Ramesses III and Tiye

**Ptah**
god of craftsmen and architects, associated with the city of Men-nefer (Memphis)

**Ptahmose**
Royal Scribe of Memoranda

**Pwene**
the Land of Punt, modern day Ethiopia, Somalia

**Qebehsenuef**
a protection god of the Canopic jars, son of Heru

**Rahmes**
a physician of Men-nefer

**Rahotep**
Egyptian name adopted by Rath

**Ramesnakht**
King's Son of Kush

**Ramesses**
(1) King of Egypt (Ramesses III)
(2) son of Ramesses III and Queen Tyti

**Ramose**
Egyptian name adopted by Goloth

**Rath**
eldest son of Ti-ament and Zeben the Kaftor

**Re**
(Ra) sun god, often worshipped as Amun-Re or Atum-Re

**Remaktef**
Overseer of the tomb builders

**Retenu**
Canaan, present-day Israel, Jordan and Lebanon

**Ribu**
a tribe in eastern Libya

**Rina**
daughter of Dov & Adara (known later as Dvorah)

**Ruma**
Overseer of the Treasury to Year 4 of Ramesses III

**Sanakht**
nephew of Panhesy

**Scarab**
mythical ancestress of the House of Ramesses

**Shechem**
a tribe of the Land of Sin where Ament once sought refuge

**Sea Peoples**
a loose amalgamation of sea-faring tribes from around the Mediterranean. Included the Phoenicians, Greeks, and Philistines. Other tribes include the Ekwesh, Denyen, Teresh, Peleset, Shekelesh and Sherden.

**Sekhmet**
warrior goddess and goddess of healing

**Seneb**
a soldier in the Hapi corps, an axeman

**Senedje**
Commander of Amun corps

**Senet**
a popular game involving a board and pieces

**Sepat**
a nome, or administrative district

**Serket**
goddess of healing venomous stings and bites

**Set**
Seth, god of desert, storms, disorder and violence, Lord of the Red Land (desert)

**Setau**
a naval commander

**Seth**
god of the desert, storms, disorder and violence

**Sethirkhopeshef**
fifth son of Ramesses III and Tiye

**Set Ma'at**
The Place of Truth, village of the tomb builders

**Setnakhte**
First king of the 20th dynasty, father of Ramesses III

**Shekeleth**
one of the tribes of the Sea Peoples

**Sherden**
one of the tribes of the Sea Peoples

**Shere**
Troop Commander, Loyal Set corps

**Siese**
(1) head charioteer under Goloth
(2) a sailor in the Heron Squad

**Sin**
The Land of Sin, the Sinai Peninsula

**Sobek**
the crocodile god, a protective deity

**Taita**
King of the Peleset

**Takhat**
wife of Mentuhirkhopeshef, also granddaughter of Takhat, the wife of Userkheperure Seti

**Ta Mehu**
Lower Egypt (in the north)

**Taremu**
Leontopolis, city in Ta Mehu, modern day Tell al Muqdam

**Ta-sekhet-ma'at**
The Great Field, Valley of the Kings

**Ta-senet**
a city south of Waset, modern day Esna

**Ta-set-neferu**
The Place of Beauty, Valley of the Queens

**Ta Shemau**
Upper Egypt (in the south)

**Tau**
adopted name of Tausret in exile

**Taui**
eldest daughter of Ti-ament and Zeben the Kaftor

**Tausret**
last king of the 19th dynasty, wife of Ament in exile

**Taweret**
goddess of childbirth and fertility

**Ta-ynt-netert**
Dendera, a city north of Waset, near modern day Qena

**Tentopet**
eldest surviving daughter of Ramesses III and Tiye

**Ti-ament**
sister of Ament

**Timna Valley**
a copper-mining site in the east of the Land of Sin

**Tiye**
first wife of Ramesses III

**Tiy-merenese**
wife of Setnakhte, mother of Ramesses III and Tyti

**Tjamet**
the site of the palace and Mansion of Ramesses III, Medinet Habu

**Tjaty**
Vizier, the highest official to serve the king

**Tjayiri**
Great Overseer of the Per-Khemret in Men-nefer

**Tjehenu**
the tribes of Libya

**Tjeker**
one of the tribes of the Sea Peoples

**Tjenu**
Thinis, a city north of Waset, possibly near modern day Girga

**To**
Tjaty of the South after Hori

**Tyti**
sister and Queen of Ramesses III

**Userkhaurenakht**
(aka Tjayiri) Great Overseer of the Per-Khemret in Men-nefer

**Usermaatranakht**
Steward of the Estate of Amun

**Usermaatre**
throne name of Ramesses III

**Usernakhte**
Captain of the Palace Guard in Waset

**Wadjet**
goddess, patron and protector of Ta Mehu, protector of kings and women in childbirth

**Waset**
capital city of Ta Shemau, Amun's holy city, Thebes

**Wawat**
province of Northern Kush

**Wepwawet**
the opener of ways, a wolf deity, son or brother of Anapa

**Yeshua**
father of Dov, a Khabiru

**Zau**
the town of Sais in the western Nile Delta

**Zawty**
a city north of Waset, modern day Asyut

**Zeben**
husband of Ti-ament

**Zephan**
a Shechem tribesman who guided Ament in the Land of Sin

**Ziphah**
mother of Dov, a Khabiru

**You can find ALL our books up at Amazon at:**
*https://www.amazon.com/shop/writers_exchange*

**or on our website at:**
*http://www.writers-exchange.com*

**All our Historical Novels**
*http://www.writers-exchange.com/category/genres/historical/*

# About the Author

Max Overton has travelled extensively and lived in many places around the world--including Malaysia, India, Germany, England, Jamaica, New Zealand, USA and Australia. Trained in the biological sciences in New Zealand and Australia, he has worked within the scientific field for many years, but now concentrates on writing. While predominantly a writer of historical fiction (Scarab: Books 1 - 6 of the Amarnan Kings; the Scythian Trilogy; the Demon Series; Ascension), he also writes in other genres (A Cry of Shadows, the Glass Trilogy, Haunted Trail, Sequestered) and draws on true life (Adventures of a Small Game Hunter in Jamaica, We Came From Königsberg). Max also maintains an interest in butterflies, photography, the paranormal and other aspects of Fortean Studies.

Most of his other published books are available at Writers Exchange Ebooks, http://www.writers-exchange.com/Max-Overton.html and all his books may be viewed on his website:
http://www.maxovertonauthor.com/

Max's book covers are all designed and created by Julie Napier, and other examples of her art and photography may be viewed at www.julienapier.com

## If you want to read more about other books by this author, they are listed on the following pages...

# A Cry of Shadows

{Paranormal Murder Mystery}

Australian Professor Ian Delaney is single-minded in his determination to prove his theory that one can discover the moment that the life force leaves the body. After succumbing to the temptation to kill a girl under scientifically controlled conditions, he takes an offer of work in St Louis, hoping to leave the undiscovered crime behind him.

In America, Wayne Richardson seeks revenge by killing his ex-girlfriend, believing it will give him the upper hand, a means to seize control following their breakup. Wayne quickly discovers that he enjoys killing and begins to seek out young women who resemble his dead ex-girlfriend.

Ian and Wayne meet and, when Ian recognizes the symptoms of violent delusion, he employs Wayne to help him further his research. Despite the police closing in, the two killers manage to evade identification time and time again as the death toll rises in their wake.

The detective in charge of the case, John Barnes, is frantic, willing to try anything to catch his killer. With time running out, he searches desperately for answers before another body is found...or the culprit slips into the woodwork for good.

Publisher: http://www.writers-exchange.com/A-Cry-of-Shadows/

Amazon: http://mybook.to/ACryOfShadows

## Adventures of a Small Game Hunter in Jamaica

{Biography}

An eleven-year-old boy is plucked from boarding school in England and transported to the tropical paradise of Jamaica where he's free to study his one great love--butterflies. He discovers that Jamaica has a wealth of these wonderful insects and sets about making a collection of as many as he can find. Along the way, he has adventures with other creatures, from hummingbirds to vultures, from iguanas to black widow spiders. Through it all runs the promise of the legendary Homerus swallowtail, Jamaica's national butterfly.

Other activities intrude, like school, boxing and swimming lessons, but he manages to inveigle his parents into taking him to strange and sometimes dangerous places, all in the name of butterfly collecting. He meets scientists and Rastafarians, teachers, small boys and the ordinary people living on the tropical isle, and even discovers butterflies that shouldn't exist in Jamaica.

Author Max Overton was that young boy. He counted himself fortunate to have lived in Jamaica in an age very different from the present one. Max still has some of the butterflies he collected half a century or more ago, and each one releases a flood of memories whenever he opens the box and gazes at their tattered and fading wings. These memories have become stories--stories of the Adventures of a Small Game Hunter in Jamaica.

Publisher: http://www.writers-exchange.com/Adventures-of-a-Small-Game-Hunter/

Amazon: http://myBook.to/AdventuresGameHunter

## Ascension Series, A Novel of Nazi Germany

{Historical: Holocaust}

*Before he fully realized the diabolical cruelties of the National Socialist German Worker's Party, Konrad Wengler had committed atrocities against his own people, the Jews, out of fear of both his faith and his heritage. But after he witnesses firsthand the concentration camps, the corruption, the inhuman malevolence of the Nazi war machine and the propaganda aimed at annihilating an entire race, he knows he must find a way to turn the tide and become the savior his people desperately need.*

**Book 1: Ascension**

*Being a Jew in Germany can be a dangerous thing...*

Fear prompts Konrad Wengler to put his faith aside and try desperately to forget his heritage. After fighting in the Great War, he's wounded and turns instead to law enforcement in his tiny Bavarian hometown. There, he falls under the spell of the fledgling Nazi Party. He joins the Party in patriotic fervour and becomes a Lieutenant of Police and Schutzstaffel (SS).

In the course of his duties as policeman, Konrad offends a powerful Nazi official who starts an SS investigation. War breaks out. When he joins the Police Battalions, he's sent to Poland and witnesses there firsthand the atrocities being committed upon his fellow Jews.

Unknown to Konrad, the SS investigators have discovered his origins and follow him into Poland. Arrested and sent to Mauthausen Concentration Camp, Konrad is forced to face what it means to be a Jew and fight for survival. Will his friends on the outside, his wife and lawyer, be enough to counter the might of the Nazi machine?

Publisher: http://www.writers-exchange.com/Ascension/
Amazon: http://mybook.to/Ascension1

**Book 2: Maelstrom**

*Never underestimate the enemy...*

Konrad Wengler survived his brush with the death camps of Nazi Germany. Now, reinstated as a police officer in his Bavarian hometown despite being a Jew, he throws himself back into his work, seeking to uncover evidence that will remove a corrupt Nazi party official.

The Gestapo have their own agenda and, despite orders from above to eliminate this troublesome Jewish policeman, they hide Konrad in the Totenkopf (Death's Head) Division of the Waffen-SS. In a fight to survive in the snowy wastes of Russia while the tide of war turns against Germany, Konrad experiences tank battles, ghetto clearances, partisans, and death camps (this time as a guard), as well as the fierce battles where his Division is badly outnumbered and on the defence.

Through it all, Konrad strives to live by his conscience and resist taking part in the atrocities happening all around him. He still thinks of himself as a policeman, but his desire to bring the corrupt Nazi official to justice

seems far removed from his present reality. If he is to find the necessary evidence against his enemy, he must first *survive*...
Publisher: http://www.writers-exchange.com/Maelstrom/
Amazon: http://mybook.to/Ascension2

**Book 3: Dämmerung**
Konrad Wengler is captured and sent from one Soviet prison camp to another. Even hearing the war has come to an end makes no difference until he's arrested as a Nazi Party member. In jail, Konrad refuses to defend himself for things he's guilty and should be punished for. Will his be an eye-for-an-eye life sentence, or leniency in regard of the good he tried to do once he learned the truth?
Publisher: http://www.writers-exchange.com/dammerung/
Amazon: http://mybook.to/Ascension3

# Fall of the House of Ramesses Series, A Novel of Ancient Egypt

{Historical: Ancient Egypt}

*Egypt was at the height of its powers in the days of Ramesses the Great, a young king who confidently predicted his House would last for a Thousand Years. Sixty years later, he was still on the throne. One by one, his heirs had died and the survivors had become old men. When Ramesses at last died, he left a stagnant kingdom and his throne to an old man--Merenptah. What followed laid the groundwork for a nation ripped apart by civil war.*

**Book 1: Merenptah**

The House of Ramesses is in the hands of an old man. King Merenptah wants to leave the kingdom to his younger son, Seti, but northern tribes in Egypt rebel and join forces with the Sea Peoples, invading from the north. In the south, the king's eldest son Messuwy is angered at being passed over in favour of the younger son...and plots to rid himself of his father and brother.

Publisher: http://www.writers-exchange.com/Merenptah/

Amazon: http://mybook.to/FOTHR1

**Book 2: Seti**

After only nine years on the throne, Merenptah is dead and his son Seti is king in his place. He rules from the northern city of Men-nefer, while his elder brother Messuwy, convinced the throne is his by right, plots rebellion in the south.

The kingdoms are tipped into bloody civil war, with brother fighting against brother for the throne of a united Egypt. On one side is Messuwy, now crowned as King Amenmesse and his ruthless General Sethi; on the other, young King Seti and his wife Tausret. But other men are weighing up the chances of wresting the throne from both brothers and becoming king in their place. Under the onslaught of conflict, the House of Ramesses begins to crumble...

Publisher: http://www.writers-exchange.com/Seti/

Amazon: http://mybook.to/FOTHR2

**Book 3: Tausret**

The House of Ramesses falters as Tausret relinquishes the throne upon the death of her husband, King Seti. Amenmesse's young son Siptah will become king until her infant son is old enough to rule. Tausret, as Regent, and the king's uncle, Chancellor Bay, hold tight to the reins of power and vie for complete control of the kingdoms. Assassination changes the balance of power, and, seeing his chance, Chancellor Bay attempts a coup...

Tausret's troubles mount as she also faces a challenge from Setnakhte, an aging son of the Great Ramesses who believes Seti was the last legitimate king. If Setnakhte gets his way, he will destroy the House of Ramesses and set up his own dynasty of kings.

Publisher: http://www.writers-exchange.com/Tausret/
Amazon: http://mybook.to/FOTHR3

## Kadesh, A Novel of Ancient Egypt

Holding the key to strategic military advantage, Kadesh is a jewel city that distant lands covet. Ramesses II of Egypt and Muwatalli II of Hatti believe they're chosen by the gods to claim ascendancy to Kadesh. When the two meet in the largest chariot battle ever fought, not just the fate of empires will be decided but also the lives of citizens helplessly caught up in the greedy ambition of kings.

Publisher: http://www.writers-exchange.com/Kadesh/
Amazon: http://mybook.to/Kadesh

# Haunted Trail A Tale of Wickedness & Moral Turpitude

{Western: Paranormal}

Ned Abernathy is a hot-tempered young cowboy in the small town of Hammond's Bluff in 1876. In a drunken argument with his best friend Billy over a girl, he guns him down. Ned flees and wanders the plains, forests and hills of the Dakota Territories, certain that every man's hand is against him.

Horse rustlers, marauding Indians, killers, gold prospectors and French trappers cross his path and lead to complications, as do persistent apparitions of what Ned believes is the ghost of his friend Billy, come to accuse him of murder. He finds love and loses it. Determined not to do the same when he discovers gold in the Black Hills, he ruthlessly defends his newfound wealth against greedy men. In the process, he comes to terms with who he is and what he's done. But there are other ghosts in his past that he needs to confront. Returning to Hammond's Bluff, Ned stumbles into a shocking surprise awaiting him at the end of his haunted trail.
Publisher: http://www.writers-exchange.com/Haunted-Trail/
Amazon: http://mybook.to/HauntedTrail

# Glass Trilogy

{Paranormal Thriller}

*Delve deep into the mysteries of Aboriginal mythology, present day UFO activity and pure science that surround the continent of Australia, from its barren deserts to the depths of its rainforest and even deeper into its mysterious mountains. Along the way, love, greed, murder, and mystery abound while the secrets of mankind and the ultimate answer to 'what happens now?' just might be answered.*

**GLASS HOUSE, Book 1**: The mysteries of Australia may just hold the answers mankind has been searching for millennium to find. When Doctor James Hay, a university scientist who studies the paranormal mysteries in Australia, finds an obelisk of carved volcanic rock on sacred Aboriginal land in northern Queensland, he realizes it may hold the answers he's been seeking. A respected elder of the Aboriginal people instructs James to take up the gauntlet and follow his heart. Along with his old friend and award-winning writer Spencer, Samantha Louis, her cameraman, and two of James' Aboriginal students, James embarks on a life-changing quest for the truth.
Publisher: http://www.writers-exchange.com/Glass-House/
Amazon: http://mybook.to/Glass1

**A GLASS DARKLY, Book 2:** A dead volcano called Glass Mountain in Northern California seems harmless...but is it really?

Andromeda Jones, a physicist, knows her missing sister Samantha is somehow tied up with the new job Andromeda herself has been offered to work with a team in constructing Vox Dei, a machine that's been ostensibly built to eliminate wars. But what is its true nature, and who's pulling the strings?

When the experiment spins out of control, dark powers are unleashed and the danger to mankind unfolds relentlessly. Strange, evil shadows are using the Vox Dei and Andromeda's sister Samantha to get through to our world, knowing the time is near when Earth's final destiny will be decided.

Federal forces are aware of something amiss, so, to rescue her sibling, Andromeda agrees to go on a dangerous mission and soon finds herself entangled in a web of professional jealousy, political betrayal, and flat-out greed.

Publisher: http://www.writers-exchange.com/A-Glass-Darkly/
Amazon: http://mybook.to/Glass2

**LOOKING GLASS, Book 3:** Samantha and James Hay have been advised that their missing daughter Gaia have been located in ancient Australia. Dr. Xanatuo, an alien scientist who, along with a lost tribe of Neanderthals and other beings working to help mankind, has discovered a way to send them back in time to be reunited with Gaia. Ernie, the old Aboriginal tracker and leader of the Neanderthals, along with friends Ratana and Nathan and characters from the first two books of the trilogy, will accompany them. This team of intrepid adventurers have another mission for the journey, along with aiding the Hayes' quest, which is paramount to changing a terrible wrong which exists in the present time.
Publisher: http://www.writers-exchange.com/Looking-Glass/
Amazon: http://mybook.to/Glass3

## Hyksos Series, A Novel of Ancient Egypt

*The power of the kings of the Middle Kingdom have been failing for some time, having lost control of the Nile Delta to a series of Canaanite kings who ruled from the northern city of Avaris.*

*Into this mix came the Kings of Amurri, Lebanon and Syria bent on subduing the whole of Egypt. These kings were known as the Hyksos, and they dealt a devastating blow to the peoples of the Nile Delta and Valley.*

**Book 1: Avaris**

When Arimawat and his son Harrubaal fled from Urubek, the king of Hattush, to the court of the King of Avaris, King Sheshi welcomed the refugees. One of Arimawat's first tasks for King Shesi is to sail south to the Land of Kush and fetch Princess Tati, who will become Sheshi's queen. Arimawat and Harrubaal perform creditably, but their actions have far-reaching consequences.

On the return journey, Harrubaal falls in love with Kemi, the daughter of the Southern Egyptian king. As a reward for Harrubaal's work, Sheshi

secures the hand of the princess for the young Canaanite prince. Unfortunately for the peace of the realm, Sheshi lusts after Princess Kemi too, and his actions threaten the stability of his kingdom...
Publisher: http://www.writers-exchange.com/Avaris/
Amazon: http://mybook.to/avaris

**Book 2: Conquest**

The Hyksos invade the Delta using the new weapons of bronze and chariots, things of which the Egyptians have no knowledge. They rout the Delta forces, and in the south, the unconquered kings ready their armies to defend their lands. Meanwhile in Avaris, Merybaal, the son of Harrubaal and Kemi, strives to defend his family in a city conquered by the Hyksos.

Elements of the Delta army that refuse to surrender continue the fight for their homeland, and new kings proclaim themselves as the inheritors of the failed kings of Avaris. One of these is Amenre, grandson of Merybaal, but he is forced into hiding as the Hyksos sweep all before them, bringing their terror to the kingdom of the Nile valley. Driven south in disarray, the survivors of the Egyptian army seek leaders who can resist the enemy...
Publisher: http://www.writers-exchange.com/conquest/
Amazon: http://mybook.to/conquest

**Book 3: Two Cities**

The Hyksos drive south into the Nile Valley, sweeping all resistance aside. Bebi and Sobekhotep, grandsons of Harrubaal, assume command of the loyal Egyptian army and strive to stem the flood of Hyksos conquest. But even the cities of the south are divided against themselves.

Abdju, an old capital city of Egypt reasserts itself, putting forward a line of kings of its own, and soon the city is at war with Waset, the southern capital of the Nile Valley, as the two cities fight for supremacy in the face of the advancing northern enemy. Caught up in the turmoil of warring nations, the ordinary people of Egypt must fight for their own survival as well as that of their kingdom.
Publisher: http://www.writers-exchange.com/Two-Cities/
Amazon: http://mybook.to/TwoCities

**Book 4: Possessor of All**

The Hyksos, themselves beset by intrigue and division, push down into southern Egypt. The short-lived kingdom of Abdju collapses, leaving Nebiryraw the undisputed king of the south ruling from the city of Waset.

An uneasy truce between north and south enables both sides to strengthen their positions.

Khayan seizes power over the Hyksos kingdom and turns his gaze toward Waset, determined to conquer Egypt finally. Meanwhile, the family of King Nebiryraw looks to the future and starts securing their own advantage, weakening the southern kingdom. In the face of renewed tensions, the delicate peace cannot last...

Publisher: http://www.writers-exchange.com/Possessor-of-All/
Amazon: http://mybook.to/Possessor-of-All

**Book 5: War in the South**

Intrigue and rebellion rule in Egypt's southern kingdom as the house of King Nebiryraw tears itself apart. King succeeds king, but none of them look capable of defending the south, let alone reclaiming the north. Taking advantage of this, King Khayan of the Hyksos launches his assault on Waset, but rebellions in the north delay his victory.

The fall of Waset brings about a change of leadership. Apophis takes command of the Hyksos forces, and Rahotep brings together a small army to challenge the might of the Hyksos, knowing that the fate of Egypt hangs on the coming battle.

Publisher: http://www.writers-exchange.com/War-in-the-South/
Amazon: http://mybook.to/WarInTheSouth

**Book 6: Between the Wars**

Rahotep leads his Egyptian army to victory, and Apophis withdraws the Hyksos army northward. An uneasy peace settles over the Nile valley. Rebellions in the north keep the Hyksos king from striking back at Rahotep, while internal strife between the Hyksos nobility and generals threatens to rip their empire apart.

War is coming to Egypt once more, and the successors of Rahotep start preparing for it, using the very weapons that the Hyksos introduced--bronze weapons and the war chariot. King Ahmose repudiates the peace treaty, and Apophis of the Hyksos prepares to destroy his enemies at last. Bloody warfare returns to Egypt...

Publisher: http://www.writers-exchange.com/Between-the-Wars/
Amazon: http://mybook.to/BetweenTheWars

**Book 7: Sons of Tao**

War breaks out between the Hyksos invaders and native Egyptians determined to rid themselves of their presence. King Seqenenre Tao launches an attack on King Apophis but the Hyksos strike back savagely. It is only when his sons Kamose and Ahmose carry the war to the Hyksos that the Egyptians really start to hope they can succeed.

Kamose battles fiercely, but only when his younger brother Ahmose assumes the throne is there real success. Faced with an ignominious defeat, a Hyksos general overthrows Apophis and becomes king, but then he faces a resurgent Egyptian king determined to rid his land of the Hyksos invader...

Publisher: http://www.writers-exchange.com/sons-of-tao/
Amazon: http://mybook.to/SonsOfTao

# TULPA

{Paranormal Thriller}

*From the rainforests of tropical Australia to the cane fields and communities of the North Queensland coastal strip, a horror is unleashed by those foolishly playing with unknown forces...*

A fairy story to amuse small children leads four bored teenagers and a young university student in a North Queensland town to becoming interested in an ancient Tibetan technique for creating a life form. When their seemingly harmless experiment sets free terror and death, the teenagers are soon fighting to contain a menace that reproduces exponentially.

The police are helpless to end the horror. Aided by two old game hunters, a student of the paranormal and a few small children, the teenagers must find a way of destroying what they unintentionally released. But how can they stop beings that can escape into an alternate reality when threatened?

Publisher: http://www.writers-exchange.com/TULPA/
Amazon: http://mybook.to/TULPA

# Scythian Trilogy
{Historical}

*Captured by the warlike, tribal Scythians who bicker amongst themselves and bitterly resent outside interference, a fiercely loyal captain in Alexander the Great's Companion Cavalry Nikometros and his men are to be sacrificed to the Mother Goddess. Lucky chance--and the timely intervention of Tomyra, priestess and daughter of the Massegetae chieftain--allows him to defeat the Champion. With their immediate survival secured, acceptance into the tribe...and escape...is complicated by the captain's growing feelings for Tomyra--death to any who touch her--and the chief's son Areipithes who not only detests Nikometros and wants to have him killed or banished but intends to murder his own father and take over the tribe.*

**LION OF SCYTHIA, Book 1:** Alexander the Great has conquered the Persian Empire and is marching eastward to India. In his wake he leaves small groups of soldiers to govern great tracts of land and diverse peoples. Nikometros is one young cavalry captain left behind in the lands of the fierce, nomadic Scythian horsemen. Captured after an ambush, Nikometros must fight for his life and the lives of his surviving men. Even as he seeks an opportunity to escape, he finds himself bound by a debt of loyalty to the chief...and his own developing love for the young priestess.
Publisher: http://www.writers-exchange.com/Lion-of-Scythia/
Amazon: http://mybook.to/Scythian1

**THE GOLDEN KING, Book 2:** The chief of the tribe of nomadic Scythian horsemen is dead, killed by his son's treachery. The priestess, lover of the young cavalry officer, Nikometros, is carried off into the mountains. Nikometros and his friends set off in hard pursuit.

Death rides with them. By the time they return, the tribes are at war. Nikometros must choose between attempting to become chief himself or leaving the people he's come to love and respect to return to his duty as an army officer in the Empire of Alexander.
Winner of the 2005 EPIC Ebook Awards.
Publisher: http://www.writers-exchange.com/The-Golden-King/
Amazon: http://mybook.to/Scythian2

**FUNERAL IN BABYLON, Book 3:** Alexander the Great has returned from India and set up his court in Babylon. Nikometros and a band of loyal Scythians journey deep into the heart of Persia to join the Royal court. Nikometros finds himself embroiled in the intrigues and wars of kings, generals, and merchant adventurers as he strives to provide a safe haven for his lover and friends. With the fate of an Empire hanging in the balance, Death walks beside Nikometros as events precipitate a Funeral in Babylon...

Winner of the 2006 EPIC Ebook Awards.

Publisher: http://www.writers-exchange.com/Funeral-in-Babylon/
Amazon: http://mybook.to/Scythian3

## We Came From Konigsberg

{Historical: Holocaust}

Based on a true story gleaned from the memories of family members sixty years after the events, from photographs and documents, and from published works of nonfiction describing the times and events described in the narrative, *We Came From Konigsberg* is set in January 1945.

The Soviet Army is poised for the final push through East Prussia and Poland to Berlin. Elisabet Daeker and her five young sons are in Königsberg, East Prussia and have heard the shocking stories of Russian atrocities. They're desperate to escape to the perceived safety of Germany. To survive, Elisabet faces hardships endured at the hands of Nazi hardliners, of Soviet troops bent on rape, pillage and murder, and of Allied cruelty in the Occupied Zones of post-war Germany.

Winner of the 2014 EPIC Ebook Awards.

Publisher: http://www.writers-exchange.com/We-Came-From-Konigsberg/

Amazon: http://mybook.to/Konigsberg

# Sequestered
# By Max Overton and Jim Darley
{Action/Thriller}

Storing carbon dioxide underground as a means of removing a greenhouse gas responsible for global warming has made James Matternicht a fabulously wealthy man. For 15 years, the Carbon Capture and Sequestration Facility at Rushing River in Oregon's hinterland has been operating without a problem...or has it?

When mysterious documents arrive on her desk that purport to show the Facility is leaking, reporter Annaliese Winton investigates. Together with a government geologist, Matt Morrison, she uncovers a morass of corruption and deceit that now threatens the safety of her community and the entire northwest coast of America.

Liquid carbon dioxide, stored at the critical point under great pressure, is a tremendously dangerous substance, and millions of tonnes of it are sequestered in the rock strata below Rushing River. All it would take is a crack in the overlying rock and the whole pressurized mass could erupt with disastrous consequences. And that crack has always existed there...

Recipient of the Life Award (Literature for the Environment): "There are only two kinds of people: conservationists and suicides. To qualify for this Award, your book needs to value the wonderful world of nature, to recognize that we are merely one species out of millions, and that we have a responsibility to cherish and maintain our small planet."

Awarded from http://bobswriting.com/life/

Publisher: http://www.writers-exchange.com/Sequestered/
Amazon: http://mybook.to/Sequestered

# Strong is the Ma'at of Re, A Novel of Ancient Egypt

{Historical: Ancient Egypt}

*In Ancient Egypt, C1200 BCE, bitter contention and resentment, secret coups and assassination attempts may decide the fate of those who would become legends...by any means necessary.*

**Book 1: The King**

That *he* is descended from Ramesses the Great fills Ramesses III with obscene pride. Elevated to the throne following a coup led by his father Setnakhte during the troubled days of Queen Tausret, Ramesses III sets about creating an Egypt that reflects the glory days of Ramesses the Great. He takes on his predecessor's throne name, names his sons after the sons of Ramesses and pushes them toward similar duties. Most of all, he thirsts after conquests like those of his hero grandfather.

Ramesses III assumes the throne name of Usermaatre, translated as "Strong is the Ma'at of Re" and endeavours to live up to the sentiment. He fights foreign foes, as had Ramesses the Great; he builds temples throughout the Two Lands, as had Ramesses the Great, and he looks forward to a long, illustrious life on the throne of Egypt, as had Ramesses the Great.

Alas, his reign is not meant to be. Ramesses III faces troubles at home--troubles that threaten the stability of Egypt and his own throne. The struggles for power between his wives, his sons, and even the priests of Amun, together with a treasury drained of its wealth, all force Ramesses III to question his success as the scion of a legend.

Publisher: http://www.writers-exchange.com/The-King/
Amazon: http://mybook.to/StrongIsTheMaatOfRe1

**Book 2: The Heirs**

Tiye, the first wife of Ramesses III, has grown so used to being the mother of the Heir she can no longer bear to see that prized title pass to the son of a rival wife. Her eldest sons have died and the one left wants to step down and devote his life to the priesthood. Then the son of the king's sister/wife, also named Ramesses, will become Crown Prince and all Tiye's ambitions will lie in ruins.

Ramesses III struggles to enrich Egypt by seeking the wealth of the Land of Punt. He dispatches an expedition to the fabled southern land but years pass before the expedition returns. In the meantime, Tiye has a new hope: A last son she dotes on. Plague sweeps through Egypt, killing princes and princesses alike and lessening her options, and now Tiye must undergo the added indignity of having her daughter married off to the hated Crown Prince.

All Tiye's hopes are pinned on this last son of hers, but Ramesses III refuses to consider him as a potential successor, despite the Crown Prince's failing health. Unless Tiye can change the king's mind through charm or coercion, her sons will forever be excluded from the throne of Egypt.
Publisher: http://www.writers-exchange.com/The-Heirs/
Amazon: http://mybook.to/StrongIsTheMaatOfRe1

**Book 3: Taweret**

The reign of Ramesses III is failing and even the gods seem to be turning their eyes away from Egypt. When the sun hides its face, crops suffer, throwing the country into famine. Tomb workers go on strike. To avert further disaster, Crown Prince Ramesses acts on his father's behalf.

The rivalry between Ramesses III's wives--commoner Tiye and sister/wife Queen Tyti--also comes to a head. Tiye resents not being made queen and can't abide that her sons have been passed over. She plots to put her own spoiled son Pentaweret on the throne.

The eventual strength of the Ma'at of Re hangs in the balance. Will the rule of Egypt be decided by fate, gods...or treason?
Publisher: http://www.writers-exchange.com/The-One-of-Taweret/
Amazon: http://mybook.to/SITMOR3

# The Amarnan Kings Series, A Novel of Ancient Egypt

{Historical: Ancient Egypt}

*Set in Egypt of the 14th century B.C.E. and piecing together a mosaic of the reigns of the five Amarnan kings, threaded through by the memories of princess Beketaten-Scarab, a tapestry unfolds of the royal figures lost in the mists of antiquity.*

**SCARAB - AKHENATEN, Book 1:** A chance discovery in Syria reveals answers to the mystery of the ancient Egyptian sun-king, the heretic Akhenaten and his beautiful wife Nefertiti. Inscriptions in the tomb of his sister Beketaten, otherwise known as Scarab, tell a story of life and death, intrigue and warfare, in and around the golden court of the kings of the glorious 18th dynasty.

The narrative of a young girl growing up at the centre of momentous events--the abolition of the gods, foreign invasion, and the fall of a once-great family--reveals who Tutankhamen's parents really were, what happened to Nefertiti, and other events lost to history in the great destruction that followed the fall of the Aten heresy.

Publisher: http://www.writers-exchange.com/Scarab/
Amazon: http://mybook.to/ScarabBook1

**SCARAB- SMENKHKARE, Book 2:** King Akhenaten, distraught at the rebellion and exile of his beloved wife Nefertiti, withdraws from public life, content to leave the affairs of Egypt in the hands of his younger half-brother Smenkhkare. When Smenkhkare disappears on a hunting expedition, his sister Beketaten, known as Scarab, is forced to flee for her life.

Finding refuge among her mother's people, the Khabiru, Scarab has resigned herself to a life in exile...until she hears that her brother Smenkhkare is still alive. He is raising an army in Nubia to overthrow Ay and reclaim his throne. Scarab hurries south to join him as he confronts Ay and General Horemheb outside the gates of Thebes.

Publisher: http://www.writers-exchange.com/Scarab2/
Amazon: http://mybook.to/ScarabBook2

**SCARAB - TUTANKHAMEN, Book 3:** Scarab and her brother Smenkhkare are in exile in Nubia but are gathering an army to wrest control of Egypt from the boy king Tutankhamen and his controlling uncle, Ay. Meanwhile, the kingdoms are beset by internal troubles while the Amorites are pressing hard against the northern borders. Generals Horemheb and Paramessu must fight a war on two fronts while deciding where their loyalties lie--with the former king Smenkhkare or with the new young king in Thebes.

Smenkhkare and Scarab march on Thebes with their native army to meet the legions of Tutankhamen on the plains outside the city gates. As two brothers battle for supremacy and the throne of the Two Kingdoms, the fate of Egypt and the 18th dynasty hangs in the balance.
Finalist in 2013's Eppie Awards.
Publisher: http://www.writers-exchange.com/Scarab3/
Amazon: http://mybook.to/ScarabBook3

**SCARAB - AY, Book 4:** Tutankhamen is dead and his grieving widow tries to rule alone, but her grandfather Ay has not destroyed the former kings just so he can be pushed aside. Presenting the Queen and General Horemheb with a fait accompli, the old Vizier assumes the throne of Egypt and rules with a hand of hardened bronze. His adopted son, Nakhtmin, will rule after him and stamp out the last remnants of loyalty to the former kings.

Scarab was sister to three kings and will not give in to the usurper and his son. She battles against Ay and his legions under the command of General Horemheb and aided by desert tribesmen and the gods of Egypt themselves. The final confrontation will come in the rich lands of the Nile delta where the future of Egypt will at last be decided.
Publisher: http://www.writers-exchange.com/Scarab4/
Amazon: http://mybook.to/ScarabBook4

**SCARAB - HOREMHEB, Book 5:** General Horemheb has taken control after the death of Ay and Nakhtmin. Forcing Scarab to marry him, he ascends the throne of Egypt. The Two Kingdoms settle into an uneasy peace as Horemheb proceeds to stamp out all traces of the former kings. He also persecutes the Khabiru tribesmen who were reluctant to help him seize power. Scarab escapes into the desert, where she is content to wait until Egypt needs her.

A holy man emerges from the desert and demands that Horemheb release the Khabiru so they may worship his god. Scarab recognises the holy man and supports him in his efforts to free his people. The gods of Egypt and of the Khabiru are invoked and disaster sweeps down on the Two Kingdoms as the Khabiru flee with Scarab and the holy man. Horemheb and his army pursue them to the shores of the Great Sea, where a natural event...or the very hand of God...alters the course of Egyptian history.
Publisher: http://www.writers-exchange.com/Scarab5/
Amazon: http://mybook.to/ScarabBook5

**SCARAB - DESCENDANT, Book 6:** Three thousand years after the reigns of the Amarnan Kings, the archaeologists who discovered the inscriptions in Syria journey to Egypt to find the tomb of Smenkhkare and his sister Scarab and the fabulous treasure they believe is there. Unscrupulous men and religious fanatics also seek the tomb, either to plunder it or to destroy it. Can the gods of Egypt protect their own, or will the ancients rely on modern day men and women of science?
Publisher: http://www.writers-exchange.com/Scarab6/
Amazon: http://mybook.to/ScarabBook6

Made in the USA
Las Vegas, NV
16 July 2023

74821182R10216